"Come on, we'd better get away from here," said Gideon, "before we're crushed."

He groped for her hand in the darkness and, finding it, staggered to pull her away. Samiah held steadfast.

"What's the matter?" he said.

"You saved my life again, that's all," she whispered. She looked up into his face with saucer eyes. Gideon wiped away a smudge from the side of her mouth. Her lips slightly parted, warm and inviting. And there, amid the chill and solitude of the ancient catacombs, they kissed, the bleak and dangerous world around them lost during a moment's rapture and embrace. For a single, wonderful instant the terrors awaiting them seemed to vanish forever.

Marrakesh Nights

Graham Diamond

FAWCETT GOLD MEDAL • NEW YORK

A Fawcett Gold Medal Book
Published by Ballantine Books

Library of Congress Catalog Card Number: 83-91136

ISBN 0-449-12502-5

Manufactured in the United States of America

First Edition: January 1984

Marrakesh Nights

 AFTER HIS NIGHT'S WORK, HABIB WALKED HOME at the leisurely pace to which he was accustomed. It was not a long way to his humble house, but now, in the hours before dawn, it seemed endless. Stoop-shouldered, he crossed the narrow streets leading away from the *souk*—the vast marketplace of Marrakesh—his broom in one hand, dragging his mostly empty canvas bag along the dusty walk with the other. Both were the tools of his trade; and weary as he was, he still held them with a measure of pride. After all, he'd had them for so long they were almost a part of him.

Habib was a dustman. His duties were simple. Each night, after the stalls and shops were tightly shuttered and the merchants and shoppers long since retired to their homes, he and the other refuse collectors would ready themselves for the work ahead. Brooms in hand, they would begin the task of collecting the voluminous trash, sweeping the plaza and sprucing the market in preparation for the next day's business.

Being a dustman in the famous *Jama-el-F'Na*, the heart of the city, was no easy job. Each day the crowds thronged to the market, bartering and choosing from the greatest selection of wares available in any single place. Among the vendors and hawkers, acrobats and jugglers, philosophers and fools, madmen and poets and soldiers of fortune, the buyers would come to browse and spend money. If, at the end of a day, the square was left filthy, reeking of rotten vegetables, soured milk, and camel dung, what shoppers would wish to return upon the morrow?

The *souk* was the center of Marrakesh life, and men like Habib kept it clean. His job was not considered prestigious. Certainly the pay was small. But Habib knew it was honest work and satisfying in its way. For, without its dustmen, the fabled marketplace, greatest in all the world, would wither and die. Besides, after so many years Habib had come to like it. And the pay-packet at the end of each month had always been just enough to feed and clothe his family, shelter them decently, and even leave a few small coins for himself. As a prudent man, devout, a believer in the old ways, he needed no more. Habib the dustman was content.

In a nearby alley a pair of stray dogs barked. Habib paused, smiled, dug a calloused hand into the canvas bag and pulled out two meaty bones found earlier that night near the butcher shop. The mongrels appeared from the shadows as cautiously as always, lolling their tongues and wagging their tails in eager anticipation of supper. Habib, you see, fed them every night. He tossed the bones high into the air, and chuckled when the dogs leaped and caught them between snapping jaws. Then they were off, scampering noisily back into the alley that was their home. Habib watched for a moment, sighed, and resumed his walking. He loved dogs. Cats as well. In fact, he loved all animals, particularly those orphans who were forced to roam the back streets and alleys, unloved and uncared for. His heart was bigger than his brain, or so his dear wife—bless her soul—was inclined to say. But Habib didn't mind. Were it somehow in his power, he would gather all the city's strays, and feed and shelter them. For he was a charitable man, a kind and warmhearted man who had never known spite or jealousy in all his six decades of life.

In any event, he considered himself more fortunate than most. He had his job, his little house, and had raised a healthy family. Six children his dear wife—bless her soul—had bestowed: three son and three daughters. All the sons had gone their ways, of course, had married, and were now fathers themselves. The same for the daughters. All wedded to fine young men of promising degree, each now with her own family to raise. All but one.

At the thought of Samíah he frowned. How tragic it was. His eldest daughter, now twenty, had become a widow more than a year ago. Married to a wonderfully kind young fellow, a fine stonemason, she had seen her life shattered by his accidental and untimely death. She miscarried at the news and, grief-stricken, was forced to wear the black dress of mourning. Although the time for sorrow had passed, she still bore the scars.

Habib, of course, had immediately brought her back to his house to live with him. Samíah, though, had yet to bury her grief. Oh, she kept herself busy enough with her work; the girl was a fine seamstress, there was no denying. But it was, well, *unnatural* for her to hide herself away as she did. In truth, she was a lovely young woman who still turned many a bachelor's head, and could have had her pick of many. Taking a second husband would be normal. But no. Samíah worked diligently at her sewing, cared for her father and ran the house. She was highly intelligent; witty, and charming but she refused on any terms to consider another marriage.

Not that Habib wanted her out of the house, even if she was becoming a bit of a shrew, often scolding him for this or that. Just that he wanted her to find the same happiness her sisters and brothers knew, the same happiness he and Samíah's mother had shared. It simply wasn't *right* for her to behave like this. Yet Samíah was a woman with a mind of her own—as she frequently told him—and as strong willed and temperamental as a mule when she wanted to be.

Stubborn. Smart and shrewd. But lonely. Habib knew it even if she didn't. If only she would listen!

The winding streets of the Old Quarter were grim and silent; Habib whistled a happy tune as he walked, trying not to let his worry about his daughter get the best of him. He was an outgoing, jovial man by nature and this was reflected in his gait, even if his broad shoulders drooped a little from so many years of bending to pick up refuse.

Laundry was hung to dry over the many tiny balconies that

overlooked his street. A cooling wind from the mountains blew gently, causing the dust to swirl at his feet and the few sturdy trees to rustle their leaves. These trees were well tended by the community, providing excellent shade for grandmothers who loved to sit and exchange daily gossip during the hot midday hours.

The Old Quarter was not a wealthy neighborhood. It was made up of many families very much like his own—working-men, tradesmen, a scattering of craftsmen. The houses were far too clustered, the walks extremely narrow, the frequent arcades providing the only shade. Yet it was a clean and proud neighborhood, of which the dustman was pleased to be a part. He had lived here since his marriage some forty years before, and in many ways his neighbors had almost become a part of an extended family. Each household shared the highlights of the others' lives, through good times and bad, happiness and sadness, births, weddings, and deaths. Thus it was a good place for Habib. But not for Samíah, he knew, although outwardly the girl seemed content enough.

Habib scowled, reminding himself not to dwell so much on his daughter's misfortunes. He was only going to get upset, make himself miserable again, which was really a futile and silly thing to do. As he approached the small patch of tended grass that led to the front door of his modest, two-floor, white-washed mud-brick house, he tried to harden his heart. *If Samíah insists on becoming an old maid, let her! It's her life, isn't it? At least that's what she always tells me!*

A rooster crowed from old Mustapha's backyard; the few skinny hens began to stir in the coop. Habib glanced up at the starry sky and saw it had brightened. Dawn already, he mused, seeing the gray glow above the roofs. He should have been home an hour ago, but since tonight had been payday, as was his custom, he had lingered a bit longer at the market to chat and to drink mint tea with the other dustmen. He jingled the coins in his pocket with a smile. Samíah's own income from sewing had already matched his, and by all accounts, would soon surpass it. If nothing else, having the girl around certainly eased the financial strain. If only she weren't so fussy all the time!

Across the narrow street in the balcony directly opposite, the widow Anna, a buxom woman of Habib's age, poked her head from between the wash. "*Salaam*, Habib!" she whispered huskily, her face unveiled and broadly grinning. She batted her eyelids over her gray eyes as she waved.

"*Salaam*, Anna. Peace be upon you," he answered, then quickly hurried to his door before she got him tied up in a lengthy conversation.

That the widow had an eye out for the ruggedly gentle dustman was no secret. For years the gossips had been predicting a marriage. And why not? Mother of eight and grandmother of thirty-three, Anna had more than proved her womanly worth. There was still life in those aging bones, the old women would cackle. And at least as much life in Habib. It was a perfect match. Certainly one blessed by Allah. Habib, though, was having none of it. One marriage had been enough. Not to misunderstand him; the dustman had an eye for women, and during his youth had made himself quite a reputation with the available girls. But he shuddered at the thought of marrying again now. Especially to a nag like Anna. Better for him they remain as always—neighbors and friends.

Aware that from behind some tightly bolted shutter, one of the old washerwomen or other could be observing the little exchange on the sly, Habib duly apologized to Anna for being too weary to stand and chat; then he opened his front door and stepped inside.

"Papa, is that you?"

Habib frowned; he squinted as he peered across the shadowed room and saw Samíah standing between the opened curtains that separated her working room from the tiny parlor. The girl was almost a silhouette, soft features barely distinguishable from the patterned draperies. Her long black hair was pinned and bunched atop her head, and she wore a long robe with small white ruffles on the sleeves. The hem came below her ankles, and the toe of her slippers barely poked from the loose gown.

"I . . . I'm sorry if I woke you, child," Habib mumbled. "I was trying to be as quiet as I could."

Grinning, the girl breezed across the room and dutifully pecked her father on the cheek, leading him by the hand toward the table. "You didn't wake me, Papa. I've been up for hours, working." Her dark eyes glinted as she spoke. "Are you hungry?"

"Work, work, all the time work," he muttered, allowing himself to be pulled along like a child. His silver brows knit, and he pursed his thick lips. "It isn't right, girl! Staying up all night like this, alone, sewing in the dark—"

"I had two lamps burning," she pointed out. "Besides, I still have ibn al-Hassan's youngest daughter's bridal gown to finish." She brushed a few loose tendrils of hair away from her eyes and sighed, adding, "And Ishmael asked if his wife's *chador* could be ready by—"

Habib's growl cut off her words. "Ishmael! Ibn al-Hassan! Let them find another seamstress for their women!"

She urged him into a chair and poured him his tea. "But I *like* my work, Papa. It keeps me busy, and"—here her eyes narrowed and she pointedly looked at him—"besides, it increases our income."

"A woman should not have to work," he observed. "Her place is in the home, running the household." He sighed. "I earn enough for the two of us, daughter. More than enough. . . ."

"Drink your tea, Papa."

"But—"

"Drink your tea. I'm heating the bread."

Exasperated, Habib shook his head slowly and stared into the green brew. Piping steam wafted into his nostrils. Samíah opened the shutters, and streams of light from the crimson sun poured in. He sipped his drink contentedly. When he smelled the fresh bread ready to be brought from the oven, his mouth began to water.

Samíah was a good cook, as fine a cook as her mother had been. In fact, since her return he'd been better fed than at any time since his wife's death. Samíah was good that way. Good in other ways as well. No sooner had she come back to him and walked in the door than she'd pulled a long, troubled face.

"The house is filthy!" she had complained. "It smells!" And over his protestations she had taken command—of everything. Within weeks there were new curtains everywhere; the shutters and doors no longer creaked; the floors and rugs were washed with pine-scented cleaner; the sills and shelves were dotted with plants, all kinds of plants—big ones, small ones, tall ones, shooting ones. Then she threw out the dogs. This, of course, really made his temper flare. "I love my dogs!" he complained. To which she smugly replied, "Then sleep with them—out in the yard."

As morose as the animals who'd been accustomed to sharing both home and bed, Habib grew resigned to his fate, feeling he was somehow no longer master of his own destiny. However, all things being equal, Samíah had certainly done a fine job of it, that much he couldn't deny. His house had never looked so nice, not even when his wife had run it.

Samíah served the bread. Habib broke it in half and bit into the crust. It was delicious. So was the cheese she promptly brought. Yes, and the fresh fruit as well. Breakfast done, he slouched deeper in his seat and gazed out the window. The street was coming alive, children laughing and shouting as they played and slowly ambled toward the little school. Dogs were barking everywhere, chasing cats, rummaging in and out of the alleys, making a nuisance of themselves until broom-wielding wives and grandmothers gave chase. Habib could hear the jingle of the belled bridle belonging to the ragman's lazy mule.

Habib looked out the window for quite a while. When Samíah came back, she was dressed for the day. Her hair was down, falling in long waves over her shoulders, her shapely form modestly and properly draped in a dark-colored *chador*. In her pretty face he could see the delicate features of her mother, the wide, expansive eyes and slanting brows. Her strong features were softly offset by unblemished flesh. A small basket hung from her arm.

"I have to go out for a while," she said.

Habib's brow rose. His daughter didn't seem to leave the house very much these days. Only to deliver her dresses when they were done or to browse through the market in search of a good buy on a new roll of linen or cloth. With her sisters and friends all married and busy with their duties, Samíah rarely even chatted with other women. Oh, now and then she might spend an afternoon in pleasant company, but mostly she stayed right here, working, caring for him. That she was going out now pleased Habib.

"We need some flour. More salt, also."

Habib grimaced. "Why don't you spend the morning in the market? Browse around. Buy yourself something pretty—a bracelet or a charm? Abul the goldsmith's shop is filled with new delights. I've seen them. A new shipment of quality jewelry just came from Damascus. I'd bet he'd find you something exquisite."

"Jewelry is frivolous, Papa. I have other things to do with my money."

Inwardly he steamed. "Don't you want to look beautiful?"

Her laugh was short and caustic. "Are you hinting that I'm turning ugly?"

"Of course not, daughter! But every woman likes pretty things to show off with, to impress her friends, to please her hus—" He bit off the last word, sorry he had spoken so impulsively.

Samíah's eyes brooded. "Husband?"

Shying from her intense stare, he said, "You know what I mean." Then, finding the courage to look at her directly, he went on. "It wouldn't hurt..."

She laughed now, too fond of her well-meaning father to be truly angry. She slipped her arm around him, bent her head, and kissed his cheek. "Take a nap, Papa. You must be very tired." She turned to go.

"Your veil, daughter. You forgot to put it on."

Samíah grinned impishly. "I abhor wearing a veil, you know that. Anyway, the sultan has decreed that it's permissible for a woman to walk in public without one."

"For shame, daughter! What will the neighbors think?"

She shrugged. "They can think what they like. Lots of women, even wives, conduct their business freely without having to hide their faces. Why shouldn't I?"

8

"For modesty, daughter."

"These are new times, Papa. The sultan has decreed—"

He nodded dourly, annoyed at her refusal to adhere to strict tradition and code, but aware that what she had said was true. Times *were* changing. The whole world was changing. There was little room for men who so tenaciously clung to the old ways. Even the sultan himself had said so. A new age had begun—a Golden Age, they called it, an era of enlightenment. The holy wars were over. Trade flowed freely across the world. Why, even Christian European ships were allowed into Arabian ports!

Habib shook his head, wondering where it would all end. He was not a political man, never had been. The law was the law, period. And if the sultan, surrounded by all his wise ministers and viziers, proclaimed that a woman might walk publicly without covering her face, who was he to dispute it? The Koran itself, the Holy Book, never said a woman *must* be veiled. Yes, things were changing quickly. Soon it would probably be permissible for a woman to walk unescorted at night. Habib chuckled. Wouldn't that be something!

"Do you need anything, Papa?"

He yawned and shook his head. The warm sun was making him sleepy.

"I'll be back in an hour or so," she told him softly. Then she marched to the door, looked over her shoulder, and added as an afterthought, "Please have your bath before I come home. And put your work clothes with the dirty laundry. Your shirt is stinking up the house."

 "I FORGOT TO TELL YOU," SAMÍAH SAID WITH A big smile later that day as they sat down for dinner. It was almost sundown, and soon Habib would have to get ready for work if he wasn't to be late.

"Oh? Tell me what?" He gnashed his teeth and swallowed, putting the leg of roasted lamb down onto his plate and wiping his greasy fingers on his napkin.

"Returning home from the market, I saw Anna drawing water at the well. She asked me to remind you of her invitation." There was a coy little smile parting his daughter's thin lips, Habib noticed. The girl sipped from her teacup and put it down before her. "Something about your promising to come for supper on your day off . . ."

The dustman slapped his palm against his forehead. "I did forget," he admitted, recalling the incident. "But I didn't *promise*. All I said was that I'd try and—" He paused to dislodge a sliver of meat jammed irritatingly between two molars.

"Don't pick your teeth."

"Sorry." His hand flew to his side. "I wish Anna wouldn't keep after me like this."

Samíah's soft features glowed in waning sunlight spilling luxuriously into the tiny room. "Why, Papa, you should be flattered. It's not every man your age who's so hotly sought after by our street's most available woman. Anna receives a

10

very nice pension, I understand. Her late husband toiled for years as a palace gardener."

"I can earn my own money, thank you."

"Don't be offended. Besides, she's really quite pleasant when you get to know her."

Habib went back to eating. "She means well, I suppose. Only, her tongue never stops wagging. It's enough to drive a man mad."

"Don't talk with your mouth full. Anyway, wouldn't it be a nice change for you? A romantic dinner, a pleasant diversion, just you and her alone . . ."

"Samíah!"

She grinned. "Excuse me, Papa. I was only thinking of you."

He patted his belly, satisfied with the meal. In the yard his dogs were impatiently growling, waiting for the scraps. "I, er, thought we might spend my day off together," he said casually. "Your uncle would be most pleased if we left the city and came to visit."

"To his village?" She made a face.

"What's wrong with it? Or have you forgotten it's *my* village as well. And a bloody better place to live than inside walls. A man can breathe free, smell the mountain air, the desert sands—"

"Not to mention the burning camel dung." She shuddered on purpose. "Papa, it's been how many years since you left the village? Really, Marrakesh is our home. The only one we have."

"Still, a visit with my brother wouldn't hurt. In fact it might do us both some good. What do you say, daughter?"

Samíah regarded him dubiously. "In your brother's last letter, didn't he mention something about a young man? A son of his third cousin who recently inherited some land? What was it he wrote?" She smiled when she quoted. "Ah yes, 'a fine *eligible* fellow' . . ."

The dustman flushed under her stare. She was on to him, he saw. "So what, Samíah?" he said. "So what if I wanted to have you meet this young man? Is it a crime?" His chest swelled

11

with his hurt, his face growing stern. "Does it make me a criminal to wish my daughter wed, raising a family, happy for a change?"

"I am happy, Papa."

He threw up his hands. "*Bah!* A healthy woman of twenty who locks herself in the house and works all day and all night, has no children and no husband to care for her. Is that happiness?"

"I can take care of myself. I don't need a husband."

Habib groaned, beside himself with frustration. "Other fathers would find a husband for you, you know, barter over the dowry and set the date without consulting you at all! Is that what you want?"

She lowered her gaze. "No, Papa."

He puffed his cheeks and blew the air out of his mouth, feeling upset and angry at himself for this display of temper. Samíah knew very well he wouldn't resort to such a blind marriage. Yet the girl was being so willfully obstinate. Bullheaded and intractable! Like her mother, he mused, so very like her mother.

"Oh, Samíah, Samíah. I've seen you change so much since Rashid's death." He reached his hand out across the table and gently stroked the side of her face. Samíah pulled away, turning her head sideways so that a curtain of silky hair hid her eyes. Habib knew there would be tears forming. "I only want you to be your old self again, daughter, laughing, dancing. Remember how you loved to dance?"

Her voice was a whisper. "Please, Papa. Don't push me so much. I'm not ready for what you ask yet. I need time." She tried to smile. "It's only been a year."

"A year and a half, child. Soon it will be two." He leaned in closer and took her slim hands in his. They were trembling, and to Habib his daughter seemed like an injured fawn, healed in body but not in spirit, and, so, afraid to run again.

"I know how much you and Rashid cared for each other. I know that you can never fully forget..."

Her eyes were wet and wide. "Please try to understand, Papa. I cherish my memories of Rashid, truly I do. But I also accept the fact of his death. I know that someday another will take his place."

At this, the dustman was glad. A shadow, though, crossed his face when she said, "But I fear that time is still far off for me. It's not because of Rashid's memory that I am as I am."

"Then why, daughter? Why?"

She had no answer, and for the life of him Habib couldn't understand her. Samíah was the most intelligent woman he'd ever known. Surely she realized what she was doing to herself, spurning offer after offer and refusing to consider a new suitor. What was the reason, if not Rashid's memory? Or was it that she was frightened? Afraid of meeting somebody new and falling in love, only to have tragedy strike again?

Shaking his head with uncertainty, he said, "Very well. If it's time you need, then time you shall have."

Her eyes perceptibly brightened.

"We'll visit my brother another time. Anyway, the village bores me."

Samíah giggled girlishly. "You'll accept Anna's invitation?"

"I suppose so," he drawled.

"Good. Then I'll sew you a new shirt and—"

"Samíah!"

"Sorry, Papa." She got up from the table to clean the plates. Habib watched her work, more pleased and proud of her than he could put into words. Samíah was capable of accomplishing anything she set her mind to. Gods, what a prize she would make for the right man! How fortunate the lucky fellow would be. But it would take a strong man to handle a woman as willful as she; one stronger than he could provide. It would take . . . well, it would take someone every bit as adamant and single-minded as she.

 THE KNOCK ON THE DOOR WAS LOUD AND ABRUPT. Samíah frowned, then sewed a few more stitches before placing the nearly completed garment down.

"Yes?" she called, hurrying for the door. Outside, thunder rumbled and the wind blew wildly. The sky was a cold, chilly gray, and she hoped her sleeping father had had enough sense to shut the window in his room. The knock came again before she reached the door.

"Who is it?" she asked.

The voice on the other side was muffled.

"Who?"

He gave a name. It sounded something like "Gideon." Puzzled—for she knew nobody by that name and wasn't expecting any visitors this afternoon—she wondered if it might be the servant of a new client someone recommended. Samíah unconsciously straightened her dress and opened the door a peek. The rain pelted with dramatic fury. Standing in the doorway was a man. A rather youthful fellow, whose clean-shaven face dripped with the deluge, he was tall, lanky, and not bad looking except for the stupid, awkward grin he wore.

"Yes? What do you want?"

He lowered his head respectfully. "Er...Is this the house of Habíb?" he asked weakly, one hand covering the top of his bare head in a useless effort to stave off the rain.

"It is."

The grin expanded. "I, er, was told to come by this afternoon and collect the rent." He sounded apologetic. He certainly was not the usual image of a rent collector—that hardy breed surpassed in coldness only by the tax collectors. Besides, he was a stranger, and such men were always viewed in the Old Quarter with a measure of suspicion.

"Where's Mister al-Gamal?" she asked. On this street the landlord had been personally collecting his rent for twenty years. Odd that now someone else was here to do it for him. The whole matter seemed peculiar to Samíah, and she wondered if perhaps this fellow might be a thief. If so, he'd picked the wrong neighborhood. Patrols of sultan's guards were always close at hand.

"Mister al-Gamal broke his leg, mistress," the man who called himself Gideon told her with a slight stammer. "I'm his nephew." Here he beamed. "His new assistant."

The girl was more than suspicious. Still, the man before her, if she was any judge of character, certainly seemed anything but some cunning brigand out to falsely collect rents. Anyway, with that foolish grin he didn't seem smart enough.

Lightning lashed and the thunder crashed. Gideon got drenched by a burst of gusted rain; he took his hand from his head and looked at her lamely.

"Who's there, child?"

Stifling a big yawn, Habib ambled from his bedroom, peering into the darkened parlor. The wind and thunder had roused him from a deep, satisfying slumber.

Tilting her head sideways, Samíah called, "He says he's here for the rent, Papa. But he's a stranger."

Habib squinted at the doorway and saw the youth standing there soaked. "Gideon? Gideon, is that you, boy?"

Samíah showed her surprise. "You know him?"

"Ach, certainly I know him, child! He's our landlord's nephew! By Allah, Gideon, why are you standing there in the rain?"

The girl opened the door wider. "Come on in," she said, sighing grimly as the visitor dripped all over the rug. Gideon saw the anger flash in her eyes and tried to placate her with one of his smiles. "It's wet out there," he said.

"Sit, sit, boy!" bellowed Habib. He gestured for the young man to have a seat on the divan.

"Samíah! Where are your manners, daughter? Bring our guest some tea. Yes, and some of your pastry as well."

"Oh, please don't go to all that trouble, sir—"

"Nonsense, Gideon. No trouble at all, is it, Samíah?"

She lowered her gaze. "No, Papa."

Habib gave Gideon a towel, and the rent collector dried himself quickly, thankful to have gotten out of the storm.

Out in the tiny kitchen, Samíah turned when her father came inside. "Is he really al-Gamal's nephew?" she asked.

Habib nodded. "A nice young man, wouldn't you say? He's only been in Marrakesh a very short time, I understand. Comes from the country, they say."

Samíah's eyes lit up with amusement. "Ah, a bumpkin. That explains it."

"Explains what?"

"Never mind. Just that he caught me by surprise. I wasn't expecting him. You didn't mention that the landlord broke his leg."

Habib scratched his head. "I didn't? Hmmm. Must have slipped my mind. Nasty accident, it was. Slipped off a ladder or something. He'll be all right, though. His nephew arrived in the nick of time, don't you think? Al-Gamal would likely starve if he had to wait for his rents to be delivered." Habib chuckled darkly.

"Him? That rich old swine. Why—"

"Shhh! Samíah! Do you want his nephew to overhear us?"

"I don't care if he does! His uncle's been gouging us and our neighbors for years! Toothless old goat! This place isn't worth half its cost." She poured tea into a cup; placed it and a single piece of pastry onto a tray. "And you want to feed him, no less! Papa, sometimes I think you've taken leave of your senses."

"So how do you like our city?" inquired Habib, following

16

his daughter out of the kitchen, wiping his brow, hoping the young man hadn't heard his fiery daughter's outburst.

Gideon rose politely and took the tray from her hands, setting it down gingerly on the round table. Habib lit a lamp.

"So far, I like it very much," Gideon answered honestly. "Yes, very much indeed."

Samíah sat opposite. Making polite conversation, she said, "Where are you from?"

The young man hesitated before answering. "Oh, from the north. Beyond the mountains. My, er, father has a business on the coast." He smiled.

Samíah smiled back. "How nice for you."

"Ummmm. Your tea is delicious." He savored the aroma, took another sip. When he put his cup down, a little of it sloshed over the rim and onto the tray. Samíah hid her grimace.

"Excuse me," he stammered. "Sometimes I get quite clumsy." And as if to emphasize his words, he inadvertently knocked his arm into a hanging plant.

"Have you many rounds left today?" Habib asked.

Gideon was very careful not to bump into anything when he leaned forward. "Fortunately, no." He patted the purse tucked safely in his belt. "This street is my last."

"Will you be collecting the rent for long?" Samíah wanted to know.

Again the hesitation in his answer. "Er, that depends, mistress. My, er, uncle will have to decide. Anyway, I'm going to give this job my best. I like it."

Samíah glanced at her father with eyes that said, "He *likes* collecting rents!"

The dogs began to howl. Habib stirred and frowned. "I'd better see what's the matter," he mumbled. "No, please stay," he added when Gideon rose as well. The rent collector did it again, this time banging his head on yet another hanging plant.

"I—I really had better be going, anyway. But thank you for your hospitality." He bowed, all smiles. "Thank you both. *Salaam*, Habib. Peace be unto you, Samíah. I can call you by your name, can't I?"

The girl nodded.

17

"Then farewell for today." He stuffed the last crumbs of pastry into his mouth, unaware that several tumbled to the floor. Then he turned to go.

"Hey, wait a minute!" cried Samíah.

He looked back dumbly. "Yes?"

"You forgot to collect your uncle's rent."

AT DAWN, THE RED WALLS THAT SURROUND MARrakesh gleamed and burned with the rising sun, and a rosy haze hovered above the city like the glow of a smoldering fire. Beyond the walls stretched a magnificent belt of green, an oasis of palms and great trees that surrounded the city and pushed back the encroaching desert. To the north stood the great chain of snow-capped, glittering peaks, the High Atlas Mountains where it is said day meets the night and Atlas himself upholds the heavens.

Within the city walls nothing was more wondrous than the *souk* where Samíah had come that particular morning to purchase a pair of slippers.

The *Jama-el-F'Na* teemed with life. From the first hour after dawn it was jammed with incredible movement as a bewildering medley of people and animals carried on amid indescribable noise. Thus it had been for centuries—a gathering place, some said, as ancient as the sands of the Sahara itself. It was the meeting place for peoples of all lands, Moors and black Africans, Berbers, merchants from Damascus and Baghdad and Jerusalem, tribesmen from the mountains, Hebrews and Christians, seafaring Phoenicians, Greeks, Turks, Egyptians, and a host of nameless foreigners come to seek fortune, fame, and adventure in an ageless and fabled land.

Samíah took her younger sister Hoda by the hand, and together they pushed their way across the square through jostling crowds. Lazy mules pulling wagons balked in the heat and plopped down in the middle of the road, refusing to budge. Camel drivers hurled insults at the wagonmasters; pedestrians grumbled about the blockage and scrambled in thick knots around both beasts and wagons. The sun beat down unrelentingly. Hoda groaned. Hand to her bulging belly, for she was three months away from delivering her third child, she glanced around furtively for a shady place to rest. There were none. The places beneath the occasional trees and wide awnings were filled with others also beaten by the oppressive heat. Young mothers and whining children, old toothless men—all were sweltering and weary, while around them a host of beggars, blind and limbless, shuffled in search for alms. Sultan's guards, unobtrusive but always nearby, moved them along from time to time, but there were always a dozen more to replace them.

"Are you all right?" asked Samíah.

Hoda took a deep breath of the stagnant air and bravely nodded. "I will be," she said, peeking at the sun and adjusting her veil. "If only it would rain."

The sky was cloudless, the heat wave having lasted for a week now.

"Perhaps it was a mistake for you to come with me today," Samíah said.

"No, no, dear sister. It was my idea, remember? There are still so many things I need for the baby. . . ."

With a knowing nod, Samíah sighed. Hoda, wed these three years, already had more than a handful at home. Under the careful scrutiny of her mother-in-law, the poor girl labored endlessly to care for her children, the cantankerous, complaining old hag, as well as a hardworking husband who came home every night with an insatiable appetite. Hoda's family was steadily growing, with additions arriving each year like clockwork; and at times Samíah was astounded that Hoda was able to bear up as well as she did. But the girl was happy, and really that was all that mattered.

"We'll find a place to rest soon," Samíah assured her sister. "Perhaps in the *babouch*."

Samíah wiped perspiration from her brow and pulled Hoda away toward an area between groups of acrobats and performing jugglers. Vendors called out from their stalls for the street performers to go away, claiming they were blocking their displays. Singers loudly crooned at the top of their lungs, and Samíah carefully led Hoda over a man lying flat in the dust, his eyes tightly shut, his bony arms outstretched. Over and over he cried out the name of Allah. "Allah the merciful, Allah the all knowing, Allah the blessed." No one paid attention. Bargaining, bantering, and laughter carried on all around the fellow as if he weren't there.

A snake charmer gaily tooted a horn while a venomous cobra twisted up from an open basket. Unheard beside him, a poet spouted verse. Water boys—small children with goatskins strapped on their backs—hawked their offerings, a cupful for a penny. Many shoppers stopped to buy a drink, gladly paying the small price, for the walk to the public fountains was long and tiring.

Dressed in splendid finery, a small group of visiting nobles bullied a path past browsing housewives in search of a good price. Here and there some African slave, marked by the silver earring set into his lobe, hurried on some errand for his master. All over the square, stalls of fruit—innumerable piles of oranges, lemons, grapefruit, pomegranates, apricots, and olives hung in huge baskets—could be seen, all fresh and tasty, protected from the sun by awnings of tent canvas. The stall owners outbid each other in price in an effort to make a day's decent wage.

"This way, this way," urged Samíah, laughter still in her eyes after they had briefly watched the antics of a puppet show. She guided Hoda well away from the frivolity, past the stalled wagons, and continued the fascinating journey.

From one distant corner the reek of fish was pungent. Hauled by caravan from the coastal villages, the supply was always quickly snapped up by wise early morning shoppers, but the stench of fish remained strong and foul, as it always did until nightfall. Against an aged and crumbling wall stood a market of junk and rubbish. Here visitors rummaged through piles of cracked pots and earthenware, useless tools, old boxes, discarded clothing, and rags—ever in search of something precious amid the refuse. Across from the heaps, past another milling throng, sat the apothecaries, the red flags of their trade limply hanging from tiny wooden poles, ready to sell a prospective buyer herbs, medicines, and all the secrets of their trade. Women squatted, selling loaves of freshly baked bread from homemade baskets placed carefully beneath pieces of fan-shaped canvas, shooing flies and protecting their product like hens watching over unhatched eggs.

In the *souk* of Marrakesh there was nothing that could not be bought for the right price: weaponry of the finest Damascus steel; the finest and most expensive jewelry; artifacts of gold and silver, diamonds, pearls, fire opals, rubies, amber, bloodstones, emeralds, and every gemstone known to man; goods of leather for the rich, of cloth for the less prosperous; charms to ward off misfortune, amulets to cause it; oils and snakes; potions of every conceivable concoction. From horseflesh to human flesh, from perfume to sulfur, good luck to ill, the wares and goods of the entire world could be found in the *souk*.

Hot and sweating, Samíah and Hoda finally worked their way across the blistering square and turned up one of the countless side streets leading toward the palace. Along the Street of the Sandalmakers they paused, Samíah at last able to seek the pair of slippers she had come to buy. The street was roofed with palm leaves laid across trellis work to keep out the sun, and in the shadows was relief from the market's terrible heat. They wandered leisurely along the countless little shops and stalls, bewildered by the countless offerings. In Marrakesh men always wore slippers of yellow, women of red. Sellers eagerly called out to the two women to come inside, but Samíah's eyes had been caught by a particular pair on display, a pair worked in tooled leather and exquisitely seamed with gold thread. The shopkeeper saw her interest and openly grinned. Samíah walked to his shop as aware as he that the sale was already made except for the customary and obligatory haggling over price. As she came to the awning a man hurriedly pushed by, causing her to turn and look at him. A well-dressed, dark-skinned man who offered no apology, in his haste he nearly stumbled.

Hoda examined the offered slippers first, pleased with their softness and craftsmanship, but frowning in hopes of reducing the price. Samíah aloofly stood in the awning's shade, content to let her sister make the first offer.

Across the street, meanwhile, a deformed beggar hobbled out of an alley, as shoeless and faceless as all the rest of the city's destitute. Samíah would not have paid him the slightest attention had not something curious happened. The well-dressed man paused at sight of the beggar and, to her surprise, came slowly toward him, offering a coin for his cup. From both the finery of his dress and the assurance of his gait she assumed him to be a gentlemen, perhaps even a noble or a member of the palace court. That he was here in the *babouch* was one thing; that he stopped in his hurry to converse with a beggar another. Samíah wondered why.

The well-dressed man's eyes darted to and fro suspiciously as the beggar mumbled something in his ear. It was Hoda's gentle nudging that finally pulled her from her thoughts. "What do you think?"

"Offer him ten," she said.

"Ten?" mimicked the outraged shopkeeper, gold front tooth aglitter. "Ten? This pair is a steal at twice the price!" He rolled his eyes heavenward and wrung his hands. "Such quality is unsurpassed in the city. Dear ladies, would you rob the food from a poor man's plate? Would you—"

"Twelve and no more." Hoda sounded firm.

The merchant slapped his forehead and moaned loudly. "I myself paid more," he wailed. "Seventeen and not a penny less." And on and on they rattled, Hoda refusing and slightly upping her offer, the shopkeeper berating himself for his own stupidity as he slightly lowered his.

When Samíah again looked across the street, the beggar was

gone. The well-dressed man, though, was still there, smiling with what seemed to be satisfaction. Then, he too turned to leave, again walking briskly as he made his way from the shops of the quiet street back toward the direction of the square. Samíah was about to put the encounter completely from her mind when, to her shock, she saw a trio of hooded figures suddenly leap from the alley. It all happened so fast that events were a blur. The noble was hurled to the ground. Knives flashed. Without a sound, the noble was dragged back into the shadowed alley and out of sight.

"They're killing him!" screamed Samíah.

Startled, both Hoda and the merchant turned.

"There!" cried the girl, her lips trembling, hand pointing to the alley. "Didn't you see? A nobleman's been attacked!"

From the adjoining shops the merchants, hearing Samíah's cry, ran outside. Hoda threw down the slippers and followed Samíah out into the midday sun. Several shopkeepers and passersby dashed for the alley, ready to confront the thieves. When Samíah pantingly arrived they were all standing around perplexed and shrugging. There was nothing to be seen. No sign of the scuffle, not of victim or assailants. Save for the barking of a dog behind the wall, the alley was silent. In the Street of the Sandalmakers the commotion had spread. Shoppers were now in a near panic, and above the din could be heard the shouts for someone to call the soldiers. They were not long in coming.

Along the arched street they came, turbaned and uniformed, running out of breath, hands clutched to the hilts of their curved swords.

The captain brusquely commanded his men to cordon off the street, then brushed aside the gathered crowd and marched into the alley, keen eyes missing nothing. "What happened here?" he demanded.

Feet shuffled and all eyes were cast downward. Samíah, still shaking, boldly stepped in front and confronted him. "They—they must have kidnapped him," she said, panting, looking about in frustration.

The soldier slanted his bushy brows. "Kidnapped who?"

"I don't know. I mean, I saw him but I don't know his name. He was a noble, I'm sure. Finely garbed, dark skinned. He was here when they jumped from this alley. . . ."

The captain's face was impassive. "Who was in the alley?"

"Three men. All hooded. They carried knives. . . ."

"Assassins!" someone gasped.

The soldier's features hardened, and he glanced about sternly. There was enough trouble without having anyone jump to conclusions. "Go on."

Samíah retold the story. When she was done, the captain turned to the others. "Did anyone else witness this?"

All present shook their heads.

"Didn't *anyone* else see it?" Samíah cried. There was no answer, and she bit her lip to keep it from trembling, balled her hands into fists and held them at her sides. "Surely one of you—Someone must have noticed?" She pointed to the street. "He stopped to speak with the beggar. Didn't any of you see him either?"

Again no response, only this time the eyes of the captain seemed mocking and filled with disbelief. "I saw it, I tell you!" Samíah insisted to the skeptical soldier. She glanced to her sister. "Hoda, you were with me. . . ."

"I didn't see a thing, Samíah." Hoda's eyes were wet and worry filled. "Are you sure . . . ?"

"I didn't see anything either," added the slipper merchant. "Both these women were inside my shop when this one"—he pointed to Samíah—"started to scream."

"Aye, that's the first I heard of it as well," confirmed a second shopkeeper. The crowd mumbled.

Samíah pulled herself together, ignoring the pounding of her heart and the looks of pity she was beginning to receive. "I know what I saw," she said flatly. "A man was abducted right here, right where we're standing now. He may be dead or they may have carried him away somewhere. Whichever, I saw it with my own eyes."

Hoda put a hand to Samíah's elbow. "Maybe you were mistaken, sister. Maybe—"

Samíah pulled away sharply. "I'm not! I *saw* it!"

The captain looked over his shoulder to his men, snapped his fingers. "Search the street!" he directed. "Every alley from here to the square." His men ran off in different directions. The crowd gradually started to dissipate—one by one the merchants returning to their shops, the visitors to the street, going back to their business. After a short time only Samíah, Hoda, and the captain were left in the alley.

"I don't think you believe a word I've said," Samíah told him.

The burly soldier met her gaze evenly, ignoring the remark. "What's your name?" he asked.

"Samíah, daughter of Habib the dustman." She stood straight and tall. "I live nearby in the Old Quarter."

The captain thought for a moment, reflecting on the thousands of names and faces he came in contact with. After a time he remembered the dustman—a nice old fellow, gentle, soft-spoken. He peered about once more to satisfy himself, kneeling and sifting his hand along the surface of the dusty ground where she claimed the encounter had taken place. But if there had been signs of the disturbance, they were gone now, trampled and erased by too many fresh footprints.

He stood and sighed.

"Aren't you going to do anything?" Samíah asked.

"What can I do?" he retorted. "The victim has disappeared along with his abductors. Whatever happened here, real or imagined, is over and done. If such a man was abducted, his family will soon report it to the proper authorities."

"Then I was right. You don't believe me."

"Go back to your home, Samíah," the captain said quietly.

Hoda heaved a thankful sigh, glad to be able to leave this place at last. "Come, Samíah, there's nothing more to be done."

"But I was a witness," the girl protested. "I did see it!"

"You'll be promptly called again for questioning should anything further develop," the captain promised. "But for now, go home. I advise you to forget about this." He frowned distastefully as he glanced around. "Forget about everything you think you saw." When the girl didn't move, he put a gentle hand on her shoulder and forced her to look at him. "For your own sake, Samíah, Marrakesh can be a dangerous place—and for an innocent bystander who has seen too much, more dangerous than ever."

His voice was cold, and Samíah dumbly nodded, suddenly frightened. Long after she had left him, the warning continued to echo in her ears.

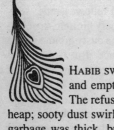 HABIB SWUNG THE TRASH-FILLED CANVAS BAG UP and emptied its contents into the loading wagon. The refuse clattered and sank into the mountainous heap; sooty dust swirled and clogged his nostrils. The stink of garbage was thick, but after so many hours of sweeping and collecting it, Habib was immune. All over the empty square the teams of trash collectors copied his act identically, each hauling his own load to the wagons, each emptying his collection quickly before continuing his rounds. The mules snorted and stamped their feet, eager to pull away and be led to the dumps.

A perfect crescent moon hung lazily in the night sky, surrounded by a plethora of twinkling stars. With an ache in his legs and a cramp in his back, Habib dutifully began to sweep another section, carefully piling the litter in a little mound before sweeping it into his waiting bag.

A whistle blew, signaling the end of the shift. Habib strained to pick up his half-filled bag, then marched in procession with his fellow dustmen. One at a time they unloaded the last of the rubbish. Moments later whips cracked in the hands of the drivers and the garbage-laden wagons groaned forward, winding their way beyond the city gates to the massive refuse dump at the edge of the desert. Cobblestone walkways gleamed wetly; Habib waved to several of the slop-bucket laborers, collected his meager tools, and with broom safely tucked under his arm prepared for the walk home.

"*Salaam*, Habib," the chief engineer of the cleanup operation called. "See you tomorrow."

Habib smiled and nodded, pausing at the water wagon to dip the ladle and drink his fill. At his side another dustman waited his turn. A small, wispy fellow named Hussein who was ragged and dirty in the best of times, he now looked and smelled as though he'd just crawled up from a cesspool. "Lookie here," rasped Hussein, standing in the shadow of the looming mosque tower.

Habib dropped the ladle and turned. Huessin was grinning broadly, sheltering something in the palms of his hands while his cat eyes narrowed and spryly danced.

Habib squinted, but couldn't tell what it was. Hussein held it out for him to see. The dustman gasped. It was a brooch, an intricately designed golden brooch with a dark bloodstone set at its center. "Where did you find that?"

Hussein chuckled as he glanced over his shoulder to where an alley cat had darted from a trash basket. "Found it," he whispered in his husky, accented voice. Hussein was a foreigner from the mountains, he claimed, and new on the job. There was little employment to be found inside the city these days, and many would have regarded the small man as lucky to have found the job he had. "Found it at the edge of the market," he went on, indicating the general direction with his thumb. Then he placed the brooch inside his soiled shirt. Broken teeth flashed malevolently. In the distant the sultan's soldiers marched smartly along the parapet of the high palace wall, standing watch and overseeing the city as they always did.

"Aren't you going to report your find?"

Hussein snickered. "Why should I?"

27

"It's the rule. You know that. Lost property is to be turned over to the gang boss for safekeeping."

The wispy man's snarl was vicious. "Safekeeping, ha! I know what they do, Habib. I know very well what they do. Don't make me laugh. They won't report it either. Lookie, the overseer's not stupid. He'll keep the brooch for himself, that's what. No, no." He patted his find tenderly. "I ain't so dumb. Not me."

"You'll lose your job if they find out," Habib warned truthfully. It would not be the first time some poor worker was fired because he had accidentally come across something of value among the trash and failed to hand it over for a report to be made.

Hussein's feline eyes glimmered with mischievous fires. "Lookie," he said, "a brooch like this is worth plenty. A year's pay, maybe more. You think I'm gonna just give it back?"

Habib shrugged. "There might be a reward for its return. . . ."

"Sure." Hussein winked lewdly. "Some fine noble's gonna pay me, eh? Forget it. I found it, it's mine. Finders keepers."

"All right. But if there's any trouble about it—"

"You'll keep your mouth shut, eh?"

Habib nodded in promise. A man of his word, he would never consider informing on a fellow dustman; still, he realized Hussein was taking a bad risk. Selling the brooch openly in the marketplace would cause many questions as to how and where a lowly dustman came into possession of such a fine piece of jewelry. On the other hand, should Hussein opt to barter it clandestinely to one of the city's unsavory characters, the outcome might be even worse. It would not be the first time some thug slit a man's throat if he thought the reward worth the effort.

Several other workers, also finished with unloading, talked in low voices and sauntered toward the water wagon. Hussein saw them and concealed the bulge in his shirt with his arm. He drank a ladle of water, then smiled secretively at Habib and went on his way, not looking back. Habib watched him dis-

28

appear into the shadows and heaved a long sigh. Then he picked up his canvas bag and started his own march home.

Dawn was yet awhile off, the night sky like velvet, the many towers and minarets looming in front of the stars like silent sentinels. He heard the rush of wind as it rustled the broad leaves in the plaza's palms and gardens and listened to shutters bang gently against closed windows. A storm was brewing, Habib was sure; he could feel it coming in the air. As he crossed the first of the narrow streets, he sensed a growing uneasiness. But what troubled him, he didn't know. Only that he somehow wished Hussein had never spoken to him about what he found.

The angry snarl of a dog sounded behind him. Habib turned sharply. From the corner of his eye he caught sight of the mangy hound, ribbed and tatter eared, as it dashed from the threshold of a deserted alley with its tail between its legs, witlessly whimpering, and fleeing as though a demon were chasing him. The wind was steadily rising, and Habib wiped particles of dust from his eyes.

The hiss of an unseen cat made him stumble and take an unconsious leap backward. When he looked toward the shadows, he saw it glaring at him from slitted green glowing eyes, its white fangs bared like a miniature lion's, its back arched and its front paws forward as if ready to jump. A cunning street fighter of a cat, wild and untamed, living in the jungle of alleys.

Tiger stripes showed on its back where the moon's silver light slanted in beams into the shadows. For what seemed a long time, both man and cat stood motionless, eyes locked on each other's. Habib moved first, reaching out with his hand in friendship. The cat drew back and hissed again.

It was plain that the feline wanted no part of human company, and Habib would have gladly obliged its request for solitude if he hadn't noticed the injury.

The cat's paw was swollen and bloody. A thistle or sliver of wood must have lodged painfully between pad and paw, Habib realized, and unless it was removed the swelling would worsen. Despite the menace, Habib felt pity for the creature.

"Let me see," he said in a soothing voice, not yet daring to approach.

The cat curled its tail and narrowed its eyes. Habib, putting his broom and canvas bag carefully down, approached gingerly. "I only want to have a look at your paw," he told the animal in the same tone he would use with a small child. "I won't hurt you. . . ."

Into the long shadow he moved cautiously, for if the cat proved sicker than he thought or rabid, it would surely attack him. It didn't, nor did it run. Slowly it backtracked deeper into the darkness, never once taking its gaze away from Habib. The dustman knelt and held up his palms unthreateningly. He wished he had some food to offer. The cat moved up against the wall, studying him with unmistakable cunning and intelligence. Instinctively it knew Habib was not an enemy, but it was not yet prepared to accept him as a friend, either.

"Let me see your paw," he said. "Perhaps I can make the pain go away."

The cat sniffed the air. Wind gusted inside the alley. Habib extended his hand. "Come on, let me have a look." He continued to speak, hoping the cat would grow accustomed to the sound of his voice. "I saw the way you handled that dog," he told it. "Made him run for his life, eh? Taught him a good lesson about the world, eh?" He chuckled. In all his years he'd never failed to sooner or later win over the respect—and sometimes love—of homeless animals, and he wished this time would prove no exception. "I had a she-cat once, you know. Yes, I did. Gave birth to a litter of seven, she did. Lovely kittens. Of course it wasn't easy to convince my wife to let me keep them until I found each a proper home." The cat seemed to relax slightly. "And I did, you know. Found a shelter for every last one of them. Loved those kittens." Flying dust tickled the hairs in his nostrils and he sneezed. The cat jumped. "There, there, don't be frightened. I suppose I must look terrible to you, eh? Smelly as well. I'm a dustman, you know. Have been for more years than I'd like to say." He touched the cat gently, stroking behind its ears. "My daughter says it's time for me to retire. Says she can take care of me in my old

30

age, she does. Can you imagine? What's the world coming to? I don't know. Women working, walking in public without a veil. Things have changed since my time. Yes they have." He grinned and urged the cat to him, quickly taking the hurt paw in his hand and examining it. "As I thought, a piece of wood. Nasty injury. Now, don't squirm. Hold still and I'll have it out in a second." His thumb and forefinger worked open the space between its tender pad and its claws. With a swift dig of his fingernail, Habib plucked the wood and burst the pus-filled swelling. The cat yelped and tried to leap out of his grasp. Habib, though, held him firm. "All gone," he said, pleased with his simple and effective surgery. "But that wound needs some salve. We don't want it to get any worse, do we?" He bit his lip and sighed. "Only one thing to do. Bring you home. I know, I know, you don't like people. Can't say I fault you for it. However, it's the only way, friend. Don't worry about Samíah. She'll understand. Anyway, it's only for a short while. Just until the injury heals. And there'll be plenty of fresh milk for you. Decent food, also. What do you say?"

He lifted himself up, ignoring the cramp in his back, held the cat to his chest, and scooped up his broom and bag with the other hand. The cat seemed docile enough, but as he began to leave the alley it began to snarl and scratch.

"Hey! That hurts!"

The claws dug into his shirt. Habib winced, and in that split second the cat squirmed free and jumped to the ground, running back into the alley. Habib pulled a sour face. Again he put down his tools. Hands on hips, he marched into the shadows. "Is that any way to treat a friend, hmmm? Come on now. It's nearly daybreak. Besides, you know as well as me what this rising wind means. A storm, my friend. Life will be much better for us both inside the house, won't it?"

The cat was arching its back again, hissing and glaring as it hovered near the edge of the wall.

"Aren't we friends anymore?"

The cat moved from his outstretched hand.

"Very well. If that's the way you want it." Habib shrugged, sorry to see the cat's mistrust come back so quickly. Still, he had accomplished what he set out to do. The splinter was gone, and with luck the injury would heal naturally. Perhaps he'd better get along home already. If Samíah was up, she would be worried by now.

"One more chance, then. Are you coming?"

The cat snapped its head back and showed its fangs. Then it jumped to the side. As it did Habib saw something glitter in the shadows.

"Hello, what's this?"

Resting at the base of the wall, half-covered with a hank of old, soiled rag, stood what seemed to be—well, what looked like—a kettle, rounded and spouted, badly rusted. Never one to leave discarded property lying around without at least a cursory inspection, Habib momentarily forgot about the cat and went to have a better look. The cat went wild, running in circles around him, hissing, growling, lashing out with its claws and scratching his ankles.

"Ouch!" said Habib, hobbling on one foot while rubbing at the other. "What did you do that for?" He hopped away from the wall and the cat backed off, leaving him alone.

"I wasn't going to attack you, you know. I only wanted to have a look at this kettle." The sting ebbed and he put his other foot down, grimacing as he walked again to the wall. Once more the cat viciously assaulted him. "Ungrateful beggar!" He pulled himself to the opposite wall and, to his suprise, the cat meekly stepped out of his way. Habi scratched his stubbled chin. Slowly comprehension dawned.

"It couldn't be," he mumbled beneath his breath.

But it was. He made for the kettle a third time. Again the cat attacked. It was preposterous! The cat was protecting the kettle!

This time Habib was determined. He left the alley, picked up his broom, and came back wielding it. The cat dodged the thistles this way and that, leaping here, jumping there, baring its teeth, glowering, snapping its jaws. In a single swoop Habib picked up the kettle and tossed aside the old rag. He stared at the object in his hand. It wasn't a kettle after all, he realized. It was a lamp.

The cat stalked around him, wary of the menacing broom. Habib sighed in exasperation. "What do you care about an old dented lamp?" he demanded. "What good is it to you?"

The cat stood still. Habib thoughtfully placed the lamp down on the ground in front of him just to see what would happen. He was astounded to see the cat grow docile and literally curl itself around it.

"It must think it's his mother!" gasped the dustman.

Certainly such a happenstance was nothing less than impossible, but at the moment it seemed to be the only logical explanation. Habib quickly amended the thought; nothing in this unfolding little drama seemed logical.

"I see," he said, hands back to his hips, the broom handle sticking up in the air like a flagpole. "You and the lamp are inseparable, is that it? It doesn't go where you don't go, and you don't go where it doesn't."

He dropped to his knees and petted the purring feline.

"All right, then. You're a pair. Now I understand." Gently he lifted both cat and lamp together, truly pleased to find that the cat gave not the slightest resistance. Were he to tell this story to anyone, they would think him mad, probably whisper that he belonged in the asylum. Yet it had happened. It was no illusion.

He came back outside of the alley, fighting the strong wind. The sky was growing light, and he could hear the first stirrings of city life as a milk wagon slowly wheeled along the next street. Habib opened his canvas bag wide and put the cat and the lamp safely inside. Then he placed the whole bundle under his arm and did what he should have done much sooner.

He went home.

SAMÍAH'S LARGE EYES WERE RED AND TEAR FILLED when Habib finally came to the house. Uncharacteristically, she threw her arms around him and buried her face in his chest.

"What's happened, daughter?" he asked. "Is anything wrong? Has anyone hurt you?" He let his broom and canvas bag drop, took Samíah by the shoulders, and forced her to look at him.

"Today, Papa," she said through a sniff, "at the market. I wanted to tell you, but you'd already left when I came home. . . ."

He eyed her questioningly. From the puffs and discolorations, he knew she'd been crying for quite some time. Most unlike the girl to show such emotion.

"What happened to you at the market?" he asked, suspecting the worst.

Samíah folded her arms as if cold. Outside, the wind was blowing with frenzy, the dust storm quickly overtaking the city now and blotting out the sky. In the yard his hounds were whining, shivering in the shelter of the lean-to he'd built to shade them from the sun.

"I saw something yesterday, Papa," Samíah finally said. "Something strange and terrible." She proceeded to recount the tale, how she and Hoda had gone to the sandalmakers' bazaar, the appearance of the deformed beggar and the noble and his subsequent abduction in the alley.

"Did you report this?" Habib wanted to know.

She nodded. "But it all happened so fast. So fast, Papa. A blur. The soldiers came, looked around, but couldn't find anything. Papa, they didn't believe me." Her lip trembled again. "No one believes me, not even Hoda. I'm sure they think I imagined it."

Habib, thankful that Samíah had not been hurt, sheltered the girl in his arms the way he did when she was a child. "It's all right," he whispered, running his fingers through her disheveled hair. "It doesn't matter. Such awful heat can do strange things to a person. Make them see lakes in the sand, cities rising from the dunes . . ."

"It wasn't a mirage!" She spun from his touch, banging a fist against her thigh. "You don't believe me, either!"

"I didn't say that, daughter. Only that maybe—" He hesitated. "Maybe things weren't exactly as you thought. After all, in your own words everything was a blur, happening too quickly to tell for sure." He scratched his head and pondered. Thinking aloud, he went on, "Possibly you did see the hooded men, but during the encounter they fled one way and this noble fled the other. A simple robbery, too fast for the eye to catch. Are you sure they dragged him away? Or could he have escaped, beat them off, and run? By the time the soldiers came all traces were gone. . . ."

Samíah regarded her father through the curtain of her spilling hair. In her heart she was positive of what she'd seen. Yet, perhaps Papa was right. Maybe things weren't exactly the way they seemed. Surely in such a quick time she could have made a few small mistakes. She reconstructed the scene in her mind, slowly shaking her head.

"I—I'm confused, Papa. I was so certain . . ."

"There, there, daughter. Let the soldiers handle the matter. Believe me, if a nobleman was indeed abducted there'll be hell to pay for it. Troops will comb the city in search of the abductors. You'll see. They'll know what to do."

She shivered involuntarily, fixing her eyes on the steaming kettle. "I suppose you're right, Papa." She faced him and sniffed, a little dimpled smile bringing a ray of sunshine to her gloom. "I guess I've been acting silly. I'm sorry."

"You did the right thing, Samíah. Now it's out of your hands. The captain will get to the bottom of this, I promise you. One way or the other."

With a long sigh she walked past the curtains and picked up the kettle. Then she poured tea for them both in small earthen cups. The minty aroma filled the room. All night she'd been awake, pacing the floor, then trying to work and put this from her mind. She couldn't, though. But now, with Papa's strong presence and calm explanation, she felt better, much better. And quite foolish for having carried on the way she had.

"The bread is ready, Papa. Shall I bring it for you?"

Habib shook his head. "Not now, daughter. It's been a very long night. I want to sleep for a while. In fact, you look as though you need a bit of rest yourself." He picked up the teacup and sipped. The dust storm swept overhead depressingly. Habib hoped it would be over by the time he awoke.

"Meow!"

Samíah's eyes darted to the canvas bag, opening wide when something seemed to move. "What's that, Papa?"

The dustman slapped himself in the head. His concern for his daughter had made him forget about his own strange experience. He picked up the bag and held it with both hands, letting it hang. Inside, the cat began to claw and move around.

"You see, Samíah," he started to explain with a wan expression, "on my way home I came across—"

"Meow!"

The girl gaped. "It's a cat!"

"Yes, child. An injured cat. Its paw—"

"Oh, Papa! I thought we agreed: no more stray animals. You gave me your word."

"And I am bound by it. But, daughter, you see, this cat wouldn't let me take the lamp. It tried to attack when I—"

"The cat *attacked* you? And still you brought it into the house? Papa, are you crazy? The animal is sick—and dangerous! Get rid of it at once!"

"Samíah, you don't understand!"

Angry now, hands balled and on her hips, she stood in a dramatic pose, cocking her head to one side, impatiently tapping her foot. Habib was desperate to explain. His words came out in a tongue-twisted frenzy, and when he was done his daughter seemed no more nearly placated than before. "Now do you understand?" he asked feebly.

She sighed in exasperation. "Only that you brought home a crazy feline who thinks its mother is a kettle."

"It's not a kettle, it's a lamp," he corrected.

"Whatever. I don't want a cat in the house." She was as firm as ever. "You gave me your word."

"But it won't leave the lamp." Then, before she could utter another sound, he poked his hand into the back and brought out the cat. The striped animal coiled itself around his arm, searched about, then poised on his shoulder with its claws digging into Habib's shirt. Emerald eyes expressively glared at Samíah.

"It looks like a tiger!"

The cat hissed.

"Yes, a bit," Habib admitted. He drew out the lamp next, blowing a lungful of air to clean off some of the dust.

"That's the lamp you found? Papa, it's junk! Look at it. Tarnished, dented. It's worthless. You might as well take it to the dump!"

At her remark, the cat snarled. Both Habib and the girl were taken aback. To the dustman it seemed—insane as it sounded— that the cat had understood what she'd said.

"Get rid of it, Papa. Get rid of both. Immediately."

Habib frowned miserably. "Daughter, you're being very unfair. The poor kitten is hurt. Look at its paw."

"Kitten? Papa, I tell you that cat is no innocent stray. And certainly not a kitten. You heard it snarl at me. Get it out of here. And take the lamp with it." She huffed. "Thinks it's his mother, ha!"

"Very well, daughter. But not until I've taken care of his wound; and not until I've had a better chance to look at the lamp. Who knows, maybe after it's been properly polished it might be worth something after all."

Samíah groaned.

Habib held out his palm. "Enough, Samíah."

"But, Papa..."

"Enough!" The obstinate girl was beginning to rile him. He soundlessly counted to ten to let his temper cool, then quietly laid down the law. "I am still master of this house," he told her sternly. "And the matter is closed. In a few days the cat will be gone, I promise. Until then, I shall keep both lamp and cat locked in my room so that neither will offend you."

Eye to eye Samíah stared at the feline, neither so much as blinking. It truly was a handsome cat, she grudgingly had to admit. Yet, still, she wanted no part of it.

"Better keep your door always shut, Papa. If once, just once, your cat gets out and disrupts the house..." Her unspoken warning was loud and clear, underscored by the flash of her dark eyes. When Samíah's own temper was aroused, Allah help the poor man who got in the way. As Habib knew personally from experience, the brooding girl could make life miserable, unendurable, a living, breathing tempest of depthless fury.

Once, mad at him over something or other, Samíah had spent the entire week giving him her silent treatment. Banging plates and pots at supper time, serving his food cold, letting all his dirty laundry pile up in a corner until he had no fresh clothes to put on—all in all, exacting an awful revenge on her poor father. But that hadn't been the end of it, not by a long shot. When the eligible son of an Old Quarter merchant had made an innocent remark about her not wearing a veil, Samíah, carrying a bucket from the well, had flung the water in his face. And when the rag man had disturbed her from work with his knock on the door, she threatened him with a rolling pin. Small wonder he never stopped at the house anymore unless he was certain she was out.

Cold as a fish, Samíah could be, with ice in her veins instead of blood. Small wonder unwed young men stopped coming around.

"All right. It's agreed. I'll keep my door shut and bolted."

A quick smile of satisfaction, and her face returned to its stoniness.

The cat and his daughter were not going to get along.

HE WOKE IN THE EARLY AFTERNOON WITH A
pounding toothache that shot pain up from his jaw
straight to the top of his head.

In a lathery sweat, Habib got up from the bed and moaned.
Hand to his face, he peered into the smudged mirror on the
wall. His cheek was swollen from the side of his mouth, and
he touched it softly with his fingertips. "Ohhhhhh." It hurt,
hurt badly.

The cat stretched out on the floor, flanked on one side by
the tarnished lamp and on the other by an emptied bowl of
goat's milk, looked up at him through curious eyes and yawned.

Habib shut his eyes and shook his head. "What am I to do?"
he groaned.

The dust had settled, the wind diminished. Opening the
shutters, he was greeted by a flood of early-afternoon sunlight
pouring into the cramped room like thick honey. In the yard
his dogs were snoring beneath the lean-to, twitching ears and
snarling as flies buzzed above their heads. He flexed his jaw
and winced with the stab of bolting pain. Tears came to his
eyes.

"Where are you going?" Samíah asked, looking up from
her sewing as he hurried from his room—after carefully shutting the door—and came into the parlor. Hand covering his
mouth, he said, "To the doctor."

Samíah put down her needle, brows raised. "It's your tooth

39

again, isn't it?" She sighed deeply. "I told you to take care of
it weeks ago. But no, you said the pain would go away. Told
me it wasn't going to bother you anymore. . . ."

"Please, daughter, don't berate me now!"

She half rose from her cushioned seat. "What about supper?
It's already in the pot."

The last thing on the dustman's mind was food. With pain
such as he was experiencing, chewing was out of the question
anyway. "I'll be back in time to collect my things for work,"
he said. Then he ran out the door, huffing down the street, one
hand wrapped around the lower portion of his face.

"You have a bad abscess," said the dour Syrian physician,
a man who had practiced his trade in Marrakesh ever since
Habib could remember. Kubla, he called himself. Curly-haired,
frail-looking, and thin as a stick, with his small, pointy beard
curling slightly upward at the tip, his profile seemed that of a
devil. The enigmatic smile he always wore for his patients
made Habib wonder if he enjoyed his work a little too much.

"Should have been taken out long ago, Habib," the physician
chastised.

Habib sat in the awkward chair with his mouth gaping wide.
His hands clutched the chair's arms, his legs were spread with
his heels firmly braced against the footrest.

Kubla took from his tray a small instrument that looked to
Habib like tweezers. "Open wide," he said. "Good."

The dustman found himself squirming like a worm. His
whole mouth felt on fire. Kubla squinted, poked around, then
withdrew the instrument and put it back in its place. "You have
a problem," he announced. "Better not to pull the tooth yet.
It could cause bleeding."

"To Hades with the bleeding. It hurts too much. Pull it,
Kubla."

The Syrian's smile expanded. "All right."

As Habib watched, the physician took a swab of cotton from
a bowl and dipped it gently into a vial of darkish, foully odorous
liquid. "A medicinal herb to ease the pain," he explained, fitting
the cotton tightly between gum and jaw. Habib fidgeted ner-

vously; Kubla went back about his business, selecting from the tray a tiny knife and pincers. "The tooth is impacted. I may have to cut." He held both up to the light, turning them in his hand. "How is your family, Habib?" he asked in a light manner, purposely making small talk.

"All well, praise be to Allah," Habib replied.

Kubla's brows furrowed. "And Samíah? How is she faring lately?"

For a very long while the Syrian had been treating the folk of the Old Quarter and come to know many as friends. In fact, Kubla himself had not only treated Hoda and her twin brother but had cared for Habib's sickly wife continuously before her declining months. The Syrian had used every potion known to his craft to make the suffering woman more comfortable at the end, and for that Habib was eternally grateful.

"If you want to know has Samíah found a husband, the answer is no." He smiled gloomily. "Samíah, well . . ."

Kubla knowingly nodded; further explanations were unnecessary. "She'll come round, my friend. Time heals the severest wound. By the way, I hear she had quite a fright yesterday. In the bazaar, wasn't it?"

"The Street of the Sandalmakers. You know about it as well?"

The physician shrugged. "Gossip travels quickly. Especially in the Old Quarter, hmmmm?" He chuckled, leaving Habib to wonder what was in his mind. "Open wide again." Habib did, and with a steady finger the Syrian applied pressure on the swollen gum until Habib cried out.

"They say the poor girl was beside herself," Kubla went on after his inspection. "That she dreamed it all up—delusions from the heat."

"Is that your opinion? I mean, do you think it was all in her imagination, then?"

"Who can tell?" the physician replied with another shrug. "But one thing I do know," and here the smile vanished, the glittering teeth disappeared and were replaced by a mask of tightlipped seriousness. "This isn't the first time such happenings have been reported."

Habib raised his head. "You mean there have been other . . . abductions?"

The Syrian didn't answer for a time. He walked back to his worktable, dipped the tiny knife and pincers into a readied bowl of antiseptic solution, then drew the curtains tightly, blunting the strong sun. "Haven't you heard?" he said in a soft tone.

Habib shook his head. "I've heard nothing."

Kubla regarded his patient doubtfully.

"Not a word will pass your lips?" he asked.

The dustman's palms moistened and his heart began to pump faster, but whether it was due to the impending extraction or what the Syrian was about to say, he wasn't sure. "My word on it, Kubla. What have you heard?"

Mouth mere inches from Habib's ear, he said, "They say a number of well-to-do citizens have been accosted these past months. Yes, many of them from the court, officials, even ministers."

Habib was shocked.

"It's true, but they say word of the assaults has been hushed. Afraid of widespread panic, they must be. Some escaped harm, but at least three are still missing—and two are known to be dead."

The dustman's mouth hung limply. "But who," he stammered. "Who would do such a thing? And why?"

Kubla laughed mirthlessly. "Fanatics will do anything to further their cause. As to who they are, there can only be one answer: Assassins."

Habib could feel the hackles rising on his neck. *Assassins!* The dreaded scourge of the Islamic world. Faceless men, drugged and crazed, who would stop at nothing to overthrow any ruler, king or sultan, if they could.

"My friend, you can't be serious!"

"But I am. They say this is their work. The Assassins are among us."

Incredulous, the dustman swallowed hard. It had been many years since the last outbreak of such mindless violence in the city, years of peace in which the thought of these dreaded

Assassins had been all but forgotten. Now, though, it came rushing back on Habib in a flood.

To this day no one fully knew who they were. Only that they obeyed the will and command of some unknown maniac bent on the total destruction of a civilization he hated. Some said their leader was from the wild and savage tribes of the mountains; others claimed him to be a defrocked holy man, a *mullah* whose warped mind was so twisted that he vowed to slaughter all those who remained believers in the True Faith. Still others said he was not a man at all but a demon, robbing the souls of his blindly devoted followers with hashish and causing them to commit the most unspeakable crimes.

Blood had spilled in the streets. Nowhere in the city had been safe, not even a man's own home, not even the palace itself. Marrakesh had lived beneath a pall of terrible fear, for no one could predict where or when the hooded fanatics would strike next. Shaven-headed, glassy-eyed, the members of the secret cult would murder openly, destroy the innocent in cold blood, yes, and laughingly throw away their own lives in the name of their leader and his cause.

Little more than this was ever discovered about them. The sultan's forces had waged a long and costly battle to wipe them out, and even at the end they had never broken the secret code that would have exposed who this leader really was. To this day it remained a mystery. No one knew what happened to him, whether he was dead or still alive, had perhaps fled far away beyond the mountains and the reach of the sultan's justice; or if maybe he lived somewhere inside the city, biding his time and waiting. It was a chilling thought.

"They say these Assassins have vowed an oath to chop off the sultan's head and display it on a spit," Kubla was saying as he worked the tiny knife into Habib's mouth and made an incision. "Yes, as well as the heads of any man or woman who dares to oppose them."

Habib jerked, feeling the cut.

"Our sultan is said to be deeply, deeply worried, and these senseless abductions have only increased apprehension in the palace." The knife went out and the pincers came in. Habib felt the pressure and the crunching of bone. Tears swam from his eyes; he fought off an impulse to scream. Then a flash of blinding light burst before his vision, and when it cleared, he saw Kubla triumphantly holding up the bloodied tooth.

"There it is," he said with professional pride.

Habib leaned over the side of his chair, spit a mouthful of blood into a spittoon. Perspiration beaded his forehead. His mouth felt swollen and still on fire, but at least he knew that the worst of it was done.

"Better a tooth than finding your head on a pole, eh, Habib?" said the Syrian with his famous smile.

"Eh?"

Kubla laughed. "Wash your mouth with warm salted water. Eat only soft foods for a day. The bleeding will stop by itself." The smile deepened.

Habib got up groggily, fumbling his way to the door. His head was pounding like a kettledrum, his jaw aching as though someone had pounded it with a sledgehammer. He knew he wouldn't be able to go to work tonight. And he also knew that bad teeth and Assassins were two things in life he never wanted to come across again.

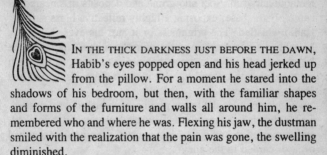IN THE THICK DARKNESS JUST BEFORE THE DAWN, Habib's eyes popped open and his head jerked up from the pillow. For a moment he stared into the shadows of his bedroom, but then, with the familiar shapes and forms of the furniture and walls all around him, he remembered who and where he was. Flexing his jaw, the dustman smiled with the realization that the pain was gone, the swelling diminished.

He tried to fall asleep again, but sleep eluded him. Hearing the cat's purr, Habib sat up and looked down at the sleeping feline. The swelling on its paw had subsided appreciably, the salve healing the injury quicker than he'd expected. Soon he would have to keep his promise to Samíah and get rid of the cat for good. A pity, for he was beginning to grow quite fond of the creature. As for the lamp, well, what with his bad tooth and all, he'd not yet even had the chance to examine it more closely.

The cat opened one eye lazily and stared as he rose and sought some polish and a rag. Maybe, once cleaned, it wouldn't prove as worn and useless as Samíah thought. And if she liked the lamp and wanted to keep it, well, then she'd have to agree to keep the cat as well. After all, the two were inseparable.

He found a clean cloth and his polish, knelt and quietly placed his hand over the lamp's spout. The cat's eyes opened wide and suspicious before he could pick it up.

45

"I'm not going to do it any harm," he muttered to the watchful tiger-striped feline.

The cat hissed, baring its fangs.

"All right, all right." He put the rag and polish down on the bed, picked up the cat and the lamp together. "Here, see," he said, indicating the cloth as he sat, "I only want to clean it a bit. Take care of it like I did your paw."

Ever mistrustful, the cat sat rigid and vigilant, unwavering in its scrutiny when Habib placed the kettlelike vessel on his lap, dabbed a smudge of polish on the cloth, and began to methodically rub. Soot and grime and deposits of smeared oil came off the base, exposing a highly reflective brass surface. Habib whistled. The brightness of it hurt his eyes. Curiously he rubbed some more. And the more he rubbed, the more the lamp seemed to shine, almost beginning to glow, as though it were filled with oil and lit. But it was a flameless glow, and Habib grew uneasy.

Within minutes the lower portion of the lamp was cleaned. To his surprise, the metal was flawless, unscratched, unnicked, and unmarred in any way. Most unusual for an object that had been discarded in the alley.

He rubbed some more; the glow was becoming more intense, the room perceptibly brightening. Habib looked at the window expecting to see daylight. There was none, only the blackness of the night. The glow was coming from the lamp, and only the lamp.

The dustman scratched his head. Were his eyes deceiving him, he wondered. Could an unlit lamp that looked like a kettle glow all by itself? Or was he dreaming? Was this the throes of a nightmare? He pinched himself. The pain was real enough. It wasn't a dream.

Hurriedly he found another clean rag and discarded the first cloth, which was already too soiled for further use. Cleaner and cleaner the brass lamp became, its shine catching starlight and its surface as reflective as a mirror. Soon Habib found himself so entranced, so bewildered, that he rubbed effortlessly, without awareness. The cat shared none of his puzzlement; with slitted eyes, it kept its gaze upon the spout and nowhere else, front paws stretched out, tail lifted high and starting to wag like a dog's.

Then a strange thing happened, a very strange thing. As Habib held the lamp for inspection he could feel his fingertips begin to tingle, felt the lamp itself grow warmer and warmer. He rubbed the cloth over the top—the last tarnished area— working now in a frenzy. Again and again he made the circular motions over the top until it, too, gleamed. The cat's eyes widened, and it drew back slightly, the glow reaching over its shadowed form.

Habib's breathing became rapid. He was sweating, and the tingle in his fingertips had spread all over his hands. Glued to the smoothed, polished surface, he found himself transfixed and awed by the eerie brightness, and now he could feel the cause of the tingling, a vibration from inside the lamp, a humming not unlike the purring of the cat, a stirring as though something, something inexplicable, was rousing...

Habib gasped. A curl of wispy green mist poured like steam from the spout. Habib threw the lamp to the floor in fear and covered his mouth with the back of his hand. Vapor jetted upward to the ceiling, billowing now, spinning dizzily above his head, thicker and thicker until he couldn't see, couldn't breathe.

The dustman stifled a scream and tried to run. His feet were like ships' anchors: leaden and unmoving. He couldn't budge from his place no matter how hard he tried. He was frozen in time and space, an unwilling participant in something without logic or explanation.

Then there was laughter, a sound not unlike the distant rumble of faraway thunder. Habib saw the cat jump from the bed and hover over the lamp. It was laughing, too, he realized; welcoming whatever was desperately fighting its way out. All around him the green haze swirled. The outside world became lost, not even a blur, and in those fearful moments he knew he had committed a terrible act. He had raised a devil! Yes, willingly brought to life that which would destroy him: a hellish demon freed because of his stupidity. He only prayed his death would be swift and painless.

THE ROAR OF LAUGHTER CEASED. HABIB, COW-ering in the corner, arms protectively crossed over his face, knew he was still alive. His heart assured him of that, thumping against the cavity of his chest like the savage beat of a procession of drums. In his horror it took all the agonizing effort he could muster to lift his head and open his eyes. When he did, the green mist was gone. Vanished. His room was back to normal, everything in its proper place, the rags and polish still atop his bed, the lamp lying on its side upon the floor where it had fallen, the window open wide and the night sky blinking back at him. Even the cat was as before. Purring and complacent at the foot of the bed. Only one thing was different: he and the cat were no longer alone.

Arms folded, standing beside the opposite wall, stood a man. Well, not exactly a man, although it did have two arms and two legs, eyes, and a human face. He was a rotund, almost jolly-looking figure, dressed in turban and white robe with silver stitching—a most beautiful garment, Habib saw, worthy of the finest sultan or even emperor. His visitor's eyes regarded him briefly, slitted eyes, as feline as the cat's, emerald and glowing in the darkness. Except for the extraordinarily bushy brows that slanted and nearly joined above the bridge of his bulbous nose, he seemed hairless and human— As human as one seems with flesh tinted just a slight shade of green. Large ears lay flat against the side of his head, and he flashed gold-flecked teeth in what was either a grimace or a smile. Habib wasn't sure which and wasn't about to ask.

The cat curled itself around the visitor's ankles, then eased under the loose robe with only its head sticking out, staring up at the trembling dustman. The demon of the lamp laughed again; it lowered its arm and the cat licked its hand, purring as it was stroked behind the ears. Then the demon straightened again, folding its arms and turning its attention back to Habib. "Who has summoned me?" it said in a deeply resonant bass voice.

The dustman, in fear, fell to his knees. "I—I . . ."

With a disdainful curl of his thick lips, it beckoned with one finger for Habib to get up. The dustman obeyed weakly with his knees knocking. "Who are you?" demanded the voice.

"Habib, O great lord. A simple man of the city. One who knew not . . ."

"Habib?" Emerald eyes narrowed, pored up and down the shaky figure. "You have woken me from my rest—a very satisfying rest."

The dustman gulped. "For—forgive me, O lord." He bowed waist-low with open hands, like a postulant. "It was an accident, a mistake, I assure you . . ."

The supernatural visitor scowled with displeasure. "Nevertheless, I am here. For what purpose was I called?"

"Called?" Habib could have fainted dead away. *How stupid I am!* he berated himself, wishing now he had taken Samíah's advice in the beginning and never brought either cat or lamp into the house. "I—I did not know, O Great One," he stammered. "I mean, no one told me there was anyone inside the kettle—"

The demon's eyes flashed like lightning, his voice rumbling like thunder. "Hrumph!" The cat hissed. "My home is not a kettle."

"Of course not, Benevolent One! Strike my tongue for my foolishness . . . The lamp . . ."

"It has been my home since the Dawning of Creation," Habib was summarily informed. "Since the days when the Overlords of Sky and Water reigned supreme over all the universe!" The demon made his point by lifting a handful of clawlike fingers into the air. "And I, Master of the Night and Sands, was charged to do their bidding."

"Are—Are you a—devil?"

The visitor laughed, then grimaced. "Do I look like a devil?" he boomed with hands on hips.

Habib lowered his gaze. "Forgive me again, Merciful One," he stuttered. "I am not schooled in such matters. . . . I cannot tell the difference."

At this, the visitor flared his nostrils, a tiny jet of dragonfire igniting in flame. "Would a lowly devil dwell in such a palace as mine?" he demanded. "Sleep amid the splendors bestowed by the Overlords themselves?"

Habib was shaking all over, unable to meet his guest's fiery glare evenly.

"Of course not!" The visitor said, answering his own question.

The dustman managed to raise his head. "You're not a devil?"

"Certainly not."

"Forgive me for asking, O Great One, but then what are you?"

The visitor was growing agitated, his frustrations with the stupidity of mortals overwhelming him. "What do you think?" he retorted, turning a darker shade of green, similar in hue to the swirling vapor that had filled the room.

Now Habib was a superstitious man by both nature and upbringing. And he believed in all the mysteries of the world; but for this he had neither explanation nor reply. Dumbly he stood there, looking at his uninvited guest, glancing at the lamp and the cat, then back again to whatever it was that was speaking with him. He scratched his head as comprehension dawned. "By Allah!" he cried. "You're a genie!"

The cat purred.

"A genie," he repeated, blurting the words. "And I've set you free!"

"In a manner of speaking, mortal. Actually, you aroused me from my rest. I have been in a deep, deep slumber for the past, oh," and here he paused to calculate, rolling his slitted eyes this way and that, "about a century of your time, give or take a few years. Yes, about that long."

Habib's mouth hung limply. "A century?"

The genie seemed apologetic. "My last calling here in your realm was quite taxing; indeed, I was thoroughly exhausted by it all." He paused again, this time yawning. "Usually I'll nap for five or six decades between jobs. After that last episode, though, I still probably need half a century more."

The dustman was astounded. It was all so incredible.

The cat was still purring, and the genie snapped his fingers, calling the feline out from beneath his robe. When it appeared the genie scooped it up into his chubby arms and petted it some more. "If it wasn't for Lucifer here, I don't know what I'd do."

"The cat is yours?"

The genie seemed surprised by the question. "Of course. Every genie has one. It's part of the regulations: section thirteen, article seven of the bylaws. We're a team, aren't we, Lucifer?"

Habib tottered, faintness coming upon him again.

"You look pale," said the genie.

"I don't feel very well," the dustman admitted.

"Must be the heat. Damnable. Always the same in these lands. Insufferable, I always said, didn't I, Lucifer?" The cat meowed in agreement.

Now it was beginning to make sense, Habib saw. At least as much sense as anything else in this peculiar matter. Suddenly it was easy for him to understand the cat's fierce loyalty, why it fought him when he tried to take the lamp home, refused to let the tarnished vessel out of its sight for even a single moment. Lucifer was no ordinary cat. No, no, no. He was a guardian of the genie, protecting his master while he slumbered through the centuries.

The genie pulled out an embroidered silk handkerchief from an invisible pocket and wiped perspiration off his neck. "Hrumph! I'll never understand how any living thing can tolerate such an awful climate."

Habib was still queasy, though he didn't believe himself in imminent danger now that he knew his visitor wasn't a devil. But the urge to run as fast as he could without looking back hadn't quite gone, either. "Perhaps you would like me to serve you something cooling to drink?" he asked lamely.

Wiping away a speck of sleep dust from the corner of his eye, the genie politely refused. "Your offer is kind, er, Habib, is it? Thank you, but no. Perhaps later, after my visit here is done and I return."

"Return?"

"To the lamp, of course. I told you; you interrupted my very satisfying rest."

"Oh," said Habib, a little confused. He was no expert in such matters, but everything he'd ever been told about genies assured him that they loathed the close confinement of lamps, bottles and the like, that they would pay any price, grant any wishes and fulfill any heart's desire merely to be released. "Then you don't intend to remain . . . free?" he questioned.

The genie laughed at him grandly. "Free? To swelter in your desert heat? Remain here decades before I've finished my rest? Don't be absurd." The bushy brows slanted harshly. "Anyway, sooner or later somebody or other will call me again. They always do, you know. The number of genies is rapidly decreasing, I'm afraid to say, and those of us still around are quite in demand." He sighed and mopped his face with the silk handkerchief. "So if you don't mind, let's be quick about our business."

"Business?"

The genie's frustration was steadily growing. He put his hands back to his hips and stared at Habib whose courage began to drain again. "You summoned me, remember? Called me to the world. Tell me what needs to be done and we can both stop wasting time."

Habib still didn't seem to understand; the genie slapped himself in the head and groaned. "Your wish, mortal! Your *wish*! Tell me what it is you seek." Here the brows lifted. "Hmmm?"

"I, er, I don't have any particular request," Habib told him truthfully. "As I've said, you were called quite by mistake."

The genie clapped his hands together in exasperation. "Well, surely there must be something? Gold? Rubies? A harem of young virgins to offer pleasurable nights of diversion?"

The dustman chuckled at the idea. "No, I'm too old for that," he conceded, although the idea of riches was appealing.

The genie mumbled under his breath as if calling upon the gods of old to deliver him from such a fool. "Listen, Habib," he said in a voice one shade short of testy. "There are laws, universal laws, that we all have to follow. Even I. And one such law commands that once summoned I cannot return to rest until the reason for my appearance has been satisfied. Can you understand that?"

"You mean you have to stay here?"

"Until our bargain is settled, yes. It's all written in the bylaws, the genie contract sealed eons ago. Now, as I've told you about five times already, I'm really too pooped to be hanging around doing nothing. Sleep rejuvenates my powers and it's going to still be some decades till they're back to maximum capacity. But I can't recharge my magic standing here chatting forever with you. Understand? Good. Now before I can leave I'll be able to grant you, oh, let's say one wish."

"Genies are supposed to give three," Habib said absently.

The visitor from the lamp pulled a sour face. "Under the proper circumstances, yes. But not while I'm rejuvenating. By your Allah, I've already explained!" He was getting agitated again, Habib saw, perspiring profusely and constantly wiping his face. "Look," he went on, "between you and me, I'd just as soon disappear. Impose on your kindness to toss the lamp into some quiet, not-too-frequently disturbed alley where I can go back to sleep and let Lucifer handle the rest. But it's not that simple. The code of our guild demands I fulfill a bargain. Any bargain. Subsection nine, paragraph three. So why don't you do us both a favor and make a wish like any other mortal, hmmmm? It doesn't have to be much. Need a mother-in-law taken care of? A boss fired? Name it."

"Oh, nothing like that," said the dustman.

The genie folded his arms, unfolded them, and fumed.

"But I'll think of something!" Habib was quick to promise.

"All right. Take your time—but not too long, mind you. This heat is making me sick."

So there it was, Habib realized. By a fortuitous blunder he'd stumbled upon an opportunity most men can only dream of, a chance to make any wish come true. *Any wish!*

Habib rubbed his hands nervously. What should he request? he wondered. What marvel to alter his life for the rest of his years? A splendrous palace in which to dwell, surrounded by servants and lackeys and voluptuous women? Perhaps a mountain of gold coins, wealth enough to make the richest man seem a pauper by comparison. Or an island; yes, an island paradise, a kingdom of his own with a peaceful citizenry to govern, an army to ride and conquer in his name a vast new empire. King Habib the Glorious! Why, the sultan himself would bow at his feet.

The genie had suggested a harem. Well, getting on in years he might well be, but only a lunatic would reject the bliss five hundred young and beautiful women could bestow. . . .

"Well, Habib?" The genie's voice was impatient.

"I'm thinking, I'm thinking!"

Oh, if only Samíah were not asleep. She might have a few suggestions of her own. Yes, together he and his daughter would select the single wish. "Would it be all right if I consulted with my daughter, Samíah?" he asked hopefully.

The genie shook his head sternly. "Only the one who has summoned me can make the choice," he said. "Asking the advice of another is against the rules. Article fourteen, subhead one oh—"

"I understand."

The dustman bit his lip in a quandary. What should he do? What should he ask for? Wealth? Longevity? Happiness? Anything, the genie had said. *Anything!*

After what seemed a very long time of debating and mulling over the sweep of possibilities, Habib looked at his visitor and smiled. Oh, empires and riches and harems were fine enough, but not for a man such as he was. A simple, hardworking man, devoted to his family and his home. It was nice to imagine himself a king, nice to envision the mountain of gems, but none of these things held much value. Life was too fleeting, too short to waste on mere possessions and pleasures. Besides, none of it would bring an iota of joy to any other apart from himself. Selfish like that Habib never had been and hoped he never would be.

"Have you chosen?"

The dustman nodded, certain that at last he had made the right decision.

"Good. What shall it be? I have only to snap my fingers or blink my eyes . . ."

Habib stared at the brightening sky, wistful as the morning stars flickered and the first glimmers of dawn pushed back the darkness. "I wish only for one small thing," he said. "One very simple thing. I have a daughter, genie, a wonderful, lovely and intelligent girl. Willful and spirited as her mother was, and as stubborn as a mule. She is lonely, you see, although she denies her unhappiness, and I fear unless something is done she will never find happiness again . . ."

"Go on," said the genie.

The tired dustman's eyes brightened in that moment when he said, "I wish for you to find her someone to love. I wish for a husband, a husband for Samíah."

"What?"

"Nothing more," Habib assured him.

The genie's brows knit and rose, knit and rose. He acted as though the wind were suddenly knocked out of him. "He *is* crazy," he mumbled to Lucifer.

Habib nodded with a soulful sigh. "Perhaps; but that is my wish. That and no other."

The cat and his master shared a baleful look, the genie putting his hand to his forehead.

"Is anything wrong?" asked Habib. "You said I could ask for anything."

"I know, I know. I have a headache, that's all."

"Then our bargain is sealed?"

The genie stood shaking his head gloomily. "Couldn't you

have requested something a little easier? How about a herd of wild horses or a golden chariot? I could build you a castle in the sky or—"

"Of what use are any of these to me when Samíah—even if she denies it—is miserable?"

"A mighty pyramid erected in your honor. A magic well, or a flying carpet to whisk you across the world..."

Habib, though, was adamant. He had made his choice and would stick to it no matter what spectacular prizes the genie offered.

"Please, er, Habib, won't you reconsider?"

The aging dustman shook his head. "Unless you can't do it," he said dejectedly. "But remember, you said all it would take was a snap of your fingers, a blink of your eyes..."

"Yes, yes; don't rub it in. But I offered you *material* things. Things you mortals lust for, die for, commit every criminal act under the sun for. But no, you have to ask for the most difficult gift of all: the gift of love!"

"So?"

"So, he says! Ha! Look here, Habib, things like this are ordained by the stars themselves! You just can't ask a genie to alter what has been preordained. It would upset the whole balance of the universe. Why, I could even risk losing my license."

"I see," said Habib sadly, disappointment dulling the momentary brightness. "Then you won't do it?"

"Hold on, hold on. Did you hear me say *won't*, eh? All I said was that it isn't easy to tamper with fate like this. More difficult than you can ever imagine. Let me put it to you another way. For Samíah the stars have already chosen someone. Crossing their scheme of things can cause terrible problems. You have no idea. You see, it has to do with fate and what is meant to be, and not even a genie, not even an *Overlord*, by your Allah, can just blatantly disregard it." He mopped his brow and sighed. "You do understand, don't you?"

"Go back to your lamp, genie. I won't summon you again, you have my word. Return to your sleep until someone else calls, someone who needs a golden chariot or a castle in the sky." The dustman meant it, too. He was through with genies. Through for good.

"Now let's be calm about this, Habib. I explained before that I can't just leave without our business being complete. I need a wish from you."

"You already had one."

"I know, I know." He frowned in consternation. "Listen, I already told you, there *is* someone for Samíah. Believe me, the stars make sure of it for every mortal. She *will* find her husband—when the time is right."

"Are you sure?"

The genie's smile was large and not too condescending. "Positive."

"Then I wish for you to help the stars in their work. Seek out who the chosen fellow is and, er, perhaps urge things along a little bit quicker. Can you do that much?"

His visitor thought for a moment, making some mental calculations, wondering about the many star charts he'd have to read and interpret. What Habib was asking was certainly not covered in the rules. Yet it wasn't quite breaking them, only bending them a bit, helping out things with a gentle magic nudge.

"Well?" said Habib. "Do you find Samíah a husband or not?"

The genie put his oversized hands to his turbaned head and groaned like he'd just been hit by a brick. Complications galore faced him, he knew, and this matter was going to take an extended amount of time—time he would have to spend here in this insufferable world, making sure everything went smoothly.

"I am going to need a few things from my lamp," he said.

"All right, if you promise to come back immediately."

He huffed. "My dear Habib, one thing you'll have to learn is that a genie never goes back on a bargain. A husband you need and—" he groaned again—"a husband I am duty bound to provide."

He blinked his eyes rapidly. Lucifer jumped away. Habib stared as the green vapor returned and filled the room. Then the genie was spinning, spinning so fast the dustman could no longer see him. But before he was completely gone, Habib merrily called, "Bring along some light clothes! Marrakesh gets much hotter than this in the summer!"

FROM THE GLOOMY DEPTHS OF THE MISTY NIGHT they saw him come, this frightened, pitiful figure, observed his every movement as he slipped inside the gates of the quarter although he did not see them. With idle curiosity they watched him traverse the narrow, darkened streets, crossing between the shadows in search of his destination. Upon shrouded roofs, lurking unseen inside the thresholds of dim doorways, sheltered among circumscribed pitch-black alleys they peered at the stranger and wondered what his business here might be. Few outsiders came into the casbah at night, and most of those who did rarely came back out. For not even the sultan's soldiers themselves dared venture alone into this city within a city, this forboding quarter riddled with criminals of every description from pickpockets to thieves to cutthroats, from escaped prisoners from the mines and quarries to deranged murderers. But this man had come, this beragged, pathetic stranger seeking, as had so many others in the past, to sell some stolen valuable among the many traffickers in contraband.

Hussein's fingers groped nimbly for the scarf tucked inside his shirt and the brooch wrapped within. Assured of its safety, he wiped the moisture from his palms and continued walking. At the end of this twisting street he turned left, remembering the careful instructions, and made his way briskly toward the rising din.

Hussein had been afraid to come, recalling Habib's warning. He knew he was the cause of prying eyes and men who would slit his throat without a question. Yet he found there had been no other choice. For days he had let it be known by careful word of mouth that he had something of value to barter. But the *souk*'s dealers in contraband offered less than a pittance of the brooch's true worth. The brooch, it seemed, had aroused a good deal of interest. Sultan's soldiers had been combing the *souk* and asking questions about it for several days. Why, Hussein didn't know, or really care. But this surge of interest in the item assured him that his find must be of far greater value than he had assumed. Also, it promised more trouble should, by chance, he be caught with it. With each day he found himself more desperate, and so when a contact had told him of an interested buyer in the casbah Hussein realized he had no choice. There was a man known only as the Dealer in the forbidden quarter, a man who for reasons unknown to Hussein had passed word of his interest in the brooch. Thus, Hussein had come, following careful instructions offered by one of the *souk*'s shady characters, and believing that at last his price would be met.

Wind rose and gusted as he shouldered his way down the Street of Harlots. No sooner had he turned the proper corner than the clamor of the busy avenue was gone and once more he found himself greeted with silence. The eerie solitude made his flesh crawl. He peered into the darkness uneasily. Before him was a tiny street, nameless like most of the others, dingy and deserted. A high wall loomed at its end, and behind it the familiar myriad of minarets and steeples of the city outside the casbah. He licked his lips and stiffened his resolve. Soon the transaction would be complete, he told himself in an effort to quell mounting apprehension. He would be out and well away from this awful place, safe and free, with the coins of gold jingling in his pockets.

He looked back another time to be sure he hadn't been

followed. Then he proceeded as cautiously as before. The single shop on the empty street was boarded across the entrance, slats of aged wood nailed in a crisscross pattern. There was no door behind them, only the black hole leading inside.

Hussein sucked in air, rapped lightly on the boards as he had been instructed. Long moments passed, unendurable, with the collector of trash growing increasingly edgy. He rapped again, knuckles white. A pair of suspicious eyes appeared from between the boards and focused intently upon him. Hussein cleared a thick throat. "I am looking for the Dealer," he croaked.

The eyes remained unresponsive and cold.

Hussein shuffled his feet. "I—I have something to sell. Something of value. The Dealer is expecting me."

Still there was no answer, only the unsettling glare.

He wiped sweat off his brow. "The brooch," he told the unshifting eyes.

Here there was a faint flicker in the eyes, Hussein imagining an unseen smile to accompany it.

"Do you have it with you?" The voice was low and soft, almost feminine.

Slowly he nodded.

Then a pause. "Come inside."

The eyes vanished before he could speak; he peered with narrowed vision between the slats but could see nothing. Heart beginning to thrum again, he glanced one last time back into the street. Then he knelt before the barred entrance and began to crawl beneath the layer of boards, a space large enough perhaps for a dog but hardly for a man.

When he cleared the doorway he rose, aware of his heavy breathing. He still couldn't see anything, and for an instant panic set in. Only the thought of the waiting money calmed him enough not to bolt, and he eased his hand inside his shirt and clutched at the small bundle.

"Show it to me," said the voice.

Hussein saw the hunched figure motionless among the shadows. He could see no face or any features, not even shape or form. The eyes, though, were clear; piercing, flashing orbs that peered out at him from the darkness.

"Do not be frightened," said the voice. "I am the Dealer. If the brooch you carry is the one I'm seeking, your reward will be greater than you ever could have dreamed."

Hussein smiled. He unwrapped the scarf eagerly and stepped farther into the shadows. He was glad he came.

"Is—is that everything?" Habib asked meekly, confusion reshaping his face.

The genie nodded somberly.

"But all you did was clap your hands a single time!"

"Twice," came the correction with a hint of annoyance. "Twice was all that was called for."

Bewildered, the dustman scratched lightly at the gray stubble covering his cleft chin and sat down at the edge of his bed. It had all been so quick, so effortless. No sooner had his friend from the lamp returned than he summarily commanded the dustman to step aside, rolled up his silk sleeves, went into some rigamorole of preparing his awesome magic. Breathless, Habib had watched, wondering what would happen next. Would there be a thunderous explosion? Would the night sky alight with fierce and inexplicable lightning? Would strange mists arise and swirl across the city, or conjured demons fly over the cloudless sky spitting fire?

The genie, after shooing Lucifer and going through his act, proceeded to clap his hands. That was it. Afterwards nothing at all took place, which left Habib feeling more than doubtful about the whole thing.

"There," said the genie with a relieved sigh, flicking specks of dust from his immaculate robe. "It's done."

"Are—are you sure?" Not that the dustman meant to question the powers of this superior being, only that earlier the genie had made so many protestations about the difficulty of the task imposed. Habib had fully expected, well, he didn't know exactly what, except that surely there would have been more than this. A few simple handclaps, which as a matter of fact hardly even made a sound.

"What's the matter?" said the genie, irritation in his stare as he gazed down at the perplexed dustman.

"Oh, nothing. Nothing. I guess I thought I'd see the world swim or the stars bursting in color. . . ."

"Trust me."

"I do, I do! Truly. But—" and here he glanced casually around the room, seeing everything in its proper place "—nothing seems to be *different*."

The genie groaned. "Because nothing *is* different."

"Samíah is going to get her husband, isn't she?"

"That was the deal, Habib. As I said, the stars usually govern such matters, but I obeyed your wish and did all I could to urge things along."

Habib's eyes fixed on him in a puppy-dog stare. "Does she know . . . ?"

He was greeted with an amused laugh. "Not yet, of course! Listen, I thought you understood; these things don't just *happen*. Fate, Habib, believe in fate. Listen, it may have seemed easy to you, but I assure you it wasn't. As a matter of fact, when I returned to my lamp and did a thorough study, examined her zodiac star chart in detail . . ." His voice trailed off.

"Then you know all about her?"

"Everything." He shuddered involuntarily.

"That bad?"

"Worse. Quite a young woman, your Samíah. Yes, indeed." He inhaled deeply. "Believe me, matching her up properly was some tough job."

"I know she's a bit stubborn," said Habib lamely.

"Stubborn? Why she's the most headstrong, intractable, pertinacious, dogged . . ." He cut off the description, not wanting to injure the dustman further. He placed an uncharacteristically sympathetic hand on Habib's shoulder. Heaven knew the dustman had his hands full. What with her combination of fire signs forever ascending, she had the makings of a sabre-toothed tiger and wolf combined. In fact, he wondered if he was doing either the father or daughter a favor by cheating the stars this way. Not to mention her husband!

"But you did, er, find someone?" Habib asked worriedly.

The genie smiled devilishly. "Yes," he drawled. "I did. Not a bad match up at all, to tell you the truth. Not bad at all. Grant the stars intelligence, at least."

Relief swam over Habib's features, and he was able to relax. "Praise be to Allah! I don't mind telling you that I was concerned. Deeply concerned. Not that I doubted your powers for even an instant—"

"I understand," the genie replied knowingly, secretly thanking the Overlords for never having been put in a similar position. "All's well that ends well, though," he said. "Samíah is going to get the man she deserves."

"You mean she'll be tamed?"

"Tame as an ocelot," he muttered below his breath, quickly adding, "subdued, anyway." He chuckled with a twinkle in his eye. "Yes, a good match. A very good match."

The dustman was beside himself with curiosity. "Can you tell me his name, genie? Who the, er, lucky fellow is going to be?"

"Afraid I can't, old boy. Not just yet, in any case. Samíah has to be the first one. Regulations, you know."

Habib frowned. "Not even a hint?"

The genie hesitated, wondering if he should again bend the rules. In truth, the dustman had no particular right to be let in on such privileged information. After all, Samíah's life was her own to lead. Habib would find out sooner or later, anyway. Still, the genie couldn't help but feel a pang of pity for the dustman; and Allah knew he had been through a lot. . . .

63

"Very well," he relented at last. "Tell you what. I'll pose a little riddle, make a game of it. Hidden in the riddle is a hint to the young man's identity. Ready for it?"

Habib was not particularly fond of games, especially riddles. Yet this one he had no choice but to play. "Ready," he said with a nod.

The genie shut his eyes and playfully rubbed his hands over one another. "He that is, is he who he is not. He that is he who he is not, is assuredly he." He looked down at the thinking dustman. "Well?"

Habib moaned. "Would you repeat that, please?"

The genie, who had a penchant for such diversions and would spend countless hours of solitude in the bottle making up and playing similar word games, eagerly complied with the request. Alas, it proved to be of little value, for when Habib tried to reconstruct the clever riddle he became hopelessly lost. *"He who is . . ."* he muttered. *"He who is not . . . Is not he who . . ."*

"Never mind," said the visitor with some open disappointment, realizing that the days ahead would probably prove even more boring than he suspected. He only hoped love would come to fruition swiftly and he could be soon back asleep. "Tell you what," he went on, making the best of things. He pressed two fingers against the lids of his tired eyes. "I see that tomorrow is going to be a frantic day for Samíah."

"She has a number of deliveries to make," Habib conceded. "Her customers expect her to finish her work punctually. And she always does," he quickly added with a measure of pride.

"Yes, yes. Whatever. According to my calculations chance will intervene and the lovers shall see one another. . . ."

"You mean she's going to meet her future husband?"

"Something like that."

A light as bright as a lamp came to the dustman's eyes.

"So all you have to do is figure out who the one the stars have chosen might be. Simple, isn't it?"

"You're on!" cried Habib.

The genie grinned. "Good, good. But don't get overjoyed just yet. I never said any of this was going to be easy. Take my word, it won't. But remember one last thing: nothing in this world of mortals ever is as it seems. Especially in Marrakesh these days."

"I don't think I follow you."

"Didn't think you would. Not that it matters, though." His hand squeezed firmly upon Habib's shoulder. "Let's just say that from here on in concerning Samíah, you and I are only observers. The stars will work their own course; and for Samíah, I'm afraid this tale has barely begun."

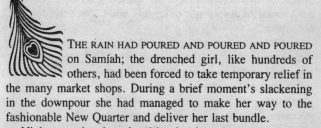

THE RAIN HAD POURED AND POURED AND POURED on Samíah; the drenched girl, like hundreds of others, had been forced to take temporary relief in the many market shops. During a brief moment's slackening in the downpour she had managed to make her way to the fashionable New Quarter and deliver her last bundle.

Night was already at hand by the time she returned to the hubbub of the *Jama-el-F'Na*. The dusty and dirtied streets were cleansed by the rain, littered with the petals of fresh flowers caught in the storm. Irate merchants and laborers grunted and hurried through the tasks of hauling merchandise inside the shops and closing up for the day. Beyond the high walls muezzins came to the balconies of the minarets and called the devout to evening prayer. The hubbub of the *souk* quickly vanished even before the rain had gone, and it was not long until the market was empty and quiet. Samíah stood beneath the gay awnings projecting from the wall along the carpet-sellers' street and lingered while the crowds disappeared. Her day's deliveries had gone well; she had already in hand a number of new orders that promised work for many weeks ahead.

When the final downpour stopped and the drum of rain slackened to a dull patter atop the canopy she left the shelter and headed in the direction of the Old Quarter. The green-tiled roofs of the mosques glittered; the rush of wet wind bent the boughs of the acacia and tamarisk trees. She walked through the public park, short-cutting her journey along a shady walkway where huge hedges of arum lillies and still larger hedges of red geraniums bloomed. On the breeze came the scent of cooking fires. Quick-stepping over a puddle, she paid scant attention to sounds of children and wailing infants from within.

She knew she was very late and that her father would be angry with her for not being home before sundown. Still, the delays hadn't been entirely her fault; the storm had caught practically everyone by surprise. Anyway, she was sure that when Habib heard about her good fortunes and the many new orders, he would forget about her lateness and be pleased. She only hoped he would not be unduly upset about the delay in his supper.

Her stomach began to growl as home became closer. Black clouds scudded across the sky, and beyond the high walls and panorama of flat roofs and fingerlike obelisks she could again see the hazy silhouettes of the Atlas Mountains lazily looming. The notes from a two-string *quembri*, a guitarlike ancient instrument, flitted from somewhere and caused her to pause. The music soon was accompanied by the sweet voice of a young ballad singer. Samíah could not help but listen, wistfully remembering. Rashid used to sing and play that very song, she knew, and hearing it now disturbed her. How much the stonemason had loved to sing! Their friends used to gather at the house and listen, saying that his voice was like—

She cut off the memory with a bitter pang of sorrow. Rashid was dead, she reminded herself. The past was gone, never to return.

Samíah quickened her pace. Her desire to reach home intensified with her wish to lock herself away from the outside world, find safety in the walls of her house and her work, where the root of her sadness need never be faced.

The old crooked gate marking the boundary of the Old Quarter stood nearby. She greeted it with a thankful sigh and passed beneath the trellis of the intersecting street, glad now to be alone, back in control of her emotions. Here and there a worker was returning home late from his job. Dogs were barking from the yards, babies crying for supper. The street was familiarly dark and almost deserted, and Samíah would have reached her own street and home in moments more had it not been for what she saw.

Beneath the lumbering shadow of an overhead balcony two hunched figures were speaking quietly. Drops of water slid down the balcony and formed a slender curtain before they splashed to the street. Neither of the men seemed aware of Samíah's nearby presence, nor did she pay much attention to them until something almost forgotten jarred in the back of her mind.

One of them was a cripple, his right shoulder higher than the left, one arm tragically bent and misshapen like the branch of a tree ready to snap. His hand was mangled, fingers crooked and turning warpedly inward. Samíah gasped. She fled into shadows and stood panting at the threshold of a darkened doorway. Her flesh crawled with sudden anxiety; she kept a hand to her throat where her heart was pounding and peered across the street with fear in her eyes. *I know that man*, she told herself. *I know him! Only when I saw him last he was ragged— a beggar!*

The events of the abduction came flooding back. He was the one! He had to be! The deformed beggar who'd whispered in secret to the missing noble!

But what was he doing here in the Old Quarter? Beggars did not belong, but now he wasn't a beggar at all. His dress was neat and clean—the robes of a merchant or an artisan. She must be mistaken, she knew. It couldn't be the same man. The street was dark; her eyes were playing tricks. But her stomach knotted and sank when he moved from the balcony, shuffling alone into the dim recesses. His movements were rigid and slow, arthritically rigid in the misty drizzle. His left leg dragged slightly behind the other in the identical way she had seen the last time. Now she was sure. This *was* the same man! She would—could—never forget him.

What should she do, she asked herself. Should she try to stop him before he disappeared again, plead with him to remember that day in the markets? Or should she shout for help, alert the patrolling sultan's guards and have him held for questioning? This man, this beggar in artisan's clothes, was her only proof; he could testify to what had happened better than anyone. . . .

She began to move from the doorway but stopped. Waves of fear came over her as she recalled the soldier's warning: *Forget everything you think you saw. . . . Marrakesh can be a dangerous place for the innocent bystander who has seen too much. . . .*

Samíah held her breath and pressed her back firmly against the wall, hoping she hadn't been seen. The deformed man hobbled away soundlessly, lost in the gloom of night. His companion lingered, a tall and lanky figure that peered suspiciously up and down the street before moving on in a long, awkward gait. Then abruptly, while she was still watching him, he slowly turned around, pulling up his collar against the breeze. For an instant his gaze settled in her direction. Samíah was unsure if he had seen her, but in that time she had caught a glimpse of him. It was the bumpkin. The landlord's nephew, Gideon.

"Ah, at last! Where have you been?"

Samíah shut the door firmly behind her. "I'm sorry to be so late, Papa," she said, catching her breath in short gulps. "The storm forced me to take shelter in the *souk* and before I could finish my deliveries—"

He held up an open palm, a twinkle in his eyes. "I understand, I understand," he said sympathetically. "I was beginning to worry, but then I was assured you were all right."

"Assured, Papa?"

He moved into the light with a quick frown. Of course it had been the genie who had told him not to fret, that Samíah's delay was all part of his magic. However, the dustman could hardly explain that to his daughter. "I, er, meant that the bad weather assured me you would be late," he corrected. "Never mind, though. Take off your wet things and dry yourself. Then tell me about your day, all of it. I'm eager to hear everything."

"I hope you're not angry about supper?"

"Supper? Heavens no, girl!" He wrinkled his nose and grinned. "Seeing you were going to be late I decided to cook it myself. For us both." He proudly gestured toward the steaming pot of stew simmering over the crackling fire. "Come on now, out of those wet things. Everything's almost ready."

Samíah hesitated, regarding him with a long stare. It was most unlike her father to behave this way. "Are you all right?" she asked.

His laugh made his belly quiver like jelly. "Never better, Samíah, never better."

It hadn't taken long for her to change and take her place at the table. And once seated, to her astonishment, she found Habib curiously doting over her, helping her to serve, pouring the tea, and acting in a way she could not recall him ever doing before.

"So then," he said, smacking his lips and plunging his spoon into the bowl of piping stew. "Begin at the beginning."

Samíah wasn't very hungry; her encounter with the deformed beggar had left her feeling shaken and uneasy. But she forced herself to eat, not wanting her father to know anything was wrong. At least not yet, not until she had sorted all these strange events properly out in her own mind.

Making casual conversation, she told him all he wished to know, about her deliveries and new orders, getting caught in the downpour so unprepared, remarking on this and that and everything she could think of. Her father, though, seemed more interested in exactly who she had met today, rather than what had happened. "Did, er, did you make any new acquaintances today?" he wanted to know.

Samíah shrugged. "I don't think so, Papa. Wait a minute, there was someone new at Ali Sa'id's household. . . ."

"Oh?" Habib leaned forward with interest, elbows up, chin cradled over his knitted hands. "Someone with, umm, a little appeal?"

"Appeal, Papa?"

"You know what I mean. Someone . . . likeable?"

Samíah smiled with deepened dimples. "Oh. Perhaps I see what you mean. Yes, a newcomer from the city of Rabat. Actually I was asked many things about the city, about my life, my work. I think we might become friends."

Habib's face lit up, only to sour when the girl hastily added, "Ali Sa'id's mother-in-law and I seem to have much in common."

The child was definitely giving him a hard time, playing either coy or stupid. But obviously she must have come across *someone* today; the genie had been positive of it. "Wasn't there anyone else? Someone, perhaps, that you've overlooked?"

For the second time she shrugged, dipping a piece of crusty bread into the rich gravy. "Like who?"

"How should I know? Maybe a man . . ." He tried to sound casual but it didn't come off very well. Samíah stopped chewing and regarded him with an odd look.

"Are you trying to match me up again, Papa? I thought we had an agreement—"

"And we have, daughter! By the Prophet's holy beard, we have! I, er, was only wondering. Being gone from the house all day, er, I just wondered if, er, during your business you might have run into someone. Accidently, of course. Someone interesting . . ."

She placed her spoon down beside the bowl, her eyes brewing as she studied him. "Are you positive you're feeling well?"

He chuckled jovially. "Go on with the rest of your story."

"That's really all there was. Except for on the way home." Suddenly she avoided his gaze, letting her eyes drift and linger on the half-filled teacup.

"What happened on the way home?"

"If I tell you, Papa, you'll only say I was imagining things again."

He reached for her arm and gently pressed a hand over her slim wrist. "No I won't."

"Promise?"

He nodded. Samíah shifted her weight and, still not looking directly at him, sighed. "Just before, Papa, as I was entering the Old Quarter, I saw something very strange. *Very* strange." She bit her lip. "There were two men beneath a balcony in the street by the gate. Speaking in whispers. They didn't see me, or at least I don't think they did, pressed into the shadows as they were."

"They must have been taking shelter from the storm. It doesn't sound very unusual to me."

Her lashes closed over her eyes. "No, Papa, perhaps not." Then she went back to eating, prepared to drop the matter entirely. She chewed her food very slowly, wondering how she would find room for the meal in her knotted stomach.

"Is that all, daughter?" Habib demanded. He waited patiently for her to answer. It was a while before she lifted her head and faced him.

"One of the men was a cripple, Papa. I recognized him. It was the man from the Street of Sandalmakers, the beggar I saw before the abduction. Only now he wasn't a beggar at all. He wore fine, well-tailored clothes, like a man of means." As she spoke Habib noticed her hand had begun to tremble slightly, her distress very real and troubling.

"Are you certain of all this, Samíah?"

Somberly she nodded, profile cameoed against the dim light. "Yes, Papa. It was the same man—I *know* it was."

A hint of starlight broke through the overcast, glittering through the opened window. Habib leaned back in an uncomfortable silence and listened to the rustle of breeze flitting among the trees, unsure what to think. Could Samíah really have seen what she claimed? Or was the girl so distraught these past days by the incident in the market that it had begun to affect her mind, causing her to see things that were not really there? Habib was a simple man; these questions were beyond

71

his understanding. He decided to discuss the matter with the Syrian; Kubla might provide an answer.

Her face seemed pale in the lamplight's glow, eyes anguished and worry filled. "You think I'm dreaming this all up, don't you?" she said.

"No, daughter." He measured his words carefully, not wanting to upset her further. "But as you said, the street was already dark, these men huddled in shadows . . ."

"I thought so." She laughed low, mirthlessly. "Then I'll tell you something else, Papa. I got a good glimpse of his companion as well—and I think he may have seen me, too, as I saw them whispering." She grimaced, standing up from the table, turning her back on him. "They were up to no good, Papa. I know it even if I can't prove it. Something is going on in the city, something bad, something evil—"

"Nonsense, Samíah! Now you really are letting yourself get carried away."

She spun around, pressing her lips, glaring at her father. "Am I?" She was shivering. "Or are the Assassins imaginary, too?"

His heart skipped a beat. "What do you know of Assassins?" he said derisively.

"I've heard the gossip, Papa. It's rife in the markets, throughout the city—"

"I don't want to ever again hear such foolish talk, Samíah!" he boomed. "These rumors are the talk of fishwives, rattling tongues who enjoy sowing the seeds of fear and anxiety."

Flaring at him with righteous anger, she said, "There is one thing that I do know: this cripple is not what he pretends to be. Neither a beggar nor—nor—"

"Even if this *were* the same man you saw before the abduction, what of it? You're letting your fantasies run away with you, daughter. All you saw were two men together taking shelter from the rain. Nothing more and nothing less."

"Then I'll have to prove to you that I'm right."

Habib lacked the inner resources to argue. "Prove it how?" was all he said.

"By confronting the beggar's companion. You see, there

was one other matter that I haven't yet mentioned. The man I saw conspiring with the cripple, the one who I think may have seen me—I recognized him as well." She paused now, her surge of temper calmed, her voice subdued and modulated again. Habib fidgeted in his place. "It was your friend—our new rent collector."

The dustman stared. "Gideon?"

"Yes. You asked me whom I met today, Papa, whom I might have run into accidentally. He was the only one—and he's my proof that I wasn't imagining any of this."

Poor Habib couldn't coax the words from his mouth. Was it possible, could the landlord's nephew, the clumsy, stuttering, awkward newcomer actually be the one the genie had foretold?

"I'm going to find him, Papa," Samíah was saying, oblivious to her father's sudden astoundment and disbelief. "Confront him and make him admit he was seen with the cripple. Take him straight to the sultan's soldiers and let them question him."

Habib snapped from his fog. "What? What are you saying?"

"That I don't believe this Gideon is who he claims to be either, Papa. What do we know about him, *really* know, I mean?"

"Samíah!" He rose from his cushioned seat, the corners of his mouth tucked down in a mixture of anger and frustration. "You'll do no such thing! Gideon is a nice young man, a stranger here, guilty of nothing except maybe seeking shelter from the rain!"

"With the same cripple who saw the nobleman kidnapped!"

"I forbid this, Samíah! This whole matter is ridiculous. Leave the landlord's nephew out of your imaginings!"

"Even if he's helping to conspire with our sultan's enemies?"

The dustman was beside himself with worried anticipation. The strong-willed girl was capable of going to any lengths necessary to prove her case, lengths that in the long run would cause a terrible ruckus and in the end leave them both looking like fools.

"Listen to me, Samíah; this Gideon is nothing more than a good-natured, well-meaning young man who doesn't yet know his way around life in the city. I admit he seems to be a bit of a simpleton, that he's naive and not too bright..."

"I wonder, Papa. I wonder."

He fumed. "If you insist on this foolishness, I'll—" He spluttered, looking for the proper threat.

"All right, Papa," she said. "I won't go to the soldiers. I'll not embarrass you or him."

Habib sighed thankfully, glad that he'd been able to pound at least an iota of common sense into her head. He sat back down and shut his eyes wearily. "Then you promise to forget all about this matter and leave things alone?"

"My word, Papa. Outside of you, him and me, no one will hear of it or get involved."

What she didn't say was that she still had something to prove to herself. Perhaps she was wrong, she conceded, about everything. Perhaps there was no cause for concern, that the cripple's presence in the Old Quarter was meaningless, that Gideon indeed was no more than an innocent bystander keeping out of the rain. There was only one way to find out—and she was intent on doing it without her father ever knowing.

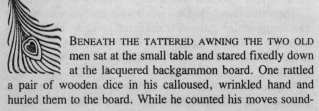

BENEATH THE TATTERED AWNING THE TWO OLD men sat at the small table and stared fixedly down at the lacquered backgammon board. One rattled a pair of wooden dice in his calloused, wrinkled hand and hurled them to the board. While he counted his moves soundlessly his companion sipped from the tiny cup of Turkish coffee, pondering his own strategy for his upcoming turn.

Another man sat alone at the next table, his concentration absorbed by the setting of the sun. The final call to devotion still echoed from the minarets, the busy market streets becoming quiet and lifeless as the throngs hurried for their homes. Evening stars glittered from above fiery passing clouds, a crescent moon hung unobtrusively above the golden dome of the palace. The man at the table displayed the same disinterested glance as all the others seated at the café each time some passerby crossed the lonely avenue. When a dark figure emerged from a darkened shop across the way his features betrayed only the mildest of absorption. Then, as their glances met in breviated acknowledgment, he quickly returned his attention to the night sky, whistling an abstract tune and drumming the fingers of his left hand on the tabletop. Nothing seemed very different or unusual about him, only that the third finger was missing, a fact frequently obscured by the way he held his hand.

The figure across the street quickly passed the café, his eyes coolly fixed ahead toward some unknown destination. The man at the table kept his gaze upward, but listened to his walk, counting the steps until they were out of hearing. A moment later he rose from his place, took a few coins from his pocket, and placed them slowly down on the table. The proprietor, a clubfooted, obese but genial fellow, hobbled to collect the payment, muttering a thank you, and the obligatory *salaam* long after his patron had departed. As he cleaned off the table and went back inside, the old men playing backgammon never glanced up once.

The four-fingered man skirted the row of empty stalls and waited at the narrow intersection while a donkey-led wagon inched its way slowly in the direction of the *souk*. The driver, swollen-eyed and gray-bearded, held the reins lazily and clicked his tongue in a futile gesture to make the animal move faster. The donkey swatted its tail to chase away buzzing flies and drooped its head lower, too wearied from the heat and the weight of its load to obey.

When the wagon rumbled away, the four-fingered man

stepped into the tiny cloud of dust and proceeded. He walked with stiff, economical movements, darting his eyes as the breeze rustled in the trees. Far up the street he saw the man from the shop pause, glance in his direction, then slip unseen into an abandoned doorway. The four-fingered man bared his lips in a smile.

"What have you got for me?" the four-fingered man was asked from the shadows.

"How much can you pay?" came the terse reply.

His companion frowned, ran a finger along the side of his angular jaw as he studied the informer. Information never came cheap. Especially from this one. But the four-fingered man had proved his worth before, and for now remained the most valuable information gatherer he had. At least since the death of the Parrot, a man whose contacts and spies infiltrated every aspect of Marrakesh life from the Casbah to the palace. A pity the Parrot had been found with his throat slit and his tongue cut off and stuffed back inside his mouth. He was sorely missed.

The man in shadows considered the arrangement. Four Fingers had many uses, as many facades and facets to his personality as he had disguises. But the only code he followed was his own, and unlike the Parrot, he was treacherous. Capable of anything, selling his information to any bidder regardless of motive, he could violate any trust at the jingle of a coin, and not bat an eyelash when those who had put their faith in him were cold-bloodedly double-crossed by his perfidy. Still, he served a purpose; especially now, this man of no name, this streetwise purveyor of information whose uncanny methods were invaluable. Other informers sold rumor and gossip; Four Fingers sold only fact.

When the man in shadows opened his fist, two tiny gold coins glittered in the darkness. Four Fingers grinned broadly, one front tooth noticeably missing.

"I have found him for you," he said with a lisp.

"Where is he?"

"In hiding."

"Alive?"

Here Four Fingers leaned his back against the frame of the

door and folded his arms; expressions of amusement and boredom broke simultaneously across his weathered, scarred face. "Not for long."

His companion glared in consternation. "He's no good to me dead," he said.

Four Fingers shrugged. "I promised nothing—only to find him. This morning he was still alive, I assure you. A weasel of a man. Spineless and cowering, useless to himself and to anyone else."

"Not to me."

The informer ran a finger along his down-turned mustache. "Then you had better hurry." His smile was sly and cunning. "There are those in Marrakesh who do not trust his wagging tongue, who know he will spill his guts and tell what he did, what he saw, the moment he is found. These men know it even as you and I do." He frowned distastefully. "Such a man is a bane. Better off silenced."

The man in the shadows narrowed his gaze at Four Fingers, despising everything about the informer. "Tell me where he is."

A dirty hand was held open. "First the money."

"First the information."

For a few long moments they stood eye to eye, Four Fingers loathing him every bit as much as he knew he was loathed. Likes or dislikes, though, played no part in the exchange. The lure of gold was all that mattered.

"He gave up his own quarters days ago. Afraid for his life. I learned his whereabouts are a hovel, a place near the Casbah where he intends to hide until it is safe to come out—safe from the questions of the sultan's soldiers." He chuckled malevolently beneath his breath, as fully aware as his companions that it was not the soldiers he needed most to fear.

"The exact location, frog."

Four Fingers winced. The term was one he did not like. It expressed the disdain all buyers of information feel for those who sell the intelligence they seek.

"It will please me very much one day to hear of your own demise," the informer wheezed. "Very much indeed."

His companion smiled. He handed over the coins and listened intently as Four Fingers accepted them and fulfilled the bargain. Then he was gone one way and the informer the other.

Hussein had been sleeping. He had not heard the lock being picked, nor seen the masked men as they sneaked inside his decrepit room and hovered over his bed. A hand nudged him awake, and the bucket carrier opened his eyes wide in terror. His arms lurched out defensively; he started to scream. The sound was quickly muffled by the pillow squeezed over his mouth and nose. Hussein's legs danced convulsively. His struggle was brief and pitiful, and when the pillow was removed he lay gaping and glassy-eyed, staring out into nothingness. His killers grinned, then hoisted the frail body from the bed, opened the window, and slipped the corpse out, where it fell in a dulled heap among the high-piled refuse in the alley. Sprawled, his limbs crookedly puppetlike, he lay alone in the darkness. No one had seen, no one had heard, no one cared. There he stayed, heaped in the garbage, a scarecrow figure who kept away the prowling mongrels.

 SHORTLY AFTER HABIB GATHERED HIS BROOM AND sack and left for work, Samíah put down her needles and threads, neatly folded an unfinished garment, and carefully put it away. Turning the lamps down low, she left the house.

For better than an hour she walked through the nearby streets, unsure exactly what she hoped to accomplish tonight but determined to find the courage to do what had to be done.

Samíah passed the gate of the Old Quarter and crossed over familiar streets. Each time a passerby hurried her way she found herself slipping among the shadows, staring from the darkness to see who it might be. Each time, though, she was disappointed. None proved to be he, the man she was intent on finding, the landlord's nephew.

Almost another hour passed uneventfully. She wandered along byways of clustered shops and empty stalls now shuttered for the night, still uncertain about this whole affair. All she knew was that no matter what she had promised Papa she could not leave matters the way they were. If only to prove her own sanity, she knew she had to once and for all cast away these nagging doubts.

A trio of drunkards spilled from the doorway of a seedy tavern and onto the ill-lighted street. Across from them a shoeless urchin huddled and hungrily ate a stolen crust of bread. A one-legged man hobbled on his crutches along a side lane. Samíah kept herself in her dark nook below the trellis and observed them all. Restless, fatigued, she started to feel more than a little foolish at her escapade, almost ready to concede that maybe her father had been right. Exactly what did she expect to prove anyway?

Back along the arched, silent byway she marched, the hour already far later than she had intended to remain. Her thoughts were confused and troubled, but home was just a short walk away and she resigned herself to giving up. Besides, there was still so much of her own work left to be done, work she had neglected in this silly hope to—

Samíah stopped in her tracks. From the entrance to the Azzemour hanging gardens she saw him. Quickly she back-pedaled into the comforting shadows and followed his every move. It was Gideon all right, his stride, his lanky frame giving him away to her instantly despite the distance that separated them. He walked briskly, his shoulders slightly hunched, away from the lane that would lead to the sprawling plaza and off in the direction of dingy streets she knew would take them to the Casbah.

She stiffened and held her breath. This time he hadn't seen her, she was sure. Here was her chance...

She followed cautiously, pausing when he did, keeping a safe range between them. There was little to distinguish him from the cascading shadows and grim forms of the trees; she paced him by instinct more than sight, now growing increasingly curious where he was heading and why especially during the dead of night.

Gideon seemed to know exactly where he was going; he made a few quick turns around darkened corners and entered a section of the city that Samíah was not familiar with—an area of moribund edifices long since decayed and abandoned. Deeper and deeper the rent collector led her into the maze of twisting, silent streets.

Along a deserted lane by a low crumbling wall the rent collector halted. Samíah pressed herself out of sight and watched. Gideon hesitated momentarily beside the crumbled arch secured by an aged, rotting doorway, then entered.

Samíah swallowed and moistened her dry lips, debating whether she should go after him. The strangeness of these streets frightened her, particularly as a sudden gust of wind eerily rustled in and out of the gloomy facades. Fear was rising in her and something tugged at her to go, to run back home and leave well enough alone. But the mystery surrounding the landlord's nephew had only deepened. Samíah wondered how he, a newcomer to the city, could possibly know these ancient streets so well. Now she was sure of her belief: the country bumpkin was not what he claimed to be. Somehow—and she didn't yet understand how—he was involved deeply in the intrigues she had touched upon.

There wasn't much time to debate what to do, not if she still hoped to catch up and discover more. She drew up her fading courage and pressed stealthily onward, following the contours of the crumbling wall until she arrived at the doorway. Then she pushed open the door and hurried inside before she talked herself out of it.

A long corridor twisted before her, the walls dank and the air foul. Her feet disturbed a thick layer of dust. She shuffled her way inside, feeling the dust scatter and rise. When she sneezed she threw her hands to her face to muffle the sound. In the distance she could hear Gideon's footsteps continue without hesitation. Samíah sighed with relief that she hadn't been heard and, on her toes, moved cautiously on.

The corridor turned abruptly and left her completely sightless. She groped her way through the blackness at a steady pace, one hand held out in front, the other tracing the wall. Breath heavy and labored, she negotiated another turn, then nearly jumped at the sound of a creaking door. Somewhere ahead, yet unseen, there was an exit. She stood still and listened as Gideon passed through. Then she found herself alone in the dark.

Panic began to replace fear; she fought the urge to turn and run back, and had there been but a single pinprick of light to guide her out, she would have done just that. The darkness encroached on all sides and numbed her, converging and rendering her helpless.

It took all her effort to get a hold of herself and proceed. There was no point in turning back, she told herself. Not now, not when she was so close to learning the truth.

Her flesh crawled when an unseen spider's web tickled the side of her face. She shuddered and squealed, pushing the silky threads away. On she pressed. Then something blocked her path, a solid wall in front. Her hand felt along the seams and she found a door. Blindly she felt for the latch, slipping it open easily, carefully pushing it inch by inch so that it didn't groan on its hinges.

Suddenly the air was fresh and clean again; moonlight flooded from above. Samíah found herself standing on the edge of a small courtyard, hemmed in on all four sides, with weed and fern growing in savage clumps everywhere like a miniature jungle. From the state of disrepair she was sure that no one had used it in decades.

Slowly Samíah stepped out into the open and stared confusedly about. High walls rose to the left and right, but before

her stood an entrance to a dim hall. Of Gideon there was no
sign at all, but there was only one way in which he could have
gone, and Samíah followed the broken path and went into the
hall.

The half light scarcely revealed the hall's shadowy and
immense proportions. The roof, to her surprise, was upheld by
slender columns of marble ranged cloisterlike around the hall,
leaving a square space in the center. The columns were cracked
from years of disrepair, and far above her head the cedarwood
roof was almost imperceptible in the dim light. Among the
cloisters, behind the columns, shafts of moonlight streamed
through the roof's fissures, highlighting aspects of the worn
marble and tiled floor. All around the tops of the walls were
incredible friezes of scenes from the sacred Koran.

It was the absolute silence that made Samíah uneasy. She
felt as though she were more than a tresspasser, that she had
innocently come across something lost and forsaken, a secret
spot guarded and sequestered from both time and memory,
buried forever within the recesses of nameless streets and byways of a quarter few ever saw.

Beyond the worn and broken tiles large blocks of granite
lay embedded in the floor. Samíah approached with a measure
of anxiety and knelt beside the first. Her hand brushed away
a thin layer of dust, and she stared at the surface. Etched into
the stone in a fine cursive writing were names of men she had
never heard of and titles she couldn't properly understand.
Standing at last, she now realized what she had discovered: a
sepulcher. The hall was a tomb.

Through a high, pillared arch she entered another chamber,
smaller than the first, whose walls were colorfully decorated
with beautiful, if worn, mosaics, a chamber virtually intact
despite the passage of time. But despite the beauty there was
something she perceived as sinister about this separate room.
She felt a chill and the desire to leave it as quickly as she
could.

The passageway out had fewer twists and turns than the
way in. When she emerged it was into another courtyard, only
from here she could see above the walls the flickering lights

of the city. A dark alley led to the street. As Samíah approached it, a huge black rat darted across her path and took refuge inside a gaping hole in the wall. Lurching back, Samíah waited until it was gone then, putting her disgust aside, made her way along the alley. The smells of the city came back to her in a rush. The tomb was far behind now, away from sight and thought, and she picked her path slowly, the high walls of the Casbah looming on the other side.

She had made her way almost to the street when once again she stopped. Ahead in the shadows she saw the figures of two men, one lying motionless atop a heap of rubbish, the other squatting grimly over him, urgently rifling through his pockets. Her shoes scraped over stone; the squatting man turned. When she saw his face she wanted to scream.

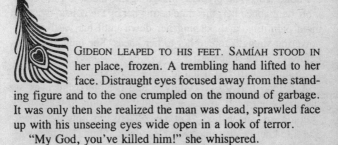

GIDEON LEAPED TO HIS FEET. SAMÍAH STOOD IN her place, frozen. A trembling hand lifted to her face. Distraught eyes focused away from the standing figure and to the one crumpled on the mound of garbage. It was only then she realized the man was dead, sprawled face up with his unseeing eyes wide open in a look of terror.

"My God, you've killed him!" she whispered.

Gideon stared at her. "No," he said, reaching out his hand in her direction. "But—what are you doing here?"

The enormity of the horror before her began to take hold. Samíah moved back, shaking, sickened, and frightened. So

83

now the truth was out—and the worst of her suspicions had been proved. She had caught the landlord's nephew in the act, and for that he would kill her as well.

She stumbled as she turned, started to run back along the dark passage. "Samíah, wait!" Gideon cried. She ran for her life. Suddenly his hand was on her shoulder and he forcefully twisted her around. She fell back against the wall, her panicked eyes confronting his, tears streaming down her face. "Murderer!" she screamed at him.

He grabbed her roughly and shook her again and again.

"Killer! You'll pay for your crime! I'll see to it! I'll find the soldiers and I'll—"

He slapped her hard, the sting of his palm breaking her hysteria and changing it into a flood of uncontrolled sobs. She struggled with him, desperate to break loose from his grasp to run and somehow reach the street, to summon the sultan's patrolling guards. Gideon, though, was holding her fast, his strong arms pinning her upright against the crumbling stone of the wall, preventing her from moving. In self-defense she lashed out in every way she could—kicking, clawing, aiming for his dark eyes in an effort to scratch them out. When she screamed he covered her mouth with his hand. Samíah bit down as hard as she could over his fingers, making him cry out and release the hold. Then she pivoted, kicked again, made to run. Once more he grabbed her, this time taking her by the wrists, twisting them painfully, and pushing her down until his vastly overpowering strength forced her to her knees. She hung her head before him and sobbed.

"Samíah, will you listen to me!" he barked.

Unbound hair tossed wildly before her bloodshot eyes as she shook her head, refusing to allow his words to reach her. "Let me go!" she wailed. "Let me go!" His grip only tightened. She tilted her head, forced herself to look at him. His face was distorted, outraged, and fearful.

"Go on then—kill me, too! Do it! Butcher! Assassin!"

"Won't you listen to me? Won't you give me a chance to explain—?"

"Help! Soldiers! Soldiers!"

Gideon glanced around in desperation. Here and there across the dark facades of buildings lights were being lit in the windows. "I don't want to have to do this, Samíah," he wheezed.

She was yelling now at the top of her lungs, berserk with fear. She did not feel it when he dragged her back up to her feet, nor see him as he drew his hand back into a fist. Stars danced across her vision; she moaned and slid to the floor.

When she awoke she was heaped at the foot of the alley. Dizzily she peered up. Gideon was still there, hovering over her like a beast, hands clutched at his sides and balled into fists. "I—I didn't mean to do that," he said, looking straight down at her.

Samíah glared up at him. When she tried to speak she felt the pain in her jaw, the throbbing bruise below her chin where he had hit her. He extended a helping hand. "Will you listen to me now?"

She pulled away, crawling into the slanting shadows along the wall. The menace of his being chilled her and she wondered why he hadn't just killed her right then and had done with it.

"I'm sorry, Samíah. Truly I am. But you were hysterical, out of your mind. I couldn't let you keep screaming like that."

"Pig." She spat on his pants, her gaze smoldering with dim fires. "You'd better kill me while you still can. Because if you don't I'm going to take special pleasure in watching the executioner remove your head from your shoulders."

"I didn't kill him, Samíah," he said. "I want you to believe that."

"Liar!" There was venom in her voice, hatred in her flashing eyes. "I saw you going through his pockets like a thief. Saw you gloat over his corpse . . ." The lifeless body was still there among the refuse, she saw. Pitiful and horrendous. A ghastly sight, mangled and crooked as it was. Slaughtered like an animal.

"He was already dead when I got here," Gideon told her. "That's the truth." He sighed deeply, wiping his sweaty brow. "Poor fellow. It was too late for me to help."

A caustic laugh parted Samíah's thin lips. "You expect me to believe that, too?"

"It's the truth."

"And because you couldn't help him, you decided to rifle through his pockets, is that it?"

Gideon turned away from her in exasperation. "It's not like you think. I, er, I was searching for something. . . ."

"His purse, no doubt."

"I'm not a thief, Samíah!" There was anger in his eyes when he shifted back in her direction. Anger and worry. Her presence here was an unforseen complication—one that could ruin everything. "Listen to me," he said, kneeling beside her. "I was coming this way on an errand. To find this very man. But I was too late. Can you understand that? He was dead by the time I reached him."

She glared at him evenly, loathing this deceitful lair, knowing him now for what he was—a cunning, cold-blooded cut-throat. Two-faced and treacherous, caught in the act of his crime and now trying to wiggle out of it like a worm.

"I want you to know I could have helped him," Gideon was saying, unaware of her thoughts. "At least forestalled . . . this." Glancing over his shoulder he peered grimly at the unmoving body. Then he hung his head, shaking it slowly from side to side, adding as an afterthought almost to himself, "If only I'd been here a little sooner. Maybe there would have been time . . ." His words trailed off into an inaudible whisper.

"You don't fool me," Samíah snapped. "I know enough about you already."

His stare became intent. "What do you mean?"

"I mean I've been following you," she said with a measure of triumph. "I've seen you, Gideon. Seen you with the cripple, whispering among the shadows. Trailed you like a hound to-night. You're no stranger to Marrakesh. You crossed through streets no one even knows about. Entered into the tombs and—"

He grabbed her arm, looked deep into her eyes. "You followed me there?" he rasped.

She smiled, nodded. "It's no longer a secret Gideon—if

that is your name. And your game is up. Once I expose you for what you are and what you've done—"

"You bloody little fool! You've been inside the tombs?"

"I told you; I've followed you all night."

Biting his lip, he grew openly anxious. "Did anybody see you, Samíah? Inside the temple, I mean?"

Her only response was a laugh.

"Don't play games with me, girl! I have to know. It's too important not to know!"

There was mocking in her eyes now, a sudden feeling that she had somehow bested him at his own game, stopped him cold in his treachery. "I'll never tell," she answered. "I'll take that knowledge with me to my grave."

And she meant it, he could tell. "Listen, Samíah," he said, his tone now belying his concern. "I haven't time to explain, but if anyone *did* observe you it could be dangerous. For *you*."

She sat up straighter, unafraid. "You underestimate me, Gideon. My conscience is clear. I've done nothing wrong, broken no laws. It's you who's the one in trouble. I've suspected it ever since I saw you with the cripple from the Street of Sandalmakers. And when the soldiers learn about it—"

Gideon groaned. "Your thinking is flawed, Samíah. Neither he nor I had anything to do with the abduction. But if you've been seen by anyone who did, it could put your own life and your father's as well in great peril." He looked at her plainly, an open frankness in his face. Samíah felt her flesh crawling again.

"What are you saying?"

He rubbed wearily at his temple, trying in desperation to put his normally coherent thought processes back into some semblance of order. The girl's prying was a greater problem than he'd realized. At best it could spell trouble for them all— at worst, disaster.

"I don't care what else you believe about me, Samíah, but this you have to know. Marrakesh is in grave jeopardy. There are those," and here he hesitated, not wanting to expose her to even greater dangers, "those who are intent on creating anarchy. Overthrowing the law and government and wresting all power for themselves. Evil men, Samíah. Men who stop at nothing to achieve their goals. Should they have their way our nation will endure the biggest bloodbath in all of history."

"I think you're just trying to scare me."

He was solemn as he denied it. "No, Samíah, I'm not. There are things afoot in our city that it is better for you not to know about. It's enough for me to tell you that should you unwittingly become exposed, your life will be as valueless as"—he indicated the corpse—"as his."

Samíah shuddered. Why was he saying all this, what was he trying to prove? "Even if what you say is so, what has any of it got to do with what I saw?"

Gideon could tell she didn't understand. But how could she, this child of the Old Quarter, daughter of simple, honest folk who knew little or nothing of the vile world of violence? "I have reason to believe this man was murdered by the very Assassins you accuse me of being a part of." She gasped, and he continued, "Like you, he was an innocent bystander. A man who saw too much and acted upon it. He didn't realize what he was up against, and he paid for his foolishness with his life."

Trembling, Samíah felt confused. For the first time she harbored doubts about Gideon's crime; she tried to reconstruct—without hysteria—everything she had seen. The cold fact was she had not witnessed the landlord's nephew commit the murder, only observed him hovering over the body. It *was* possible that another had been responsible. . . .

"If all this is true, then why don't you go yourself to the soldiers now, explain what you think?"

He shook his head. "You don't understand. It wouldn't do any good. Besides, this isn't their matter. It has to be worked out differently," again he groped for the right words, "clandestinely, in absolute secret."

She studied him for a time, then she smiled coldly. "I think you'd go to any extreme, concoct any tale to keep me from telling what I've seen, wouldn't you?"

"No," he shot back, "but there are those that would."

She stood slowly, brushing off dust and grime from her *chador*. "Then I'll just have to do it myself."

He was standing now as well, regarding her intensely. "What are you intending?"

"Only what I said from the beginning: to go to the soldiers and tell them everything. About you, about the tomb, about the corpse. If you're innocent then there won't be anything to fear, will there?" A tinge of daring was evident in her voice now.

"I—I can't let you do that, Samíah. For your own sake. Too many spies are about, even among our sultan's guards."

Hands to her hips, she looked at him scornfully. "So you *are* afraid!" she flared. "Well, you can't stop me—unless you kill me."

Gideon moved, blocking her path to the street. She was creating a difficult obstacle for him, he knew, her cleverness posing a serious threat to everything he needed to do. Events were moving too swiftly, the danger constantly mounting. And wittingly or not, the willful girl could destroy all that he had worked to achieve. "Listen to me, Samíah," he said. "Look at this man. Do you know him?"

Her eyes drifted toward the lifeless form, and she shook her head.

"His name was Hussein. He worked in the *souk* at night— with your father. A friend of your father's . . ."

"You're lying."

"Am I? Then ask him. Ask him if Hussein has been to work these past days, or if he's disappeared without a trace."

"And what if you're right? What does that prove?"

His eyes narrowed in the darkness, his stance no longer the familiar stoop she was acquainted with. "It proves that I haven't lied to you. It proves what I've tried to impress upon you is very real. Don't meddle, Samíah. Go home, and stop asking questions. If you weren't being watched then you'll be safe."

"Safe from who?" she sneered. "From your revenge?"

A small pulse throbbed along the side of his jaw. "I've never in my life hurt anyone or shed innocent blood. Don't make things worse for either of us. Just do as I tell you."

"Not a chance!" She spit the words. "How do I know that you're not one of them? Not a member of the very band you claim to oppose? How do I know Hussein was killed if not by your hand then by your instruction?" She glared at him again. "How does a rent collector come to know all these things, anyway? A stranger to Marrakesh so well informed about the intrigues of our city?"

"I can't tell you that."

She smiled mirthlessly. "Then maybe the captain of the guard can make you answer." She turned her back to him purposely, content to traverse the alley and backstep her way through the tombs.

"Stop, Samíah!"

Though her heart was thrumming she kept on walking. She was pushing him to the edge, she knew. Forcing him to commit himself one way or the other, using her life as bait.

"I'm warning you for the last time," he called out after her. "Listen to me before it's too late."

She paused in the darkness, turning around slowly until she faced him fully and could see his face.

Gideon frowned. "Don't make me do something we'll both regret."

"Then you'd better kill me now because I'm going to report everything that's happened." Her eyes burned as they fell on his. "Unless you have a lot more explaining to do."

He considered what she was saying carefully. In his mind there wasn't the slightest doubt she meant every word of it. She had already seen far too much to be satisfied, and not aware of what she was doing, she would indeed go straight to the authorities. Letting her do that though, was out of the question. Months of difficult work would be ruined, and with it the only chance of his succeeding.

The girl had him in a bind, and they both knew it. Only two options were available. Confiding in her—or killing her.

"Well?" she asked.

Gideon sighed a long sigh. He stared at Hussein's broken body and ran a hand through his tousled hair. In his business there was little room for sentiment; the bucket slinger had taken his chances and paid the price of failure. But Samíah was innocent of all of this. Could he now willingly make her a part? That question was soon to be answered for him.

From the corner of his eye he saw the shadow fleeting across the nearby roof. Instinctively he threw the girl to the floor, shouting, "Stay down!" Then he whirled, hitting the garbage heap in a headfirst dive.

The solid crossbow bolt sailed an even trajectory to where they had been standing and hit the wall behind with a fearsome *whump*! where it embedded deeply in the cracks.

Samíah dizzily spit out dust and lifted her head. "Keep low!" came Gideon's booming voice. Then he was up on his feet, loping over Hussein's corpse, straddling the clinging shadows. With amazed eyes she saw him bend and draw a secret curved dagger from inside his boot and move deftly toward the street.

The figure atop the roof was still there, hunching, searching the darkness for his prey. Gideon ran from the alley and to the low wall. The figure on the roof darted over the tiles, leaping and bounding across the flat-topped roofs, disappearing within the shadowy maze.

Seconds ticked slowly; Gideon waited in hiding and, aware that the assailant was gone, quickly made his way back to the alley and Samíah's side.

"Are you all right?" he asked, kneeling beside the shaken girl but keeping his gaze steady on the rooftops.

Samíah found her breath and nodded weakly. She gazed fretfully into his eyes. "They mean to kill us!" she cried.

Gideon sucked in air and scoured the night. "Do you believe me now?"

"I—I don't know what to believe. . . ."

"We'd better move from here fast. Now we've been spotted together we're both marked."

Samíah's eyes grew wide. "Marked?"

"No time to explain now." He yanked her roughly to her feet, pulling her away from the alley and into the unlighted street. "I know a safe place," was all he said, and Samíah blindly let herself be towed along the curvature of the high wall leading into the Casbah.

Suddenly she became aware that Gideon, no matter what his crime, was not the true enemy. There was someone out there with a crossbow, probably still hiding and watching, waiting for the opportune moment to strike. And whatever the reason, there was a bolt now marked for her as well as her companion.

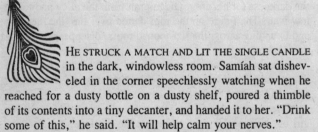 HE STRUCK A MATCH AND LIT THE SINGLE CANDLE in the dark, windowless room. Samíah sat disheveled in the corner speechlessly watching when he reached for a dusty bottle on a dusty shelf, poured a thimble of its contents into a tiny decanter, and handed it to her. "Drink some of this," he said. "It will help calm your nerves."

Absently she obeyed. The liquid was like fire; she downed it with a single swallow, gasping, struggling to catch her breath. "What is it?" she wheezed.

A thin smile parted his features. "A European concoction. They call it whiskey. It works like strong wine only far more potently."

Samíah pulled a face, her insides aflame. She fanned an open hand over her mouth, sinking deeper into the shadowed nook, her back firmly against the peeling plaster wall.

The room was musty with stale air. Where Gideon had taken her she didn't know; only that they had run and run and run in a seemingly endless journey in and out of unknown byways, cluttered lanes, deserted serpentine streets, and through gates and beneath arches she had never seen. Until at last they had arrived at this place—a subterranean room in an abandoned warehouse somewhere nestled amid the squalor and stench of the forbidden Casbah.

And now, thoroughly exhausted, she sank into melancholia, confused and frightened.

The candle's flame spluttered. Gideon seemed to ignore her presence for a few moments, keeping himself occupied first by bolting the crooked door and then by peeking through a small circular hole high in the wall which, Samíah correctly presumed, afforded a restricted view of the street outside.

Fidgeting, she scratched at her bare arms and glanced around at the dismal surroundings. The walls closed in on her claustrophobically.

"Feeling any better?"

His question was unexpected and caught her unaware. She snapped out of her gloomy thoughts. "Where—Where have you brought me?"

"Call it a safe haven. A place where no one can find us. I use it on occasion."

"I want to go home." Her pert face was smudged and her eyes wetly luminous and reddened.

Gideon hid a grimace as he turned to face her. "You should have done that when I told you to. Now we don't have a choice. We have to sit tight."

She was growing increasingly uncomfortable, the surge of panic caused by the appearance of the rooftop sniper gone, but the sense of dread about this whole affair strong and vivid. The shock of these events made her feel queasy, the smallness of the room telling her that she was trapped, with no way out. Down here anything could happen to her; she could scream and howl at the top of her lungs and no one would hear, not from a secret room in an abandoned warehouse in an area that was completely deserted. She and Gideon were totally alone, and that fact itself was more than she could come to terms with.

Besides, as she looked at him now she hardly recognized him. His shoulders were straight, the stoop with which he had carried himself mysteriously vanished. He didn't move with his clumsy, awkward gait, nor even stutter as he spoke. In fact, his whole speech and manner were different, letter perfect and articulate. And the knife, the secret dagger he'd sequestered inside his boot, what kind of man would carry such a weapon? No, this man wasn't the Gideon she knew—or thought she knew—at all. He was, well, different. The same but not the same. Another person entirely. This also scared her.

"What are you planning to do with me?" she asked feebly.

His shrug was noncommittal. "I haven't decided." He went back to the peephole and stood on his toes for a better glimpse. When he turned around again he was scowling. "There's someone out there. Lurking along the end of the street."

Samíah's heart beat savagely in the hope it might be a stray soldier on patrol, making his rounds of the silent streets. If only there were some way for her to reach the door and unbolt it before he could prevent it, she might be able to elude him and make her escape. He wouldn't dare try and harm her there, not with the risk of being confronted by the guard . . .

"You might as well make yourself comfortable," Gideon said. "It seems we're both going to have to stay a while."

The whiskey was still racing through her bloodstream, her head beginning to throb. She drew whatever courage she could muster and said, "You have no right to keep me locked here like a prisoner. I demand that you allow me to leave."

Gideon poured himself a thimble of the European drink and downed it quickly. "Too late for that," he answered curtly, his face stern and harsh, a cold look she had never encountered before in al-Gamal's nephew. "If you *are* marked then you'll be stopped. Or have you forgotten that bravo on the roof?"

She hadn't forgotten; the reminder of that hulking presence sent another chill. "Then why don't you send for the soldiers?"

He shook his head. "I told you I can't do that. Now just stay put for a while, and when things seem clear—"

"Kidnapping is a serious offense, rent collector!" She huffed her way into pretending she wasn't afraid. "Now, either you let me go, or the authorities will hear about it!"

There was a sharded slat bench set along the opposite corner and Gideon settled onto it. Hands folded between his open legs, he looked at her evenly and said, "Samíah, if I thought there was any chance of your making your way home alive, I'd let you walk out this door right now."

She took the challenge, standing, the hem of her *chador* swaying as she turned. "Good. Then I'm leaving—and don't make the mistake of trying to stop me. I'll scream so loud that every patrol between here and the *souk* will hear."

He extended his hand toward the exit. "All right, go then. But remember what I said: someone is out there. Not one of mine, and probably one of *theirs*."

"Theirs?"

His demeanor was cool. Too cool. "An Assassin."

Samíah tightened her gaze and swallowed. "You're bluffing. Likely as not it's a sultan's soldier on patrol. Probably looking for you."

Their eyes met in an icy stare, neither flinching from the other's gaze. Gideon didn't respond to her taunt; instead he sat impassive and rigid on the slat bench. Testing him, she moved from the corner into the open and then to the door. Still he didn't budge, not even when she took hold of the rusting latch and slid the bolt. At the last moment before walking out she glanced back over her shoulder. "Were you telling me the truth?" she demanded.

Gideon's eyes dilated in pain as he glared past the candle's flame, clinging to his truculent silence. Then, after a time, he said simply, "I wouldn't lie about it. Step out into the open and you'll be fortunate to be found as intact as Hussein was. These people don't play games, Samíah. A dustman's daughter has no part in involving herself in such matters." His jaw firmed. "Find out for yourself."

She hesitated now, debating what to do. Was he lying to her, using her fear to his advantage, to keep her here for his own purposes? Something told her to run, run while she had the chance. Get away and seek the protection of the soldiers as quick as she could. Yet something else nagged at her the other way, instilling in her a thought that perhaps he was right, perhaps he was telling the truth after all . . .

She snapped the bolt back into place dramatically and marched back to her corner, resuming her place and glaring at him with flashing eyes.

Observing her anger and sheer frustration, Gideon could not help the small grin that parted his lips. "Samíah, that's the first intelligent thing you've done all night."

"Go sleep with a camel, rent collector!"

She dropped her gaze and stared disconsolately at the saw-dust floor, Gideon meanwhile paying no attention to her mood as he casually examined his cuticles.

The candle's wax dripped and melted in its sconce, the thin wick sagging further with each successive minute. At length Samíah couldn't stand the overbearing silence any more. "My father is going to be fuming when he hears about this," she told him suddenly.

Gideon nodded as he watched her raise her head. "And I don't blame him, either. If I had a daughter who thought she could meddle at whim into things that don't concern her I'd be livid as well. You did a stupid thing, Samíah. A very stupid thing."

She flushed with the insult, inwardly simmering. How dare he call her stupid? This arrogant . . . bumpkin, this awkward, sneaky, idiot collector of rents who had to depend on his vile landlord uncle for work.

"I'll show you who's stupid!" she rattled. "After tonight you're going to be out on your ear, understand? I'll make al-Gamal too ashamed to ever show his face again! I'll make him the laughingstock of Marrakesh, that's what. And you," here her face darkened perceptibly and her lips trembled with rage, "as for you, you'll lose a great deal more than a job, rent collector! This little gambit is going to cost you your head! Murder and kidnapping aren't taken lightly in this city, my friend, and—"

"Shut up, Samíah."

"What?" She spluttered.

He regarded her blankly, the way he would a spoiled child that didn't know when to quit.

"Don't tell me to be quiet, you driveling, incompetent,

corpse-robbing moron! What a fool I was not to have summoned the soldiers the first instant I ever laid eyes on you!"

Gideon forced himself to keep calm and contemplative, clearheaded and reasonable. Her unexpected presence tonight had altered things conclusively, and now because of it someone had to do the thinking for them both, to find some way to extricate themselves from a mess she'd essentially created. Only her constant berating was making it hard for him to concentrate.

"If you don't keep your mouth shut I'll have to tie you up and gag you."

Her brows rose exactly like her father's whenever his wrath was incurred. "You wouldn't dare!"

He glanced over to the shelf where a cord of hemp rested in a knotted circle. Samíah saw it as well and groaned. Gideon, it seemed, was serious.

"Look," he said, "I don't very much care what you think of me right now, or ever for that matter. But we're both here now because of your meddling, understand? You put me and you in possible great danger—and maybe even your father as well. If there's anyone to blame, blame yourself."

"This is my fault? Was it me that was stealing from a dead man? Me who's been sneaking around the city in places that even Allah Himself has forgotten? Don't tell me that the killer on the roof was my doing—or that his arrow was aimed for me!"

Leaning forward, Gideon said, "That's exactly what I'm saying. That crossbow bolt, unlikely as it seems, was meant for you."

Samíah bit her lip, the horror of what he was telling her twisting her stomach into a knot. She wanted to cry again, to burst into tears and sobs, but she was determined not to let Gideon see her weakness, not to give him the satisfaction of knowing he'd frightened her even more. How much she rued this awful night. It was a nightmare. Why hadn't she just heeded Papa and stayed put at home?

"I really didn't mean to upset you," he went on with a sigh. "But I think it's time you understood something. When you followed me and crossed through the tombs you violated more than sacred ground. You walked into a place held in such secrecy that defilers often have lost both their eyes and tongues so that they may never see again or recount what they have seen. My guess is that the tomb was already being watched, and when you came into the open you had been marked."

She sneered. "That's ridiculous! You crossed the tombs, also. If someone was after me because I trespassed, then surely they were after you as well."

He shook his head. "Not in the way you think." Then he leaned toward her again, his features betraying a measure of urgency belied by his tone. "The tombs are a gathering place, Samíah. Headquarters for a highly secret group that only allows their followers inside—"

"You mean the Assassins! And you're one of them!"

Gideon banged a fist against the slats; a cloud of dust rose and slowly settled. "No, that's not what I mean!" he shouted with anger. "Don't question—and don't jump to conclusions! Just listen, that's all. *Listen!*"

Certain that at last she had trapped him into admitting his guilt, she drummed her fingers and said, "I'm listening."

"There is a group in Marrakesh, a tribe of wanderers that has traveled the length and breadth of the known world. They live among us, frequently passing themselves as our own. But they obey not the laws of the sultan nor any other liege, only the strict and rigid codes of their own people. Tell me, Samíah, have you ever heard of the Karshi?"

"Religious fanatics," she replied promptly. "Everyone has heard of them. They travel in caravans, like nomads, gypsies. Thieves, they say. Fortune tellers and mystics." She frowned with distaste, recalling many stories she had heard.

"Yes," Gideon drawled. "The Karshi are all that you say. They live lives that we cannot understand. And like gypsies, of which their own tribe is said to be an offshoot, they are almost universally despised. But misunderstood would be a better word."

There was surprise in her eyes as he talked about these strange people so gently, and a touch of cynicism in her voice when she said, "Are you telling me that you're a Karshi? A member of their sect?"

"No. Only that, er, for reasons, they have to come accept me—"

"Those tombs look like no one's used them for ages," she retorted. "Deserted and worm riddled. Are you telling me now that they're a Karshi sanctuary? Anyway, what has this got to do with murder and assassination? You're the one entangled in these crimes, not me. I don't rob corpses. I don't sneak around the city with crippled beggars."

Pressing the bridge of his nose with thumb and forefinger, Gideon heaved a long sigh. The problem of what to do with Samíah was becoming increasingly difficult, he could see. With the few pitiful facts she had assembled she was capable of concocting all sorts of notions, any of which—if passed into the wrong ear—could get them all killed. Gideon knew he could not procrastinate any longer. The time for a decision was at hand. He would have to admit to her what was happening. Not everything, of course, for that would be too great a hazard, but enough to placate her and make her understand the enormity of what he was doing. At least until a better option came his way.

"Listen and listen carefully," he said. "You really don't know anything about me, who I am or why you saw me doing the things you did. You have a distorted picture."

"Do I? I think I know enough—at least enough to make the sultan's soldiers curious. I'm sure they'll want to find out how a stranger to Marrakesh knows so much, how he comes to be acquainted with Karshis, and I'm equally sure when they drag you to the dungeons you'll answer far better to their satisfaction than to mine."

"You'd only be wasting your time, Samíah. Believe me. True, my arrest would take time to straighten out, but when it was, you would be sorely disappointed. No harm would come to me. What might transpire during my absence, though, is that a great many innocent people could get hurt. Even lose their lives—including you and all those you profess to love."

There it was, she knew. He was threatening her. Telling

her in so many words that if she dared inform on him her life would not be worth a copper coin. She eyed him suspiciously, softly taking up his challenge once more. "And if I take that risk?"

"What if I told you that turning me in might make you responsible for the downfall of our entire civilization?"

She huffed. "I'd say you were insane."

"Then let me try and explain." He paused, wishing against all logic that even now he might find some other way to deal with her. But there was none. "You're too young to remember," he said when he was ready, "but not so many years ago Marrakesh underwent a terrible, violent and bloody siege. Not by foreign armies or bandit hordes, but by a highly regimented and skillful cult of mad fanatics intent on creating anarchy. Bringing our land to its knees by brute force."

"I know about the Assassins. Everyone knows."

"Then you know they stopped at nothing. Under the banner and misguided beliefs of their crazed leader, the Assassins and their zealot followers intended to destroy the very fabric of order and society, to create total havoc, and then by cunning design to wrest control of our nation under the guise of a new messianic order. A satanic and corrupt order that demanded the annihilation of all those who opposed it. Enslavement for all as a new empire was to sweep the world, eradicating religion and the belief in God, based not on the principles of law and justice but upon a devilish code of terror and abject evil.

"And had in fact these madmen won their holy war, their jihad, we would all be condemned. Human sacrifice, incredible cruelty and tyranny, these were and are the tenets of the Assassins."

Samíah shifted uneasily in her place. Although she was as familiar with this account as anyone, it still sent chills crawling up her spine. To think that such insanity had almost succeeded.

"You haven't told me anything that I don't already know," she said after a moment.

"No, perhaps not, but my story isn't finished." He looked at her earnestly. "As history tells us, no one has ever learned how this cult began or who its leader was. What history often doesn't tell is that without the help of another group of fanatics diametrically opposed to this evil, our sultan might never have been able to vanquish them. You see, it took the zealous beliefs of one sect to hold out against the Assassins. They and they alone stood between them and us. No matter what else, we owe these people a great debt. . . ."

Samíah looked at Gideon with rising interest. "Are you speaking about the Karshi?"

"Yes. You see, because of their deep convictions, which to even a holy mullah may seem strange, the Karshis swore a blood oath against the terror of the Defilers, as they call the Assassins. And in turn, the Assassins hate their devout counterparts more than any other. It is a blood feud, and Karshi assistance years ago, although never officially recognized, served our own cause well. In return they have asked little of the sultan; only the right to continue in their ancient ways, and to keep from prying eyes their Tomb of the Dead, where their most revered clansmen rest in peace."

"I—I never knew any of this," whispered a stunned Samíah.

"Few do or ever shall. For that is the way the remaining Karshis wish it to be." Gideon stared at the flickering candle. "Though now I fear we have need of them again."

"I still don't understand any of this. You've spoken to me about Assassins and Karshis, the feud to the death between them. But what has any of this got to do with me?"

"Be patient, Samíah. Let me continue. As I told you, no one knows what happened to the Assassin messiah after his forces were finally trapped and wiped out. All we can say is that he seemed to have vanished off the face of the earth, perhaps fled beyond the High Atlas, perhaps slain by our forces or even by his own hand during the final moments of battle. For more than twenty years now Marrakesh and the rest of our land has known only peace. Until now. Until the first dark clouds started to gather again." Gideon narrowed his eyes into slits, and as he spoke he seemed to be gazing into some far distance beyond Samíah's comprehension.

Clearing a thick throat, she said, "If my father were here

he would accuse you of spreading old wives' tales, malicious rumors, and midnight gossip."

Gideon smiled thinly. "Perhaps it would be better if I were," he conceded. "Unfortunately, I am not in the rumor business. I deal only in fact—and the stirrings have proved all too real. Abductions, killings, seemingly senseless murders until you scratch below the surface and begin to dig. And we are not just speaking of palace nobles, Samíah, but the horrible deaths of everyone who by the faintest implication finds himself involved. Like that poor, hapless bucket slinger..."

Her laugh was low and mirthless, intended more to ward off the goose bumps that had started to crawl up her flesh. "Surely you're not serious! Are you intimating that Hussein was the target of Assassins? What value could *he* possibly be to them?"

His mouth turned down at the corners in a frown of bitterness and futility. Though his voice remained cool and objective, Samíah could tell that inside he was deeply troubled. He stood and turned his back to her, clasping and unclasping his hands. "A short while ago there was an abduction in the Street of Sandalmakers." She gasped and put a hand to her face, Gideon not seeing as he continued. "The man taken was on a vital errand. Around his neck he wore a golden brooch, and inside the locket lay hidden an urgent message for my friends. The message detailed a new plot afoot to kill publicly an unnamed official. Also included, we believe, was the name of the man who may be the mastermind of the coming jihad."

"You mean the Assassins' messiah?"

"Exactly." Gideon smacked a fist into his palm in frustration. "In the proper hands this information might have prevented wholesale slaughter and smashed the uprisings before they started, dealing a final blow to this cult's aspirations for once and for all. Sadly our carrier was taken before he could reach us. But during the scuffle the brooch was lost, perhaps torn from his throat, perhaps tossed away purposely in hopes of our finding it. We may never discover which. In any case, both our side as well as the Assassins and their agents have been frantic to find it. The man who wrote the message, a trusted agent, was found drowned in the canal; only his note can tell us what he had learned."

Samíah pushed locks of mussy hair away from her face and looked at her companion plainly. "What has this got to do with Hussein, though?"

"I have reason to believe that the bucket slinger accidentally came across the brooch, maybe in the *souk*, maybe in some gutter. Whichever, he saw only the gold content, never dreaming that there was a far greater value inside. Hussein quickly slipped from sight and no one has been able to locate him for days. We know he tried to pawn the brooch in the markets because our agents were later told about it. But he couldn't find a buyer to meet his price, so he did the only thing a desperate man could do—seek to sell it in the Casbah. Finally when I was able to have him traced it was too late." His expression soured; he dug his heel into the sawdust. "The other side visited him first."

Shock and disbelief marred Samíah's features. Gideon had confirmed what she had believed all along: the abduction had been real, and not a figment of her imagination. It had been exactly as she said—only far worse and far more terrifying than she dared suspect. The crosscurrents of intrigue were steadily deepening; only now they were dragging her along with them.

In a weak tone, she asked, "How is it that you know so much about all this?"

Gideon stood directly before her and blew the air out of his mouth. "Because these matters are my business: to gain Karshi acceptance, to utilize all my skills in seeking out the messiah and preventing the worst bloodbath Marraskesh has ever known."

"A peculiar job for a rent collector . . ." She stood as well now and focused her gaze on his. On the shelf behind the candle continued to flicker, suddenly dying with a last spurt of brightness and leaving the room in grim shadows.

"You're not really a collector of rents, are you?"

He shook his head.

"Or al-Gamal's nephew?"

"Your landlord is a man with a great many debts. He reluctantly agreed to give me my cover."

He couldn't see her faint, feline smile. "Then you're not the country bumpkin you pretend to be?"

"It keeps the wrong eyes from looking too closely. Marrakesh has always been my home."

"Is your name really Gideon?"

"That much about me is true."

"If you're not al-Gamal's nephew and not a stranger here, then what are you?"

"What do you think?"

Her heart began to beat more rapidly again. "I think I would call you a spy."

Gideon's eyes danced with laughter. "In my trade they refer to it as something else. In reality I'm little more than a procuror of information, a middleman for political dirty work. I deal in secrets, hunting and paying for information, and making certain it's delivered into the proper hands. Sometimes, when I'm unlucky, I also deal in murder—self-defense. It comes with the job."

Samíah wasn't totally sure why she now believed him; but she did. Still, it was going to take a great deal of time for her to accept that bumbling Gideon was a secret agent.

 "I THINK OUR SCAVENGING FRIEND IS GONE AT last," said Gideon as he moved from the peephole, brushing dust off his hands.

Samíah held her breath. "Then it's safe for us to leave?"

"Nothing is for certain; these rogues are like roaches, coming up out of the woodwork when you least expect them. But we might be lucky, it's getting close to daylight." He knelt briefly, slipping his dagger from the sheath in his boot, adding, "Best to move now, while it's quiet." He held out a hand for her to take. Samíah hesitated, then gave him hers.

"Where are we going?" she asked as he pulled her away.

"Somewhere else that's safe. Where I can get word out about what happened. Assassins are reluctant to make any moves during daytime unless they must, so for a while we'll have the advantage."

Dumbly she nodded, quickly saying, "What about Papa? He'll be home from work soon, and when he finds me missing he'll be frantic."

"Don't worry. We'll get word to him as soon as we can. Letting you go home now, though, is still too dangerous. First we have to be sure that they don't know your identity. For now it's better that you come along with me."

"Are—Are you sure your friends will help? They may not want to get involved. . . ."

"I've trusted them with my life before—and they're no strangers to trouble. Anyway, they're on our side."

"I see. So they're undercover also?"

He grinned as he soundlessly slid the bolt and opened the door a crack. "Not exactly. But you're learning fast."

Samíah pulled a sour face. "You haven't given me very much choice."

Then out of the hovel and up the rickety steps they hurried, soon stealing back across the main level of the warehouse until they retraced their steps to the street, blending silently among the slanting shadows.

Behind an unlocked street-level door an old woman sat cross-legged upon a tattered cushion on a threadbare Persian rug. Heavy drapes clung to the peeling walls all around, one curtaining off the entrance to the tiny adjoining rooms. In front of the woman a small oil lamp burned on a pedestal; she held her wrinkled hands over it and firmly shut her eyelids, long dark lashes closing gently across folding flesh. Under her breath she mumbled an ancient Romany incantation that few in Marrakesh would have recognized. Her heavy body swayed slightly as her lips mouthed the words. The pinned bandana over her head covered a mass of white stringy hair once silken and auburn, the loose-fitting ruffled blouse and darkly embroidered full skirt she wore well-concealed large sagging breasts and fat shapeless legs. To see her now it would be difficult to realize that many years before she had been a woman of exceptional beauty, spirited and willful, the pride of her family and clan, who had brought her Gypsy father a handsome price for her marriage. Fortune-teller, healer of the soul, curer of any illness and malady, Queen Yana was all this and more: a true *boojo* woman who commanded fear and respect. It was said enormous cunning lay behind her cold, sunken eyes, and a fertile mind that improved with the passing of time. Even now, in her waning years, she held a firm grip on the Gypsy clans of Marrakesh.

The rapping upon the street door was low but firm. Yana's eyes snapped open wide at the noise.

"The door is unlocked," she said in her husky, hoarse voice.

Hinges creaked as Gideon eased inside, Samíah nervously right behind. The strong smell of burning incense assaulted Samíah's senses; the sight of the withered, hollow-cheeked woman was disturbing.

Yana saw her uneasiness. She spoke not a word, peered up at Gideon before letting her eyes wander suspiciously over Samíah. A sheen of perspiration dotted her forehead, and she shifted anxiously under the scrutinizing gaze.

Yana fanned herself, satisfied that in these brief moments she had learned much about the unknown visitor. She brusquely made a gesture dismissing his apology when Gideon begged the queen's forgiveness for the unusual time of the visit. "You are welcome," she told him, then returned her stare to the girl.

"She is a friend," Gideon said. "You need not be troubled."

A hairline smile cracked across Yana's fat, painted lips. "It is not I that am troubled, but you," she said matter-of-factly. "What has happened?"

Gideon glanced around the room, focusing on the curtain that divided it from the other chamber. Samíah saw that he was familiar with this place and had probably been here many times. "I need to see Wanko," he said.

"The *boojo* woman put down the fan and clasped her stubby hands. "He is not here." She fondled the large silver medallion hanging from her neck. "You can tell me." Then she added something in a dialect that Samíah couldn't understand but Gideon could. The secret agent sighed and nodded.

"I have found the man I sought. He is dead." There was little surprise in Yana's face. Gravely she nodded. Gideon continued. "The girl followed me tonight, innocently I am sure. But she has trespassed through the Tomb of the Dead and was observed. Afterward an attempt was made on her life. This is all I know."

Yana's tired, watery eyes flickered coldly; she glared at Samíah with a look that made the girl cringe. "Are you certain this one is as innocent as she claims?"

Samíah swallowed as she waited for Gideon to answer.

"Yes. She knows nothing." Here he hesitated. "Until now. I was forced to tell her."

"*Forced*, young friend?"

"There was no other way. She . . . interfered. It was too late for me to prevent it."

The Gypsy woman listened impassively. "Then the Assassin's failure was yours as well. Her death could have spared you much trouble." She made a guttural sound as she sighed, curling her hands slowly over the lamp. Her eyes shut and for a time she returned to her trance, muttering her strange phrases as though her visitors were not there.

"Don't be afraid," Gideon whispered to the trembling girl. He nudged her by the elbow. "Gypsy ways are different than ours, tradition bound and ritualized."

"She—She mistrusts me," Samíah said. "You heard what she said about the Assassin's failing to kill me—"

"Sit, both of you." It was a command, not a request. Gideon hushed the girl and bade her take a place at Yana's left. He sat on the Gypsy's right.

"Tell me what it is you want of me," the *boojo* woman said when they were settled.

"Wanko's assistance. The girl is in jeopardy. I think she's been marked. I need to find a safe place for her, Yana. At least for a while. Also, a message must be sent to her father, assuring him she is safe."

Yana appraised Samíah anew, this time deciding that the girl was far too skinny and too pale, that her back was weak, and that surely her life was too soft. Definitely not the stuff of which Gypsy women are made.

"She means that much to you, this girl?"

"She means nothing to me, Yana."

Samíah squirmed.

"Then why go to such bother? Wanko can dispose of her in a suitable fashion."

Samíah looked about ready to faint when Gideon quickly added, "Her father is a good and just man. He has befriended me, and I have returned that friendship. I would not dishonor him by robbing him of that which he so dearly loves."

The *boojo* woman was clearly satisfied with his response. "Very well. Perhaps I can help. I can give this one cover for a time, that is if she will willingly do as must be done."

Gideon shot Samíah a glance that told her to bite her tongue and say nothing.

Yana turned and faced him squarely. "But you have not spoken of yourself. Has the girl compromised your own position?"

"I think not. The Parrot's information has been lost. With the knowledge of the Karshi I hope to retrace his steps. But time is short. The attack we have feared may come at any time, any place." Outside, it was beginning to grow lighter, the new day all but arrived. "Today the sultan appears from the gallery. The plaza will be packed with pilgrims and well wishers. I must send word to the palace of the bucket slinger's death. They need to be warned of my failure."

"Wanko shall have that done for you, though what is to be cannot be altered."

Gideon stood. "We still must try." Then he turned to leave.

Samíah's arm shot out. "Hey, where are you going?"

"I've lost enough time," Gideon answered, facing her. "With luck, I'll be back tonight."

"But what about me?"

"You'll be safe, I promise you."

"You mean I have to stay here. Alone with . . . *her*?"

Yana the Gypsy queen smiled thinly. "What is your name, child?"

"Samíah."

Yana fondled Samíah's hair, thinking it felt as her own once did. "You have nothing to fear, Samíah." She looked to Gideon. "Go, young friend," and she made a few designs in the air with her hand to ward off evil. "Do what you must. Meanwhile I shall do my best to make the child one of us."

 THE CITY WAS IN A STATE OF GREAT EXCITEMENT, streets and plazas seething with people to greet the benevolent sultan upon his return to visit with his elder cousin, the caliph of the ancient city of Meknes. Outside the massive gates throngs gathered in jubilation along the sandy hills. The earth was covered with a softly scented carpet of springy turf and glorious wildflowers—narcissus, hyacinths, iris, lavish daffodils—many of which had been gathered especially to toss joyously at the first sight of the approaching caravan. From beyond the orchids and groves of pear trees the approaching train was first sighted. Immediately a tremendous roar went up across the hills, carried on into the winding streets of Marrakesh itself as word of the beloved sultan's return quickly spread.

Near the gates of the central plaza, Gideon took refuge at the fringes of the jostling crowd. The gathering was enormous, citizens came from all points of the compass to do homage to their respected ruler. Soldiers quickly cleared a narrow avenue for the oncoming horsemen—the Caids, vanguard of the approaching retinue.

One by one the Caids splendrously entered the city. They rode high upon their magnificent steeds, a pair of slaves running along on either side with hands holding onto the stirrups of their masters. Garbed in desert white with an occasional flash of color embellished on their turbans, their scimitars hung proudly from jewelled sheaths, catching the glint of perfect sunlight in dazzling display. They sat tall, these noble guards and protectors, upon peaked saddles which were themselves each a work of art, crafted from the softest and most beautiful leathers, exquisitely colored and decorated and embossed in true Moorish fashion. Each was a priceless heirloom passed on from father to son in time-honored tradition.

As the Caids moved along the road and headed toward the motif-covered walls of the grand palace, the soldiers again pressed in on the overflowing torrent of humanity. Gideon, pushed back as well, peered up casually and grimly took note of the troops stationed across the roofs and crenellated walls overlooking the plaza—a thousand soldiers and more standing vigilant duty to make certain the sultan's arrival remained unmarred. Yet Gideon also realized the enormity of their task; for a handful of fanatics buried unseen within the throngs was all it might take to turn this perfect day into disaster. And until the sultan himself was safely inside the confines of the palace his apprehension only grew.

The sounds of native music rose everywhere; all sorts and conditions of people were present. Keeping close under the high walls surrounding the square a huge group of veiled women clustered at one side of the gate, eagerly waiting to greet the sovereign with their high, shrilling cries. Others gathered in their holiday garb, full skirts of crimson, green, and purple; silk shawls crossed over their breasts; brightly colored kerchiefs twisted among their dark hair, the fringes of which hung far down their backs. Here, also, stood unveiled women of the hills; tribeswomen adorned in long burnouses of camel's hair in white and red stripes secured around their head, concealing beneath their folds the infants strapped on their backs. Water carriers sang out from among the crowds, fruit vendors and sweetmeat sellers all pushed their way amid the myriad of people.

At the far side of the great square Gideon saw the silent group of pashas, patriarchs garbed in fine flowing garments, on hand to personally welcome the sultan home before he reached the gallery and addressed the people. The royal procession was now close to the gates. A troop of black Senegalese soldiers on foot smartly marched to the cadence of pounding drums. Immediately behind them came four horses, superb animals, each carrying the royal saddles, heavily embroidered with threads of silver and gold, each horse led by a standard-bearer who proudly bore aloft the flags with the sultan's royal insignia. Moments later the advance members of the private bodyguard, the Mokhaznis, appeared, dressed in long white robes and cone-shaped, scarlet hats.

In the center of this dignified group came the sultan himself. The crowds went wild. Racing upon a gray, white-maned, Arabian stallion, he sat regally upon the state saddle of his forefathers. Simple tooled leather, virtually without decoration save for the narrowest threading of gold. Two fierce and somber Mokhaznis walked on either side of his stallion and held the stirrups, while two more ebony-skinned bodyguards waved long silken scarves to keep away the flies. Directly behind the sultan came the carrier of the royal umbrella, a small green canopy of velvet, held on a high pole to shade the liege from the blistering sun.

From head to foot the sultan was garbed in robes of the purest white, unrelieved by any jewel or decoration. His bulky figure slightly swayed with the movements of his horse, and he inclined his head gravely, greeting his happy subjects as he passed through their midst. Gideon looked on intently as the procession made its way slowly across the plaza. Most of the citizens sank to their knees as the sultan passed. When the procession arrived outside the high gate, the veiled women en masse began to screech, clicking their tongues and creating a sound almost like the screams of birds in flight.

The sultan smiled; he held up his hand and the roar subsided. His bodyguards cleared the path anew, and while the Sultan patiently waited, out of the gate rode a magnificent figure, a dark-skinned courtier on a coal-black horse, hailing his lord and giving signal to the quiet pashas that they might now advance and do reverence to their liege.

The old men came forward in small groups of three, hands to their hearts, making the solemn bows of the *salaam* with inclined heads. Then they prostrated themselves on the earth, and in homage kissed the dust at his horse's feet. "Welcome, O Sultan!" they hailed in unison. "Your city greets you!" When they stood, the aging sultan had tears in the corner of his eyes. He loved his people, and they loved him. For more than three decades he had reigned in Marrakesh, through strife and drought, war and times of trouble. It gladdened him to see the throngs today more than he could say. For deep inside his heart he knew that they and he were one, inseparable.

"It is good to see you all, old friends," he said wearily to the pashas. "Coming home has never been better than now. I thank you all deeply for this display of kindness and affection you have shown."

"You deserve no less, sire," said the eldest of the pashas, and as the throngs picked up their chant the patriarchs bowed. The sultan glanced across the overflowing plaza, the avenues littered with fresh flowers, the honest faces of the thousands of men and women and children whose names he did not know but whom he nevertheless loved as well as he did his own sons. Finding a smile again, he lifted his arm for silence. It was time to withdraw to the palace, he knew, but only for a brief while until he was ready to speak from the gallery. There were so many things to tell his people about the success of the new alliance formed with Meknes . . .

"Sire, we must hasten," said the captain of the Mokhaznis, leaning in close to his liege.

The sultan nodded, reluctant to depart from such a happy sight. But he took firm hold of the reins and prepared to ride on.

Gideon breathed a sigh of relief. All had gone well this morning. His fears were unfounded after all. As he turned his head, though, he saw a figure emerge across the blue tiles of the mosque's dome—a hooded figure who momentarily blocked the sun. Gideon gasped.

"Death to the tyrant!"

Bodyguards sprang to life, soldiers drawing their swords. But it all happened so fast there was not even time to think. A woman screamed from somewhere behind. From the shadows atop the wall another hooded figure kneeled and fired. The arrow missed the sultan but struck the throat of the dark-skinned courtier. His coal-black horse reared in panic, the rider tumbling from the saddle and sprawling in the dirt.

"Assassins!" came the awful cry.

Gideon whipped out his dagger; all around him panic was breaking loose. A third figure jumped from the arch above the gate. Eyes blazing from the effects of hashish, he toppled the sultan from his stallion and straddled his fallen form. As his bare arm lowered to plunge the poison-tipped dagger through the startled sultan's heart, a bodyguard heaved his scimitar and slashed off the attacker's head with a single stroke.

Everywhere there was screaming and pandemonium. Wild-eyed citizens broke through the barricades and ran in frenzy for shelter. A barrage of snubbed arrows loosed from the roofs. Other hooded men appeared and disappeared as if from nowhere. They clambered across the roofs and hurled daggers. Two Mokhaznis staggered and fell. Behind Gideon a misdirected blade sank into the back of a screaming woman. Those around her froze, then ran for their lives, trampling everything and everyone. Mounted cavalry tried to restore order. One's horse reeled beneath the impact of an Assassin's crossbow bolt. The animal snorted insanely and fell with a thud. A second soldier ran to his comrade's aid. Before he could shove his way through the tumult a drugged fanatic appeared and lunged. The soldier never had time to protect himself. The knife gutted his belly; small children witnessing the murder started to scramble for cover. A line of archers across the wall aimed and pounded the offender. The Assassin wheeled around, nine arrows piercing his body. And amid the screams and wails he laughed, lifting his bloodied arms to the heavens and shaking his fists in triumph. Again the soldiers aimed. The zealot staggered backward as new shafts ripped through his face and his groin. He fell in a heap, convulsively jerking in spasms as he died.

Gideon looked on in horror. Within seconds the entire plaza was a shambles of yelling and wailing humanity, numbed thousands scattering for their lives, spilling into adjoining streets and spreading the panic.

"Guard the sultan!" shouted Gideon, barreling his way toward the fallen liege.

Already a strong cohort of Caids and Mokhaznis had formed a wall around the fallen sultan, captains barking terse commands at the top of their lungs for the plaza to be secured and all Assassins rooted out. The damage, though, had been done. While the sultan was lifted to his feet and sheltered, the dazed throngs ran rampant. Gideon saw another Assassin leap from one low roof to the other. Snipers aimed and caught him before he could pounce below. The crossbow hurled from his hands and he screamed a horrible scream. Then off the narrow ledge he fell, bones shattering as he smashed down on the ground ten meters below, the tip of a markman's arrow lodged inside his ear, piercing his brain. A colorless liquid oozed from the wound.

"Cordon the city!" Gideon heard someone shout. "Shut the gates!" cried another. "Treble the guards along the towers and walls! Marrakesh is under siege!"

Wagons turned over, witless citizens scrambling over them mindlessly and dashing helter-skelter. Fires were beginning to burn in every direction, the flames and rising smoke only adding to the total confusion. One pilgrim, caught unaware underneath a smoldering awning howled as the flames licked at his clothes. He ran into the street a human torch, screaming at the top of his lungs for someone to help. The rolling wagon could not be stopped in time; the pilgrim was hurtled into the air and sent slamming among the stalls, his fiery garments quickly setting ablaze the dry wood.

Still in a fog, the aging sultan pushed away the stout bodyguards hovering around him and looked on in disbelief. Where minutes before there had been joy and harmony, now there was utter dismay and dread, corpses littered with the flowers, trampled souls crawling and crying out in anguish, blindly choking in the thickening smoke. Alarm had turned to terror, spreading like tinder from one side of the city to the other. "My people, my people," muttered the sultan with hands outstretched. But the only response was the wails of the dying and injured. Instead of garlands at his feet there was blood—and the heaving, gasping form of the eldest pasha, who lay sprawled with a feathered shaft protruding from his lung.

It was for barely an instant that his eyes and Gideon's met; whether there was recognition in them Gideon wasn't sure. Barely having escaped with his life, the sultan was now being forcibly pulled from the carnage, a hundred soldiers around him and hustling him away.

Gideon spun, a hand placed on his shoulder. In front of him stood a young woman, dazed and in shock. Cradled in one arm rested a lifeless infant, its head crushed by the stampeding mob. "Please, help me . . ." she muttered incoherently. "My child, my child . . ."

Moved to pity, Gideon cradled her and pulled her away. His ears were bursting with other like sobs and cries for assistance. Mounted Mokhaznis thundered across the plaza, heaving scimitars and chasing down fleeing Assassins. With the alert troops now regaining control a semblance of order was being restored.

Gideon gently guided the benumbed woman away from the carnage and hurried her to the physicians' station the guards were hastily trying to set up. He left her there in the care of a helpful guard and staggered among the huddled groups of crying, trembling people.

Tears of anguish streaked Gideon's face as he walked amid the terrible wreckage. Stunned and petrified citizens ambled aimlessly now. Everywhere he looked it was the same, butchery and slaughter, screams mingled with the weeping, the people like sheep, turned into a frenzied mob and suffering the aftermath.

This was exactly what the Assassins had intended, he knew: to spread fear and dread into the hearts and minds of everyone. This bitter victory was a prize worth more than the murder of ten sultans. For if the fanatics were to succeed in wresting complete power they must first instill paralyzing terror in the populace, shatter all illusions of trust and confidence in those that governed. Only then could the way be paved for the final thrust, the ultimate victory. Today had gone a long way in meeting that end.

Gideon searched the roofs again as he recalled the initial glimpse of the man upon the dome, the one who had commenced the bloodbath. And something in that memory made his blood grow cold. How or why he didn't know, only that something assured him that the hooded figure had been the messiah, personally directing the onslaught, then disappearing as mysteriously as he had come.

We will meet again, you and I. In another time, another place . . .

From this moment forward no one was safe. No quarter would be asked and no quarter given. Marrakesh was as shattered as the sultan's broken dreams and heart. But for Gideon, the war had only begun.

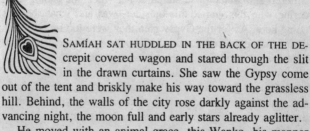

SAMÍAH SAT HUDDLED IN THE BACK OF THE DEcrepit covered wagon and stared through the slit in the drawn curtains. She saw the Gypsy come out of the tent and briskly make his way toward the grassless hill. Behind, the walls of the city rose darkly against the advancing night, the moon full and early stars already aglitter.

He moved with an animal grace, this Wanko, his manner deceptively relaxed and his hawkish features as immobile as a family portrait. Wide-shouldered and quite powerful despite his years, he had a full head of curly dark hair, a clean, unblemished, desert-tanned skin, and a pair of deep-set luminous black eyes that gave the impression of looking right through you. He sported a luxuriant brush mustache that curved sharply downward along the sides of his thin mouth. His hands were uncalloused, large and almost femininely soft; an indication that hard, manual labor had been unknown to him throughout his life. If asked, Wanko would proudly give his occupation as a trader—but in reality thieving was the only trade he had ever known—stealing anything from purses to jewelry to goats and sheep. Horses, though, were his true specialty, and horseflesh he understood better than anything else. Within the severe and structured confines of Romany society a horse trader—which to a Gypsy automatically meant a horse thief, the two being interchangeable—was something of an aristocrat.

Samíah had been afraid of him from the beginning, although her fears were mostly unfounded, for Wanko had been quite gentle with her, barely lifting his voice above a whisper when he spoke and never resorting to threats even when at first she had refused to leave Yana's rooms and be taken to a safer place. "A Romany woman does as she is told," Wanko had said quietly but sternly, and that had been the end of her protests.

Without a fight she had allowed him to whisk her away, to bring her under the cloak of dark out of the city to this small Gypsy camp along the outskirts of the main gate. The Gypsy children and women had stared at her when she came, wondering who this *gadjo*, this outsider, was and what she was doing here. As for the Gypsy men they were too immersed in their games of chance and drinking bouts to pay much attention. That Wanko had brought her was enough; the Gypsy king had his own reasons, and for them that alone was sufficient.

Wanko had taken her to the empty wagon, ordered her to stay put, then returned a short while later carrying a bundle under his arm. "For you," he had said. "New clothes. Gypsy clothes. Put them on."

"I don't need Gypsy clothes. I have my own—"

"Put them on." It was a command. Samíah took the bundle and nodded. Wanko left, another Gypsy came in, a young woman of Samíah's own age. She helped the girl out of her *chador*, smiled thinly and mysteriously as Samíah dutifully put on the black flaring skirt and crimson ruffled blouse. Samíah frowned when her companion pulled back her hair and tied the scarlet bandana around her head. Then she stood back and pouted.

"You still look like a *gadjo*."

Samíah stared at her. The girl was slender and pretty, with black hair and blacker eyes. A bevy of copper bracelets adorned her bare arms and wrists; she wore rings on almost every finger and tiny jangling bells on her toes. Both finger- and toenails were gaudily painted a shade of crimson which matched her dress. Long curling hair fell below her ample breasts, and a pair of huge circular earrings, like finger rings, dangled from her ears. To Samíah she seemed wild and untamed.

"Here," said the girl, taking off the earrings and giving them to Samíah.

"No, thank you, I don't think—"

The gypsy girl put her hands to her hips and glared askance at her, shifting her weight so that one hip rose higher than the other. "I was told to dress you like one of us. Now don't cause trouble."

Samíah bristled beneath her condescending tone. "Now listen, this has gone about as far as it will. I'm *not* a Gypsy, and I have no intention of—"

The girl spun, pulled open the flimsy curtain and called, "Hey, Wanko! This one won't listen!"

A group of men had been sitting around a nearby campfire, Wanko among them. At the call he lifted himself and sauntered over toward the wagon. Two toothless old Gypsy women sitting by themselves grinned as he passed.

Wanko poked his head between the curtains; he looked first at Samíah, then at the Gypsy girl. "What's going on?"

"I was only doing what you said," the Gypsy told him. She displayed the earrings. "I told her to put on these, but she won't do it."

"Why not?"

Samíah huffed. "This whole thing has gone far enough. I

only came with you because Gideon forced me into it. But now I think I'd like to leave. Give me back my *chador*; I'm going home."

The girl looked at Wanko. "Burn the *gadjo* dress," he said.

"Don't you dare!" flared Samíah.

The Gypsy girl grabbed the fallen *chador* and hurled it from the wagon. Then, hands to her hips again, she barred Samíah from trying to get out and retrieve it.

"You're going to be in big trouble for this!"

His eyes were cold. "Rosa, give her the earrings. Make sure she wears them."

Rosa smiled. "Yes, Wanko." The curtains snapped shut; Wanko went back to his friends. Samíah was left standing in the middle of the wagon face to face with Rosa.

"Now listen, honey, you think that maybe you can deal with us like you deal with other *gadjos*. But you can't. See? So why not make the best of it for us both and do as you're told? Anyway, these earrings are the best I have. Gold."

"They look like copper."

Rose gritted her teeth. "Gold, honey. I stole them myself so I should know. Now do you listen or what, because if I have to call Wanko again the old man is going to be plenty mad. And when Wanko is upset he makes life pretty bad for everybody. Is that what you want, trouble on your first night here?"

Samíah pulled the earrings out of Rosa's palm and put them on. Rosa stepped forward a pace and considered. "Not bad. Turn around, honey. Let's see how you look." Samíah complied, but only because she didn't want to have to deal with the king again.

"Well?"

Shrugging, Rosa said, "You'll pass for now. Maybe tomorrow I can start giving you a few lessons so that you'll learn how to talk and act more like us."

"Wait a minute! I was only supposed to be here for a day!"

"That ain't that way I understand it, honey. Wanko says to keep you here and to make sure nobody spots you for a *gadjo*, otherwise it could cause problems."

"You mean I'm supposed to . . . *stay*?"

Another shrug. "It ain't up to me, honey."

"Are—Are you really going to burn my clothes?"

"Sure. Wanko wants it that way and around here what he says goes. If you know what I mean."

Samíah nodded. "He's your king."

"Not just mine, honey. Of all our tribe. And I've known the brute long enough to know that when he tells you something you don't argue, you just do it. Like I said, we don't want to get him riled. He's got a temper like you never saw." She shook her hand in a gesture to indicate how bad it really was. "He's a devil, that Wanko."

"Rosa!" The voice was clear and loud.

"Gotta go, honey. The men are getting restless for their supper. Now if you behave maybe after the men are finished you can come out and eat with me and the other girls. Would you like that?"

It only dawned on Samíah now that she hadn't eaten all day. The smells of the cooking fires were enticing, skewered lamb hissing as it turned over the flames. "I am hungry," she admitted.

Rosa smiled. "You stay put till I call for you." Then she turned to leave, glancing back over her shoulder, saying as an afterthought, "Don't be worried, honey, we ain't so bad."

That had been Samíah's induction upon arrival at the camp. For hours afterwards the Gypsies had eaten, drank, sang songs, and played their instruments while some of the girls danced and entertained them all. Now the hour was late; most had retired to their wagons and tents, a few of the men still lingering around the ebbing fires, the women silently slipping between them and finishing the chores—cleaning the pots, tending to the chickens and goats, watering horses tethered beside the clump of trees.

Returned to the wagon, Samíah huddled in the shadows and marked the time. Dawn was not very far away, and still there was no sign of Gideon. For a moment she wondered if the spy had abandoned her, purposely left her here without any thought of coming back. But soon those thoughts changed and she began to wonder if something had happened. If, during this long day and night, he had been found by the Assassins and was now sharing the same fate as poor Hussein. It was a disquieting thought. For next they would be coming after her.

 "I HAVE BEEN PRAYING FOR YOU," SAID YANA AS she sat kneading the string of beads between her wrinkled fingers.

Haggard, exhausted, Gideon stepped into the heavily draped room and sat opposite the queen. As always the reek of incense was thick, the lamplight flickering and the room bathed in dancing shadows.

"Have you taken care of things for me?" he asked.

"Yes. The girl is safe in Wanko's hands. Word has been sent to the father."

Gideon shook his head slowly. Poor Habib. The dustman must be fraught with worry. Concern for his daughter was paramount above all else, including his own safety. He only hoped Habib would trust that she was in good hands and, Allah willing, no harm would come to her.

"I expected you hours ago," Yana said, pulling him from his thoughts.

"There has been much to do, and still much left undone. Things have gone badly."

The Gypsy queen nodded knowingly. After hearing of the

slaughter in the plaza she had read the tarot cards. And what she saw had made her shudder and abruptly end the reading.

"Do you understand how critical the situation is, Yana?"

"The omens are evil."

"Yes." He heaved a sigh and rubbed at his tired eyes. He could not recall when he had slept last, and right now didn't know when there might be time to sleep again. "A Karshi has sent word to me," he said. "The Defilers have taken this action as a sign of the righteousness of their cause." He leaned forward and met Yana's eyes, the Gypsy woman's bulk seeming all the more massive in the pallid light. "They have seen how fragile our defenses are, seen the weakness of the sultan and intend to act upon it."

"To seize the moment is their way," Yana observed. "Do you know what they scheme?"

"Only that it will be dramatic and fast. Ruthlessly, they will lose no time in solidifying the grip of fear that already prevails."

Yana hung her head, avoiding his gaze.

"What is it, Yana? What's the matter?"

"I fear for you, Gideon. I have read the tarot . . ."

"What did it say?" Gideon was not a superstitious man by any means, but his Gypsy and Karshi friends were. More than once he had scoffed at their secretly gleaned predictions, and more than once he had been astounded to see them come true. Gideon no longer derided that which he didn't understand.

"I saw only from shadows," Yana began. "For evil always crouches in darkness. But the numbers of death came to me again and again. Each time portending the same dangers." She touched his arm lightly and lifted her face. There were tears in her eyes.

"Night Masters," he whispered.

Yana put a hand to her heart and gasped.

"The messiah has turned them loose. Secretly, under the cloak of dark, in small numbers throughout the city." His voice was cold and devoid of emotion as he spoke of this. These skillful, highly trained merchants of death had been sent to create havoc. Unknown and unseen, this regimented vanguard of the Assassins would bleed Marrakesh. They had done as

123

much in other places. They would infiltrate the subterranean world of the city, striking not randomly but at well-placed targets in a slow bath of infamy. And when they were done Marrakesh would be helpless.

"How much time is left?"

Gideon shook his head. "Their agents are everywhere. A week, two weeks. By then they will be prepared."

Hardly enough time for even the most rudimentry counter plans to be drawn, Yana knew. The sultan's forces could mobilize and triple their vigilance, but still it would not be enough to deter such a motivated cadre of fanatics.

"What are you going to do?"

"As much as I can. If the Karshi can infiltrate one of their cells, then I can try and discover the messiah's overall plan."

"How?"

"By posing as a zealot myself."

Yana was aghast. Placing himself among them might be possible—it had been done before. But the price, if caught, was one too ghastly to contemplate. His end would be slow and agonizing, death a blissful release from the pain and torture they would impose.

"Is there no other way?"

Grimly, he said, "None." A man's fate could not be denied, they both knew. He looked at the aged Gypsy woman and tried to smile. "I have one more favor to ask. The girl, Samíah. You must keep her with you a while. . . ."

"Arrangements have already been made."

"I don't want anything to happen to her, Yana. Having discovered the Tomb of the Dead she is special to the Assassins. Through her they know they can get at the Karshi." His face turned hard and harsh. "That must not happen."

"Wanko will look after her, young friend. Among the Gypsies she is safe."

"With Night Masters on the prowl no one is safe. They will spare no effort."

"Already she is being instructed in Romany ways. Wanko will make her one of us."

There was kindness and genuine concern in her eyes, and

Gideon thanked Allah for giving him such good friends. Once they had given their word the Gypsies would guard Samíah with their very lives. It was their way.

"I shall not see you for a number of days," he said at length. "Four Fingers has found out the name of the man Hussein bartered the brooch. If I can find him perhaps some of the pieces of the puzzle will fit together. He is a Casbah thief, known among his fellows only as the 'Dealer.' Does the name mean anything to you?"

Yana shook her head. It was a common name; the Casbah and the city were rife with such men of no identity.

"Look for me within a week's time. I will come to your camp at night. Perhaps then I'll know what to do with the girl."

"And if you don't come, young friend?"

His smile was mirthless. "Then remember me in your prayers for the dead."

"I'M NOT GOING TO DO IT AND YOU CAN'T MAKE me!" With that, Samíah angrily plopped herself down on the damp grass beside the wheel of the covered wagon and refused to budge.

Rosa groaned in consternation. She looked over her shoulder and called, "Hey Wanko, she says that she ain't gonna do it no matter what!"

Samíah folded her arms and gritted her teeth. The pluming smoke from the scattered Gypsy fires was making her eyes sting. The Gypsy men, preoccupied as always, paid no attention either to her or to Rosa's flustered call, but the Gypsy women around the camp paused in their various tasks and turned their heads.

The *gadjo* woman was giving the king problems again, as she had for each of the three days she'd been with them. Always refusing to do as she was asked; becoming abusive when told to serve the men their supper, sulking when given a basket of dirty wash and told to scrub it in the pond, scowling and groaning when Rosa had tried to instruct her in the most basic womanly duties. Poor Wanko. Why was he showing such patience with her and her *gadjo* ways? Surely all that needed to be done to rectify matters was to give her a good strapping on her fleshy backside. That would bring her into line.

"Now listen to me, honey," Rosa was saying, her hands to her hips as she stood in the shadows over Samíah, the flames of the nearest fire illuminating her face. "I thought that you and me understood each other and that we wouldn't have to go through this anymore."

Samíah looked at her with a sneer. "We understand each other very well. For three days I've been kept here like a prisoner, washing dirty laundry, scrubbing pots, shining Wanko's boots, mending socks. Next you'll expect me to go out and steal!"

"Not yet, honey. You ain't ready yet."

Samíah moaned beneath her breath.

"What's wrong now?" It was Wanko's voice.

Rosa turned and faced him. "You told me to teach her to dance, didn't you? So when we go back into the city she'll pass as one of us." She paused in her monologue to catch her breath. "Well, when I tried she laughed at me and said it was insulting for me to think that she'd put herself on display like this and—"

"That's right!" flared Samíah. "If you think, either of you, that I'm going to cavort in front of strangers like a belly dancer you've got another think coming. Both of you!"

"See, Wanko? See what I mean? Thinks she's too good for us. Doesn't want to do anything to her earn her keep."

Samíah got up, daggers shooting from her flashing eyes. She glared from one Gypsy to the other. "*Earn* my keep? What else have I been doing? From morning till night without a stop. Do that, do this, like a slave. Well, let me tell you I'm *not* your slave. And now you tell me I have to learn to *dance*? Like a *Gypsy*?"

"It is important for you to pass as one of us," Wanko said softly.

"I don't *want* to pass as one of you! I want to go home!"

"You can't go home."

Samíah spluttered in outrage, wanting to choke the king and the girl both. Instead, she pulled off her gold earrings and hurled them savagely to the ground at Rosa's feet.

Rosa flushed crimson. "Let me at her, Wanko! Let me at her!"

Wanko stepped between, blocking the fiery Gypsy girl from lunging.

"Let her go!" hissed Samíah. "I'm not afraid. She's bullied me long enough!"

At the noise of the heated exchange even the men around the campfires began to turn. A fight was brewing for certain, and there was little Gypsies enjoyed more than a good brawl. Especially among women.

Another figure approached. It was with surprise that Samíah recognized her. It was Queen Yana, only just arrived at the camp.

"They are at each other's throats," explained Wanko. But the explanation was hardly needed. The king regarded his queen with a wan expression that asked, What should I do?

Yana, though, seemed to have none of his hesitation. "It must be settled in the traditional fashion."

"But we gave Gideon our word that no harm would come to the girl . . ."

"I can handle myself well enough!" shot Samíah.

"And this one has already challenged me!" bristled an equally livid Rosa. She indicated the fallen earrings. Wanko nodded; the *gadjo* had indeed insulted Rosa.

"Then there is nothing further to discuss," Yana said. It would be better to let both women vent their anger now.

"Very well," said Wanko. "The matter will be settled once and for all."

Rosa bared back her lips in a snarling smile; Samíah balled her fists and looked forward with gleeful anticipation to the coming encounter.

"A fight!" one of the men happily yelled, and within seconds all the Gypsies of the camp were up on their feet, grinning and beginning to make wagers on the outcome. The early odds were three to one that fiery Rosa would finish the match in less than three minutes.

"Down there," said Wanko, pointing towards the farthest campfire which had been set at the edge of a small grassless field. Rosa marched toward it, Samíah on her heels.

"The rules are simple," the king informed Samíah when they had come down to the selected site. "As this fight is not a vendetta it shall be only until one or the other yields." As he spoke the Gypsy men hurriedly gathered, forming a large semicircle away from the fire. The women and children huddled behind and alongside them. Samíah and Rosa stood opposite each other, glowering.

"There are to be no knives or razors used," Wanko went on. Rosa openly frowned, and beneath the stern scrutiny of the king she sighed, kneeled, and pulled out a small razor that was carefully hidden inside the hem of her skirt. She handed it over to another Gypsy girl for safekeeping. Wanko hid a smile and turned to Samíah.

"I have no weapon," she said.

"There are no other rules," he added loudly so that all could hear. "Kicking, scratching, and biting are allowed." Rosa's smile expanded as Samíah saw the length and sharpness of her fingernails—like a cat's claws. "Choking an opponent is only permitted up to the point of unconsciousness. Rocks may be flung but not concealed inside a fist. This is to be a fair fight. Do you both agree to the terms?" He glanced from one to the other, and they both nodded simultaneously.

He stepped away from the combatants, leading them to the

field where there was plenty of open ground to maneuver on. A few Gypsy men held torches, and Yana gave the word by calling, "Let the fight begin!"

Samíah took a step toward her adversary and extended her hand in a gesture to show there would be no hard feelings no matter what the outcome. Rosa drew back her fist and hit her squarely in the face. Samíah staggered briefly backward, nearly losing her balance. She felt something warm oozing from the side of her mouth. Blood. The watchful Gypsies greeted the scene with humor as she wiped it away. There was to be no fair fighting in this match.

"Come on, come at me!" hissed Rosa. The Gypsy grinned as she beckoned with an open hand; then she went into a crouch, balling her fists in a boxer's stance and tensed for the attack.

Regaining her footing, Samíah started to weave slowly in a broad circle around the girl. The sting of Rosa's blow and the humiliation she felt at the genial laughter of the Gypsy band made her temper begin to boil. If that little vixen wanted a dirty fight then a dirty fight she would get!

A barrage of punches lashed Samíah's way; she sidestepped them all, managed to grab hold of Rosa's wrists and grappled. They went round like wrestlers. The Gypsy pivoted, kicked, entangled Samíah's legs with her own. Then with a shove and a quick slanting motion Rosa pushed Samíah to the ground, sending her sprawling across the earth. Amid howls of delight Samíah picked her head up, spitting out bitter dirt. Rosa pounced on her back and straddled her like a pony, pinning an arm around Samíah's throat and starting to squeeze.

"Break her arm, Rosa!" someone gleefully shouted. "Make her eat mud for supper!" called another to the general hilarity of everyone. "Show her how a Romany woman fights!"

The grip tightened, Samíah gasped for breath. Lungs bursting, she struggled to break free. But Rosa's grip only strengthened with the Gypsy girl's heightened anticipation of a quick victory. Samíah managed to lower her head into the crook of her adversary's arm. Then she bit with all her might. Rosa yowled and let loose. In that instant Samíah rolled over, made it to her knees, and lashed out. The punch caught Rosa below the eye; the Gypsy wobbled back, still on her knees, while Samíah's body pushed forward. She took hold of Rosa's tousled hair with both hands and yanked as hard as she could. The Gypsy girl tumbled beside her. Then with a laugh of sweet revenge she forcefully pushed Rosa's face into the mud, rubbing her nose into it.

Rosa spluttered and squealed. When the hold was released the Gypsy came up for air, caked in dark soil. "You—You bitch!" She lurched bodily and knocked Samíah over. Grappling again, they rolled over and over on the ground, skirts flaring, fingernails digging like talons into each other's flesh, spittle flying as they cursed and screamed.

"Ooof!" groaned Samíah when a swift kick caught her in the belly. She doubled over. With the grace and speed of lightning Rosa was back up to her knees, behind Samíah now, dragging her down by the hair and elbowing her every which way. Dizzily, Samíah fought back to her senses. Squared off on their knees, the Gypsy took a severe fist to the jaw. As her head snapped back reflexively Samíah clenched her hands and swung her arms like a bat. The blow sent Rosa careening. But like a cat she was back up and on her feet before Samíah could finish her off. With astute footwork Rosa paced, jabbing and hitting Samíah in the side of the face before she could stand. Samíah grabbed her by the legs, bit into a fleshy calf, and down went Rosa.

Most of the Gypsies were enjoying the fight immensely; some seemed surprised at Samíah's tenacity, while others laughed and passed a jug, constantly changing the odds now that it seemed Rosa's victory was anything but assured. Glumly Wanko watched from the sidelines. He wished one or the other would win already and put an end to it. Injured women meant they wouldn't be able to work, and without women to labor a Gypsy man's life was made pretty miserable.

Samíah's palm hammered a terrific blow under Rosa's chin. The Gypsy girl groveled, momentarily stunned, then heaved herself up. Back over the ground they tossed and tumbled. Rosa allowed her adversary no time to gain the upper hand; she swiped at Samíah, delivered a fist to the ribs. Samíah returned in kind by gouging at Rosa's ears, so angry she was tempted to rip them off. They swarmed over each other, clothing tattered, bodies battered, faces bruised. A large purple welt had formed under Rosa's eye; likewise Samíah's lower lip was swollen to twice its normal size. Scratches and bite marks crisscrossed their arms and legs, and both their jaws bore dark discolorations.

Exhausted and panting, neither was yet ready to yield. Courage may not have been lacking, but by now strength surely was. Still on their knees, Rosa's punch sailed harmlessly by. Samíah's lurch missed the target and she found herself flat on her belly, choking for air. Rosa tried to take advantage but couldn't. She crawled to Samíah and made to knock out a few teeth. The half-hearted blow widely missed, and the Gypsy collapsed in a heap at Samíah's side.

The crowd became quiet and sullen. Disappointment carved into the faces of the bettors. With obvious anguish they cajoled either of the women to get up and finish things properly, but when neither one seemed able to move they turned and looked at one another dejectedly.

"Enough!" cried Yana, stepping from the gathering and onto the field of battle.

"But how are we to decide the winner?" cried a slender Gypsy called Flacco.

"There is no winner," snapped the queen. She knelt in between the panting combatants and pursed her lips. "Are you both satisfied with this outcome? Has honor been defended?"

Rosa rolled onto her back and stared at the weathered face above her. Slowly she put her fingertips to the bulbous welt below her eye, wincing with the pain. Then she nodded.

Yana turned the other way. "And you?" she demanded.

Samíah made it to her elbows and moaned softly. Her jaw was aching, it felt like her mouth was on fire. Her legs and her hands felt numb. "I—I suppose so."

A big, thankful smile parted the queen's cracked lips. "Good. Now before you tend to your wounds get up and show me there are no more bad feelings."

It took a long minute until they were both able to find their feet. Wobbly, they regarded each other.

"Shake hands," said Yana.

Samíah hesitated, recalling too vividly what happened the last time. Rosa, though, showed none of her reluctance. With a big smile of her own, she said, "You fight dirty, honey. Like a Gypsy."

It hurt Samíah when she grinned. "So do you."

Wanko laughed good-naturedly; gently he led them by the elbows away from the field. "You had both better get cleaned up," he said. "It would be a shame to miss the party."

"We're having a party?"

Rosa threw back her head and shared Wanko's mirth. "Of course!"

Throughout their long history the Gypsies never have needed much reason for a celebration. Tonight was certainly no exception. The feud was over; now it was time for the festivities.

By the time Samíah and Rosa had crossed back into the camp the music had already started, Gypsy men and women cavorting around the fires to the rhythm of the mandolins and the clatter of the tambourines. Reaching the wagon, Samíah shook her head bemusedly.

Being here with Wanko, Rosa, Yana, and the others was proving to be quite an unforgettable experience. She might even come to enjoy it. And she would certainly tell Rosa so when the Gypsy girl finally taught her to dance.

IT WAS LATE; WELL BEYOND MIDNIGHT. THE LAST of the campfires were ebbing in the darkness. Everyone was at last asleep. Everyone but Samíah. She had tossed and turned, then sat up, pushing aside the flimsy curtain. From the back of the wagon she listened to the sighing wind as it rustled through the palms, heard the distant cry of a loon above the lake, stared at the massive walls of the city above the sloping hills. A smear of moon appeared from behind passing clouds and its silvery light slanted and washed softly over Samíah.

The Gypsy men, drunk and snoring, lay scattered throughout the camp, the children and most of the women now taken to their tents. Gazing out at the peaceful scene where only an hour before bedlam had seemed to reign, Samíah tried hard to clear her confused thoughts. It had been a wild and frenzied night, like nothing she had ever before experienced. The music and singing and dancing had seemed to last forever. Yes, and the wine as well. Tambourines in hand, the Gypsy women had whirled with flaring skirts, the men joining in and taking part. But it was when Rosa had stood to dance that all eyes turned. Hauntingly seductive, the vivacious young Gypsy captivated them all with her sensual movements. Spellbound, Samíah had watched.

When Wanko became her partner everyone formed a circle around the couple and clapped hands in time to the music. The

133

rhythmic swaying had reminded Samíah of Spanish flamenco dancers, whirling and gyrating in sweaty unison, foot-stomping to the savage, untamed beat of the Gypsy song. When they had finished the Gypsies had cheered wildly, hailing the king and the princess, the Romany queen-to-be. It had been only then that Samíah, to her astonishment, learned that Rosa was Wanko's daughter.

For a time Samíah had felt herself becoming a part of their culture and tradition and enjoying every moment of it. But then reality had taken over again and she was unable to share the ebullience she'd been feeling. Suddenly she felt separate from them, different, untouchable. The nagging fears returned. Fear for her safety and for her father, fear that somehow her presence here and the dangers it brought would reflect on them all. The drama of life and death was still being played out within the walls of the city, she knew; the perils were far from over. Gideon had still not come back for her, and once more she began to wonder if he ever would.

Soundlessly, she slipped from the wagon to walk among the trees. There didn't seem to be any guards posted around the camp; for a moment she thought about making her escape, here and now. After all, it wasn't very far to the city gates, and beneath the cover of darkness she had an excellent chance of making it without being seen. A better opportunity was not likely to come again. Samíah sauntered between the trees.

"You cannot sleep, child?"

Heart thumping, she turned; a silhouette appeared from among the leafy palms. A woman. Queen Yana.

"You startled me," said Samíah, gulping for breath. "I was just taking a walk. . . ."

The old Gypsy woman came closer, her eyes calmly burning into the jolted girl. "Forgive me, child," she wheezed. "I did not mean to alarm you. For far too many years my own nights have been sleepless. Sometimes I find comfort in walking beneath the sky, listening to the songs of the leaves, the tales whispered upon the wind." Her frown turned into a stretched smile. "I hope I didn't frighten you too much."

"Oh, no," Samíah lied. "Perhaps I'd better return to the wagon. It's becoming chilly."

"Stay," said Yana. "Come, sit here with me. It is good that we have a chance to speak." Then, with some difficulty, the Gypsy woman made herself comfortable on the grass, shaded by the overhanging boughs of an ancient poplar. "These trees and I have passed many a long year together," she remarked absently. She gestured for Samíah to take a place opposite. Hesitantly, Samíah folded her legs under her and shied from the old woman's gaze. The queen unnerved her, as she had that night Gideon had brought her to Yana. She felt strangely uncomfortable, as if in the presence of some superior wisdom, someone who, by magic or otherwise, was able to see right through her, know her every thought before she knew it herself. She didn't feel this way with Wanko or Rosa or any of the other Gypsies. Only Yana. And she wondered if the rest of the band felt it, too; perhaps this was why all the Gypsies held the queen in such awe.

"You seem unhappy, child," said Yana, looking straight at her.

Samíah shifted beneath the piercing scrutiny. "No, it isn't that. Truly it isn't." She made herself confront the questioning eyes. "Just that I've been so . . . frightened these past days. I miss my home, my father. . . ."

Knowingly, the queen nodded. With an effort that seemed coldly formal, she said, "It is for your own good, daughter of Habib. The city is unsafe for you now." Then, perhaps in a reference to Samíah's thoughts of flight, she added, "Leaving us now would only cause you harm. Great harm."

Her words were chilling, and Samíah trembled slightly. "Why hasn't Gideon returned as he promised?" she asked suddenly.

Yana pursed her lips. "He shall come when he is able. . . ."

Samíah leaned forward. "Is he all right? Has anything happened? Has he been hurt?"

The old Gypsy stared hard into her eyes. Fondling the chain of beads dangling from her throat, she said, "So many questions, child, so many questions. Does his absence trouble you so greatly?"

Samíah felt embarrassed. "He is nothing to me," she answered. "Not even a friend. But he promised to come back and take me home. . . ."

"Ah, I see. It is your eagerness to leave that causes you to ask."

"Yes. No." She seemed flustered. "I mean, yes I want to return to my family—but I also hope that nothing ill has befallen him. He's tried to help me, after all. I wouldn't want to see him harmed on my account."

The queen's smile was enigmatic. She sat stiffly in the sylvan setting, the folds of her flesh seeming to droop with weariness. "He is unharmed, I promise," she said after a time. "But events are such that his arrival is yet delayed."

"Oh." Samíah felt a little foolish. In recent days she had been thinking about Gideon a great deal; at times hating and loathing him for getting her involved in these intrigues, yet at other times finding herself truly apprehensive that maybe something bad had indeed happened. No matter what her personal grievances against him she still didn't like the thought of him lying dead somewhere with an Assassin's blade in his back. "Well, I'm glad he's safe," was all she said.

"As I'm sure he is pleased that you are."

This time Samíah flushed, and she was glad it was dark so Yana couldn't see her. "I think you have the wrong impression," she told the Gypsy. "Believe me, Gideon and I are strangers to each other. Why, I've only seen him a handful of times."

Yana grinned, exposing a glimmering gold tooth. "Yes, child. Of course you are right."

For a while there was a silence between them, Samíah listening to the brush of wind teasing the leaves, Yana lost within her own unfathomable thoughts. Samíah, after a time, broke the quietude by saying, "Did you arrive from the city tonight?"

The Gypsy nodded.

"And are matters . . . resolved? Will it be safe for me to leave soon?"

Lifting her head, staring at Samíah again with those ageless eyes, Yana made a guttural noise that turned into a long sigh. "There is tonight a foul curse upon Marrakesh," she said, gazing now toward the distant high walls. "A cancer that cries out to be rooted, plucked before it can spread beyond control. No, child, matters have not been 'resolved.'"

Samíah followed the queen's gaze and looked out at the darkened city. The only outlines she could discern were the dome of the great mosque, its minarets, and beyond them the looming towers of the palace itself. Dim lights burned an orange glow from the tower windows; she wondered if the sultan and his ministers were as sleepless as she tonight. No one had told her of the massacre in the plaza.

"Yana . . ."

"Yes, child?"

"You were right. I am unhappy, troubled."

"I know."

"Why, Yana? Why are these Assassins doing these things? Why do they wish to destroy our nation?"

"No one knows. But the lust for power is a cruel appetite to sate. Better for you not to dwell upon such questions. Leave it to those who can deal with it."

"You mean like Gideon?"

"Like him—and others."

Samíah wrapped her arms around her knees and shuddered. It was all so incomprehensible to her, so totally confusing. "Please, Yana, tell me what you can. About the Assassins, I mean."

The queen shook her head. "Let it be, child. Too much knowledge can be dangerous."

"Everyone is always telling me that. My father, the soldiers, Gideon, and now you."

"Then you should listen."

"But how can I?" Her eyes widened as she leaned forward. "If it's true that I'm marked because of something I saw, if my life is threatened, then don't I at least have a right to know? Isn't it worse to remain in the dark, not knowing, seeing danger behind every shadow, unable to tell an enemy from a friend?

Did you know that until three days ago I suspected Gideon of being an Assassin?"

Yana looked at her quizzically.

"I did, truly I did! With the way he was sneaking around the city, what else was there to think?"

Here the Gypsy woman smiled, even as she sighed in sympathy for the poor girl's predicament. "Gideon is many things, child. Many things. But a Defiler he is not."

"Then you do know about him?"

"Some things, yes."

"But nothing you would tell me?"

A small light came to her eyes, quickly extinguished. "He must tell you himself." There were some secrets not to be shared.

"And about our enemies? This man who calls himself messiah, and would rule the world?"

At the very mention of the despised name the Gypsy visibly flinched; she lifted a hand and thrust two fingers out into the darkness to ward off evil.

"Please," Samíah beseeched. "I want to know."

Yana resumed her rigid posture, inhaling deeply. The wind gusted around the trees, and the old Gypsy wondered which spirits traveled upon it and were listening.

"He is the devil incarnate," she began, speaking in hushed and revered tones. "A tyrant who hungers for savagery, who commands his followers to kill and kill again. They say this man has slain more than three thousand of his enemies *with his own hand*. They say that his own high priests and generals are in constant danger of their lives, that anyone who dares cross his will or speak in contradiction is immediately put to death upon his altar. His unholy court is a place of terror and abomination such as the world has never known. . . ."

"Then why do they follow such a madman?"

"In blind belief in his cause—the Black Empire and the everlasting life assured to them in service of the dark lords." Yana paused, stared into her open hands. "Legend claims that once he had a son, an embodiment of the father. One time and

138

one time only the child spoke against him, sought for the right to claim the bloodied throne of Defilers for himself. . . .

"They say the messiah learned of the plot and came upon his flesh and blood during the night, and there, accompanied by a dozen of the masked executioners we call Night Masters, revenge for the blasphemy was wreaked. The wayward youth groveled at this father's feet, imploring forgiveness. But the messiah's will was resolved—insurrection could not be tolerated, and as an example to all his followers he showed no mercy.

"Dragged to the unholy temple where no outsider has ever set foot, the child was bound to the altar while hundreds of hooded fanatics solemnly gathered. Then one at a time the father severed the limbs of the son. First the offensive right hand, then the left, then his feet. As the boy screamed, the bleeding stumps were cauterized, and he was left upon the black altar in agony while the messiah and his followers offered his flesh as a gift to their foul lords of the dark. Slowly he perished, painfully slowly. . . ."

"It—It's ghastly," muttered Samíah.

The Gypsy woman nodded gravely. "Yes. And from that day forth a word against the messiah has never been uttered among his flock. For if their leader might do such an unspeakable thing to his own flesh and blood, would he do less to any other who disobeyed his will? No, child. The messiah reigns supreme."

Samíah sank back in stunned silence. Only now did she understand what Gideon meant when he said poor Hussein had been fortunate. "Then," she stumbled for the words, her mouth suddenly very dry, "then this is why Gideon sent me here, to spare me. . . ."

"If the messiah has his way, then no one shall be spared," Yana told her fatalistically. Her eyes searched toward the grim walls of the city. She studied the silhouetted outlines, looked out at the waning palace lights. Inwardly she prayed that it was not too late.

"I am sorry for my behavior, Yana," Samíah said quietly.

"I give my word I won't think of escape again. And I'll do everything you want me to."

The old Gypsy smiled. "Then let Rosa be your teacher; listen and do everything she asks. And let us all hope that Gideon returns before too long."

SEVERAL OF THE HORSES SEEMED UNDULY REST-less, stamping their hooves, neighing and shaking their manes. Other than that, the Gypsy camp remained immersed in night silence. Wanko snubbed out the last burning ember with his boot; he stretched wearily, put his hands to the small of his back and rubbed at the tight muscles. Then, as he always did before retiring, he began his final inspection of the campsite. Along the perimeter of tents he saw the Gypsy standing watch. The guard waved from the shadows in recognition, and Wanko waved back. All was well.

After soothing the horses briefly the king paused at the back of the old wagon and on an impulse quietly slid the drawn curtain aside. Rosa and Samíah were both fast asleep. Wanko smiled at the sight. It was good to see how well the two headstrong young women were getting along together. Since the night of the feud there had not been a single altercation between them, Samíah doing as she was told without a murmur of protest. And now, in the ninth night since her secret arrival even he had been surprised to see how quickly the girl was adapting to the Romany way of life. Outwardly at least, Samíah already was beginning to look and act the part of a Gypsy. The king was pleased; more than pleased. Soon her own father might have difficulty in recognizing her. Rosa had done a good job. For the first time since her arrival Wanko was resting easy, feeling confident for the moment of her safety.

The Gypsy on guard atop the crest of the hillock paced back and forth. Wanko drew the curtains again, stepped into the open, and walked slowly toward his own tent. A few chickens in the coop started to gobble. Dawn would not be many hours away.

Deep among the thick cluster of trees three cowled men crouched and hid frozen among the shadows. Not even their eyes moved. Patiently they remained, carefully aware of the two Gypsies on watch, but not yet ready to make their move. Trained expertly in their craft, the Night Masters waited. After a while, when the first of the sentries seemed to grow weary, the leader of the three silently motioned for his companions to make ready. Three knives slipped out from within the folds of their loose sleeves—small knives, curved and double-edged, killing knives.

One slunk away from his cover and approached the first sentry from behind. The Gypsy didn't have time to turn. The blade sank deep into his back between the shoulder blades, the Assassin's hand quickly over his mouth to cover the squeal. The Gypsy slumped noiselessly.

The other two Night Masters circled from the opposite side, approaching the hillock. They waited until the second guard came into proximity, close enough that they could scent the odor of strong wine upon his breath. Ticking off seconds, eyes never wavering, they waited until his back was turned to them. Then the Assassin sprang. The Gypsy sensed the disturbance in the wind and whirled. His head snapped back with the thrust of powerful hands; back broken he slid to the ground. Before his groans could be heard, the second Night Master straddled and gutted him. Blood stained the short grass.

Holding their breath, the three Assassins turned their attention back to the campsite. All remained as still and peaceful as before. Behind the king's tent the four black hounds rested, the chickens were silent in their coops.

There would not be much time for them, they knew. They would have to move and act fast—search the tents and wagons and find the girl, then deal with her swiftly before the Gypsies had time to group and sound the alarm. Amid the general panic and melee that was sure to come, though, they were certain of achieving what needed to be done: eliciting from her the information they needed, then dispensing with her once and for all.

With grips tightened around the hafts of their knives they were ready. Two moved down from the hillock, the third from his position near the tethered horses, converging in the darkness.

Samíah stirred from her slumber. Rosa lay huddled in her blanket, curled like a small girl, her face resting against her hands. Smiling at the image of her Gypsy friend she turned on her side, yawned, tried to fall back asleep. The whinnying of a restless horse disturbed her. Glancing through the partially pulled-aside curtain she peered from the back of the wagon. The camp was patterned with shifting shadows thrown by a crescent moon playing peek-a-boo between the clouds. As always, there was the dim butter-yellow glow of lamps in the faraway towers of the palace. Samíah sighed, stroked her fingers through her mussed hair, and thought of home. Then with a quick grimace she put these thoughts aside. *This will all be over soon*, she assured herself. *Gideon will come, I know he will. The nightmare will end. . . .*

The horses' noise pulled her back again from the verge of sleep. Wide-eyed now, she felt her heart start to quicken its beat. Rosa wriggled her shoulders and turned over onto her stomach, nestling her head down deep in the blanket. The Gypsy girl was lost in a dream. Samíah shut her eyes and tried to put worry from her mind. Morning would come soon. There was nothing to be frightened of. Horses are always restless.

A pair of narrow flat eyes surveyed the camp; the leader soundlessly indicated the different directions for his companions to take. The Assassins nodded and followed his direction.

The first tent was entered; moments later the Night Master came out with his knife bloodied. The Gypsy family lay motionless inside, throats carefully slit as they rested in their beds. The second Assassin skirted the open wagons and came to the tent opposite Wanko's. He lurched inside. A woman jumped to her feet. His curved blade flashed. The Gypsy slumped without a sound. When the Night Master came out he signaled his leader with a shake of his head. The girl had not been there.

It was the sudden bark of the hound that brought Wanko to his feet. Sleepy-eyed and shirtless he pushed aside the flap and stared. Everything seemed quiet enough—but his sharp Romany senses told him something was fearfully wrong. He pulled his knotted leather strap from the hook and stepped out into the open. A foggy image dashed across the periphery of his vision. A hooded, grim image.

"Defilers!" he cried. "We're under attack!"

With lightning speed the leader of the Assassins slipped among the steeds and slit their reins. Then with a whoop and a slap he set them free, sending them surging through the camp. The panicked horses raced helter-skelter, stampeding across the campsite, kicking over the chicken coops. The hounds snapped up, yapping and barking, straining at their leashes. All at once Gypsies came rushing from their tents.

"To your weapons!" hollered Wanko. "To your weapons!"

Caught amid their stealth, the Assassins had now no choice but to fight. Outnumbered two hundred to one, the dreaded and feared legendary killers of the night showed no fright or emotion. Killing was what they lived for, and now they would create the bloodbath that could not be stopped.

Gypsy men swarmed outside, dashing among the running steeds. With frenzied yells calculated to strike terror into the hearts of their opponents, the Night Masters no longer hid from view. Cowls thrown back, they came charging, brandishing their knives, slitting open the flaps of every tent and carving death wherever they could, still intent on finding the girl before they were stopped.

They pressed the onslaught, overwhelming those who got into their way. Knives flashed and were thrown. Gypsies staggered and fell beneath the furious charge, two of the raiders purposely creating a bloody diversion while the third slipped away and searched to locate the victim they had come to kill. Women screamed hysterically, small children crying and fleeing without direction. Wanko hastily tried to form his men into order, but amid the wild panic there was little he could do.

One Gypsy ran toward the buried fires in an effort to hurl down the nearest attacker. The Assassin saw him, whirled, tossed his knife. The blade sank with a heavy *thunk* into the Gypsy's chest. As he staggered he was knocked down by a racing mare and trampled. Bleeding, he crawled for safety— but the hooves of another horse crushed his skull and sank it deep into the soil.

Wanko, still shouting commands, ran past the overturned chicken coop, glancing over his shoulder when a woman screamed and tottered, seeing a Defiler drag her from her tent, slitting her throat before he butchered her small son. The hounds were insane in their urge to break loose. Fowl were running free and frantic everywhere, squawking, fluttering wings, feathers flying as they too were trampled and slaughtered. He reached the straining dogs, knelt with his own knife in hand. These mongrels were the product of five years hard training, black-muzzled, short-haired dogs trained for the hunt. Killers with traces of wolf in their veins, they were eager to be set on their prey. With agile fingers he untied the choke collars and slashed their leashes. "After them!" the king shouted. The hounds leaped and bounded off into the grim darkness.

A sickle-shaped knife wedged violently into the bowels of a club-wielding Gypsy. His nearest companion reeled with the blow of another knife between his shoulder blades. Wanko hurried to the scene, ducking as a dirk came sailing over his head and stuck into a tent post behind.

An Assassin came racing from another tent where he had just butchered an entire family. Amid the swelling pandemonium he did not see the hound. The killer dog leaped by instinct, its slitted nostrils aflair, fangs gleaming in the silver of moonlight. The dog's weight brought the Assassin to his knees; he rotated, stumbled, slashed his dagger wildly. A second dog drew in for the attack while the first growled and bit into his calf. Then, tearing at his flesh they brought him flat on his back. The Night Master thrashed and screamed. It was not long before his face was carved into a pulp, his eyes blinded amid a sea of blood. The dagger fell from his grasp and life ebbed quickly as he vainly sought to crawl away. Only his twitching fingers still moved, helplessly clawing into the soil.

Wanko and his men cut off the path of the second Assassin before he could reach the covered wagon. The king, knotted leather strap in one hand, flashing knife in the other, drew himself up squarely opposite the raider. No novice to violence or death, he swung the strap fiercely and caught the oncoming Defiler across the face. The shaven-headed, drugged, glassy-eyed killer hardly winced. He came on with expert footwork, holding his balance against the sting of the whip and jabbed with his dirk, transforming a bitter thrust into broad slashes through the air that pushed Wanko back.

So fast were his movements that Wanko did not even see the ruthless blow, but he grimaced with the pain of the cut, felt blood as it seeped across his forearm. With an inhuman wary cry of victory the Assassin plunged for the kill, his strokes keeping the other Gypsies at bay at the same time. The curved dagger sent tracing patterns through the air. Wanko rolled to the side and kicked out. The toe of his boot caught the assailant in the belly, momentarily stunning him and halting the advance. With his wounded arm, Wanko lashed out with his strap. Again the knots ripped across the Assassin's face, causing huge welts to rise instantly. But again the devil-worshipper showed no sign of pain. With a Gypsy's boldness Wanko lurched leaving no time for his opponent to regain the advantage. Wanko struck forcefully; he rammed his knife cleanly through the cloth of the Assassin's bloodied robe, the blade punching between ribs. Then the king dug it deeper, in right up to the guard, twisting the knife upward in a single stroke. The Assassin's muscular form fell against Wanko. The king was unable to withdraw the knife and plunge again; he struggled hand to hand with the Night Master, sought to push him away. But the fearless Assassin, life's blood draining from his body, still would not fall.

His calloused hands closed firmly around Wanko's throat and squeezed. Wanko fought for breath, to break free of the grip. Together he and the Assassin tumbled to their knees. The king's wounded arm hung limply now, all feeling gone, the numbness spreading as he gasped for breath. The world began to spin around him. The screams and wails of the dead and dying dimmed in his ears and his vision darkened. He was helpless against the dying man.

Suddenly the Assassin's head snapped back. A hand tore across his throat; his head lolled sickeningly to the side, dark blood pulsing like a fountain. The Assassin slumped crookedly at the king's knees. Coughing, still gasping for air, Wanko peered up foggily. In a daze he saw Rosa. The Gypsy girl was standing numbly over the corpse, a razor in her hand, her nightclothes splattered with blood.

Flacco and a number of the others had begun to restore a semblance of order. Some of the stampeding horses had been gathered up, others had fled far away and off in the direction of the desert. Slain Gypsies lay scattered throughout the camp; wives, mothers, children hunched over the victims and softly wept. Gypsy men had taken to the perimeters of the campsite and were, in teams, vigilantly searching for any other attackers.

Wanko struggled to stand. He glared around at the carnage with disbelieving eyes. Death and destruction was everywhere. At least twelve of his band had been slain and half again as many wounded.

Rosa stared at the shirtless figure of her father. "Your arm, Wanko," she said. "You must take care of it. . . ."

The king shrugged off the notion with a quick gesture. There would be plenty of time for that later—but not until he was sure the camp was secure.

A squat, square-faced Gypsy came from the wagon, two yapping hounds flanking him. "The raiders are dead, Wanko," he said glancing at the fallen Defiler sprawled on his belly where the hounds had left him.

"Are you sure?"

"As far as we can tell," replied Blinco Rascola as he wearily sheathed his knife at his belt. "We think there were only two—and both have been accounted for." He smiled grimly.

"Good, good," mumbled the king. "And the girl, Samíah?"

"Safe, Wanko. In the wagon. We'll have someone stand guard over her for the rest of the night."

The sounds of weeping were beginning to flood the king's ears. "Have Flacco post sentries every ten meters along the perimeter. We don't know if they'll strike at us again." Once more he looked around at the terrible loss of life.

"It was fortunate you gave the alarm when you did, Wanko," Blinco Rascola told him. "Otherwise it could have been worse. Much worse."

Wanko grimaced sourly, the pain beginning to take hold now. "Best to bury our dead quickly. Tomorrow shall be a day of grief and mourning for us all."

The scream turned all their heads. From the shadows, the figure of the third Assassin came leaping recklessly for the wagon. "Catch him!" yelled Blinco Rascola.

Demonically the Night Master wielded a small hatchet, cutting down two armed men before they had time to move. With almost superhuman effort the Assassin jumped to the buckboard. A hound lurched. The Defiler swung out with the hatchet in both hands, catching the animal broadside. The dog's skull gave way, brain and colorless humor splattering in every direction. As the animal fell in a heap the Night Master ducked a sally of thrown knives and, using the hatchet now like a dirk, shredded the canvas and pushed his way into the darkness of the wagon. Only seconds remained before the Gypsies would swarm and kill him he knew. But that did not matter; nothing mattered—only that he reach the girl first and slay her, succeeding at the messiah's task and thereby earning himself an exalted place among the dark gods forever.

He saw the blankets, saw the slender figure cowering in shadows beneath them. With a gleeful cry proclaiming victory he brandished his weapon above his head and brought it down with a fearful blow. The ax head sliced through cloth and pillows, embedded fast into the wooden floor. Chicken feathers flew through the air. For barely an instant the Assassin stared

147

uncomprehending, then he pulled the hatchet free and grinned. Samíah stood against the back of the wagon. Rosa's knife wobbled in her hand. Seeing her, he lurched; she threw the blade and it toppled off him harmlessly. On he came, an insane gleam in his drugged eyes. She pushed open the flimsy curtain and tumbled out. The hatchet came sailing a hairbreadth from her face.

She was on the ground, trying to get up. From the corner of her eye she saw him in pursuit, jumping out the back as well, a tiny dirk pulled from the folds of his bloody robe and now in his hand. Samíah looked up and screamed.

Wanko, Flacco, and Blinko Rascola hurled him to the ground. The Assassin swung the dirk, got back to his feet. With a frenzied shove he pushed Flacco against his companions and made to run. Other Gypsies came from the sides. The Night Master pivoted, spun, jabbed out savagely and tried to clear a path. Still other Gypsy men came and blocked the way. They held clubs and sticks of wood and hatchets of their own, slowly closing the raider inside a circle with no avenue of escape.

"Don't kill him!" screamed the Gypsy king. "We want him alive!"

Menacingly, the ring tightened. The Assassin knew he was trapped—dozens of angry, grieving men were ready to pounce and cut him apart like a slab of beef. His dark eyes darted, first to the girl, who now was well protected by at least six men standing over her, then to the line of swarthy men pacing toward him. He had failed, he knew. Disgraced himself before the gods, disobeyed the law of the messiah. There was no way out. No way out—but one.

Before Wanko could have the others stop him, the Night Master ripped open his robe and, holding the dirk tightly with two hands, plunged it into his belly, digging the blade up toward the heart. He fell silently.

Wanko kneeled beside the gasping figure and shook his head. The Defiler was dead. Too late for them to prevent it. Too late for them to keep him alive and make him talk.

The king stood up, watched as Samíah shakily was helped to her feet. Though it was too late to learn how and why, one

thing remained paramount in Wanko's mind. The attack had
been directed to search for her and her alone. The Defilers now
knew where she was—and even here among the Gypsies Samíah was no longer safe.

STARTLED, SAMÍAH TURNED AT THE NOISE, SAW
the tall figure move cautiously inside the tent. Gideon saw her and stood motionless. "Samíah. Are
you all right?"

Tears flooded her eyes. "Oh Gideon, where have you been?"
Then she flew into his open arms and rested her head against
his shoulder, crying softly. He comforted her for a time, stroking her unpinned, disheveled hair, letting her weep, then holding her at half-arm's length. Dressed as she was in Gypsy
clothes he hardly recognized her. Her eyes were luminous and
bloodshot, Gypsy mascara smeared over her lids and lashes.
Her low-cut blouse of bleached cotton was soiled and torn, full
skirt rumpled and caked with mud; she appeared every bit the
part Yana and Wanko had set for her to play despite the fact
that her delicate features were now filled with pain and anguish.

"I came as soon as I received word from the queen," he
said: "Were you hurt?"

Her borrowed gold earrings bobbed as she shook her head.
"No, but some of the others were. Killed, Gideon. Slaughtered
like lambs. I saw them die." Her lips began to quiver again,

and she shut her eyes but still wasn't able to blot out the imprinted images.

Wanko stepped away from the corner where he had been quietly standing. "I thought it best to keep the girl here with me until you arrived," he said.

"You did the right thing. Thank you, friend." Gideon glanced at his injured arm. Wanko self-consciously held the sling, flexed his fingers. "They took us by surprise," he said. "It was bad. Very bad."

Gideon did not need to be told. From the moment of his arrival he had seen for himself, seen the pain and anger flicker in the faces of the Gypsy sentries, heard the soft weeping of widows in their tents as they mourned their losses. The sadness of the scene had overwhelmed him. He didn't know what to say, how to tell them that he shared their loss.

"Are you badly hurt?" he asked the king.

Wanko scowled, typically downplaying his injury. "It will heal," was all he said.

Once, Gideon recalled, Wanko had been badly wounded in such a skirmish—stabbed, on the verge of death. Yet the king had refused assistance until all of the other Gypsies had first been tended, only then permitting himself to be treated. It had been a noble gesture—but one that could have cost the brave Romany king his life.

Wanko rubbed at the nape of his neck and narrowed his eyes, casting his gaze skyward. "They shall pay dearly for this night." He clenched a fist with his good hand, sucked in air angrily between his teeth. "I vow it to God. They shall pay for what they have done."

Gideon understood his enemy well enough; nothing would prevent them from trying to get at who had discovered the Karshi tomb. They would be relentless in the hunt, tracking her anywhere to learn what she knew. Too much was at stake for it to be otherwise.

"Wanko, do you feel she is no longer safe under your protection?"

The king stiffened, seemingly hurt by the question. He focused harshly on his friend, the corners of his mouth turned down. "I have given my word to protect her—and no less shall I do. With my own life if need be."

He meant it, Gideon realized, meant every word. His pledge had been solemn, and he would never go back on it, not even at the cost of those he cherished the most. Such was the Romany way.

"Thank you, friend. One day I shall find some way to return the favor."

Wanko brushed off the thought of payment with a flippant gesture. But more darkly he was quick to add, "Nevertheless, Gideon, I still fear for the child." There was a sudden disturbing undertone to his words, an undertone that made the secret agent uneasy. "What do you mean?"

Wanko's voice fell to barely above a whisper. "The wind has ears," he reminded his visitor, referring to a Gypsy fable. "There are too many unanswered questions that trouble me. I ask myself why, why did they strike as they did? Search our tents one at a time? What gave them reason to know?"

Gideon's eyes narrowed. "You suspect treachery?"

"I suspect nothing and everything. Trust everyone and no one." His smile was cold. "Sometimes not even you. All we can say with certainty is that these Night Masters chose their timing well. Too well, perhaps. They knew Samíah was here—and had reason to think she could be taken."

Samíah felt chills as he said that. "This is all my fault," she said, eyes downcast and fretful. "If it wasn't for me none of this would have happened."

The king forced her to look at him. "No, girl!" He gazed at her in a way strangely reminiscent of Yana. "The Defilers are our sworn blood enemies also. Every Gypsy woman and man knows it. What befell us tonight was not your doing or fault. The men of Romany are not afraid. No." His gaze shifted to Gideon, the mask of impassiveness replaced by a look of deep anger. "Perhaps, though, there are others who do share the blame.... Others that have forsaken our code of honor."

Gideon studied his old friend, unable to recall when last he had seen the king so bitter. "A traitor," he whispered. "There is a traitor among you."

The very idea of it made Wanko's flesh crawl with revulsion. The Gypsy code was strong and unbroken for a thousand years— until perhaps now. The shame of it was unthinkable, yet Wanko was no fool; how else could he explain the well-timed attack and the search for the girl who had seen too much?

"The blood of my kinsmen cries out for revenge," he said. "Should there be one among us who has broken the code of the Gypsies it is my matter and mine alone. The offender shall pay as dearly as those who struck the blows. These deaths will not remain unavenged. This also I have vowed to God."

A long silence ensued, Gideon well aware of what a spy among the Gypsies could spell for them all: a direct line to the messiah and potential disaster. Yet that line was a two-edged blade. . . .

"What do you want me to do?" Gideon asked.

"Go back to the city and do what you must. I will take care of things here. Trust me for that."

"And Samíah?"

Wanko considered. "Take her to Yana."

"Back to the Casbah?" cried the girl.

Gideon squeezed her hand. "Only for a short while, I promise. It will be safer for you there."

"Yes," agreed the king. "I shall have Rosa accompany her. There is still much she needs to be taught before she is ready."

"Ready?" Samíah searched each of their faces briefly, uncomprehendingly.

"You have not told her?" Gideon inquired.

The king shook his head.

"Listen to me, Samíah," Gideon said softly, brushing aside locks of hair away from her questioning eyes. "I'm going to ask you to trust me again. Can you do that?"

"I—I don't know."

"I need you, Samíah. That's the truth. Having you brought here was my idea, and so was having you trained to learn to be a Gypsy."

"But why?" she asked, astonished, not understanding at all. Nothing seemed to make any sense again. "I thought I was here to be protected—"

"And so you were," chimed the king.

"But you have a very great value to these Assassins," Gideon went on. "Tonight only proves that more than I realized. I want you to do as you're asked, Samíah. Not for me, but for our home, for Marrakesh. Together we may yet be able to learn the secrets of our enemy. Smash them at last so that nothing like what happened tonight can ever happen again. Do you understand me?"

She nodded slowly. "You want me to be your accomplice . . ."

"Fate, it appears, has given either of us little choice. What do you say?"

The horror of the attack would never leave her, she knew. It was a nightmare too real, too frightening to forget. Wanko and the others had indeed risked their lives in her behalf, no matter how much the king might deny it. And too many good Gypsies had already paid the price. No, she could not refuse her help. Not when she owed such a debt. Some of that blood was indeed on her hands, and like the king she was now sworn to avenge it. "All right, Gideon. I'll do what you want. No questions asked."

"You know it can be dangerous for you . . ."

She smiled without humor. "Worse than what they did tonight?"

Gideon turned to Wanko. "Have Rosa gather both their things," he instructed. "I'll bring them safely to Yana before dawn. For the next three days I want Samíah to learn everything she can. I not only want her to look like a Gypsy but to think and act and talk like one as well. One slip up could be fatal. Do you think she can do it?"

The king let his gaze pour up and down the shapely young woman. Already she had learned much, but there was still so much more, and Gideon was not providing very much time for it. "She can learn," he said at last.

"Good."

"What must I do?" asked Samíah.

"For now, just be a Gypsy," he told the dustman's daughter. "Play your role so well that not even your father will know you in a week. And that will be the test—for Habib as well as for us all." He took her hand again, this time enclosing it within his own, looking deeply into her eyes. Somehow they both knew they were riding with destiny.

INSIDE THE *OFISA*, THE GYPSY FORTUNE TELLER'S room, it was quiet, while outside the hubbub of the *souk* clattered on this busy market day. Rosa, sitting on cushions, her long hair severely pinned back, leaned forward with folded arms and stared long and hard at the paying customer come to have her fortune told. The dowager was veiled, dressed in good quality garb, although the clothes did seem old and out of fashion. With a Gypsy's quick eye and keen sense the girl lost no time in appraising her visitor. Not a noblewoman, certainly; probably the wife or widow of some prosperous merchant who now had fallen on hard times. But Rosa knew she would have to delve deeper, much deeper, to learn just how much money or what other valuables the dowager might be persuaded to part with.

"I can see that basically you are a good and kind person," Rosa told her flatteringly. "You have an honest look, and your face smiles for me now, but I think that deep down inside maybe you are not as happy as you seem. . . ."

The visitor squirmed self-consciously, avoiding the Gyspy's piercing stare by glancing around at the heavy curtains hanging from the walls. Although it was still daylight outside, the room was dark, save for the tiny burning lamp in the corner. Thin sticks of incense permeated the air with a thickly sweet and pungent odor.

Rosa tapped her finger against her arms impatiently. "I think that maybe you toss and turn in your bed at night," she went on, feigning deep concentration as she turned back to the roughly cut glass cube strategically placed before her. Her crystal "ball." "I feel that something is troubling you, that's for sure. Something that you've never told to anybody before, am I right?"

Eye contact was made and held; the visitor bit tensely at her lip. "Yes," she muttered to the *boojo* woman. "Everything you said is true. How did you know?"

Rose inwardly smiled; in truth she had said very little that wasn't obvious or true of everyone. However, the visitor did not know this.

Sighing with the insight of one who knows and understands everything, Rosa said, "The secret sadness inside you glows with your aura." She leaned forward, lightly touching her visitor's hand. Physical contact was important, very important— a sign of trust. "Listen to me, honey, I want you to make two wishes, only two. Then keep one of these wishes to yourself and confide in me the other, okay? But," she was quick to caution, "don't make wishes for possessions, for such things are unimportant in life. It is only a woman's happiness and health that counts, see?"

The visitor glumly nodded. As she shut her eyes and thought the wishes, Rosa took out her tarot cards, placed them carefully atop the astrological chart.

"I can see that you are undergoing a personal crisis," said Rosa when her visitor opened her eyes. "One that is very painful for you and has altered your life so that you no longer know the peace of mind you once did."

"Why, yes!" cried the startled visitor, the dowager's eyes wide and expressive. She was utterly amazed at the young Gypsy's insight. At first she had scoffed at the idea of consulting a fortune teller with her unspoken problem, but now, *having seen and heard for herself*, she was glad she came.

Rosa smiled with wisdom well beyond her years. "Tell me the second wish," she asked softly.

"I—I wished that I would not have to spend the rest of my years alone," she replied hesitantly, embarrassed at having admitted this to a total stranger. "And that—"

Rosa held up her hand, palm forward. "Say no more, honey, because I know what you mean." She stared cryptically into the glass cube. "You are a widow; your husband is dead and now you are frightened as you have never been frightened before. You feel guilt and shame and anger, and you don't understand the feelings that crawl around your belly like a cancer, am I right? You loved this man with all your heart. But now he is gone and you are left in a world that is cruel, and you don't know what to do. You wish that somewhere there might be another man, as kind and as gentle as your husband—"

"Yes, yes! And as loving as well!"

"Of course. A man who will love you for yourself and not for the little bit of money your husband's estate left to you to take care of you in your old age."

This time the dowager was really flabbergasted. The Gypsy had read her mind completely, speaking not only her second wish but her first, unspoken one, as well!

"Can—Can you help me, then?" she asked hopefully.

The Gypsy shrugged. "Maybe I can and maybe I can't." Her eyes narrowed dramatically. "If there is no curse put upon you, then I can help. But if there should prove to be such a curse, then not even I or anyone else in the whole world can help, do you understand? The curse may be too strong, and only a special prayer that I know can possibly remove it. Such is the way with spells and curses."

"Oh, please," implored the dowager, falling for the ploy hook, line, and sinker. "I'll do anything to be happy again. Anything! Just tell me what has to be done."

"Good. First we gotta learn if there *is* a curse. Understand?"

Another nod, this one serious and trouble filled.

Rosa held out her hand. "Give me a coin of gold. Place it face down on my palm."

The dowager took out her leather purse promptly and removed a coin. Her hand trembled as she placed the gold into Rosa's waiting hand. No sooner had the gold touched the girl's flesh than Rosa cried out in theatric pain. "Ah, it burns!" she wailed, squeezing the coin tightly. Then she threw it to the mat, spitting at it. "A curse! Your husband's money that he left you has been cast with evil!"

The visitor gasped. A hand went to her pounding heart. Rosa quickly stood, wringing her hands in the best performance of her young life, tears filling her dark eyes. Over and over she mumbled an incantation in the mysterious Romany tongue. To the dowager it all sounded very mystical, unaware that the girl in fact was only repeating over and over again what she'd had for breakfast. Then, in the finest display of all, she swooned, fainting to the floor. The visitor gulped, rose to help. Rosa was up before she could.

"I'm all right," she said, taking a deep breath, fingertips to her temples. Slowly she resumed her place on the pillows, reaching out and touching her visitor's hand again, only this time more forcefully. "The bad magic that you are carrying around with you is very powerful. Very, very powerful. The evil has been with you a long time. Tell me, honey, how long has your husband been dead?"

"Two years."

"As I suspected," said Rosa calmly. "Then it is the evil of the double rotation of the Earth around the Sun. See, it is all here in the tarot cards." She demonstrated a quick sleight of hand that the dowager couldn't follow. She shook her head ruefully, saying, "If only you had come to me sooner...."

"You mean it's too late to remove the curse?" The visitor held her breath.

Rosa stared into the glass cube for a long, disquieting time. "I see a gift," she said, ignoring the question for the moment. "Yes, I see a very special gift was given to you by your husband that you are wearing now." She looked up. "Inside that gift there is a poison, a poison that has tainted everything in your life, yes, and is also responsible for your misery and inability to find the man you seek. Tell me truthfully, honey, what is the gift you carry?"

The dowager seemed befuddled; she thought long and hard trying to see if she could discover what it was. Then her eyes brightened. "The gold locket," she said. "The one I always wear around my neck. The diamond-studded locket!"

"Quick, give it to me!" snapped Rosa. "Give it to me now before it is too late and the double rotation is complete and all will be lost!"

The visitor fumbled with shaking hands to remove the heavy gold chain inside her dress. With great effort she managed to unclasp it and hold it out in her hand. Rosa stared at the fine piece of jewelry. Worth a small fortune, far beyond her initial expectations. "Place it in my hand," she said. "But be careful! The magic is strong!"

The dowager did as told. Again when it was in Rosa's possession she went into her act, wailing and moaning, groaning, clutching at her stomach, and throwing herself to the floor. The dowager watched her gyrations in awe and fear. Finally Rosa was able to free herself from the burning evil, fling it away. She stared together with the dowager at the fallen chain and they both shuddered.

"There is the evil!" cried the Gypsy, pointing. "You must be rid of the gift! Remove it forever! Only then will you be free of the wickedness it carries!"

"But my husband gave it to me for our twenty-fifth anniversary!" she protested in shock.

"Listen to me, honey, do you want the curse removed or not? It doesn't matter to me one way or the other because I'm not the one unable to sleep at night, and it's not me that has to live alone for the rest of my life. Make up your mind, honey; it's up to you." Patiently now she waited for her visitor to reply.

The dowager hung her head. "Very well," she said, wiping a tear from her eye. "I'll put the locket away in a safe place and never wear or look at it again."

"No good, honey. Listen. Because it was your husband that gave you the gift, and because you accepted it with love and open eyes, the curse cannot be removed until it is given back to the giver."

"Give it back to my husband? But he's dead!"

"I know, I know," said Rosa consolingly. "But it's the only way. Your husband loved you, honey, and he had no idea that after he died his gift would place you in such unhappiness. He would die again if he knew the grief it has caused, isn't that so?"

The visitor nodded mournfully.

"All right. Then the answer is simple. You must take the locket to the graveyard, at the stroke of midnight, and put it on the grave."

The dowager trembled again. "I can't do that! Not in a *graveyard*!"

"It's the only way, honey, remember I told you. Until the locket is back with him the curse will not be lifted."

With a groan, the visitor nodded. "All right. I'll do it. Tonight, at midnight like you said."

Rosa smiled warmly, proudly. "Good. You will never regret it. No. I see that once the locket is gone only happiness shall fill the rest of your days. One other thing."

"What's that?"

"Because you've already worn the chain for almost the two full years of rotation you must enter the graveyard as a newborn babe enters the world for the first time. This will purify you."

"I—I don't think I understand."

"You must enter the graveyard naked, honey. Without any clothes."

"*What?*"

The gypsy was somber and serious. "Yes. Only a naked woman can do it. Otherwise it is futile. A waste of time."

The dowager thought of herself slipping unseen at midnight into the sacred burial ground of her deceased husband without wearing any clothes and cringed. "I can't do that," she wept. "Not like that. Not *naked*."

"The Book of the Ancients commands it, honey. It says so. Only a naked woman..."

Looking up with hope in her eyes, the dowager said, "Must it be me—or can another do it for me?"

"Sometimes another can replace the wife, yes. Why do you ask?"

The visitor shied her eyes from the gypsy's. "I, er, I thought that perhaps . . . perhaps you could do it for me. Oh please! I'll pay whatever you ask!"

Rosa sighed, mulled over the matter. "You know that you are asking a great deal of me, much more than I usually do for my visitors. It is not my body that is being poisoned, not my mind that cannot find peace. . . ."

"Your sign in the window says that you help all those who are in need," the dowager craftily reminded. "Would you turn me away?"

Rosa shook her head in pity. "No," she admitted. "I would never turn from the aid of another. Especially one as kind and good a person as you are."

"Then you'll do it?"

The gypsy regretfully nodded. "Yes. Leave the gold chain with me and I shall take it at midnight to the graveyard."

"Naked, like the Book of the Ancients commands?"

"Naked, I promise."

At that, the dowager jumped to her feet and cried with tears of happiness. At last the curse was going to be removed! At last she would find the man and the happiness she was seeking! "Oh, thank you, thank you." Her fingers slipped into her purse. "How much do I owe you for your kindness?"

"Nothing, honey," said Rosa to her surprise. "My business is in helping people, and when I do it is payment enough. Now go, return home. The hour is getting late." She made a Romany sign to further bless the visitor.

With a happy smile, feeling like the burdens of the world had been lifted off her shoulders, the dowager said good-by and left, certain now that all the bad talk she'd heard about Gyspies was totally unfounded.

When she was gone and well away Rosa looked to the drawn curtains. Samíah poked her head out. She had been listening all the while, astonished at the con, the speed and cleverness that Rosa had employed. Not only had she managed to steal the gold chain and locket but left the visitor feeling glad for it. Better than she had felt in two years!

Rosa laughed boisterously. She scooped up the "evil" chain and pranced in front of the mirror. The tiny diamonds sparkled.

"See, Samíah? That's how it's done! Now I've got me the best necklace in all Wanko's camp! And if I ever have to sell there'll be a dozen dealers eager to buy." She let the chain dangle from her wrist, put her hands to her hips. "Well, what do you think?"

Samíah scratched her head; she didn't know if she could ever learn all this. "Remarkable," was all she said. "Remarkable." Then they both went back into the inner chamber to where Yana was quietly waiting.

 "I THINK SOMEONE HAS BEEN TRYING TO BREAK into my house," said Habib after Kubla finished poking his index finger inside the dustman's mouth. "Oh, yes?" muttered the dentist. "Hmmmm. Open wide again."

This time it seemed to Habib that half the physician's face must have slipped inside as well. When Kubla stood back up, after a period of time that made Habib's jaw ache, he smiled and rubbed his hands together. "All better. The gum has healed quite well. Yes, quite well. Are you having other pain? Another aching tooth perhaps?"

Kubla seemed a bit too eager to pull out something, Habib

thought as he shook his head. And for a split second it almost appeared that the physician's eyes flickered with disappointment.

"So then, what's all this you were saying about your house?"

The dustman sat up fully in the chair and fingered his tender gums. "Last night, when I came home and was getting ready for bed I heard noises." He frowned. "Actually I didn't hear them at first; it was, er, my cousin from the home village who is spending some time here with me." In fact he meant the genie, but how could he possibly explain that to Kubla? Besides, part of the agreement was that no one would know about his presence.

"What sort of noises?" Kubla inquired.

Habib scratched at his head. "Low, scraping sounds. As if someone was at the door and trying to force it open."

"I trust you keep your door well secured at night, my friend? These are bad times in Marrakesh. This would not be the first time that some poor innocent man has awoke in his bed to have his throat slit." The physician made a gesture with a finger across his throat. Habib fidgeted uneasily.

"I've kept everything locked these past days. Even gone so far as to bolt my windows at night. Ah, it is sad to see what our city is coming to, isn't it? Where are the soldiers? The sultan's guards who are supposed to protect us?"

"They can't be everywhere at the same time," Kubla observed. "I should think they have their hands full already, what with all the terrible things that are going on." He turned to wash his hands in the basin. Outside in the vestibule a waiting patient sat groaning, his face swollen like a balloon. "Yes, bad times," he mumbled again. "Ruinous for us all."

Habib looked at him with interest. "Then you really are afraid?"

Kubla shrugged. "Isn't every man of common sense? I tell you it's a sad but unavoidable sight. Folk are fleeing the city by the hundreds. If I had a family, wife and daughters and sons-in-law, I would certainly send them away. As far away as I could. To Meknes, or to the coast, or even to Rabat..."

"If things are as bad as the gossips say then nowhere is

safe," answered Habib. "These Assassins seek to win far more than our own city. Some say they will conquer the world."

"Yes, I've heard that, too. Tell me, how is your eldest daughter coping with all this?"

"Samíah?" There was no way Habib could explain that in truth he did not have the slightest idea where the girl was, that he had not seen her for almost two weeks, and that the landlord's nephew had sworn him to secrecy, telling Habib only the barest facts that she was in peril but for the moment still safe. It had all been so strange, Gideon coming to him at dawn as he did, imploring the dustman to trust him, and definitely not to go to the soldiers about her disappearance. Most reluctantly Habib had agreed, although fraught with worry. And only then because the genie had assured him that things were continuing as the stars ordained. Samíah was in no danger. But even these assurances had not eased the burden he carried; each night he prayed that the morrow would bring the girl back. A distraught father can only be so patient. Yet what else could he do? He hadn't the slightest inkling of her whereabouts. Trying to find her in Marrakesh was like trying to pick out a particular straw from a bundle on a camel's back—an impossible task.

"My daughter, er, is staying with friends," he told Kubla after clearing his throat.

"Oh?"

"Yes. She needed a rest. Working too hard, poor child. She'll be coming home any day now."

"Is she in the city or sent to your village?" The physician asked casually as he prepared for his next patient.

"What? Oh," Habib stalled to think of an answer. "Nearby. Yes, close."

"Well, I hope not too close to those damn Gypsies. There's a whole caravan of them camped outside the walls, you know. Bunch of thieves. Stealing us blind. I tell you I wouldn't be a bit surprised if they weren't part of the reason for our troubles."

"The Gypsies?"

"Of course. Wherever they go they bring trouble. Horse traders, ha! I don't know why the sultan doesn't have them all

163

thrown back into the desert. Anyway, for your sake I hope your daughter doesn't have any dealings with them."

Habib was mirthfully chuckling as he got up from the chair. Samiah involved with Gypsies! What an absurd thought. Really, sometimes Kubla did get carried away with himself.

This time Habib heard it first. His eyes popped open, and he rested on the bed staring up at the ceiling. On the mats in the corner, the genie stood on his head with his feet up against the wall in a yoga position. Eyes open in one of his trances, he was unhearing and unseeing.

The scratching sound came again. Habib slipped his feet onto the floor and sat up, listening. There was something going on downstairs, all right. Last night the prowler had gotten away before he could catch him; tonight, though, Habib was prepared.

He scooped up the hefty stick he'd purposely placed within easy grasp, tiptoed his way to the door, and opened it soundlessly. Lucifer's head snapped up, the cat uncoiling from around the genie's head.

"Shhhhh," said the dustman, a finger to his lips. Then he tiptoed to the stairs and crept down them as silently as he could.

Habib pressed himself beside the curtains dividing the sitting room from the kitchen. His gaze scanned the windows and doors, lingering at last upon the back window overlooking his yard. Why were his dogs so quiet? If there *was* an intruder about they should be yapping and straining on their leashes. . . .

More noise. He clenched the stick tightly, beat it softly into his palm. When the pane of shutter cracked the noise was so muffled that he could barely hear it. The tip of a crowbar appeared and slowly pried loose another slat. Habib held his breath and watched as half a hand came inside and probed for the bolt. Whoever was on the other side was a professional, all right, doing his work expertly. Sweat popped out across the dustman's forehead; he swallowed and tried to wet his lips with his dry tongue. He would wait, he decided. Wait until the intruder had gained entry—then he would strike. Bash the scoundrel over the head with his stick and render him unconscious before he ran out into the street in search of the sultan's guards.

But what could this thief want here? Surely there was nothing of value: no hidden jewels or cache of gold. Only the simple belongings of a poor man. Why didn't the thief spend his efforts in the fashionable New Quarter? Why bother the humble folk of the Old?

Habib's anger was rising with the thoughts. This dastardly fellow would rue the day he decided to tangle with him! He'd show the beggar a thing or two, all right!

The figure moved like a shadow; lithe, barely noticed against the backdrop of darkness, as slippery as an eel as Habib watched his frame slither through once the bolt was successfully unlatched. The thief held his gloved hands against the window's frame, arched one leg over and onto the floor, then the other. Once inside he stopped glanced around.

The dustman surged forward with the stick in his hand. The thief ducked, took a glancing blow off his shoulder. Enraged, Habib came at him again. In the dark they grappled, knocked into the divan, and fell over it. The intruder saw the stick come swinging again; he crouched, grabbed Habib's arm and stopped the blow completely. Then he pushed the dustman off; his skinny frame belied his strength. Habib reeled, then hit the wall shudderingly. With murder blazing in his eyes he charged.

"Wait!" cried the intruder. "I'm not here to harm you!"

Habib came coming. Spryly, but with a sigh, the intruder pivoted and stuck out his foot. The dustman tripped and sprawled.

"I didn't want to do that," rasped the villian, backstepping as Habib dizzily lifted himself up. "Listen, I'm a friend, not a thief!"

Habib glared at him. "Friends don't break into houses in the middle of the night."

"It was the only way, believe me. Coming to your door was too dangerous. This street is being watched all the time."

"Yes, by sultan's soldiers! And they'll come running the minute I call." He brandished the stick again.

The intruder put up his hands, palms forward. "Listen to

me, Habib the dustman, I came to speak with you, deliver a message."

Stopping in his tracks, Habib scrutinized the man more carefully. He had a long and thin face, a face he didn't recognize. "You know my name?" he said.

The thief nodded. "That's what I'm trying to tell you. Put down your stick; I'm not an enemy."

"I don't believe you."

"Not even if I say I'm here to bring you to see Samíah?"

At that, Habib dropped his stick-hand to his side. "What? You know where Samíah is?"

"I do. And I was told to find you tonight. Take you to her unseen, without rousing any suspicions—"

"Stay as you are," ordered the dustman. "Move one muscle, and I'll still crush your skull like a melon." The intruder obeyed; Habib fumbled for a match and lighted a lamp. Dim yellow light filled the parlor. "Who are you?" he demanded as he gazed at the ragged looking man before him.

The intruder bowed. "I am called Flacco, right hand to the king."

"King? What king?" Habib was perplexed.

"Wanko, King of the Gypsies."

"Gypsies?" The dustman strained for a better look. Dressed in baggy trousers and garish shirt, a bandana wrapped around his forehead, the intruder did look like a gypsy.

Flacco glanced around nervously. "Listen, there isn't much time to explain everything. All I can tell you is that the king got a message to find you and take you from the house as quickly as possible. All I do is obey orders, like any good Gypsy does. Now hurry, please. My friend Blinco Rascola is waiting for us down the street—"

"Where are we supposed to be going?"

"I can't tell you that."

"Does Samíah expect me?"

"I can't tell you that, either."

Habib growled in frustration. "Then by Allah, what *can* you tell me?"

The skinny Gypsy shrugged. "Only what I already did. Now hurry. Soon it's going to be light."

From the yard Habib heard a low moan, the moan of one of his dogs. "Don't worry about them," assured Flacco. "They're not harmed. I only used something to put them to sleep, that's all." His face twitched with unease.

"How do I know you're telling me the truth, eh? How do I know this isn't some Gypsy ruse to get me away from the house so that you and your friends can rob me blind?"

Flacco peered around at the meager furnishings, thinking that only a fool of a Gypsy would work such an elaborate ploy to steal from a man who has nothing. "You'll have to trust me," he said, quickly adding, "Wanko says that if you refused I should tell you that Gideon wishes it as well."

Habib came close enough to smell the wine on his breath. His calloused hand grabbed the gypsy's collar. "Are you telling me that Gideon is a part of this, too?"

"All right," Habib said at length. "Wait for me; I'll be right back."

"Hey, where are you going?"

"To wake my friend from his trance, er, his nap. I'm bringing him with us."

"You can't do that!" cried Flacco. "Wanko, he says to get you but didn't say nothing about your friend."

Habib glared at him. "Well, if you think I'm going to go traipsing around by myself with you and this . . . this Blinco Rascola, whatever *he* is, at an hour like this, you're sadly mistaken. Either my friend accompanies me, or I don't come at all." He said it with finality.

Flacco scratched his dark curled hair and sighed at his dilemma. Now what was he supposed to do? Wanko didn't count on this; for sure the king was going to be most upset if some other *gadjo* came along uninvited. But he'd probably be even more upset if he and Blinco Rascola came back empty-handed.

"Okay, but make it quick."

Habib ran up the stairs, wheezing by the time he reached his room. He had a devil of a time rousing the genie from his inner peace and tranquility, and when he did he found his companion more than a little riled at the thought of leaving the house. But Habib insisted, cajoling and pleading so much that the genie sighed and relented, agreeing to come. Anyway, as long as it didn't break the rules, there was no harm in it.

His bushy brows slanted sharply and, with his turban askew and fine white robe badly rumpled and in need of a good ironing, he came grumpy but docile behind the dustman, Lucifer curled in his arms.

"This is my, er, cousin from the village," Habib said to Flacco by way of introduction.

The Gypsy took one look at the genie and gasped. "Hey, is your cousin sick?"

"Sick?" said Habib in surprise.

"Not that it's any of my business, but he looks like he just got up from his death bed."

"Hrumph!" said the genie. I've never been healthier. What's he talking about, Habib?" The dustman shrugged.

"Look at his complexion," cried Flacco. "His skin is . . . *green!*"

"Oh, *that*. Pay no attention," Habib told him. "it's only, er, a condition from too much sun. Common among the folk of my village, isn't that right?" He pinched the genie on the sly, and the genie nodded.

Gadgo's were certainly a peculiar lot, Flacco decided. Especially those in this part of the world. "Okay, if you say so." He was just glad he'd persuaded Habib to leave. "Follow me," was all he said.

As they slipped from the back door, Habib asked, "Can't you at least give us a clue as to where we're going?"

"It isn't very far, I promise. Only a short walk from the *souk*. But listen, we've got to move fast but cautiously. Since your sultan has imposed the curfew and martial law, we don't want to run into any stray patrols, eh?"

"We'll do as you say, eh cousin?"

The genie groaned and nodded, and Lucifer hissed. Together they noiselessly moved in single file out into the quiet and lightless street. Flacco put two fingers to his mouth and whistled softly. From beneath the trellis, amid the shadows, another figure appeared.

"It's about time," grumbled Blinco Rascola to Flacco. "I was getting worried."

"Just a slight delay. Now we're ready."

Blinco Rascola stared at the turbaned man with the slightly green skin. "Don't pay him no matter. He's from the village. Too much sun or something."

Then without another word they all hurried from the Old Quarter and towards the grim enclosure of the Casbah.

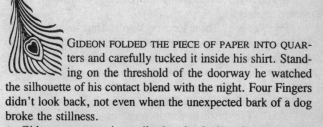

GIDEON FOLDED THE PIECE OF PAPER INTO QUARters and carefully tucked it inside his shirt. Standing on the threshold of the doorway he watched the silhouette of his contact blend with the night. Four Fingers didn't look back, not even when the unexpected bark of a dog broke the stillness.

Gideon wore a grim smile; he clutched at the paper and, fighting off his fatigue, thought ahead to the coming night, perhaps the most important night yet. For scrawled on that paper was the identity of the one man that, next to the messiah himself, he wanted most. The one called the Dealer, the buyer of Hussein's brooch.

Early glimmers of gray were threading the eastern sky. At the sound of distant marching boots, a squad of sultan's soldiers on patrol, he darted away from the arch and quickened his pace. At the far end of the street the dull lamplight spilling from the closed door shone like a beacon. Gideon hurried for it, knocked in the proper sequence. It creaked open and he went inside, past the standing guard and into the draped chamber.

"Gideon, lad, have they dragged you into this too?"

"*Salaam*, Habib. It's good to see you again."

The dustman rose to his feet, ignoring the extended hand and giving the landlord's nephew a great bear hug. There were tears in his eyes when he looked at Gideon and said, "By Allah, you look awful! Like you haven't had a good night's sleep in a week."

"I haven't."

"Poor lad! What have they done to you, boy? Eh?" He peered around the room with a scowl, sickened by the pungent smell of the incense. "What is this place, anyway? Where have they brought us?"

Blinco Rascola who was leaning against the wall said, "The dustman doesn't like Gypsies very much."

"Not when they break into a man's house after midnight!" snapped Habib.

"It's all right," assured Gideon. "Don't be concerned. We're among friends."

"Friends, is it? These Romany devils! They lied to me, lad; told me I was coming to see Samíah. Then they shut me up in here like a bloody prisoner and won't let me go." His eyes drifted to Blinco Rascola, who now had his knife drawn and was using it to clean his dirty fingernails.

"I'm to blame, Habib. I asked that you be brought here."

"You?" The dustman was incredulous. Suddenly he began to have doubts about his young friend. "Where is Samíah? What's been done to her?"

"Safe, Habib. You have my word."

"I took your word two weeks ago when you asked me to trust you and not go to the authorities. Then you said she would be home in a few days. Now it's turned into weeks. Where is she, Gideon? Where is my daughter?"

"The Gypsies didn't lie. You were brought here to see her. And you shall. Soon. Very soon."

Samíah's burly father began to pace the room like a panther, wringing his hands, seething under his breath, trying to keep his temper under control. Damn these Gypsies! Damn Gideon. Yes and damn the genie as well! Life was a great deal simpler before he'd had the misfortune to meet any of them. They were playing games with him, making vague promises, hinting at dire events if he didn't keep his mouth shut and go along, yes, and now even holding him hostage in the same way they were probably holding Samíah. But what did they want of him and the girl? *What did they want?*

"Fetch him something to drink," said Gideon to Blinco Rascola.

"I don't want anything."

"For your nerves, Habib. You need it."

The dustman scrutinized the younger man carefully. "You wouldn't be trying to drug me, would you?"

"Told you he doesn't trust us," muttered Blinco Rascola.

"It's understandable after what he's been through. Bring the wine anyway. I'll drink first; that should assure you there's nothing in it."

Habib didn't respond. As Blinco Rascola left to fetch the bottle he turned back to Gideon and said, "By the way, this one didn't come alone. He's brought a friend with him. Someone from his village, he says, but I don't know. He's the strangest man I ever saw."

"You should have come alone," Gideon told the dustman with a sigh. "There are enough people implicated in this as it is."

"Oh? Are you afraid then? Afraid that my friend might get away and expose this whole affair?"

"Sit down, Habib."

"I will not. I'll do as I please."

He was beginning to sound more like Samíah all the time. "All right, have it your own way."

Blinco Rascola didn't come back with the wine. Instead, Yana did.

"I know you!" cried the dustman. "I've seen you before, in the *souk* on market days! You tell fortunes."

Yana bowed her head politely. "And I have seen you as well. In the evenings with your broom and bag. And at night when you pause on your way home to feed the strays."

Habib was astounded. Had the old hag really seen him throw bones to the mongrels? But how, surely she wasn't up at the hours when he came home? The streets were deserted—or were they? Habib started to feel confused and troubled.

"Drink this, old man," said Yana, offering a small cup filled to the brim.

"What is it?"

The gypsy woman smiled her big mysterious smile. "Some have named it whiskey. In Marrakesh they call it 'Gypsy poison'." Then she swilled a slug of her own, shutting her sleepless eyes and smacking her lips as the fire burst through her innards. "That'll help bring the dead back to life," she chortled.

Habib sipped his slowly, amazed as she downed the last of her cup.

"Yes," said the queen, turning her attention back to the dustman. "I can see the resemblance well. Looks exactly like him, she does. Don't you agree?"

Before Gideon could say anything, Habib spoke. "Are you taking about Samíah? Do you know my daughter? Have you seen her?"

"Your child and I have become good friends these past weeks, old man," she chuckled mirthfully. "Yes, good, good friends. And don't you worry a single gray hair, old man. Samíah is doing fine, just fine."

"Then why can't I see her?" There was weariness and desperation in his eyes, a father's pleading.

"Oh, but you shall. Yes, this very day." Here Yana glanced to Gideon before looking back at the dustman. "Although I think you'll find her changed a great deal. You may not even recognize her."

"Not recognize my own child? My eldest daughter who has badgered and hounded my life for years? Preposterous, woman! I'd know her anywhere!"

Yana said nothing but continued to smile.

"It's almost daylight," said Gideon. "Soon the *souk* will be crowded."

"Yes," agreed the Gypsy queen. She offered her hand to Habib. "Come, old man. Let's you and I take a walk in the market. Then we'll see if you are as clever as you think."

THE SKY IN THE EAST DISPLAYED A PALE ORANGE tint as Habib allowed the strange Gypsy woman to lead him to the *souk*. Even at the hour of dawn the nearby streets had already started to fill: wagons rumbling along the winding lanes, merchants opening shops and setting up stalls for public inspection, *chador*-clad veiled women with baskets on their heads scurrying to market. To the snort of camels and grunts of lazy mules, Yana and the dustman crossed from the gates of the Casbah to the great square. Blue tiles of the Kotoubia glimmered bewilderingly. The high walls of the palace were rosy pink and contrasted breathtakingly with the rich green of the parks and gardens that were magnificently beside it.

Habib's darting eyes missed little of the awakening life all around. "This way," the queen had told him, leading him by the elbow away from the stalls and unloading camels and toward the market's fringe. There, where snake charmers and bread sellers, alchemists and jugglers had begun to gather, he saw the tent of of the fortune-teller, exactly in the same spot it had been for as long as he could remember. Nearby, perched atop a saddle of worn rugs thrown over the back of a flop-eared donkey, sat a Berber, a mountain tribesman wearing the traditional wound white turban of his tribe. A small square of cloth hanging behind his head marked him as a bachelor in search of a bride. Other Berbers had also begun to gather in the area, mostly fathers with their veiled daughters, come here to barter the girls with the eligible young men. The man on the donkey looked on impassively as the bevy of giggling prospective wives crossed back and forth in a time-honored pageant of public courtship.

"Why have you brought me here, woman?" Habib asked in growing frustration. "If I were seeking a wife, I could have come by myself," he growled.

"Hey, mister! Mister!"

The dustman turned to find a well-curved young Gypsy women tugging at his sleeve. "Hey, mister," she implored. "Come with me into the tent and I'll explain for you the future and all the things that are gonna happen in your life." Her eyes were wide and expansive, outlined with kohl, saffron-colored powder on her thin brows, carmine rouge rubbed into her cheeks and apparent through the blue veil she wore. As for her dress, it was decidedly Gypsy—long black flaring skirt draping around her ankles, brightly dyed red cotton blouse unbuttoned at the collar, a shawl over her shoulders, and a yellow scarf wrapped around her pinned-up hair. "Come on, mister; I can show you things that maybe you never seen before, huh?"

Habib tried to pull away but the girl clung to his arm, grabbing his hand and turning the palm upward. "I see that you are a noble and generous person," she went on, unperturbed as her potential customer grimaced in irritation, "and that secretly, inside, you are unhappy. Yes, there is a sadness in the lifeline of your hand that tells me you think something bad has happened to someone very close to you that you deeply love and miss but who is not here to let you say these things in person."

"No, no, please," said Habib, looking now to Yana in hopes that the queen would shoo her zealous kinswoman away. The

Gypsy girl laughed with a twinkle in her eyes. "For a few coins, mister, I can solve all there is that is bothering you and make you at peace with yourself again. In your troubled mind—"

"Tell her to leave me alone," the dustman grumbled.

The girl winked at him outrageously. "You think that maybe I can't help you and that all I want is your hard-earned money? The money that you work so hard for every night cleaning these very streets in which we stand . . ."

Habib was startled; he stared long and hard at the girl. "How . . . How did you know that?"

The gypsy grinned and twirled. A child tossed a tambourine, and she caught it with one hand, instantly beginning a little dance to the beat of the cymbals and drum. She shook her hips and her shoulders, tapping the tambourine above her head as the tiny bells on her shoes jingled and her golden earrings gleamed. Several of the Berber bachelors turned their heads away from the parade of tribal girls and looked on at the dancing Gypsy with growing enthusiasm. Soon there was a sizeable crowd gathered around. Habib tried to leave, but with her skirt aflare the Gypsy entertained directly in front of the flustered dustman, blocking his path.

Loud applause rose when she had finished, a smattering of copper coins was tossed at her feet. The Gypsy girl scooped them up with a grin and tucked them for safekeeping inside her red blouse.

"See, mister?" she said to Habib, her forehead dotted with beads of perspiration.

"I've seen more than enough, thank you," he replied dourly. "Now if you'll please excuse me, I have others matters to attend to that cannot wait." He started to leave.

"You think you are clever and you know so much," she called out after him. "But you don't know nothing!"

Habib stiffened and turned. The cry of merchants hawking pots, rugs, pottery, and tools faded into the background. The gypsy smiled crookedly, standing with her hands on her hips as she fixed her gaze intently upon his. "That's right. But if you are too cheap or too afraid to let me read for you the tarot cards that never lie, then it is none of my doing or fault whatever may happen."

Habib stared in confusion. Who was this brazen child of nomads? Why did she single him out like this, and what did she want of him? Didn't he have enough problems already? He fumbled to open his purse and took out a small coin. "Here," he told her with the resignation of a man too weary to be badgered like this any further. "Go on, take it. You dance very well."

She had no hesitation in taking the coin and putting it away with the others. "Thank you. But if you think this will help you with your troubles, it will not."

"Please, child. Another time, perhaps. Read your cards for me another time."

Her smile deepened. "Then you *are* afraid!"

Here the dustman began to feel his neck swell. "Who did this girl think she was to talk to him like this?"

"I am afraid of nothing!" he shot back.

The Gypsy regarded him smoothly. "Oh, no?"

"No."

"Not even when you left your pants out on the line in the yard and it started to rain and the widow Anna saw you running naked to fetch them before they shrank?"

"Of course not! I was embarrassed, that's all—Hey! How do you know about that, eh? What *are* you, a witch?" His heart had started to thrum.

"Or the time you misplaced the money for the rent and you thought that pig of a landlord al-Gamal was going to confiscate your belongings and throw you out into the street?"

Habib's jaw dropped like his hound's. Breathing shallowly he gulped and looked at the Gypsy anew. He shook his head bewilderedly. "No," he mumbled, "no, it can't be. . . ."

Tears filled her eyes; she pulled away the veil and cried, "Oh Papa, don't you know me?"

"Samíah!"

And there, as the morning sun washed over them goldenly, the dustman threw his arms around his daughter and squeezed her as hard as he could. Both the girl and her father burst into tears.

Yana stood watching the reunion with tears of her own. She glanced up at the Berber atop the donkey, and the man caught her gaze and nodded. Quietly he steered his animal away into the crowds, unnoticed by all save the queen. Gideon would be pleased, they both knew. Samíah's disguise was perfect.

THE DARK MAN SAT ALONE, PUTTING AS MUCH distance between himself and the handful of other patrons as possible. He sat with his hand clenched around the neck of the wine bottle and stared fixedly at the low beamed ceiling. The tavern was ill-lighted and shadowy. Purposely so, for few who ever frequented this dingy Casbah hideaway wished their faces to be recognized. When they spoke to each other—which was infrequent—it was always in whispers, their words brief and to the point, transactions and agreements made swiftly. For if there were honor among thieves, there was certainly none to be found in this place. Only the dregs of humanity: opium peddlers, murderers, traffickers in human flesh. Yes, and those special few who dealt in them all. Like the Dealer.

The wooden chair creaked as he shifted his weight. Wisps of tobacco smoke wafted in his direction from the table in the corner where a ragged, humorless, glassy-eyed fellow sat in a drugged stupor. Occasionally the keeper would pass by, distastefully propping him up like a mannequin before he collapsed onto the sawdust floor. At the far table across from him a yellow-wigged prostitute stared into her empty glass. Her eyes sagged with advancing age, the Dealer saw, unhidden even by the layers of makeup she wore to make herself seem young again. When a drunken sailor got up from his place and paid the keeper his bill, the whore got up also and followed him out into the street. From the corner of his eye the Dealer watched her leave. A small frown showed at the sides of his mouth.

Biding his time, he poured another drink into his glass and sipped at it slowly like a man who, having tasted all the pleasures of life once too often, was now bored with existence and the promise of a future that held nothing more but the same.

The curtains from the back room parted; the slim figure of a woman stepped out into the open, caressed by the softened shadows. She was a Gypsy, he saw; young, dark-eyed, her well-proportioned body filled with the vigor of youth. Her shoulders were bare, the linen of her tightly fitting dress bulging with the swell of her breasts. Her arms and wrists were adorned with bracelets and trinkets that clinked as she moved. Her eyes danced, teasing as he caught her gaze briefly. Aroused, he looked on with interest while the girl moved toward him. Hips swaying gracefully, she came to his table and stood, unspeaking, staring down at him intently.

The Dealer wet his lips, indicated that she should sit. She took her chair without breaking eye contact. "I have been seeking you," she said.

He showed no emotion. "You know me?"

"You are the Dealer. Everyone knows you."

"I think you've mistaken me for someone else."

She smiled with her eyes and shook her head. "No, you are he. I've invested too much time and trouble to be mistaken."

Intrigued by her boldness, he leaned forward, elbows on the table, his hands folded and his thumbs pressing lightly up against his lower lip. "Who are you?"

"A Gypsy." Her flesh glimmered goldenly in the dim candlelight. The cleavage between her breasts was deep. The Dealer glanced briefly at the gold chain and locket that hung from her neck.

"If I were the Dealer, the one you've been looking for, what do you want?"

Another smile, this one barely hinting at her secret. "I have something for you, something to sell. . . ."

"Your locket?"

She laughed lowly, enticingly. Was she offering him her body, he wondered. Like her perfume, her appeal was strong.

"No, not my locket. Something far more valuable. Something worth the ransom of a king."

Now it was his turn to laugh. "And what would a Gypsy have that is worth so much?"

"Information."

He made a flippant gesture. "I deal in material things, things of quality that can be touched and seen." He touched her wrist with his fingertips. "Things I can feel." If he expected her to flinch, she didn't. Instead, she sat straight and kept her gaze steady.

"You mean like the brooch you bought?"

His brows slanted; for only a moment did his eyes flicker and betray a hint of uneasiness. "What brooch is that?"

"Do not play games with me, Dealer. The one given to you by the man called Hussein. The brooch you were so eager to purchase."

He looked away from her stare. "I have no idea what you mean. I know nobody by that name."

Yet another of her enigmatic smiles confronted him. "Perhaps, Dealer. . ." She paused, noted his growing discomfort. "But I have something to sell to you of even greater value," she quickly went on. "Value not only to yourself but to your friends."

The Dealer leaned back, drummed his fingers on the table. A small beetle scurried between the cracks. "I still don't know what you're driving at."

"Information, Dealer. Priceless information. Worth to you, say, one hundred gold coins."

"Preposterous! Nothing is worth so much."

She eyed him slowly, drawling, "No? Not even to learn the secrets of the Karshi tomb?"

His fingers stopped tapping, and he stiffened slightly, studying the Gypsy once again. You know about the...tomb?"

"Enough. And about the zealous cult that has sworn a vendetta against the messiah." Again his eyes flickered; she spoke more rapidly now, pretending not to notice. "Or haven't you heard? The Karshi are sworn to root out their enemy—and they are prepared to do so."

He studied her for a while, wondering how this, this common daughter of Romany thieves could possibly have learned about such things.

"I think that maybe your friends would pay a very handsome price to learn at last the sacred tomb's location. Such knowledge would be vital to their interests, wouldn't it? The opportunity to at last blunt the threat?"

Her companion chuckled lowly. "You take me for a fool girl," he snapped. "My business is merchandise—not blood feuds among rival fanatics." He filled his glass. "We're both wasting our time."

The Gypsy glared, began to stand. "Then you *are* a fool! Others will be glad to close my offer." Abruptly she turned to go; the Dealer reached out and grabbed her arm, forcing her back around. "Wait a moment," he said in a hushed voice. "Perhaps I was, er, a bit hasty. Sit down."

"Then you want to buy what I have to sell?"

He regarded her coldly as she resumed her seat. Could she possibly have access to such information, he asked himself. Was it possible? Or was all of this merely an act, some elaborate, wild Gypsy scheme to gain some quick money?

"I may know a few people who would be interested in what you have to offer. But you must be aware that Marrakesh is riddled with labyrinths and secret places. You do understand that I am skeptical about how someone like you comes to possess such information. Other men have given their lives in a fruitless search to discover the tomb."

"Then I suppose you'll not be satisfied until you've seen it with your own eyes."

The possibility of her actually knowing the hidden location so long sought by the messiah and his followers fired his interest—inwardly. Outwardly he behaved with his usual calm. He must not trust the Gypsy, but he also must learn more.

"They say the tomb rests deep, deep below the ground," he remarked, testing her.

"Above ground," she corrected. "But lost in a maze of alleys and hidden lanes that only I can lead you through."

If indeed she was telling the truth—and strong doubts remained in his mind—then the girl knew far too much for her own well being. The risks of having such knowledge were great, even for him. A cautious man should never dare tread into dangerous waters such as these. Not if he valued his head. The Assassins would kill him for this knowledge—if the damned fanatical Karshi didn't do it first to prevent him from telling. Yet, there was no question but that his contacts among the zealots would pay handsomely for this information, reward him beyond his wildest imagination. Not that he trusted them, not that he trusted anyone. But the fools had paid him well for the delivered brooch and the location of the man called Hussein. Exposing the sacred holy ground of the Karshi to them would further their gratitude. In truth he loathed them all: the Assassins, the Karshi, the sultan, the people in the city, even these crude Gypsies. But Dealer they had named him, and Dealer he was—taking the cause of any side if the price was adequate. This girl was no exception. He didn't know her motives nor did he care. Whatever, they were of no concern to him. Only that now, for a while, she might be useful. Later he could deal with her in another manner. Yes, when there was time.

"If you do know the location of the tomb how is it that the Karshi didn't kill you? It's always guarded against trespassers."

"Because I entered under the protection of one of their own," she quickly replied, hiding the fact that had it not been for Gideon they surely would have. "One of their number is my lover."

"And you would risk exposing his life by coming to me?"

The Dealer locked his gaze with hers and, unspeaking,

they stared into each others eyes. "Does gold mean more than love?" he asked.

"Not for gold, Dealer. For revenge." Her brooding eyes simmered now with icy hatred.

"Ah, I see. This Karshi has jilted you."

She spat the words. "Spurned me for another woman whom he took to wife."

So that was it! The Dealer could hardly keep himself from gloating. The worst water tortures invented by man had not forced a single karshi to betray his sacred trust. How these Assassins had once tried! But now, because of love and jealousy the secret was about to be handed to him on a platter. How ironic. How strange the ways of fortune that he of them all could now hold the key.

"Will you meet my price?" she asked impatiently.

"You must hate this lover very much."

"As much as I hate all men."

"It will take me a little time to raise the money," he said.

"How much time, Dealer?"

"By tomorrow."

"Tonight."

His features tensed. "I thought the money meant nothing to you."

"Fetch it tonight. Until you do I'll tell you nothing." She glared at him mistrustfully. "And no tricks. None of your friends hiding among the roofs with crossbows."

"You'll point out the location for me before the transaction is made? Giving me proof that you're not lying?"

"You have my word." She rose, leaning over the table with her palms down on the wood. "Meet me in two hours at the arch of the Street of the Harlots. And don't try and shortchange me—I have a quick eye for counting."

"No doubt you do," he answered dourly in grudging admiration of her boldness. "Two hours it is." He smiled without humor, fondling the hilt of his hidden dagger. By dawn this Gypsy was going to make him a very wealthy man.

 THE BERBER ASCENDED THE BROKEN STAIRS OF the abandoned house and reached the flat roof. There, he squatted among the long shadows slanting from the higher walls behind and patiently cast his gaze along the deserted street below. Inside the garden courtyard opposite Gideon stood sheltered within the shade of the orange tree. Tiny flowers pushed up wildly between the cracks of the crumbling walkway, creating in daylight a colorful carpet which now seemed lifeless in the dark of the night. The scent of jasmine was fresh in the air, and the secret agent breathed deeply as he waited. A soft mist had begun to descend over the city; a glowing white pall that veiled the grandeur of the distant spires and palace towers, nestling gently over the great blue-tiled dome of the Kotoubia and creeping slowly across the ten thousand terraced roofs.

Gideon heard the first wails; he peered to the trellised edge of the street and watched the sad little funeral procession march his way. There was a litter on which the dead man lay, uncoffined, covered with a sheet of linen which left his feet bare and the form of his body plain to see. The litter was carried high on the shoulders of four weary men, and they proceeded toward the nearby cemetery with slow steps, relatives and friends following after; dressed in the wretched garments of the poorest classes. All joined in the melancholy, haunting strains of the funeral song.

It took a very long time until they had passed, but long after they had turned the corner he could still hear the weeping and moaning of the women. Then the street became quiet again, and he resumed his vigilance. He saw the Berber cross to a better position and slink his way down onto the empty balcony. The mist continued to settle, fanned suddenly by the onset of a strong gust. A mongrel barked from an alley.

The time was late, he knew; the two hours already passed. Had something gone wrong? Had his mark changed his mind, decided not to come after all? Or could he have been warned, tipped off by one of the many faceless spies of the Casbah that this affair was a ruse? A trap carefully laid . . .

He tensed at the clink of a walking stick. From the darkness the crippled beggar emerged, a blind man with stiffened arms and stiffer legs who proceeded to casually walk sightlessly to the corner of the street—the very corner of the appointment.

Gideon cursed beneath his breath. This beggar could ruin everything, he realized. His presence might easily frighten the Dealer, send him scurrying back to the safety of the Casbah before anything could be done. The secret agent hissed between his teeth. *Damn him!* Why is he standing there? Why doesn't he move?

But the beggar held his ground. Lost in the shadows of the empty doorways, Samíah looked on apprehensively. She glanced down the street at the solitude and silence, bewildered. Still there was no sign of the man she had come to meet. Like Gideon, she began to suspect that something had gone wrong. Comprehension, though, slowly dawned, and she moved from her nook out into the open.

"You're late," she said, standing face to face with the blind man from the opposite side of the street.

The Dealer smiled a small satisfied smile. He tapped his walking stick in front of him and crossed. Gideon stared on in wonder. The disguise couldn't have been better. His mark had perfectly and expertly acted the role, one of many he regularly assumed to avoid detection.

"Do you have the money?" she said.

He didn't respond until he was on the other side and concealed once more by the total darkness. "First the proof," he answered. "Show me the location of the tomb. Walk twenty paces in front of me—slowly. One quick move too many and I'll be gone by the time you turn around. Understand?"

"You don't take many chances, do you?"

"Only fools and Gypsies take chances. Now do as I say. Move!"

Samíah glanced to the dark garden, then shrugged. Hips swaying, she started to move along the deserted street, her heart pounding inside her chest. When she heard the clink of the walking stick behind, she breathed a sigh of relief. He was following, exactly as he said he would.

The arch at the end of Harlot Street loomed closer. The mist had started to swirl all around, encompassing her like a blanket. Samíah began to feel frightened. Where was Gideon? Why didn't he show himself? He was supposed to apprehend the Dealer the moment contact had been made. What was he waiting for?

She passed beneath the arch trying to keep her nerves from shattering. The tap of the walking stick remained hollow and distinct behind. Once they crossed into the gates of the Casbah it would be too late; the Dealer would be on his home ground— with his own agents surely waiting.

"Stop!" came the command.

Samíah's heart leapt into her throat. She turned around to see the so-called blind man lift his walking stick, unscrew it and expose a tiny glittering razor at the tip.

"What—What are you doing?" she gasped.

The Dealer grinned malevolently. "So you are going to take me to the Karshi, eh? Show me the secret entrance, eh?"

She stood there shaking, her eyes darting for someplace to run. There was none. Only the walls of the arch on either side, the misty gate of the Casbah behind, and him before her.

"Of course I'm going to take you there," she said weakly, swallowing as he fondled his weapon with both hands and wielded it before her eyes.

"For a while I believed you," he told her, approaching. His grin turned into a frightening scowl.

"And now you don't?" She gulped, unable to catch her breath.

His eyes glinted with malice. "Now I know better. Who you are and what you are."

"Now listen, honey," she said, trying to smile and be seductive again. "Maybe you think that I lied to you and that I just wanted to make some quick money. But you and me we're the same, see? We want the same things, the *nice* things you told me you like. We ain't so different, you and me. And we can have some good times together, alone. . . ." She thrust back her shoulders, brushed hair from her face, all the while back-stepping into the arch's gloom. "What do you say, huh? You and me? I can please you, honey. Please you like you never been pleased before. The Gypsy way, honey . . . the way I was trained."

His eyes danced with merriment. "I'm going to carve out your heart, bitch," he seethed. "You were sent to betray me."

"Betray you? Say, honey, you been talking to the wrong people."

"Fortunately for me, yes. But not for you. I did some checking, *honey*," the words rolled off his tongue like venom, "and found out the truth." He jabbed with the razor-tipped walking stick, amused as she flinched.

"No, no. You're wrong . . ."

"My contacts with the Gypsies are never wrong."

With the Gypsies! Samíah froze. So it was true after all! There was a spy in Wanko's camp! A traitor who had not only tipped off the Assassins as to her whereabouts, but now had exposed her to him!

As if reading her thoughts, the Dealer said, "Now I think you understand. One of your own, Samíah, one of your own."

He lunged and she screamed. From the balcony the Berber leaped. The Dealer spun around, but before he could stab him the Berber cracked his jaw with his fist. As he collapsed she saw Gideon come racing from the shadows. Samíah fainted before he could reach her.

 "YOU *BASTARD*! YOU SET ME UP!"

"Listen to me, Samíah. I—"

With glowering hate in her eyes she slapped him hard across the face. "You knew!" she cried. "You *knew*!"

Gideon grabbed her arm before she could hit him again. "Not for certain, no," he answered truthfully. "But we had to find out. One way or the other we had to be sure."

"So you used me as a guinea pig! Knowing all along that he might suspect. That he knew I wasn't who I pretended to be. He could have killed me—and you didn't try and stop it."

"You were never in danger, Samíah. I swear it to you. We would never have let him touch you. But we had to hold back and wait—at least until he gave himself away."

"You used me, Gideon!" She spat the words. "I trusted you, wanted to help—and you used me!" She was shaking now, tears flooding down her face.

"I didn't want to tell you sooner because I knew it would only frighten you more," he said. "But there was a double purpose in our seeking out the Dealer. Foremost we need to find out his contacts to whom he sold the brooch, but almost equally important—"

"To learn if there really is a Gypsy spy," hissed Samíah, finishing the thought. "So you decided to let me hang alone, without protection, just so you could bide your time, listening while he threatened me."

187

"Only because we needed to hear him confess it," assured Gideon. "Now we know, Samíah. There *is* a spy among us— and without your help we might never have found it out."

She wanted to spit in his face, somehow get back at him for this; but all she could do was to turn away from his pleading eyes, cry with the pain of it. For a while she had really started to like Gideon; respect him, have confidence in everything he told her. Now, though, it was plain that he was exactly like the others, all the others. Hardly different and no better than those he opposed. To them and to him her life was cheap; worthless once her purpose had been satisfied.

"Please, Samíah, won't you believe me?" He reached out to touch her but then thought better of it and pulled back his hand.

"I hate you!" she seethed. "Get out of my sight!" She flared at him with inflamed eyes, desperately trying not to let him see her cry.

Gideon looked lamely over to Wanko. The king sat with folded arms, his face devoid of any emotion. Yana scowled and cradled the upset girl in her arms, letting her bury her head against her shoulder.

"You should not have done this," the queen told Gideon sharply. "Why didn't you tell her the truth from the beginning? The child has done her part; she has been more than faithful to you, and in return you willingly risk her life as though she were chattel."

"Are you against me, too, Yana? Surely you above all should understand why I acted as I did. Don't you see, telling her beforehand might have made it far worse for her, scared her enough to unwittingly betray herself—"

"Gideon is right," said the king evenly. "He only did what needed to be done."

The queen shot the king a harsh glance. "All men are fools," she pronounced with a lofty growl. She stroked Samíah's tumbled hair gently, saying, "There, there, child. It is all right. Sometimes a woman's fate is to be guided by the stupidity of men."

Gideon sagged his shoulders dejectedly. For once he could

not seem to find the proper words to explain himself. But then, how could he possibly explain to his friends that Samíah was far more important to him than they realized? And not because of her possible usefulness. From the very first moment he had seen the girl he had liked her instantly. She was spunky, brash, sure of herself, and as feisty a woman as he had ever known. It had hurt him greatly to be responsible for her becoming entangled in all of this. None of it should be her affair; she should be home now, safe and secure with her father—or with a husband to love and cherish her.

No, he could never admit any of these feelings to Wanko or Yana. They wouldn't understand. They would think he'd grown soft, become too involved—a dangerous affliction for one in his line of business.

As Samíah dried her eyes, Gideon turned as another figure emerged from between the curtains. It was Flacco, the Gypsy just come from the camp where the Dealer had been secretly taken. Flacco nodded to Gideon, then glanced around nervously, finally settling his gaze upon the king.

"Have you questioned him?" came the query.

The Gypsy nodded slowly. "So far he has admitted nothing. He is a sly one, this Dealer. Too clever for his own good." He would have spat had it not been for the presence of the women. "I think it is going to take a great deal of time."

"We don't have a great deal of time," said Gideon. "I must learn to whom he delivered the brooch."

Wanko, the picture of repose, examined the dirt beneath his fingernails. He seemed to settle into a comfortable introspection, watching as the evening shadows behind the curtain lengthened. When he looked up at the worried faces around him, he said simply, "He will talk. I promise it. He *will* talk."

"We have to hurry," said Gideon. "Four Fingers tells me that another Assassin daylight attack is imminent. We have to find out where and when—and prevent it."

The king stood up lazily; he pressed his hands against the taunt muscles in the small of his back, gritted his teeth. "Stay here with Samíah," he told Flacco. "I am returning to the camp."

"I'll go with you," said Gideon.

"Is it safe for Samíah to remain alone?" said Yana with concern. "The Dealer is perfidious. Who knows which of his contacts may have already been tipped off before the rendezvous?"

"She will be in no danger tonight," Flacco assured. "Me and Blinco Rascola'll guard her with our lives, you can be sure."

The promise of Wanko's number one lieutenant was enough to put Gideon at least temporarily at ease. Yana and the king quickly prepared to leave the city. Gideon lingered a moment and found the courage to face Samíah again. "This isn't going to take very long," he said. "When I return," and here he hesitated, "maybe we can straighten things out."

Samíah regarded him contemptuously. "There's little we have to discuss, Gideon. All I'm concerned with now is my father. Where is he? What have you done with him? He promised to be here."

"I had him brought to the campsite. But don't worry, he's safe."

She sneered, saying, "And I suppose I have your trusted word on that as well?"

Her words stung, she saw. Good. So much the better!

Gideon turned slowly and followed Wanko outside. Once again Samíah found herself alone to decide who her real friends were.

SAMÍAH'S HEAD BOBBED UP FROM THE PILLOW, HER eyes popping wide open. Sitting upright now, she shivered in the cool night air. Her heart was still bumping at the memory of the nightmare, as she stared out at the unfamiliar walls of her tiny room.

Only a dream, she muttered to herself. Only a dream. But the hauntings of her sleep left a vivid impression. Again she was being chased, cornered by dreaded Night Masters with no avenue of escape. She dug her hands deeply into the embroidered quilt wrapped across her lap. The thick curtains hung darkly over the shaded window. Too edgy to fall back asleep, she made to strike a match and light the wicker candle set beside the sleeping mat.

"Don't touch it!"

Samíah nearly jumped out of her skin at the voice. Suddenly before her there was a figure, an eerie disembodied spirit in the fancy of her imagination. "Who—who's there?" she gasped, reaching rapidly for the curved dagger Flacco had provided her.

"Aw, honey, I didn't mean to scare ya. . . ."

Samíah blinked; the shapely figure took solid form. "Rosa! What are you—How did you—"

The Gypsy girl threw back her head and grinned in darkness. "I figured that maybe you would appreciate a little company tonight, that's all."

Samíah scratched her head. "But you were supposed to be back at camp. Yana told me yesterday—"

"I was at camp," Rosa agreed, drawing closer and crouching beside the confused girl. She glanced around glumly, putting a finger to her lips. "Shhhh. Speak in whispers. I don't want them to hear me."

Listening, Samíah heard the squeak of boots nearby, the muffled sound of someone clearing his throat.

"That's Flacco," said Rosa. "And Blinko Rascola is covering the door outside."

"Then they don't know you're here?"

"Of course not. Think I want to have to face Wanko when they tell him about it?" She shuddered. "The king'll strap me to my wagon for sure. Only tonight he said to me, 'Rosa, I want you to stay put, hear? Not budge an inch from the wagon. It isn't safe anymore.'" There was amusement in her dark Romany eyes. "But what Wanko don't know ain't gonna hurt him, is it honey?"

Groggy, only now fully brought back to reality, Samíah mumbled, "No, I suppose not. But why did you come?"

The Gypsy girl laughed spryly, a devilish glint in her eyes that betrayed her adventurous pride. "Wanko ain't got no right to keep me locked up, honey, not when he knew your papa gave me a message."

Samíah stared wide-eyed. She grabbed Rosa's ruffled sleeve. "My father gave you a message, Rosa? For me? What did he say? Tell me! Is he all right? No one's hurt him have they? Did he sneak out of camp with you, and did—"

Rosa groaned. "So many questions at the same time! Honey, your tongue is faster than a Gypsy's. Take it slow, honey. I'll tell you everything." She looked around again. "Say, you got anything to drink? My mouth is parched." Samíah obediently directed the girl to where the pitcher and cup rested. Rosa poured herself a drink. "Ugh! Water. Ain't you got no wine?"

"I don't think so . . ."

"Doesn't matter. Don't bother yourself." She resumed her place beside her distraught friend, her fingers nervously toying with the frills of her shawl. "Listen, your papa—say, he's really a nice man. I was talking to him and he told me all about you." She chuckled. "*All* about you."

"Is he all right?"

"What? Oh, sure, honey, sure. Think Wanko'd treat him any different than you, huh? The king gave him the royal treatment, he did. An honored guest. Yea, him and his friend."

Samíah's eyes narrowed. "What friend?"

"You know. The one with the cat. The one from the village. Say, I don't mean to be rude or nothing, but folks sure are funny in that place your papa comes from." She slapped the side of her face. "What a weird fellow. Looks green, with ears pressed against the side of his head like, well anyway I suppose I shouldn't poke fun at your relatives."

"Rosa, have you been drinking 'gypsy poison'? I have no idea what you're talking about. What relative from the village?"

The Romany princess shrugged. "Oh, maybe you weren't there. Since you been with us, your father says someone came to stay with him in the house. This green guy in a turban and the whitest robes I ever seen. An' that cat! What a strange cat!"

"Never mind all that," Samíah pressed, thinking there would be plenty of time later to get all this straightened out. At least Papa was safe and well. That was all that really mattered.

"The message, Rosa. You said he gave you a message."

"Oh, that! Sure, honey. He said if I was going to see you, I should let you know that he understands now what's been going on. That you don't have to worry and that everything's gonna be fine cause his friend assured him this was the way things were meant to be."

Samíah shook her head slowly. What in the world was Rosa talking about? What in the world was Papa talking about? "Is that all, Rosa? Isn't there anything else?"

The girl thought for a minute. "No," she mused. "I don't think so. Just that everything is gonna be okay. Oh! He also said to say he'll be waiting for you at the camp. Says maybe he should explain it personally."

"You came all this way for that?"

"Well, partly. Listen, honey, I heard about what happened. How you played a role to get the Dealer to meet you and how he almost had you killed." She pulled a sour face. "Wanko figured you'd be okay by yourself, but he's only a man, and what do men know, huh? I thought that maybe you'd be frightened still and that if I came it would make things a little better, see what I mean? Us girls gotta stick together, don't we?"

Samíah had to smile at her friend's childlike presentation. Rosa had put her own life in jeopardy, risked walking the city after curfew—not to mention facing the wrath of Wanko once the king heard about it, as he surely would—just to come here now and keep her company so she wouldn't be so scared. It was an insane, totally dumb thing to do—but Samíah loved her for it. She squeezed the Gypsy girl's hand, saying, "Thank you for coming, Rosa. I have been frightened. Having you here makes everything seem all right again."

"Aw, honey; you don't have to get all sentimental about it. That's what friends is for, ain't it?"

"Sure, Rosa," she said, tears coming to her eyes and adding in the Gypsy vernacular, "That's what friends is for."

"Still, it ain't right. I mean it was a nerve to put you in so much danger without even knowing about it. Yana told me the whole story. Says it'll serve Gideon right if you ain't never gonna speak to him again. The louse." She balled her hands into fists. "If that was me, would I make him pay!"

"You mean get even?"

"Sure. What's he think us girls are, anyway? I'd do plenty more than just not speak to him."

Samíah smiled; how she would have liked to even the score with the clever secret agent! Bring him down a notch or two. "But how, Rosa," she said ruefully. "Gideon doesn't even know I exist—until he needs me for some dirty work. Other than that, I'm less than nothing to him."

Rosa stared questioningly at her companion. "Honey, you gotta be kidding."

"Why? Have I ever been anything more than a pain to him? A pest who's always getting in his way, fouling up his little plots and schemes. No, Rosa," she sighed as she answered her own question. "Gideon would probably be delighted to see me out of his hair. I'm just a nuisance."

The Gypsy, to her amazement, could see that Samíah meant everything she was saying. "You got the wrong impression, honey. Listen to me; I mean, don't you know, can't you tell?"

"Tell what?"

With a loud groan, Rosa said, "Oh honey, I seen it myself. And Yana, she seen it a long, long time ago when he first brought you to her. Anybody with eyes in her head can tell, for heavens sake! Don't tell me you still don't know?"

Samíah wrapped her arms around her knees. "I wish I understood what you're talking about," she said haughtily, brushing back her long hair. "What is it that Yana's seen? That you've seen?"

Clearly befuddled at the blindness of *gadjos*, Rosa shook her head in a blend of amusement and pity. Then she faced Samíah evenly. "Hey, I'm gonna say this once so there won't be any misunderstanding, okay? The guy is crazy about you."

Samíah laughed.

"Hey, I mean it," protested the Romany girl. "Sure, maybe he don't know it himself yet—men are like that sometimes—but I ain't the one that's blind. I seen the way he stiffens whenever you're around, how his eyes, they don't focus on anything going on but you. He cares for you, honey. Really cares."

"Ridiculous." The very thought of what Rosa was saying was absurd. Gideon caring for her, ha! That was a joke indeed. Nothing but ice water ran through his veins, she was sure. His profession was his entire life, stalking the streets night after night after night in search of who-knew-what. Why, the whole world could rot or crumble around him and he wouldn't give a tinker's damn. Not Gideon, not as long as he could manipulate both friends and enemies to get what he wanted.

"You're wrong, Rosa," she said at last. "Gideon is already wed to his work. Deceit and double-dealings, these are the only things he worships. You and me and the others are only pawns in his little games. I see that now—even though I'll admit that for a while I was as fooled as the rest. Maybe one day you'll discover all this for yourself."

Rosa could see the fires burning in her eyes, the swell of

her breasts beneath her night clothes as she spat out the words. "You talk like you hate him, honey."

Samíah smiled without humor. "I do," she hissed. But the Gypsy did not seem to take her seriously. With that remark Rosa tilted her face toward the ceiling and soundlessly clapped her hands. "I knew it!" she cried laughingly. "Yana was right all along. Boy, you still gotta give the old lady credit all right. She knew from the beginning!"

"I fail to see the humor in this, Rosa. What did the queen know all along?"

With a grin, Rosa said, "About you, honey. About Gideon, too." She looked at Samíah askance. "So now you are telling me you hate him, and maybe you can't stand the sight of him, huh? Well, let me tell you I don't need no tarot cards to read you, honey. Oh, you can lie about it all you want, to me and maybe even to yourself for a little while, but deep, deep down inside you know it, too."

"Know what?"

"That between a man and a woman hate and love are the same thing."

Samíah stared at the vibrant, earthy girl with a strong measure of shock. "You're crazy," she spluttered. "Me—love *him*? That worm! That snake in the grass, that viper? Why, he's the lowest thing I ever met!"

"Tut tut, honey. It ain't me you gotta convince." She winked bawdily with a girlish giggle, leaned in slightly closer. "You know your papa he seems to suspect the same thing also. But listen; your secret's safe with me. I give my oath as a Gypsy. You do the right thing, honey, make the oaf squirm and moan a little for what he's put you through. Allah above knows he deserves it. *Men!*"

Samíah tried to protest, to explain, to convince Rosa that she certainly did not intend such a lovers' ploy. The girl, though, did not seem to hear or care about her objections. All she did was to continue her little smile of two friends sharing the same secret of the heart. Samíah saw it was a losing battle.

She propped up her pillows and leaned back fuming. What was it in her life that everyone was trying to match her up?

First Papa, now Rosa and Yana and lord knew who else. She didn't need a husband by God, and if she did—which she. didn't—it certainly would not be a pig-headed two-faced arrogant rat like Gideon! No, sir. She was too smart, too independent, too *free*.

Then she smiled. Ah, but wouldn't it be great if she could pay him back for the indignity he'd heaped upon her. . . .

"Anyway, honey," Rosa was saying as she snapped out of her musings, "you don't gotta think about it for a while. At least not until everything is over." The Gypsy said that with an uncharacteristic tone of seriousness.

"What do you mean?"

Rosa looked away from her glare. "Sometimes I got a big mouth, honey, saying things I shouldn't. Forget it."

Samíah held her breath. "You know something, don't you?" Her hand lifted the Gypsy's chin, forced her to look at her. "What is it? Have they made the Dealer talk? Tell me Rosa! Please, I want to know!"

"Aw, honey, I shouldn't be saying any of this. Wanko's gonna be mad enough as it is. . . ." She sighed, unable to avoid Samíah's intense stare. "Aw, what the hell. Okay. I overheard Gideon talking with your father in the king's tent. I think there's big trouble ahead. Big trouble. He says that Habib, he better lay low for a while, not go home, not even go to work, keep himself conveniently missing."

"Is Papa in danger?"

The Gypsy's eyes were suddenly dull and worry filled. "Maybe. Maybe we all are. The Dealer, he's a cunning one, all right. He knows much more than he's telling that's for sure. But Wanko got him to admit that the attack against the city is closer than any of us dreamed. Now Gideon, he's gotta risk his life again—and this time the odds ain't with him."

Samíah's heart almost stopped with her gasp.

"Likely as not in a day or two, Gideon ain't gonna be no more." She grimaced. "Not once he tangles with the messiah. . ."

The news hit her like a strike of lightning. So the Dealer did talk! And Gideon was taking it upon himself to reach the source of Assassin power. "Has he learned the messiah's identity, Rosa?"

"Naw, only the location of—say," Here she stared at her friend. "I thought you couldn't care less about him. Didn't you just tell me he was a worm? The lowest thing that maybe you ever saw on the earth?"

"Yes, but—" Her face turned crimson.

Rosa laughed. "Okay, okay. Anyway, there really isn't much more I can tell you. Only that sometime before dawn Gideon's going to leave camp. Yeah, him and your papa, too, I think."

"Papa? Papa's going with Gideon? But why, Rosa? What has my father got to do with any of this?"

"Beats me, honey," she answered with a shrug. "But your papa and Gideon are up to something maybe. Even the green guy is tagging along. That's why your papa he gave me the message for you not to be concerned."

Samíah ground her teeth. What was going on? What knowledge or secret did Papa possess that now he, too, had been dragged into Gideon's little game of cat and mouse? Her mind raced with apprehension. Something sinister was up, she knew. Something that perhaps she should be a part of. But instead of learning what it was she was stuck here like a helpless fool with Flacco and Blinco Rascola acting as her jailors. "Isn't there anything else you can tell me?" she asked.

"Nothing that seemed to make much sense, honey. But your papa, he was mighty disappointed to learn that you wouldn't be at camp tonight. Like I said, that's why he gave me the message."

Samíah bit her lip tensely. Events were beginning to quicken now, the mystery unfolding before her. "Oh Rosa, I don't want to be locked up like this. I'm the one that's involved, not Papa. If Gideon is in danger and really needs help then it should be me beside him, not my father."

The Gypsy patted her hand consolingly. "I know how you feel, honey. But I suppose..." She stopped speaking, tilted her head and stared wonderingly out into the darkness. "Say, what if..." She shook her head. "Naw, it'd probably never work. But maybe, just maybe..."

"What's in your mind, Rosa?"

"You really wanna get out of here, honey? Get back to camp, see your papa and maybe Gideon, too?"

"I'd give anything, yes! But how?" She peered gloomily around at the curtained walls.

"Maybe I can help." Her fingertips brushed Samíah's perspiring palm. "Wanko, he ain't gonna like it none. Gideon, either. But what the hell. Maybe they ain't never going to find out—at least not until it's too late."

Samíah lifted her brows in speculation. "What are you cooking up?"

Rosa grinned. "A little womanly revenge, that's all. Listen honey, you think that maybe you can slip by the soldiers even though it's curfew? Act like a Gypsy, think like a Gypsy? Cause if they catch you, you've had it."

"You mean now?"

"Right now. You think you can do that?"

"I . . . think so. Why?"

Rosa laughed with luster in her eyes. "Hey, sure you can, honey. I taught you everything, right? You can be back at camp in less than an hour." She smiled a decidedly feline smile. "Listen, honey, and listen carefully. You and me we ain't so unalike, huh? Same height, same build almost, same age. What if I stay here in your place, give you my clothes? Hey, already we can pass as sisters, no? In the dark no one would be able to tell us apart, certainly not these cretins Flacco and Blinco Rascola. All I have to do is put on your night clothes, wrap myself in the blankets and snore a little."

"And if Flacco comes inside the room for a closer inspection?"

Rosa thought fast. "Give me your earrings, honey." Samíah started to unhook them reluctantly. "You been wearing these ever since the day I lent them to you," Rosa went on. "They've become almost your trademark. With these," she took them in her hand merrily, "ain't nobody gonna think I'm anyone but you."

"It sounds awfully risky," whispered Samíah.

"You wanna see your papa or not?"

"You would really do all this for me?"

"Us girls gotta stick together. What about it?"

It was an offer Samíah couldn't possibly refuse. Without speaking both women began to take off their clothes and pass them to the other. Samíah buttoned the flaming scarlet blouse, dutifully wrapped the flaring black skirt around her waist, looped Rosa's belt and tied the bandana around her head. A touch of rouge and eye makeup made the transition almost complete.

"How do I look?" she asked, slipping into Rosa's comfortable shoes.

"Priceless, honey. Priceless. Take it from me." The Gypsy leaned across the sleeping mat and curled up with the blanket around her. The earrings gleamed as Samíah unpinned her hair. Leaning beside Rosa, she whispered, "Now tell me how to get out."

Rosa winked again. "No problem, honey. No problem." And she whispered into Samíah's ear the exact way to elude her guards. Samíah listened and grinned, sneaked to the far window, pushed aside the curtains and peered into the deserted street. When Blinco Rascola turned his back and marched from the doorway she eased herself out, not hearing as Rosa spryly called, "Good luck!"

PANTING, STUMBLING, SAMÍAH MADE HER WAY
along the darkened boulevard, hugging the tree
walks, darting in and out of the shadows. On either
side the stoic towers and crenellated walls surged high into the
starry night. Mindful of the sentries whose watchful eyes even
now would be scouring the streets and nearby countryside for
offenders, she summoned her courage and broke for the gate.
Shoot to kill was the order of the night. Marrakesh was under
siege—and anyone caught after curfew without a pass would
pay with his life.

Her shoes grated against the worn stone. She bolted to
freedom without daring to breathe. Ahead, unfriendly stars cast
a silvery pall; she cleared the gate and dashed for the covering
protection of the swaying palms and into the darkness of the
groves where, gasping for air, she clutched her arms and stood
silently waiting. In the still grimness of midnight her searching
eyes could not find the path leading to the meadow and the
Gypsy camp. There were no glows of Gypsy fires to beacon
her way, no sounds of festive laughter or gaiety to direct her.
An unusual solitude seemed to have captured everything, with
only the buzzing of insects and the hoots of an owl to break
the strange silence.

Samíah rested with her back against the trunk of a great
palm and glanced back in the direction of the gate. She could
see nothing except for the gaping black hole and the towers

above from which pinpricks of torchlight dully glimmered. She grew uneasy as the wind shifted and rustled through the boughs.

At times during her journey from the Casbah she had been sure she was being followed. Unseen eyes had seemed to bore straight through her, a constant presence that followed through every one of the dark streets and alleys, pausing when she paused, running when she ran, breathing when she breathed. Yet each time she had turned to see, there had been nothing there, only shadows and more shadows crawling along the endlessly winding byways. But still she felt the presence of those eyes—Mocking and scorning eyes . . .

She moved out from the palms. Waiting and watching would only make it worse, she knew. If there was some interloper about, it would be here among the groves that he would make himself known, here in the eerie quietude where she could scream as loudly as she was able but still no one would hear.

Breaking into a steady trot, she crossed from the palms to the rows of mangroves and acacias, taking deep breaths as she charted her course. The ground was soft and furrowed beneath her feet, the scent of plum and apricot trees steadily stronger as she made her way up the slope of the first hillock. The path stretched before her, a series of graduated hills leading to the meadow. A relatively short walk, peaceful and serene in daylight, but one which at night left her filled with dread and foreboding.

Every few seconds she glanced back over her shoulder. As always there was no sign of her hunter. From the position of the half moon she judged the lateness of the hour. By this time all the Gypsies would be asleep—except of course for Yana who never slept and Gideon who rarely seemed to, either. Since the attack of the Night Masters the king had tripled his guard along the campsite's perimeters. Thus slipping into her father's tent unnoticed was going to harbor risks of its own. It was one thing to maneuver from sight of patrolling sultan's soldiers, she knew—Rosa had taught her how to achieve that easily— and quite another to be able to sneak past fellow Gypsies.

Fellow Gypsies! Samiah had to grudgingly smile at the

thought. By Allah, she was already beginning to think of herself as one of them!

The path weaved and coiled downward from the crest. One last time she peered behind to the leafy obstacles of the thick-rooted trees motionless across the contours of the groves. Dense foliage permitted only the faintest rays of star- and moonlight to show the way she had come. Again there was nothing. No sight of the unknown stranger.

It's all in your imagination, she assured herself. *You're not being followed. If you were, he would have shown himself already, struck at you before you made it to the path.*

A hulking silhouette appeared and vanished between two great trunks. Samíah stifled a scream. Then she ran down the slope as fast as she could, twisting her ankle as she stepped into a rut, sucking in air and biting her lip to blunt the sting. She limped in pain through the wilderness, fighting back tears, cursing herself for her accident. Scudding clouds passed before the moon and temporarily blocked the only light. Samíah fled blindly now, fighting the growing sense of panic. Somewhere behind she heard the snap of a twig, the quickening pace of heavy footsteps.

Dread overtook her. Who was behind? There was only one answer: Assassins. Combing the midnight streets of Marrakesh, they had seen her as she escaped from Yana's quarters.

She tripped over a rock and came tumbling to the ground. Instinctively her hand went for her knife. It wasn't there. Cursing, she remembered leaving it in the room for Rosa. The footsteps were louder now, closer, and she was unable to defend herself. The hulking silhouette of the stranger appeared grimly outlined between the trees. She fought to her knees, crawled in the darkness. The figure stopped and searched, unable to see as she huddled beside the gnarling roots of a huge oak. He stepped away a few paces in one direction, then in the other. Samíah watched his every move, never letting her eyes stray. Her shallow breathing only increased the fearful pounding of her heart, so loud she was mystified why he couldn't hear the sound, the telltale giveaway of her presence. If only she had a weapon! Something, anything, with which to defend herself.

He changed direction and now moved directly toward her. Her hand shot out and groped over the ground in search of a stick or a rock, anything at all. Gravel sifted through her fingers; mindlessly she tugged at a plant and uprooted it.

The stranger stood stock still and glared. It was all Samíah could to to keep from screaming in panic. Suddenly his voice cracked the still air, a loud whisper.

"Rosa! Rosa where are you?"

Goose bumps crawled up Samíah's arms and neck. *Rosa?* He was calling for the Gypsy girl. But why? How?

"Don't try and hide from me, girl! It's me! It's safe. Don't worry. Why did you run?"

Samíah shuddered. The clouds briefly passed overhead, and the moon came back into view, light slanting softly among the boughs. She gasped when she saw him. It was a soldier, an officer of the sultan's guard, his crimson sash and insignia unmistakable. She saw his face, heard him call for the Gypsy again. A note of vague familiarity jarred something in her memory, something about his face, his eyes, the sound of his voice.

And then she knew. It was the captain of the guard—the soldier on duty that day in the market, the day of the abduction. The captain who hadn't believed her story, who told her to go home and forget everything she saw.

But what was he doing here now? Why was he following her? But of course he wasn't following *her*, he was following Rosa, or at least he thought he was. For wasn't she wearing the Gypsy girl's clothes?

"I know you're here somewhere," came the anxious voice. "Please, Rosa, this isn't a time for games. I've been worried about you for days. When you didn't come to the arch I slipped away from the barracks and watched Yana's rooms." Clouds covered the moon again, and she could no longer see his face. "Rosa, why are you doing this to me? You know how dangerous it was to sneak around the city at night like that. I saw you slip from the window; I had to follow you."

Samíah's mind reeled with confusion. Rosa and the captain? What connection could she and the young soldier possibly have? She shook her head in wonder as the truth came before her. Lovers! They were secret lovers. But Rosa was her friend, perhaps her best friend now, why hadn't she confided in her? Or was she afraid that breathing a word might put her in some trouble?

A flicker of starlight gleamed. The captain saw her. She had barely moved her head above the twisting root but he had seen. With one hand resting easily on the hilt of his scimitar, he said, "It's all right to come out. I promise it is." There was a distinct measure of relief in his tone.

Shaking, Samíah didn't know what to do. Should she try and run again? No, there was no point in that. Not now. He would follow and catch her, perhaps finding himself spotted in the process by Wanko's keen-eyed sentries, thus placing both of them in peril. So she did the only thing she could: got up slowly, and hoped for the best.

He sighed deeply at the sight of her. "Oh, Rosa, how I've worried about you."

Samíah stood awkwardly in the shadows; she straightened her skirt, brushed fallen leaves from her blouse. There was caring and concern in his deeply set eyes, she saw as he looked at her, so far still not aware she was an imposter.

"So you thought I wouldn't find you, eh?" he was saying with a foolish grin. "Thought I wouldn't search hard enough to find you? Oh, the irony of fate! Did you believe I loved you so little? That when last we met I'd listen when you warned me to stay away?" He pounded a fist against his heart. "A thousand times I would die for you, Rosa. A thousand times!"

Samíah, in a quandary, shook her head. "No, you don't understand. . . ."

"Understand?" His brows knit. "What more is there to understand, my beloved? Would that I were a poet, a man of words and emotion rather than what I am. Come," he held out his hand, "take me now to your father. Let me proclaim my love. Yes, let the king cut out my heart and my tongue if that be his wish. But never, *never*, shall we be parted again. This I have vowed to Allah—and may He be my judge."

Abruptly he pulled her to him before Samíah could protest.

His lips were upon hers, his embrace nearly crushing the life out of her in his passion. She squirmed and wrenched herself free. The bold captain stared in perplexity. The cloud cover passed again, and now his look of hurt turned instantly into one of shock and horror. "You... you're not Rosa!" he stammered.

"No, I'm not."

Flabbergasted, he stepped back a pace. His eyes narrowed; his mouth twitched. The perfume was the same, the clothes were hers, right down to her shoes and trinkets adorning her arms and wrists. Yes, this imposter even did resemble his beloved Gypsy greatly, he conceded. But it wasn't her!

"Where's Rosa?" he rasped, reaching for his weapon. "What have you done with her?"

"Hey, listen, I haven't done anything with her. She—"

"Then why are you dressed in her clothing? Speak!"

"I would if you'd only give me a chance!" She glanced around furtively, frightened that someone might overhear their voices. "Rosa's well, I promise you. Safe, back at Yana's. These clothes are hers, yes. Rosa lent them to me...."

"Then it wasn't her I saw slip from the window?"

"No. It was me."

A curious look came over his face; he scratched his head as if trying to stir some distant memory. "Who... who are you?" he muttered. "Haven't I seen you somewhere before?"

"Once, yes. In the marketplace. A few weeks and a thousand years ago."

He thought long and hard for a moment, then snapped his fingers. "Of course! You're the dustman's daughter! The girl who claimed she saw the abduction! What's your name—"

"Samíah."

"Yes, Samíah!" Then his features darkened. "What were you doing in the Casbah?" he demanded. "You're not a Gypsy. Why were you with the queen? And why were you sneaking around the city like that, breaking curfew?"

Samíah shook her head at his questions. "Listen, I haven't time to explain now. I have to reach Wanko's camp immediately. Find Gid—find my friends. Now, please excuse me, there isn't time."

She turned to leave, and he grabbed her by the arm. "Just a minute! You've broken the law, Samíah daughter of Habib. I suppose you realize that for yourself." He stood erect, saluted smartly. "In the name of the sultan I order you to come with me for questioning." His hand returned to his scimitar. "Follow me."

She groaned in anguish. "Look, captain, I can't come with you now, understand? I just told you, I *must* reach Wanko's camp. It's too dangerous to go back now."

"Dangerous, is it? What are you hiding from me, girl? Out with it! Who are these friends you must see at such hour?" He cocked his head to the side and gazed with speculative eyes. "Or are you working secretly for them?"

"Them?" she said in puzzlement.

"The Assassins."

Samíah put both her hands to her hair and sighed. The soldier's exuberance in his duty had led his mind to unbelievable fancy. She, whose very life had been in danger for so long, who had nearly been killed twice by the Defilers, was now accused of being one of them!

"You don't know how wrong you are," she told him.

"Am I? Then why are you trembling? What have you got to hide?" His face grew stern and unyielding. "You can come with me quietly, daughter of Habib, or you can come screaming. Either way, it's my duty to take you back. The choice of how is up to you."

She took a single step backward, her ankle still sore and hurting. Should she try and make a break for it, she wondered, run as fast as she could, go yelling into Wanko's camp and alert the sentries? What good would that do, though? Likely as not the keen-eyed Gypsy guards would spot the soldier and cut him down before he had a chance to speak. This naive but innocent soldier's blood would then be on her hands—and Rosa's undying hatred.

"You have this all wrong," she said, pleading her cause. "I haven't done anything wrong, committed any crime."

"Tell that to the magistrate. All I know is that I saw you break curfew, dressed in someone else's clothes, sneaking away from the city like a common thief."

"Is that what you think?"

"Maybe Rosa will have something else to add. Maybe she didn't *lend* you those clothes after all." He hissed as he spoke, wondering if perhaps this girl was more cunning than she seemed. "If one hair on Rosa's head has been injured," he warned, "I'll take you personally and—"

Samíah tried to run. His quick reflexes pushed her to the ground. "You bloody fool!" she cried as he grabbed her by the arms and tried to haul her back to her feet. "At least hear me out!" she begged. "You don't know what you're doing! Do you want to get us all killed—Rosa included? Let me go, I tell you. Let me go!"

"So now you're threatening Rosa as well! Not this time, daughter of Habib. This time you've got too many questions to answer for."

Struggling to break loose from the overzealous soldier, she kicked wildly; the toe of her shoe caught him in the groin and as he staggered back in pain she jumped up, free of his grasp. As Samíah turned to flee he lurched, spun her around, sent her tumbling again. She squirmed to her knees; he drew back his fist ready to knock her into unconscious submission.

"Leave her alone, captain!"

The soldier spun in the direction of the sudden, unexpected voice. He whipped his scimitar from its scabbard with a single motion and clutched it tightly, glaring into the darkness. The blade gleamed in faint moonlight.

A tall figure emerged from among the trees behind. Silvery light fell upon his features as he stepped into the open. Both the girl and the captain gasped. It was Gideon.

"You can let her go," he said quietly. "She's no danger to you."

At first the captain wavered, unsure; then, as recognition fully dawned, he dropped his sword to the ground, his mouth hanging limply open. He started to speak, but Gideon gestured for him to hold his silence.

"Thank Allah you came in time," panted Samíah while Gideon helped her to her feet. "This fool wanted to arrest me and drag me back to the city." He stared at her coldly, angered she had disobeyed orders and left Yana's quarters.

"She broke curfew," said the captain.

"And you broke your own orders. Why aren't you on duty in the streets?"

Samíah looked at the soldier with a smile of satisfaction as he stumbled for an answer.

Gideon scowled. "Never mind. Both of you have behaved very stupidly." He looked harshly at the girl. "You'd better have a good explanation for leaving the *ofisa*," he said.

The captain scratched his head in perplexity. "You know this woman, then?"

"She's, er, one of us," he replied. "Captain Enos, this is Samíah, daughter of Habib the dustman."

"We've already met."

"You know this soldier?" asked the girl startled.

Again the captain wanted to say something, and again Gideon gestured for him to keep quiet. "Certainly I do. Captain Enos is one of our most loyal and trustworthy officers." Captain Enos grinned and bowed slightly.

Samíah rubbed at her bruised wrists. "You'd never have thought we were on the same side," she grumbled.

"I think you'd both better start doing a lot of explaining, though. Now, why are you here?"

Samíah and the captain started to speak at the same time, flinging charges and countercharges at each other. Gideon groaned in consternation. The appearance of the captain and the unexpected connection between him and Rosa had served to add another complication, he saw as the truth unfolded. Only as yet he didn't realize how much.

 THE DEFORMED BEGGAR WALKED CROOKEDLY. CUP in hand, his twisted arm and bent fingers kept close at his side, he wandered seemingly aimlessly out of the alley and toward the end of the dark street. His face seemed as deformed as his body; blotched and severely pock-marked, as if as a child he had suffered with the plague. His eyes blinked uncontrollably, and his mouth twitched in spasms. When the squad of turbaned sultan's soldiers passed, his arm jerked out, the cup with its pitiful few copper coins jingling as he thrust it in their faces.

"Alms for the love of God," he begged in a voice so broken that the words were barely distinguishable. "Alms."

"You've been told to get off the streets after curfew," one of the soldiers told him curtly. "Go home before we have you arrested."

The squad commander took his companion by the elbow and nudged him away. "This one is harmless," he said, not bothering to look at the pathetic man standing bent and in tatters before him. "His mind is as deranged as his body is broken. Besides, he has no home to go to. He sleeps in alleys and doorways. Isn't that right, old man?"

The deformed beggar grinned toothlessly at the soldiers. He nodded, but no one seemed certain whether he really had understood what had been said or not.

"He still shouldn't be in the street after dark," said the second trooper.

"He can't hurt anyone. Look at him. Poor soul." The commander searched his pocket for a coin and dropped it into the cup. "Find yourself something to eat, old man. A doorway to sleep in. You won't find many more soldiers so understanding."

The beggar bowed in his fashion, the structure of his backbone too rigid for him to properly bend. He stared into empty space as the commander led his patrol away in the direction of another lonely and deserted street. When they were gone the beggar shuffled slowly towards the crumbling walls of the Casbah.

Samíah, cradled in the nook of the low wall between the two buildings opposite, watched the scene unfold in fascination. Beside her, Gideon huddled in silence. The deformed beggar was grinning now, and with total amazement Samíah looked on as he slowly began to straighten. The hunch vanished, the stiffened, useless arm lifted and the crooked fingers uncurled. The shuffle remained until he had crossed the street, but then his legs seemed to firm, the joints bending normally at the knees. Even his face changed; the mouth ceased its twitch, the eyes no longer blinked. It was a scary sight, and she shivered. The beggar, the one she had recognized from the abduction in the market and then later had seen whispering beneath the balcony with Gideon, was no longer deformed.

He approached the low wall and stopped. Both Gideon and the girl stood. Still hidden by shadow, the beggar opened his mouth and proceeed to pull off the black putty covering his teeth. Then, while Samíah's eyes grew wide, he started to peel off the blotchy flesh, layer by layer. Removed, too, were the false brows, pocks, and scars that had covered his face, the theatrical makeup that had sunken his jowls and eyes. With a rag from his back pocket he cleaned himself of the dark smears which had added to his overall ghastly appearance. The disguise was removed; Samíah found herself looking at a completely different individual, mellow-faced, clean-shaven, unwrinkled despite his middle years. The face of a man she had seen a hundred times before since as long as she could remember. A

211

man who had passed her street and her house once every week with the regularity of a clock. A man whom her father referred to as a friend. The face of—the rag man.

"You!" gasped the girl.

He smiled fully. "Good to see you again, Samíah. I hear you've been getting yourself into trouble again."

She was lost for words. Her eyes saw, but her mind still couldn't quite accept.

"Don't seem so shocked," he said. "Spying is still considered an honorable vocation."

"All these years, since I was a child, selling you my rags and other junk, all these years, and I never *dreamed*..."

"Ah, but if you had then I wouldn't have been doing my job very well, would I?"

"So you're not really a rag man after all."

His laugh was quite jovial. "Ah, but you see I am. Yes, and a beggar at times as well. I am many things."

"A master of disguises," Gideon interjected. "Our sultan's most reliable agent among the people."

"Do you recall the night after you saw me with Gideon?" he asked, a disturbing twinkle now in his eyes. Samíah nodded that she remembered very well indeed. "And when you followed him inside the sacred ground of the tomb? Then know that I was there also. Observing your every move."

"But you couldn't have," protested the girl. "The tomb is holy ground—forbidden to all!"

"All, save members of the sect, Samíah. You see, I am also a Karshi. A keeper of our holy place. It was only because I was present to prevent it that other guardians did not slit your throat for trespassing."

Samíah felt her face drain of blood; for a moment she was about to totter and pass out. Gideon's arm around her propped her up as she recalled her trek through the forboding sacred grounds, the sinister feelings and dread she'd felt in the far chamber, feelings of being watched...

"I received your message to meet me here only an hour ago," Gideon said, changing the drift of the conversation. "You caught me barely in time."

The spy smiled. "Then the Dealer has informed on his friends?"

"Only enough to learn the location of his contacts. Had it not been for that I would have been on my way to it now."

The master of disguises frowned with the news. "I fear then you must take another detour in your journey." He glanced to Samíah, then back to Gideon.

"What's wrong, my friend?" said Gideon.

"The *ofisa* of the queen has been . . . violated."

Yana's quarters! thought Samíah. "Rosa—has anything happened to Rosa?"

The spy's features remained grim. "Perhaps you had both better come and see for yourselves."

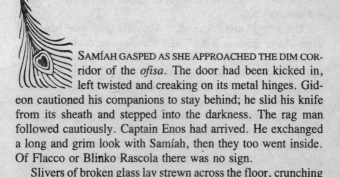

SAMÍAH GASPED AS SHE APPROACHED THE DIM CORridor of the *ofisa*. The door had been kicked in, left twisted and creaking on its metal hinges. Gideon cautioned his companions to stay behind; he slid his knife from its sheath and stepped into the darkness. The rag man followed cautiously. Captain Enos had arrived. He exchanged a long and grim look with Samíah, then they too went inside. Of Flacco or Blinko Rascola there was no sign.

Slivers of broken glass lay strewn across the floor, crunching beneath their soft footsteps. The curtained main chamber was a shambles, the heavy curtains pulled from the walls and thrown randomly about; Yana's potions were smashed, along with her lamps and incense burners. Tarot cards were scattered every-where.

"Look," whispered the soldier. He pointed to the forced-open window. Samíah grimaced at the twisted shutters, the soft whine of wind as it whistled through the mangled slats.

With a hand to her mouth she entered the sleeping quarter and peered into the shadows. There was Gideon, rigid, the knife still in his hand and his expression turned to stone. He stood over the sleeping mat—Samíah's sleeping mat—fixing his gaze on the torn blanket. Nearby, the feathered pillows lay ripped and gutted, the work of quick flashing daggers in the dark.

"She must have given them a hell of a fight," muttered the rag man.

Gideon nodded.

Samíah peered across the room with growing trepidation. "Oh, God. What have they done with Rosa?"

"And Flacco and Blinco Rascola," added the secret agent.

"The Defilers must have tread most silently to have caught them all by surprise," the rag man said. "It was exactly like this when I first arrived. No sign of anyone. The enemy knew exactly what they were after."

Gideon regarded the master of disguises coldly. "Night Masters always do."

"But what?" cried Samíah. "What did they want here? Of what use to them is Rosa?" Her companions made no reply. Samíah's lip began to tremble as the truth dawned. "God's mercy, it was me they were after, wasn't it? Me. And they thought..." She looked to the mat, filled with fear, and torment. "Rosa—they thought Rosa was me!" Tears flooded her eyes. "What have I done? Oh God, forgive me! It's my fault, it's all my fault. I let Rosa change clothes with me like that, allowed her to pass herself as me—and all the time they were waiting!" She sobbed as Gideon put his arms around her.

"It's not your fault," he said.

Samíah shook her head. "It is! I wanted to see Papa; Rosa knew how desperately, so she changed places, took my iden-tity...."

"As you took hers," Gideon said as the captain looked on with shock.

"But she did it because of me! As a friend; she said it was the only way I could get back to camp. She said it would be all right, that no one would ever know." She put her hands to her eyes and wept in grief. "And now they have her—thinking her to be me. It *is* my fault, Gideon. It is!"

"Listen to me, girl," Gideon said, taking her by the hands and forcing her look at him. "Rosa knew exactly what she was doing."

"But how could she? How could anyone have expected—"

"She *knew*, Samíah."

The conviction in his voice left her puzzled and troubled. With watery eyes she stared at the secret agent.

"The blame isn't yours," he told her. "It's mine."

"What are you talking about?"

Gideon heaved a sigh, glanced to the rag man. The rag man's eyes soundlessly told Gideon to tell her everything.

"Listen to me, Samíah. Rosa didn't come here tonight because of a message from your father." Samíah stifled a gasp. "No, she was sent here on purpose—by me. To play a role and do exactly as she did. We wanted her to be you tonight, Samíah."

For a moment Samíah couldn't speak, couldn't find words to erase the terrible sinking feeling rising from deep inside.

"Rosa lied to you," Gideon went on. "She did her job and did it well. What happened here is evidence enough."

"You tricked me again! Used me again!"

"No, Samíah. Kept you safe from harm. Safe from the Assassins."

"And what about Rosa? Is she safe now? Or doesn't her life count for anything, either? Only another chattel for your little game? Her death is on your hands, Gideon—your hands!"

The thought of the Gypsy girl lying dead somewhere sent the lovestruck captain into a rage he couldn't control. Something was going on here, something he didn't understand or comprehend. All he knew was that his beloved was gone— and Gideon was the man responsible.

"Gideon, look out!" called the rag man.

The secret agent spun around, knife drawn as the enraged captain lunged and made to draw his sword. Before he could whip blade from scabbard the rag man pounced from behind and with the side of his hand delivered a nerve-shattering chop to the soldier's neck. Captain Enos staggered and tumbled to the ground.

"I'll kill you, Gideon!" he vowed, groveling in pain as the rag man hovered over him. "If Rosa's been harmed I'll kill you with my bare hands!"

"Now listen to me, all of you!" snapped Gideon. "Rosa's not dead. She's been taken captive, but she's not dead!"

There were tears in Captain Enos' eyes. "I don't believe you. How do you know? How can you be sure?"

"Because they think that she's Samíah, and they'll keep her safe and well until she gives them the information they want!"

"But she doesn't know anything," cried Samíah. "You've sent an innocent girl to be slaughtered. Why, Gideon, why? Why did you do it?"

"To catch the spy." His voice returned to a soft tone. He was met with blank faces. "Rosa volunteered for this gambit," he went on. "She knew the risks as well as anyone. That's why it was imperative for her to reach Yana's quarters unnoticed, vital that she manage to get inside the *ofisa* without being spotted by anyone." He stressed the word. "Not even Flacco or Blinco Rascola. Even they had to believe that it was you inside this chamber, sleeping."

"Are you telling me that Rosa knew all along the Assassins were going to come?"

Gideon met her puzzled eyes coldly. "That is exactly what I'm saying. She knew they would come for her. So did I, and so did Wanko."

Samíah stood dumbfounded, shaking her head, tousled tendrils dancing before her eyes. "No, Gideon. She couldn't. How could anyone have anticipated? How could...?" She cut off her thought mid-sentence, feeling a sudden chill. "Unless..."

"Unless our enemies had been forewarned of your presence. And they were, Samíah—by the Gypsy traitor."

"No, no! You're lying!"

"It was no secret, Samíah. You must believe that. We knew they would come, but this time we were determined to prevent it, prevent it in a way that would expose the traitor for once and for all."

Samíah swallowed, sick in the pit of her stomach. "So you had Rosa concoct this whole tale for me, knowingly send me away in the dead of night, and knowing her own life was on the line for it."

"Rosa is a soldier, Samíah. She did what she had to do."

Fear was evident in her features as Samíah glanced chillingly around the grim chamber. "But no one knew I'd be here," she protested. Only you, Wanko, and Yana."

"Yes." His features tightened into a grimace. "And Flacco and Blinco Rascola."

She held her breath. Flacco, Blinco Rascola?

"One of them is the spy."

It was incredible, beyond belief. Hands at her sides and beginning to tremble, she was unable to move, unable to believe that one of the Gypsy king's most trusted lieutenants had been the one to break the sacred Romany code. But which one—and why? All she knew was that yet again the web of intrigue in Marrakesh was drawing tighter and tighter. Faces, countless faces, swam before her vision; faces of friends who now it seemed were secretly enemies, faces of those she thought as enemies who were really friends. Nothing seemed to make sense anymore. No one in the city seemed above suspicion. The game of spies and counterspies had turned to one of treachery and double crosses, and she was caught in the middle of it as never before.

Captain Enos stumbled his way slowly to his feet, the numbness from the blow easing at last. He glared at Samíah, then at Gideon, also no longer knowing who he could trust. "What have they done with Rosa?" he said, rubbing at the dulled ache in his neck.

"She's been taken to a safe haven, of that I'm certain. A place where she can be questioned about the Karshi and everything else she knows."

"But she doesn't know anything!" cried Samíah.

"We know that, but our enemies don't. Rosa is buying us time—and that's what I'm counting on. You see, we've learned now more than we hoped. Wanko had ways to pry loose the glib tongue of our friend, the Dealer."

Samíah clutched at his sleeve. "Where Gideon? Where have they taken her?"

This time Gideon smiled thinly, a small pulse throbbing in his throat as he lowered his tone and spoke rapidly. "All this time and we never suspected, all this time and the Assassin staging area has been right under our noses. Even as we speak the messiah is gathering his forces for the biggest assault yet. He plans to strike simultaneously not just at the city but the very center of power itself—the sultan's palace."

"Then what are we waiting for?" growled the hotheaded captain. Enos squeezed his hand around the hilt of his sword. "Let's attack them now. Alert all our forces..."

"Not so fast, my bold friend. We have to move slowly and cautiously. An open attack now would only serve against our interests. No, we have to be as cunning and careful as they."

"And Rosa? What about her?"

"We'll free her, Captain. And then we'll smash this messiah and all his forces once and for all."

"Then the Dealer has told you where she is?" said Samíah.

"She's closer than you would have dreamed. Right here in the heart of the city." He moved among the shadows and faced the rag man. "We have less than twenty-four hours," he said. "By tomorrow's dawn the messiah is going to move against us in force. Can your men be ready?"

The master of disguise ran a finger along the curve of an old scar. "You don't give me very much time." He paused, smiled. "But I will be ready."

"Good." He turned his attention back to the lovestruck soldier. "I hadn't hoped to have you involved in this," he said, "but now you are. So I'm going to ask your help."

"What do you want me to do?"

"Not breathe a word of what happened tonight to anyone—

including your superiors. Go back to the barracks like nothing has happened, and wait."

"But I can't just stand idly by! Not when—"

"One whispered word in the wrong ear could cost us everything. Is that what you want? Rosa's death?" The soldier's eyes shied from the secret agent's glare. "Trust in me, Captain. You'll receive word from my contacts, and when you do I'll want you to lead as many men as we can muster for the final fight."

"You promise to take care of Rosa?" he asked weakly.

"Personally—tonight. Now go back to your post."

Captain Enos drew a long breath and snapped to attention, saluting briskly. Though his heart was breaking at the thought of the dire predicament his beloved was in, he knew he had no alternative. He turned on his heels, marching from the barren *ofisa* back into the desolate street. When he was gone, Gideon looked to Samíah. "I want you to go back to Wanko's camp with the rag man," he said. "Alert the king, and give your father my instruction to meet us at dawn by the arch of the Street of the Harlot."

"You mean Papa is going to be involved in this after all?"

Gideon frowned. "I need him. If what I suspect is true, then his knowledge of the *souk* and the city is invaluable."

The rag man nodded, gently urged Samíah to leave with him. The fiery girl pulled away and faced Gideon squarely. "And what are you going to do?"

"As I promised. To try and save Rosa, and then," his features grew taunt, "to deal with the traitor. Now please go, Samíah. Time is running out."

"Not this time!" she flared with flashing eyes. "Rosa's life is in peril because of me, and I'm not about to forget. What if they already know about the ruse? How long will she be safe then? They'll be looking for you, Gideon. Expecting you."

"I have to take that risk."

"Then I'm going with you."

Stunned, he regarded her with disbelief. "What are you saying? Don't you know how dangerous this is going to be?

219

Where I'm going no one has been before. It's closely guarded, rife with Assassins."

"All the more reason you'll need another pair of eyes. You can't talk me out of this, Gideon. Not this time. Not when Rosa's life is at stake. Like it or not, I'm sticking to you tonight like glue."

She was adamant, he realized, and nothing he could say or do was going to change that.

The rag man moved toward her from the shadows. Samíah spun, ready for a fight. "Call him off, Gideon, or I'll scream all the way back to camp. I'll have soldiers breathing down your neck in no time."

The spy shared a furtive glance with the master of disguise. "I can gag her," said the rag man. "Put her to sleep if I have to..."

"Don't try it," snapped Samíah. "Or I'll start screaming right here and now." Her gaze pivoted back and forth between the two men confronting her.

"Leave her," said Gideon.

"Then I can come?"

The secret agent didn't reply; he looked at the master of disguise and said, "Give her a knife," adding as the rag man hesitantly complied, "Before the night is done she's going to need it."

"Hey, what is this place, anyway?" said Rosa.

The young Gypsy found herself on the floor of a dark, dank chamber. As she stumbled to her knees, she heard the heavy door shut behind with a metallic *clang*! Bit by bit, very slowly, she let her eyes adjust to the new surroundings. It was a small room with neither lamp nor window. The only light came from the space under the door. The floor was made of stone, the walls of thick, decaying wood. A sulfurous odor tickled her nostrils.

Rosa stood and wriggled her bound hands behind her back. But the more she struggled to loosen the bonds, the tighter they became.

"Damn," she muttered, feeling an itch in her nose she was unable to scratch. She sneezed, then craned her neck to peer about. She paced for a moment, then satisfied herself that there was no route of escape. Sullenly and stiffly she sat with her back straight against the wall opposite the door, resting her head on her raised knees. The bruise on her chin where the cowled oaf had punched her still smarted. So did her arms from the squeezing of her captors' grubby hands when they had shoved and pulled and pushed her about like a rag doll. When she had started to scream in the *ofisa*, another of the faceless brutes had rudely forced open her mouth and stuffed it with dirty rags, so deep that she gagged and could barely breathe. After that, they dragged her into the street and away.

221

But to where? She couldn't be sure. The only thing she knew was that she was still in the city, and probably not too far from the Casbah and the *souk*. The smells of the marketplace were vivid up until the last minute when they brought her into this place—probably a factory of some kind—and then tossed her for safekeeping into this chamber. Of either Flacco or Blinco Rascola there was still no sign.

Thought suddenly gave way to reality when footsteps outside grew shudderingly louder; she could hear the dull jingling of keys, one of them being placed clumsily into the lock. The metal door opened with a creak. Momentarily blinded by the brightness spilling from the hallway, she could make out the images of three or four cowled figures huddled together. So they've come, she thought. My inquisitors—or are they my executioners?

The Assassins chuckled among themselves; and to Rosa's surprise they didn't enter to interrogate her, but rather they hurled a man inside and laughed as the fellow spun dizzily and sprawled face down on the stone floor. The door clanged shut; she found herself alone with the new arrival.

Rosa scrambled onto her knees and hovered over the prostrate figure. Groaning, the man rolled slowly over onto his back and peered up through glazed and bloodied eyes.

"Blinco Rascola!" she cried, her heart beating a mile a minute. Once more she squirmed to break her wrist bonds, and once more the taut leather straps only tightened. "Blinco, are you all right?"

The Gypsy stared up at her but didn't quite seem to hear or understand. Lost in the fog of pain from the severe beating Rosa knew he had undergone, he looked at her mindlessly. But suddenly he became aware of the dim glitter of gold earrings, the faint outline of a face he still couldn't make out. Slowly, slowly, recognition crept back.

"Samíah!" he gasped.

"What happened, Blinco? What happened?"

"Samíah . . . I—I'm sorry. Forgive . . . me. They caught me by surprise, no chance to fight or warn you. . . ." He began to cough; a moment later, he tilted his head sideways and spit out a mouthful of phlegm. When he wiped his mouth with the back of his hand, Rosa realized that he wasn't bound.

"They came down from the roofs," Blinco went on as he faced her again. "I guess I was beginning to doze. I didn't see or hear a thing." Then he grimaced, part from his pain, part from his failure. "Before I could even draw my knife from its sheath, they were all over me. They hit me over the head. . . ." His fingertips lightly brushed over the blue-black lump bulging from his temple to his hairline.

"What about Flacco? Did they capture him as well?"

Blinco Rascola could only shake his head in puzzlement. "I don't know. He was inside the *ofisa*, guarding the entrance. Perhaps he fell asleep, or perhaps they overwhelmed him also. Maybe they killed him."

Killed him indeed! thought Rosa. So now the truth was out, even if poor Blinco Rascola didn't know it yet. Flacco had been the one all along. He had clandestinely tipped off the Assassins, then quietly disappeared when the time came for the attack. No wonder Blinco Rascola was caught by surprise! No wonder Flacco hadn't been there to come to his aid. Gideon and Wanko were right all along.

"Listen to me, Blinco," she whispered, leaning her face closer to his. "I think we was set up, understand? I think that maybe it was meant for you and me to be captured like this."

Blinco Rascola sat up and scratched his head. "What . . . what are you talking about?"

"About the spy, Blinco. The Gypsy traitor. And it all points in one direction—Flacco."

"You're mad! Flacco loves the king! He'd give his eyes before breaking the Romany code, Samíah. Laughingly give up his life. . . ." The Gypsy stopped speaking abruptly, narrowed his coal-black, shifting eyes at the girl as clarity came. Then he gasped. "You . . . You're not Samíah!"

Rosa grinned widely, her face like an orange with a slice removed. "Surprised, huh?" She laughed, throwing her head back while Blinco Rascola was left with his jaw hanging.

"But, but," he spluttered, "where did *you* come from? Samíah was fast asleep in the *ofisa*. I saw her—"

Outside, they could hear footsteps again. "Listen," said Rosa quickly, "there ain't much time."

When she had finished explaining everything, Blinco Rascola walked across the room and plopped himself down uneasily against the wall. He put his head to his hands and groaned. As Rosa stared in wonder, he suddenly began to chuckle, then to laugh, quietly at first more and more loudly after a while.

"Hey, Blinco, what's the joke? Gideon's plan may be clever, but it ain't so funny."

"The joke?" said Blinco Rascola absently, looking up through his hands at the girl. "We're both dead, Rosa, that's all. You and me are as dead as dead can be." His voice was calm and even, his features stoic, not even his eyes blinking.

"Hey, did that knock on the head affect your brains or what? How many times I gotta spell it out for you? All we gotta do is continue to fool these clowns for a while. Easy stuff for a Gypsy, no? Feed 'em nonsense and sit back and wait."

"We're not going to be rescued, Rosa. Never. Don't you realize that yet? Even if Gideon does come, by the time he gets here we'll both be dog food."

"I think maybe you don't feel so good, honey. Listen, why don't you just take it easy for a while, huh? Tomorrow maybe we're both gonna have a good laugh about this whole thing, right?" As she tried to ease his duress, she saw his eyes fix coldly on her, strange and chilling. And suddenly she felt a chill of her own. "I think maybe you better tell me what's bothering you. Is it Flacco? Are you concerned about what'll happen to him? Cause if you are—"

"You little fool!" He spat the words. "Do you know what this ruse of yours has done?" Spittle flew from his mouth as he raised his voice, his face twisting into an ugly parody of itself.

"Hey Blinco, I can handle the interrogators. I told you, it ain't your problem—"

"It ain't my problem," he mimicked. Then he shook his head and buried his face in his hands once again.

Something was very wrong, Rosa realized, only she couldn't tell what. Was it possible that Blinco Rascola had known about

Flacco's treachery all the time? Perhaps, because of friendship, been unwilling to expose him? Or could it be that Blinco Rascola was himself aiding Flacco in some way, involving himself with the spy—only now to find himself turned on by his friend?

"Listen," she said desperately, "Gideon's gonna take care of the traitor by himself. You an' me don't have to do anything about it. I know how you feel. Flacco was my friend as well. Almost like an older brother. But his punishment is well deserved, and we don't gotta feel so bad, see?"

Blinco Rascola was still shaking his head. This time when he looked up at Rosa he sighed. You still don't get the picture, do you? Still can't get the truth through that thick Gypsy skull of yours?"

"Hey, Blinco, that knock on the head really did jar your brain, huh?"

"There was no knock on the head."

She stiffened. "What?"

He stood up, hovered over her in a way that made her flesh crawl. Then he began to grin, veins bulging from his sinewy neck, throbbing across his forehead. "You and the king made a bad mistake for us all," he said huskily. "Better you had left Samíah alone where she was, where my friends could find her."

Rosa began to feel afraid for the first time. Blinco wiped away the congealed blood from his lump and rubbed it into his fintertips. "This was part of my game, Rosa," he wheezed. "To make you believe they'd beaten me. To let you convince yourself that Flacco must have informed on us. Yes, Samíah would have taken me into her confidence, trusted me enough so that when I questioned her she would have gladly told me everything I needed to know. . . ."

"You ain't making a whole lotta sense, Blinco," Rosa said with a gulp.

"Ain't I? Let me make it plain as water, then. Me, Rosa. I'm the one you were expecting to interrogate you. But you spoiled all of that by changing places with Samíah. My friends have little need of you—and now, less need of me. I've failed to deliver the goods one time too many. This was my last chance. And now you've ruined that one as well. So like I said, Rosa, you and me are dead. It's too late, too late for us both."

"Then . . . Flacco isn't . . . the traitor?"

Blinco Rascola smiled thinly. "It was me all the time—and you just gave your confidence to the wrong man. Gideon won't have a chance in hell once I spill the beans."

 HOLDING SAMÍAH TIGHTLY BY THE HAND, GIDEON paused ankle-deep in the muck and peered ahead into the darkness where the tunnel forked off into two directions. He furrowed his brow as he pondered which course they should follow. Between the twin granite pillars wound the passage through the ancient, labyrinthine cellars and dungeons of the old palace: the hidden catacombs constructed by the famed engineers of the first sultans, where the first armies of Marrakesh secretly withdrew to do battle with the many enemies sweeping down from the mountains. Indeed, if these tunnels could speak, what marvelous tales of courage and valor they would tell—of times gone by when men were honest and pure, and an enemy was known by the banner he flew or the uniform he proudly wore.

"Where are we now?" asked Samíah as she gazed about in the grim darkness of the passage. The stone walls glittered wetly, seeping a trickle of raw sewage that oozed down from unseen ducts. She wrinkled her nose in disgust at the foul odor, tightening her grip on Gideon's hand when a small, lizardlike creature scuttled out of one recess and inside another with amazing speed.

"Nothing to be frightened of," he told her as they passed between the granite pillars. "We've already crossed under the market, and by now"—he glanced up at the concave ceiling—"we should be, oh, directly beneath the Street of the Carpet-sellers." His boots swished through the thinning layer of slime along the floor; for a while they didn't speak, continuing through the eerie stillness textured by the soft whistling of wind pushed down through the vents above.

It was damp and chilly in the catacombs—like a grave, Samíah thought. The reek of sewage became worse; the constant drip-drip-drip of water got on her nerves. Overhead, iron pipes, rusted red from dampness and age, clung from and crisscrossed the low ceiling. Here and there she could hear the scratching of tiny feet as mice and rats clambered over the pipes in search of morsels of food.

"You still haven't told me where we're supposed to be going," said Samíah. The sound of her voice echoed metallically as it reverberated off the walls.

"Does it make any difference? You said you didn't care."

"I suppose not . . . but I'd still like to know."

Gideon drew his lips into a tight line. "This tunnel should lead us to the end of Harlot Street, to the old warehouses and factories along the edge of the old canal."

"You mean that the messiah's headquarters are hidden in a factory?" Samíah said, astounded.

"Not exactly. Only a center of operations, a staging area above." He paused, glanced around at the featureless and unbroken curve of the tunnel. "Very clever, those ancient engineers. They created a whole world of subterranean passages which spilled into every sector of the city, from sewers to aqueducts, all interconnected and accessible from one central point."

"What point?"

"What are now the ruins of the original palace. You see, the original sultans were a very insecure bunch. Frightened of siege, they constructed their inner fortresses underground. Far underground, into secret chambers long forgotten but which even now still exist."

Suddenly, Gideon pulled her hard into the closest recess. "Shhh!" he said, closing his hand over her mouth. "Don't speak! Don't even breathe!"

Samíah nodded in terror and froze. From far ahead, where the tunnel gently sloped and turned, she heard the sudden low rumbling of what sounded like distant thunder. Only it wasn't thunder. A circular stone slab rested in place in the center of the floor. With a mixture of dread and fascination, she watched it begin to move, to lift slightly and slowly, and then to slide from its place. The hackles rose on the nape of her neck as a grim robed and cowled figure began to emerge from the hole. The Assassin lifted himself out and, holding a small torch whose flame fanned wildly in the subterranean gusts, proceeded to huddle beside the black orifice and extend a hand back inside. A second robed man lifted himself out, then a third, then a fourth. Gathered together, as the brightness of the flame exploded light like a sun amid a universe of darkness, the Assassins methodically lifted the slab and carefully positioned it back in place.

Samíah looked on with bated breath; her heat skipped a beat when the one with the torch started to lead the others directly toward her. Gideon's knife glinted as he raised it higher. They were coming this way.

Less than twenty paces away, the group stopped, abruptly turned to the side. One of them groped along the wall, and to Samíah's total shock, she heard something click and a spring give way. Before her eyes, a new door, hitherto unseen, opened within the wall of granite. One by one—the torchbearer last— they passed through. And when they were gone, the stone slid shut.

"My God," rasped Samíah.

"So that's how they've been doing it," wheezed Gideon. "Striking above, then vanishing underground."

"They've been here all along. Right under our feet." Samíah shuddered. The whole Assassin army, crawling about in this underworld like roaches, burrowing like rats, living amid the horror of this lightless world of tangled catacombs, scheming and plotting for the day of resurrection of their unholy messiah.

Samíah followed on Gideon's heels as he turned away from the recess and headed back out into the murky light of the tunnel. "Where are you going?"

"Likely as not this passage is filled with Assassins," he replied thoughtfully. "They must be constantly coming and going from the ruins below to the world above. And that secret door"—he pointed to the smooth wall ahead—"undoubtedly is going to take us to the staging area and—if my guess is right—to the very place they've taken Rosa."

He slid his knife easily back into its sheath and moved cautiously to the wall. Hands lifted, he began to examine the curvature, probing lightly with his fingers, running them up and down and along the granite in search of the hidden catch spring. "There has to be one somewhere," he mumbled, gently tapping for some unseen hollow worked into the surface. But nothing happened; the wall remained as smooth and mysterious as before. Gideon cursed softly under his breath.

"Now what?" Samíah panted, brushing aside curls with the back of her hand.

Gideon peered around gloomily. A maze of caverns and narrow defiles led in every direction. "Sooner or later another of those insects is going to crawl up from the slab," he told her. "And when he opens the door, we'll be waiting."

"We could spend the whole night down here like this," she complained. "There's got to be another way, another exit."

"Sure. Only which is the right one? Show it to me and I'll be glad to follow."

Stepping lightly, Samíah bypassed the slab and let her eyes scour the near distance. But Gideon was right, she saw; there were so many different tunnels, crawl spaces, and endless passages that traversed these abominable sewers like a spider's web.

She turned back dejectedly to find Gideon moving away from her. "Hey, where are you going?"

He looked over his shoulder. "Back to the recess. They

won't see us from there, and it's as good a place to wait as any. Are you coming or not?"

Groaning, Samíah quickly followed.

Time passed all too slowly. Huddled opposite each other, they sat glumly in the damp chill and listened for footsteps. Samiah sat with folded legs and arms, staring mindlessly at the wall behind Gideon, tracing with her eyes the beads of dirty water as they trickled one by one down over the rock. "How long have we been here now?" she asked.

"About an hour."

She rubbed at her cold arms. "Feels like a whole night."

"You're too impatient, Samíah. In this business you have to learn forebearance. Losing composure and acting hastily has cost more than one good agent his life."

"But what about Rosa?" she answered. "Have you considered what they might be doing to her this very minute? And what do we do about it? Nothing. Just sit here like fools in the darkness." She peered up at the jagged ceiling, wondering if perhaps Rosa was directly above, almost close enough to reach out and touch. She fidgeted, sickened by the thought of being so close but unable to do anything. Gideon, on the other hand, seemed the picture of repose. Even down here with the Assassins only a hairbreadth away, he remained calm and relaxed, as tranquil as a mild summer's day.

"You know the trouble with you?" she blurted. "You have no feelings for anyone. Everyone is expendable as long as it serves your cause."

"I don't allow myself the luxury of personal feelings in my work, Samíah. They diminish clear thinking. If I thought about what might be happening up there now, I'd probably be as restless and testy as you. But right now clear thinking is what we need most—for Rosa's sake. What good to anyone would storming the staging area be? Most likely we'd all wind up dead."

She sneered at his complacency, his self-assurance. "Well, let me tell you something, Mister Secret Agent: One day it's going to be you on the wrong side of things, you who'll need help. But don't look to me to come to the rescue. If I had my way..."

Gideon met her angry eyes, aware of the frustration and helplessness Samíah felt now. She'd face any peril and any odds to help her friend, he knew. Spit in the eye of the devil himself, if it came that; and go down fighting without a whimper. Dying if necessary for what she believed in—and in that way, Samíah was little different from him.

"Nothing you're going to say will get me worked up," he said with a smile. "I know what you're up to, and I can't even say that I blame you for it. But the answer is no; you won't succeed in getting me angry enough to make us go raging through the tunnels like a pair of snorting bulls, right into the waiting arms of our foes."

Flustered, Samíah pouted. "If *I* were a man," she seethed, "I'd know well enough what to do. And it wouldn't be sit here in a sewer with you!" It was hard for Gideon not to laugh at her outburst, though her anger was well motivated. And when she did catch his mirth, it only served to arouse her ire further.

What's so funny, Gideon? I don't find our predicament something to laugh about."

"Ah, Samíah, you never do really give up, do you?"

She set her jaw, glared. "Not when I'm in the right."

The secret agent sighed as he leaned back against the rock, shaking his head. "I suppose it was this same determination that got you entangled with me in the first place. And"—here he turned the corners of his mouth downward in a frown—"after your father warned you not to get involved."

"How did you know about that?" She tilted her head, looked at him with curiosity.

"Oh, Habib and I have been doing a little talking. In fact, your father was eager to tell me quite a bit about you. Says you were even more headstrong when you were younger. I guess you've mellowed with age." He grinned boyishly.

Samíah stuck up her nose. "*Pfff!* Papa's like you: doesn't have a high opinion of women with minds of their own. Too old-fashioned, I suppose; thinks a woman's place is to be dutiful and charming, a perfect wife who cooks and cleans and slaves and dotes over her husband without a single complaint even when she's being abused." She studied him for a moment, licking her lip. "Hey, what business is this of yours anyway? What right do you have to go prying into my private life?"

"I didn't pry, Samíah. Like I said, Habib was happy to talk about you. In fact, except for your stubbornness and hot temper, he'd probably claim that you're the fairest, most interesting and eligible woman in all of Marrakesh. And he may even be right."

Unable to stop from blushing, Samíah pulled a face. Damn Gideon for all his snooping, she thought. Why couldn't he just stay out of her life?

"Don't be annoyed with me, Samíah. Your papa didn't mean any harm in telling me these things. Besides, if I know Habib, he had some ulterior motive."

At that, her eyes widened expressively. She stared at him, wishing she could wipe that silly grin off his face. Poor Papa, still lost in his fantasies of matching her up with someone.

Water continued to drip, penetrating the porous rock overhead in the slow erosion that had already made the underground system perilously faulted with fissures and schisms. Samíah knew very little about such matters, but it seemed to her that sooner or later this entire subterranean cavern was liable to collapse. As if to give fuel to her thought, something above groaned and scraped, sending rusted flakes drifting downward.

"Nothing to be frightened of," Gideon assured her as she nervously jerked her hand upward. "It's only a section of pipe loose in its braces. These walls have held firm for centuries, and it will be twice again as long before they begin to cave in."

Unsure, Samíah continued to stare and watch the particles fall. With a sudden, sweeping down draft, the pipe groaned and shifted again, this time more dramatically. Gideon glanced up tensely. In a few seconds the shifting ceased and he resumed his normal composure, looking at her with a satisfied smile. "See, I told you."

"Seems you know everything there is to know about everything and everyone," she answered with sarcasm. Leaning forward, she wrapped her hands around her knees and sniffed as the dampness penetrated her bones. "Is there anything you *don't* know?"

"I don't know how to open that secret door," he replied dryly.

"Or have any human feelings. Tell me, Mister Secret Agent, did you ever care about anybody? Have any friends—real friends, I mean. Not just useful contacts and fellow conspirators. Is there something of lasting value to you in the world, Gideon? Or is the whole world always the same, filled with traitors and foes, plots and evils to uncover? If I could scratch below that stony exterior, what might I find?"

He laughed, but this time with little humor. "What do you think you'd find?"

"Truthfully?" She shook her head and pondered the mystery of him, the different Gideons she had seen over the past weeks: from the thoughtful and tender man who cried at the scene of the Gypsy massacre to the cold and calculating man before her now who would willingly expend human life in service of his cause. Ruthless and cunning, but at times kind and sensitive— an enigma she could never learn to understand. "You have ice water in your veins. Was it always like that, or did it come with the job?"

"We see things from different points of view, Samíah," he said quietly. "But it hasn't always been like that. Once"—he smiled wistfully—"you'd probably have found me no different from you. I guess time and circumstance changed all that." He glanced around forlornly and sighed. There was no way to make her understand, he thought. Nor could he blame her. Samíah was still innocent, and he had lost his own innocence long before.

"Who are you, Gideon?" she asked. "Who are you really?"

He snapped out of his thoughts. "What do you mean?"

"Call it a woman's curiosity, but it occurs to me that you seem to know everything about everyone. Yana, Wanko, Rosa, even me. How we think, how we act, what we're likely to do next."

The thin, tight line of his mouth worked slowly into something of a smile. "Knowing about people is part of my business, Samíah. Like you said, it comes with the job."

"Yet no one seems to know anything about you. You're a secret to me, Gideon. A puzzle I haven't been able to solve since the first day you walked into my life."

"Seems to me that it was you who came tumbling into mine," he answered wryly. "But now you think it's time to even the score, make me tell everything you've been wondering."

"Something like that, yes. You owe me at least that much, don't you think?"

"Fair enough. Perhaps I do. But the truth might surprise you. My story really isn't very fascinating. I doubt it will hold your interest for long."

"We seem to have plenty of idle time on our hands," she said, glancing around the chilly darkness of the tunnel. "And seeing that you know so much about me . . ."

He leaned back as comfortably as he could, folding his arms, drumming his fingers lightly. Where should he start? Was it really only a short time ago that so much began to change? Or was it a lifetime ago, a dim and distant memory of a past that now seemed to belong to another person? Had someone told him he'd be where he was now, he'd have laughed and called it ridiculous. But time and circumstance had indeed taken their toll, and here he was no less trapped by the same quirk of fate as Samíah. . . .

"Where were you born?" she asked.

"Here in the city. But most of my youth was spent away from Marrakesh, in the summer home of my parents. My father, you see, had very little time for his family in those days, and he was always sending my mother, sisters, and my brother and me to the north. Not that I could fault him for it, though, because my family's . . . er . . . business and affairs demanded all of his time. Still, it wasn't an unhappy childhood, and my mother saw to it that I was educated by some of the finest tutors in all the realm."

"You must have been very rich," said Samíah.

He shrugged. "Money was never a consideration in my family. I spent most of my time dabbling in the arts, studying everything from classical history to modern philosophy, poetry to military tactics."

"Ah, so you became a soldier?"

"Not exactly. I traveled quite a bit in those days, sailing to exotic lands other boys could only dream of. But it seems I could never quite decide what I wanted to do with my life. As the second son, I knew I could never aspire to head my father's business. That, of course, remains the prerogative of my brother. Everything will one day belong to him."

"I understand," Samíah told him. "Our laws are harsh concerning second sons."

Gideon nodded. "Anyway, I remained away for several years, and when I returned I was old enough to start making some decisions. My mother betrothed me to a young girl, distantly related—"

Samíah's eyes grew large. "Then you're married?" she said.

Gideon laughed heartily. "No, it never came to that, although both my parents were angry that I refused such a good prospect. So my father than asked me to come back and remain with him for a while, sort of learning the business. But I quickly found that I couldn't be happy in his line of work so I left of my own accord. My mother has a brother who is fairly influential in the military, and through my uncle I received my first appointment—stationed in a desert garrison. I soldiered for almost three years, gaining small rank, but I still wasn't satisfied. It was about then that I sought a new position with the sultan's special services...."

"Then you served in the palace itself?"

"I resigned my rank immediately and came back. I was made an adjunct to several ministers."

The sultan's palace! Samíah was more than impressed. Gideon must come from a very influential family indeed to have merited such privileged duty. Even among the city's wealthiest families such a post was virtually impossible to attain, she knew. What father wouldn't give his right arm to have his son achieve such honor?

"Then," she said with a measure of true awe, "you must have on occasion seen the sultan himself, in person?"

He grinned at the question. "Quite often, Samíah. I was frequently present at meetings of state. But to be honest, politics bore me."

"But to have been at court! What's he like?" she implored excitedly. "Really like, I mean."

"Who?"

"The sultan, of course!" He winked at her, "I'd be willing to bet you'd like him, and the Sultana too. Perhaps one day, when all this is done, I can arrange to bring you to the palace."

"Me—come to the palace?"

"For an audience, why not? Our sultan will be more than pleased to meet the young woman whose work helped so greatly in our effort against the Assassins. I daresay you'd probably be in line for a quite handsome reward."

Samíah was awed and dumbstruck by what he said. Imagine, a lowly dress maker being invited to the resplendent halls of the grand palace of Marrakesh! Seated among the vivacious and sophisticated ladies and gentlemen of court, amid the pomp and splendor and bejeweled nobility. Servants to cater to every whim, musicians playing beneath the blue-tiled marble roofs, while she was treated in the same manner as royalty. The very idea of it was preposterous! A dustman's daughter could never hope to attain such an honor. Surely Gideon was only saying that.

"I'm quite serious, you know," he said as if reading her thoughts. "And if my guess is right, the sultan would probably enjoy having someone like you around for a while to speak your mind. It would be a nice change from the pompous and self-serving lot you usually find in court these days. You'd be like a breath of fresh air—Allah knows there's enough staleness around that place already." Her eyes were dancing as he spoke; Samíah was mesmerized. "And I'd wager you could straighten out a couple of those presumptuous, bombastic old ministers. Put them in their place, all right."

Samíah laughed. "You bet I would! Why, I'd see to it that women were given the same rights as men, that we'd never again be treated like—" She cut off her words and peeked at

236

Gideon with embarrassment. "You . . . you were making fun of me, weren't you?"

"No, Samíah, I wasn't. I meant every word of it." His voice was soft and gentle now, something in his eyes assuring her that he hadn't been only teasing her. "I *will* take you there, Samíah. We'll go together—proudly."

She could feel herself beginning to flush. *"Poof!"* she said in her sudden discomfort, teeth glistening against her darkly tanned features as she forced a smile. "I think we're both getting carried away."

He countered with a smile of his own. "I know—but isn't it nice to dream once in a while?

'Hey, I thought you were the one whose feet never left the ground."

"I told you I wasn't so different from anyone else. Even secret agents like to have dreams once in a while." He shrugged. "But I suppose there will be time enough to speak about these things later. Once we get, er, more pressing matters out of the way. Anyway, at least now you know the story of my life."

"Not quite, Gideon. You still didn't tell me how you became a spy."

"Well," he said, drawing in air and becoming serious again, "my work at the palace was the beginning." He tilted his head up toward the ceiling and shut his eyes, recollecting events he rarely thought about anymore. At the time," he went on, "I was adjunct to our minister of state, the grand pasha. Through him I became involved with the chief magistrate and the heads of our secular courts—"

"Police work?" asked Samíah.

"Intelligence. Next thing I knew"—he spread his palms in a furtive gesture—"I found myself volunteering for undercover assignmnets. There aren't many benefits in this branch, and an agent's longevity depends solely on his wits and good fortune. Believe me, if I knew then what I know now . . ." He laughed quietly and looked at her again. "Three of our best men were killed in as many months recently. The minister called on me and asked me to take command of the case. At the time neither of us suspected what was behind their deaths. But the rumblings had been there all along, I suppose, only we hadn't been able to hear them clearly. After the surge of kidnappings, I dropped out of sight, found a new cover as al-Gamal's rent collector, his nephew from the country. It was a near-perfect cover for me, occupying my days and allowing me easy access to places I'd never normally be allowed. By night I did my real work, though. I had finally learned what happened to our contact's brooch when you appeared on the scene—"

"And nearly ruined everything for you," Samíah said softly.

"You didn't exactly make things easy," he replied with a grin; then added more darkly, "But there were benefits. You see, Samíah, by drawing attention to yourself, you took attention away from me. While our foes were busy trying to get their hands on you, it freed my own hands, allowed me to move unrestricted."

"I see," she said, feeling slightly bruised. "I've been your lightning rod."

"No. Nothing was ever going to happen to you, Samíah. For that you can thank Rosa. From the very beginning she was being primed to take your place."

"You mean she knew all along that sooner or later . . . ?"

"From the very night you were brought to Wanko's camp. The king saw the resemblance at once; he knew we could deceive the Assassins. So, although Yana was against it, he offered his daughter's life to save yours."

A lump was rising in Samíah's throat as she said, "Why didn't you tell me this before? Why has everything always been a secret?"

"First we had to be sure we could trust you."

"Trust me? You thought *I* might be an Assassin spy?"

He looked at her evenly. "Not you—Habib."

She was shocked and outraged. "My father? Are you crazy? He would never—could never—"

"Hear me out, Samíah, then judge. The night of Hussein's disappearance your father was seen by one of our agents speaking with him. Hussein showed Habib something on the sly, something we now know was the brooch. It was only natural to conclude that perhaps the dustman had a hand in Hussein's dropping from sight. But we weren't sure. So we had him followed. . . ."

Samíah listened, incredulity in her widening eyes.

"Meanwhile," he continued, "a report had been filed that very day by Captain Enos that a woman—you—had caused a commotion in the market, claiming to have seen an abduction. It was very puzzling for us, Samíah. Coincidence? Maybe. But we needed to be sure."

"And now?" she asked weakly.

Gideon sighed. "Now we know the truth. Habib had nothing to do with any of these things, although—and he doesn't know it himself yet—he unwittingly has been a greater help than you could ever have dreamed."

"I don't think I understand."

"It's not important now, but you will. But I wanted to tell you everything, be as honest as I could for a change. At least maybe now you'll see I'm not the ogre you made me out to be."

Looking deeply into each other's eyes, they shared a smile. "I guess you're not, Gideon," she said. "And I—I'm sorry about some of the things I called you behind your back. I think I misjudged you after all."

He offered his hand. "Friends at last?" he said hopefully.

Grinning broadly, Samíah said, "Special friends. Who knows, maybe the old queen was right after all."

"Yana?" For a moment he looked at her with puzzlement, then they both sparkled with laughter. "Has the queen been talking to you about me?"

She nodded, recalling vividly the private conversation they had shared that night in the woods. What was it that Yana had said—something about how, when the time was right, only Gideon himself could answer her questions. And then Rosa in the *ofisa: Anybody with eyes in his head could see . . . that between a man and a woman love and hate are the same thing. . . .*

"And Yaya was speaking to you about me, too?" she asked.

"Constantly. She's been saying that I'm too old for this sort of thing, that I should settle down, find—say, don't you know?

I really thought Yana would have told you." He shook his head in amusement. "Gypsies!" he grumbled. "Bunch of mindless matchmakers and—"

Something gave way above. Samíah screamed. The section of pipe broke free of its brace and clanged as it hit the wall. Gideon threw himself and Samíah into the deepest part of the recess. The rusted chunk of iron came crashing down, falling at a sharp angle and hitting the stone floor where they had been. On her knees, Samíah coughed and waved away the cloud of dust.

"It would have killed us!" she gasped.

Gideon helped her to her feet and cradled her closely. The noxious dust swirled. Glancing upward, he heard another scraping noise, another section of pipe dangling in its brace and almost ready to fall. "Maybe those engineers weren't so clever as I thought," he mused. "Come on, we'd better get away from here before we're crushed."

He groped for her hand in the darkness and, finding it, started to pull her away. Samíah held steadfast.

"What's the matter?" he said.

"You saved my life again, that's all," she whispered. She looked up into his face with saucer eyes. Gideon wiped away a smudge from the side of her mouth. Her lips were slightly parted, warm and inviting. And there, amid the chill and solitude of the ancient catacombs they kissed, the bleak and dangerous world around them lost during a moment's rapture. For a single, wonderful instant the terrors awaiting seemed to vanish forever.

THE SLAB GAVE WAY GRUDGINGLY. IT INCHED AND scraped along the wet granite floor, and when the cover had been removed from less than half the perimeter the movement stopped. A flicker of torchlight pushed back the looming shadows. A hand took hold of the lid, a cowled head appeared from the abyss.

His mouth hanging wide open from the strenuous climb, the Assassin wriggled free and hunchingly edged his way into the tunnel.

From where he perched among the shadows, Gideon could make out the straight linear descent down the hole. A length of cable was securely tied to the handholds embedded in the rock. Had he been able to peer down the circular shaft, he would have realized the great distance between her and the innermost secret chambers whence the fanatic had come.

The Assassin paused to catch his breath. Then he placed his small torch in a sconce in the near wall before gathering his strength to fit the slab back into its place. When that was completed, he straightened, adjusted the small bow slung crosswise over his shoulder, then started to move silently toward the wall. Gideon saw him lift the torch and place his left foot against an unseen niche where floor and wall joined. The toe of his boot nudged gently against the catch spring. Something clicked; rock rumbled, the door slid slowly open.

The Assassin poked his torch through the widening opening

and hunched to pass through. Gideon lurched from behind, and grabbed the end of the horned bow. The fanatic wheeled around. The tightly nocked bowstring gnawed into his bare throat. Samíah heard him squeal as Gideon tripped him. He shoved the torch at Gideon's face, hoping to break free of the grip, but it was too late to counter the attack. With a flick of his wrist Gideon looped the bowstring tighter around the Assassin's throat. He choked and stumbled to his knees. Inside the hood Samíah could see his eyes bulge and his lips sputter as his mouth vainly sought to suck in air. The torch fell; the Assassin struggled to pry loose his attacker's hands. Gideon slid his arm under the fanatic's chin and jerked his head backward. Bone snapped; the fanatic's eyes grew mushroom-large with astonishment, his features expressionless as the facial muscles slackened. He slumped in a heap at Gideon's feet. He sightlessly stared up at the man who had killed him. His legs twitched spasmodically, and a long, deeply guttural gurgle emerged from his throat. Then he lay dead in the muck.

Without losing a moment, Gideon slid the corpse to the recess and propped him up among the shadows. Then he scooped up the fallen torch with one hand, waving it to keep the yellow flame alight, and reached out into the darkness for Samíah with the other. "Come on," he rasped, "we don't know how long the door will remain open."

Samíah felt herself being pulled through the low entrance. Hunching inside, she stared back at the recess and the grim lump that had only moments before been a living thing. Before she could utter a word, the secret door started to rumble and slide shut.

Gideon held the torch high and narrowed his eyes. Before them stood a stone staircase spiraling upward. Shadows danced in retreat from the flickering light as the torch was thrust forward. Holding tightly onto Gideon's sleeve, Samíah let him lead her up. Numbed by what had happened, she made no protest when Gideon urged her to hurry. They negotiated the crumbling steps two and three at a time. An acrid, flinty smell assaulted her nostrils. It was cold and damp in the stairwell, but as they attained height it grew warmer. Several times they spiraled around on the coiling steps, seemingly on a never-ending journey upward. Out of breath, they reached the final landing, finding themselves suddenly standing in a large, quiet anteroom with a single wooden door at the far end.

"Where are we?" she managed to speak between gulps for air.

Gideon put a finger to his lips. He doused the torch, then slipped quietly to the other end of the room. The door creaked open with the slightest touch of his fingertips. All he could see was a looming corridor with entrances to multiple chambers on either side. The thick dust over the floor had been disturbed by the crossings of recent footsteps.

Glancing back over his shoulder, he beckoned for Samíah. The girl came to his side, and together they peered into the empty corridor. Gideon pushed gently, and the door opened wide. Then they tiptoed into the corridor.

It was dank and musty, and the distinct smell of sulfur grew steadily stronger and more pungent. Pausing at the unbarred entrance to the first side chamber, they saw a dim room half-filled with boxes and crates in the center, the walls lined with shelves. Crusted mold and hardened streams of candle-wax were everywhere, as were flecks of colored powders mingled with the heavy dust scattered over the floor. They stepped inside the chamber side by side, gazing about.

"This place is a factory," mumbled Samíah.

"Yes," Gideon agreed in a whisper. He removed a vial from a shelf, uncorked the stopper and smelled. The odor was foul and decayed. "But it looks like it hasn't been used for years."

Samíah paused alongside one of the crates and gazed down into it. Small wrapped objects rested along the bottom, and she plucked one out and held it with both hands. "Look what I've found," she said, handing it to Gideon.

The secret agent crouched in the shadows and quietly tore off the paper wrapping. "Well, look at that," he muttered.

"What? What is it?"

He grinned lopsidedly, fondling the object with amusement. It was oblong, easily held in the palm, had a blunt charcoal head on one end and a small curling fuse on the other. "A rocket," he said.

"A what?"

"Fireworks. This place is a fireworks factory." He went to examine the shelves again, randomly reading the scrawled, faded labels on the assorted flasks and vials. A veritable alchemist's list of ingredients greeted him: salts of antimony, sulfur, arsenic, potassium chlorate. As he scanned the moldy bottles, his thoughts raced back to his childhood when the fabulous fireworks displays had been the highlights of his life. Originally, travelers from Cathay and the Orient had brought by caravan the concoctions used for fireworks. Later, with the rapid expansion of trade, the secrets of the craft passed to the hands of local craftsmen. For decades Marrakesh and many other cities had reveled in the delights these skyworks had provided—the celebrations of victory or peace, or coronations when the night sky came alive with exploding colors.

"I remember the night of the sultan's eldest son's wedding," Samíah mused in recollection of her only encounter with the spectacle. "I was still little, and my father took me to the roof of our house." Her eyes danced with the memory. "The heavens were lit up with shooting stars of flaming colors, so brilliant they almost blinded me."

"I remember that night, too," said Gideon. His expression turned sour. Those joyous and peaceful times were gone now, perhaps forever.

Samíah took the rocket and looked at it briefly. She also felt the bittersweet pang for the years when life was happy. Carefully she placed it back in its place. "Do you think we might have made an error?" she asked, facing him. "This place is deserted. Surely we missed a turn off somewhere along the stairs. . . ."

Gideon kneaded the stiff muscles in his neck. For the first time he began to doubt himself. Had there been a secondary passage, a secret doorway not unlike the first, which would have taken them somewhere else? "I was so positive," he said, lost in thought. "So certain that we . . ."

The cry was short and pain wracked, like the wail of some

wounded animal. Gideon took hold of Samíah's arm and pulled her away roughly. "Quick, down!" he said.

They hid behind the crates, not daring to breathe. The silence that resumed was short-lived. Suddenly there were noises in the corridor: the sound of a heavy door being opened and shut, followed by footsteps. Gideon inched his way around the stack of crates and peered at the entrance. Three hooded figures appeared, briskly, unspeakingly, walking back down the corridor in the direction of the stairwell to the catacombs. The sight of the long, curved daggers they brazenly held made him cringe.

A minute later the footsteps faded. Samíah could hear the clatter of boots on the landing, the slow, arduous descent of the Assassins back into the underworld.

Gideon leaped to his feet. "I'm going to see where that scream came from. Stay here until I come back for you."

"Not on your life!" she flared, right beside him. Determination was in her eyes. "You're not leaving me now. I'm coming with you, like it or not."

He shrugged, then moved catlike back into the corridor. Samíah followed on his heels. A maze of storage and workrooms stood silent on either side. The groaning was low but distinct, coming from the farthest chamber. Gideon slid his knife from its sheath. The metal edge glinted in the dim light.

"Over there," said Samíah, pointing to where a thick metal door was shut among the shadows. The small window in the door was barred, and she crept up to it slowly, then peeked inside.

It was hard to see anything. Gideon nudged her aside and felt for the door. With a single movement he pushed it open and came bursting inside, ready to cut and slash at anything in his way.

In a corner, a figure slithered farther into the shadows, whimpering. The secret agent stared at the pitiful form crouched with hands before face as if preparing to stave off a volley of blows.

Samíah came closer, trembling. "Allah's mercy," she whispered, making out the features for the first time. Round, frightened eyes stared straight at her from a face scarred, swollen, and as badly injured as the trunk and limbs of his body. The broken figure gave his visitors a careful inspection, but showed no sign of recognizing them. The beaten man only cringed and shivered.

Gideon knelt beside him and shook his head as he put away his blade. "In the name of God, what have they done to you, man?" he whispered. There was no response, only Flacco's glassy stare seemingly looking right through him.

His face was covered with welts and blisters; Samíah, using a piece of cloth torn from her skirt, wiped away a smear of oozing blood from the corner of the Gypsy's eye.

"It's me, Flacco," said Gideon with despair. "Don't you know me? It's Gideon."

Vacant, dazed pupils regarded him; then a hand like a lobster claw rose, bleeding fingers clutching at Gideon's shirt. Flacco was hurt, hurt badly, put through pain and torture that no man should be made to endure. Yet, through his suffering and agony, the familiarity of the voice sparked some dim recognition in his fevered brain. "Is . . . Is it really you, Gideon?" he croaked in a barely audible tone.

"Yes, my friend." He cradled the Gypsy closer, glancing around the cell with burning hatred for those whose cruelties had done such a thing. "But it's all right now, I promise you. They won't hurt you again."

There was no clean water for him to sip between his cracked, bloodied lips, no bandages or salve to help heal the awful cuts that disfigured him. Samíah soothed his brow with another rag. He coughed up blood.

"D—Don't be angry with me, Gideon," Flacco managed to say after his coughing fit had ended. "It wasn't my fault. Took me by surprise . . . no chance . . . had no chance . . ."

Don't try to speak. It's all right."

The Gypsy strained to lift his head. "They took her, Gideon. Blinco Rascola, also. Never had a chance, none of us."

Gideon's face hardened as he looked at Samíah. Poor, poor Flacco, he thought. Even now he didn't know it had been his lifelong companion, his cousin of the same blood, who had been responsible for their capture. The man whom he—and Wanko as well—had trusted with their lives.

"Never mind that," Gideon told him. "Can you understand me?" Flacco nodded weakly. "It wasn't Samíah sleeping in the *ofisa* last night. See, Samíah is here with me now." Flacco gazed at the girl beside Gideon with uncomprehending eyes.

"It was Rosa they captured," the secret agent went on quickly. "Rosa was in the *ofisa*. We tricked them, Flacco. With your help we tricked them all. But now the Defilers have taken Rosa. Where is she, man? Have you seen her? Are they holding her in the factory?"

Flacco tired to clear his foggy thoughts. Everything seemed so blurred, so distorted. How long had he been here? he wondered. How long had he been questioned and tortured? Was it hours—or days? He didn't know.

"I didn't talk, Gideon. They tried to make me, but I spat in their faces. . . ." He tried to grin bravely. "No matter how much they hurt me, I didn't talk."

"And Rosa, man? What have they done with her?"

Again the Gypsy tried to think, to constuct thoughts. Shudderingly, he recalled the terrible screams, the frantic shouts of the Defilers as they dragged her from her cell.

"She's gone, Gideon," he said, groaning. "Gone."

"Gone where, man? Think, Flacco! Try to remember."

Flacco shook his head. "Earlier, not too long. I heard them, saw them open the cell . . ." Then he stiffened, the recollection flooding back. "They took her away, Gideon. I heard her screaming."

Samíah bit her lip. "Where, where did they take her?"

"Below, they were saying. Beneath the city . . ."

The dustman's daughter exchanged a long, furtive glance with the spy. "They've brought her to the catacombs," she whispered. "To the messiah's underground fortress."

Grimly, Gideon nodded. It was the only answer, he knew; and it meant that the secret was out. The Assassins had learned it wasn't Samíah they were holding. But how? How could they have found out the truth? Rosa would have never admitted her real identity, of that he was sure. No matter what they said or how much pain they inflicted, the Gypsy girl would never have talked.

He looked at Samíah darkly. "Blinco Rascola," he said through gritted teeth. "The informer. It must have been him. Somehow he must have discovered the truth."

Samíah gasped. It did not require much imagination for her to conjecture what would happen to her now, a hundred meters and more below Marrakesh among the clandestine chambers of the messiah's inner sanctum.

"What do we do?" she asked.

"Find our way down there. Remember, I sent word with the rag man to have your father meet us at dawn beside the arch of the Street of the Harlots?"

"I remember," she replied unsteadily. "But what has that got to do with any of this?"

Gideon smiled one of his enigmatic smiles. "Have you forgotten what I told you before? That Habib is of greater help to us than we ever dreamed? Your father has worked the streets of Marrakesh for most of his life, Samíah; he's as familiar with them as any man living. Not just above the ground but below it as well."

"The sewers!" she cried, snapping her fingers. "He used to work in the sewers."

"Yes—and he knows the tunnel system. With his help we're going to reach the messiah's fortress and expose the Assassins once and for all." He glanced around tensely. "How long before dawn?"

Samíah could only shrug. "An hour, maybe a little more." she guessed.

"That should be enough time if we act fast."

She lowered her gaze and her voice. "What about Flacco? We can't just leave him here like this. They'll kill him."

She was right, he realized. By most standards, a lesser man would already be dead after suffering such brutal punishment. That the Gypsy was alive at all was remarkable.

"Save yourselves," Flacco mumbled in his semi-delirium. "Get away from here as fast as you can. Don't worry about me."

"Too late for that, my friend," said Gideon with a grin. "We'll get you out of here with us."

"But how?" His grip tightened on Gideon's stained shirt. "They're everywhere, Gideon. Everywhere. We'll never make it out the door."

"Can you move?" the Gypsy was asked.

Flacco unbent his fingers and stared at his bloodied hands. The pain was still there and in his legs. But his bones weren't broken, nor had they yet robbed him of his courage. He nodded.

"Good," said Gideon. With Samíah's assistance they helped the Gypsy to his feet. Flacco hobbled behind Samíah to the cell door, and Gideon peeked outside. The way seemed silent and clear. With their arms supporting the Gypsy, they inched back into the grim hall, unaware they had been seen.

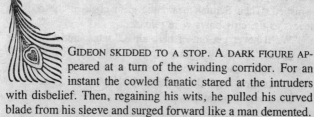 GIDEON SKIDDED TO A STOP. A DARK FIGURE AP- peared at a turn of the winding corridor. For an instant the cowled fanatic stared at the intruders with disbelief. Then, regaining his wits, he pulled his curved blade from his sleeve and surged forward like a man demented.

Gideon parried the thrust, and countered with a lightning series of quick jabs. His knife gleamed; the Assassin's blade fell to the floor, the fanatic suddenly clutching at his chest. A subtle smear spread over his black robe. He gurgled as he turned, shouting one final scream of warning before falling.

"Quick! Back to the landing!" shouted Gideon.

Another door banged open; from a side passage came two more Assassins, weapons drawn.

Blood streaked Gideon's cheek where the dagger's tip had grazed him. Badly off balance from the surprise attack, he wheeled around and led Samíah and Flacco to a bond in the corridor. Behind, they could hear a flurry of quickening footsteps, the hectic shouts that the staging area had been breached.

Up the hallway they ran. The dim corridor gave way into a large open storage room, huge and filled with hundreds of dusty boxes neatly stacked and forming narrow, crisscrossing avenues. High along the rafters, on wooden balconies running the entire length of the room, stood several more grim figures, deadly crossbows in hand.

Whump! The bolt slammed into the box directly behind Flacco, the impact so forceful it jolted the half-empty box and nearly sent it toppling over. A second bolt sailed a trajectory through the shadows and smacked into the wall, cracking plaster.

Gideon, Samíah, and Flacco scotted along the narrow aisle seeking better shelter behind a row of triple-stacked wooden crates. Above, the snipers scanned the murky chamber. The Assassins gripped the palm swells of their crossbows and snugly cushioned the cheek pieces against the sides of their faces. At the scurry of a rat they fired in unison. The bolts lurched and whistled. Then Samíah heard the grim click of the cocking levers as the crossbows were reloaded.

"We'll never get out of here alive," whispered Samíah as she glanced fearfully up and across the high, flat ceiling. The storage room was enormous, spanning perhaps fifty meters in every direction from the center. All the Assassins needed to do was keep them successfully pinned down, and then methodically sweep the rows one by one until they were caught. But because of the enormous size of the area, it was going to take time—and that was exactly what Gideon was counting on.

More footsteps broke the silence—running footsteps. Gideon spun, then crept cautiously to the edge of the aisle. Dimly in the distance he could see the open entrance and an armed squad of cowled, cloaked men swarming inside. They began to fan out in small groups, several taking one route along the wall, others spreading thinly in a single line, working their way slowly toward the room's center. Most held gleaming daggers in their hands, a few were armed with crossbows.

"Stay down!" Gideon hissed to his companions as the fanatics started to encircle them.

Samíah huddled beside the wounded Gypsy. Flacco was breathing heavily, gasping for breath; he rested with his back propped up against a splintered crate, his legs stretched wide apart across the aisle. A small gash on the side of his head had reopened. Samíah soothed his brow.

"We'll never make it," the Gypsy wheezed, shutting his eyes. "Too late. It's too late." He mumbled incoherently in his fever.

The ordeal of the escape had been more than he could handle, she saw. It had taken Flacco's last burst of strength and courage to make it this far; but now there was no longer a reservoir from which he could draw. He was depleted, unable to go on.

"Leave me, Samíah," he implored hoarsely. "By yourselves, you and Gideon might still have a chance. I'm too much of a burden. Go on. Go to him. Make a run for it."

Tears of pity were streaking down her face and she brushed them away deftly. "Don't speak, Flacco. Save your strength. Gideon will find a way out for us." She tried to smile and sound brave.

"No, not this time." He grimaced with a new surge of pain. When his eyes opened again, there was resignation in them. He searched the overhead vastness and sighed. He could not hear the approaching steps of the Defilers but was all too aware of their closeness. His Romany senses were still sharp enough to feel the presence of the evil that surrounded them all, and he knew and understood that only a few precious moments remained before they were trapped and caught. Flacco also knew he would rather die by his own hand than risk being tortured by them again.

"Give me your knife," he demanded.

Samíah looked at him, startled. "What are you saying?"

His hand closed gently over hers. "For a friend, Samíah. For a fellow Gypsy. Please . . ."

She pulled away and shook her head, unable to control her crying. Still she refused to believe that they were lost. Not after so much, not after coming so far . . .

"Samíah, look out!"

The Assassin lunged. Samíah fell back against the crates. Crossbow bolts sang from the balcony, aimed at her. But as she pivoted and lost her footing the attacker became the unwitting target. With sheer horror she saw the Assassin reel back with the blow. His cowl flew back, and Samiah saw where the bolt had crashed into his skull, cracking it in half. She screamed at the sight of bloodied chunks of brain spinning in dozens of directions while the stricken torso jumped about like a puppet.

A second Assassin reached the aisle. With crazed, gleaming eyes he saw his companion fall, and nearby, the girl whirl away in horror. Pulling his dagger, he bellowed a war cry and lurched for Samíah. Gideon dived over the corpse and brought him down. The cocked crossbow skittered along the floor and into the darkness beyond the aisle. The Assassin slashed wildly, the flat of his dagger rattling as it hit against the crates. Hauling the dreaded Defiler around, Gideon spiked him in the throat and left eye with two swift punching motions of his knife. The Assassin gurgled and stumbled back, falling over the helpless Flacco. His hands shot out and grabbed the secret agent, pulling him down with him. Gideon's weapon clattered to the floor. Before he could scoop it up, the Assassin used his overwhelming weight to pin him. Warm blood pulsed from the fanatic's punctured eye socket and throat. Vocal cords pierced, he squealed like a pig as he bore his thumb like a rivet into Gideon's windpipe and blocked his supply of air. Gideon gasped and writhed, pummeled him with his fists. A wave of helplessness engulfed him; he could not break the stranglehold. The pain-numbed Assassin roared in his triumph, hovering over the secret agent while blood sloshed down his face in sickening waves.

Samíah reached to gain Gideon's knife. A lever cocked

somewhere above, a bolt sailed down from the rafters. She dived as the missle punched its way clean through the crate above. Then, without thinking she caught hold of the weapon and, on her knees, stabbed. Steel grated against backbone. Instantly a dark smear spread over the back of the Assassin's robe. His fingers quivered and loosened. Gideon, gasping, slid out from underneath. She withdrew the knife just as the fanatic turned. The sight of his face made her wretch. Tendons in his throat were ripped and dangling, his eye socket now a cankerous blob of black and purpled ooze. The Assassin opened his mouth as if to scream. But the sound that came was the wail of a pathetic beast. Oily bile spewed from his mouth. His hand jerked to grab the girl, but he fell flat on his face in a heap, a puddle of blood forming beneath him.

Gideon fought to refill his empty lungs. He pulled Samíah away, the two of them racing for the edge of the aisle. Flacco came crawling after them, the two corpses shadowy humps behind.

"Are you all right?" panted Samíah as Gideon knelt beside the highest stack of crates.

His hand massaged his throat; he could still feel the deathly grip of the fanatic. "I . . . think so," he answered. Both of them were well aware of how close the encounter had been. And he knew that if it hadn't been for Samíah's quick action, he, too, would be lying among the lifeless bodies.

"This time I owe you *my* life," he told her.

"We're still not even," she responded dryly. "But I'll never live to repay anything I owe you with those snipers on the balcony."

That much was certain, Gideon gloomily acknowledged, quickly scanning the rafters. On ground level, hunters and prey were equal to the shadows. The snipers on the balcony, though, posed a more immediate threat. Sooner or later some of those bolts were going to find their marks—and he was powerless to stop them.

Or was he?

He narrowed his eyes and gazed beyond the aisle, past the

corpses. The second Assassin had carried a crossbow, he recalled, fallen during the struggle. If only he could reach it...

"What are you doing?" cried Samíah as the secret agent began to slither away.

"We need that crossbow," he shot back hoarsely. "It's our only chance."

"They can see you from up there, Gideon!"

"Don't...don't be a fool," rasped Flacco. "The moment you move out into the open..." He didn't need to finish the sentence.

Paying no attention to their protests, Gideon crawled against the walls of crates and dragged himself over the limp figures. His hand slowly maneuvered out beyond the aisle, groping. Nothing; his fingers closed on empty space. Hunching his shoulders he eased himself forward, dangerously out into the open. He froze at the sound of a lever being cocked again. Above, the snipers were biding their time until he was in their sights.

Like a snake he slithered ahead, frantically reaching out. As despair began to take hold, his fingertips suddenly brushed against something solid: wood—the stock of the crossbow. His heart thrummed with danger. In a bold movement he pulled the weapon and fell flat on his back. A bolt whizzed and barreled through the slat of a crate. Gideon wiped perspiration from his forehead. He fondled the weapon, feeling first for the palm swell and then the hair trigger. The bulk of the crossbow rested gently against him. It was still loaded but uncocked, a magnificent instrument of death, carefully grooved and fitted with sights. No stranger to such weaponry, he grudgingly admired its quality and craftsmanship, thinking that a few dozen men armed with such weapons might indeed be able to hold off several cohorts of the finest cavalry.

He worked his way back down the aisle, retracing his steps until he returned to Samíah and the injured Gypsy.

On one knee, he positioned the crossbow against shoulder and cheek, then turned his gaze slowly above to the rafters. Deep shadows alone greeted him. There was no way he could make out the forms of the slinking snipers who were systematically moving along the balcony. He only had one shot—and he would have to make it count. But how when he couldn't see a thing?

He put the crossbow down gently beside him, started to pry open the closest crate with his knife.

"What are you doing now?" whispered Samíah.

Gideon did not reply. When he was able to reach his hand inside he gently took out the first object he encountered. It was crude and tubular, cased in many layers of tightly wrapped paper, coated with shellac, pointed at the top, rounded at the bottom, and had a short length of stiff fuse protruded from the casing.

Flacco's eyes widened when he saw it, Samíah pursing her lips in wonder as the secret agent examined it carefully.

"What in the name Romany hell is that thing?" mumbled Flacco.

"A fireworks rocket." A smudge of finely ground carbon mixed with sulfur rubbed off on his fingertips as he tilted it. The rocket had been in its crate for quite some time, he saw; the encased powder might be damp. Frowning, he began to search his pockets.

"What are you looking for?"

"The only thing I don't seem to have—a match."

"Are you planning to light that thing?" Samíah asked in wonder.

He shook his head, but Samíah's relief turned to trepidation when he said, "No, you are."

"Don't be a fool, man!" croaked Flacco. "Likely as not it will explode in your faces."

"It's our only hope." He looked sharply at the girl. "Samíah, if we can ignite it, fire it to the rafters, I can pinpoint those snipers . . ."

"Or blow up the whole factory in glorious splendor," Samíah wryly added. She grimaced sourly.

"We can't do anything without a fire to light it."

Flacco stirred restlessly. "In my pocket there's a flint," he said. "A Gypsy always keeps one handy to start a fire."

Gideon grinned. "This may be one blaze you'll really be proud of, my friend. Can you give me the flint?"

Weakly, Flacco struggled to take the small stone from his baggy trousers pocket. Gideon reached over and clasped the stone in his fist. Then, instructing Samíah, he said, "Hold the rocket for me while I light the fuse. Aim it high—over there." He indicated the general direction of the ladders leading to the balcony.

"And then?" she asked breathlessly.

"Duck, cover your head, and shut your eyes. Leave the rest to me. Ready?" She nodded.

Cupping his hands, Gideon sat cross-legged and placed the flints in front of him. Sparks flew as he scraped the flint against his knife. Samíah lowered the rocket. The fuse took a spark and began to hiss. A tiny flame sputtered. "Now!" said Gideon.

On her knees she cocked back her arm and tossed the cylinder as far as she could. The flame of the fuse traced a blue line in the darkness, pushing back shadows. Without warning a dizzying array of color shot out into the air. The warehouse burst into bright, sparkling light.

Gideon shouldered the crossbow and leaned over the nearby crate. A stunned, mystified image appeared; the sniper was leaning all the way over the rail of the balcony, his bow already cocked. The popping and hissing continued all around. Gideon shut one eye and screwed the other; his finger barely nudged at the hair trigger. The forceful snap of the windlass jerked his head back. Amid the array of spiraling sparks, the bolt instantly found its mark. Surrounded by a frenzy of bursting color, the sniper screamed and was hurled backward. His crossbow flew from his grasp and, lifted off his feet, he whirled, slammed against the rafters, dislodged a carefully stacked pile of boxes, then tumbled forward with them and rebounded over the edge of the balcony. He crashed down among the crates, the bolt embedded straight through his heart.

From the other side of the balcony the second sniper aimed and shot. The snub bolt slammed into a crate a quarter inch from the back of Flacco's head. Its impact knocked over the crate, spilling its contents over the floor. Flacco dived to the floor.

Another bolt sallied too far overhead to do any damage. Gideon threw himself over Samíah. Fanatics had started to run helter-skelter through the aisles, aided in their search by the light of the blazing rocket. The missile sailed across the ceiling, smashing through a skylight where it petered out above the roofs.

Gideon struck the flint again; the cluster bomb in his hand virtually exploded the instant it left his hand. In three different directions the firework hissed and whined. Streaming tails of orange, ultramarine, and violet shattered the darkness the length of the warehouse.

A dagger wielding Assassin raced down the aisle, stumbling over the corpses of his companions. Samíah grabbed a rocket with shaky hands. The Assassin loped to reach her. Gideon struck the flint. The rocket shot off like a surge of white lightning, hissing in a beeline for the Assassin. Contact was made; the fanatic reeled backward, the flare ramming into his gut. Black powder ignited and exploded. A torrent of fiery flame surged with incredible fury and engulfed him as he screamed. Turned into a human torch, he fell back against the crates, waving his arms wildly, howling like a hyena, his features gruesomely reflecting his pain and terror. Neatly piled stacks came crashing around him. He rolled on the floor in a futile effort to smother the flames. Up on his knees he witlessly crawled forward. The sight of him sent other fanatics quickly scrambling away. Cowl and robe ablaze, he tried to run while the fire burned him. He fell again and writhed, exposing the boxes and crates on either side to the flames.

"Hit the floor!" cried Gideon, aware of what was about to happen.

From every side came the hiss and whistle of detonating rockets. They mushroomed in vivid eruptions of flaming color, every tint of the spectrum. Flaming missiles spewed and ricocheted, their burning compositions producing maximum combustion. More skylights shattered, the entire factory shaking with a roaring din of fireworks gone berserk.

Samíah lifted her head from the floor and stared through amazed eyes. Stick-guided missiles cartwheeled, fluttering in broad bands and circular patterns. Fantastic pins of colorful brightness danced, shooting off fiery balls of orange and crimson flame, surging and pulsing, smashing into yet more packed crates which, in turn, set off other fires and explosions in a never-ending carousel of light. Everywhere, the missiles sailed and careened, like arrows and spears.

A huge sunlike orb of yellow-blue incendiary powder was launched from behind her. A shooting star, it coursed insanely without direction toward the heavens, blasting anew as it was struck time and again by flying rockets. Screaming phantasms of speeding missiles blasted through the roof, propelled with increasing fury as they screeched into open sky and lit up the night and the city like it had never been lit up before. It seemed to Samíah she was trapped in the middle of a new and expanding universe of countless raging suns and stars, each in dizzying orbit around the next, expanding with unimaginable power. The vortex of dancing fireworks created an uproar that sent citizens by the tens of thousands to the streets and roofs to gasp in awe at the fantastic display. From one corner of Marrakesh to the next, from the groves to the desert, as far away as the Atlas mountains, numbed and dumbstruck masses stared with incomprehension.

Inside the factory, Gideon took Samíah in his arms, and together they shuddered at the tempest they had unleashed. There was no stopping it now; no shelter or protection they could find. Yet through it all they were joyous—for at last the signal had been given, and their friends would know what to do.

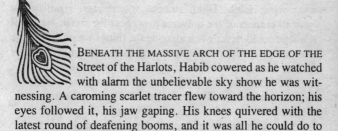

BENEATH THE MASSIVE ARCH OF THE EDGE OF THE Street of the Harlots, Habib cowered as he watched with alarm the unbelievable sky show he was witnessing. A caroming scarlet tracer flew toward the horizon; his eyes followed it, his jaw gaping. His knees quivered with the latest round of deafening booms, and it was all he could do to keep himself from fleeing at once.

"By the sacred robes of the Prophet!" he exclaimed. "What's happened to the world?"

The genie lackadaisically stroked Lucifer's fur as the cat snoozed in his folded arms. Rather a pretty display, though, wouldn't you say?" he commented absently.

"But what—how—?"

"My dear, dear Habib, you really should learn to control your emotions a little bit better. It's most unbecoming for a man of your age to be so upset by a common fireworks extravaganza." He stifled a yawn as he observed the flight path of a fiery comet of hissing yellow flame that streaked above his head. When the missile finally dipped from sight behind the towers of the distant palace, he turned his attention back to the dustman. "Not very long until dawn," he mused, shivering briefly. There was a decided mountain chill in the predawn air. "So, any moment now we should be hearing from your contact."

The reference to Gideon went in one ear and out the other.

259

Lost in a fireworks-inspired trance, Habib had all but forgotten the reason for this sojourn in the first place.

A cluster bomb shattered magnificiently, spraying meteorites across vast areas. Unconsciously Habib ducked.

The genie chuckled, unimpressed. "You know," he said, speaking to Habib but resting his gaze on the contentedly purring Lucifer, "those mortal displays are quite puny. Boring. I can remember one time when the Genie Guild put on a demonstration in the heavens that made tonight seem little more than schoolboys running around a yard with sparklers. *That* was a night, Habib!! Djinn, demons, witches, and wizards came from all corners of the universe to witness the show. Hrumph! Humans could never even imagine the things we did! Why we took the planet Mars and tilted it on its axis, then sent Jupiter reeling like, like—Habib, are you listening to me?"

"Eh? What did you say?"

"Never mind, Habib. Never mind." He went back to stroking the cat.

"Say, what time is it?" asked the dustman as he glanced to the east where a tracer flare had just disappeared, and noticed the first flickers of gray light.

"Almost time. I've told you not to worry so much, haven't I?"

"But Gideon promised to be here at first light." He was growing nervous again. "Are you sure Samíah is all right?"

The genie burped. "Be a good fellow and go back to gawking at the fireworks, will you?" he said in irritation. Everything is in order. There's nothing to fret about."

"Easy for you to say! You're a genie; one snap of the fingers and poof! Your problems are solved. But it wasn't *your* daughter that was whisked away, sent traipsing around the city with Gypsies, getting into Allah-knows-what-kind-of-trouble." He shook his head and grimaced. "Gideon should have known better than to take Samíah with him tonight. What's the matter with young people today? Why don't they listen? Don't they have any regard for their parents anymore? Don't they value their own lives?"

With a small smile that annoyed Habib, the genie said condescendingly, "Things are different today, my friend. Young people have their own minds. Besides, they must follow their stars, precisely as you yourself did long ago."

"Bah."

The sky show was abruptly coming to a close. The final bursts of rockets bulleted overhead, leaving behind pluming trails of ashen smoke. Two ragged figures came stumbling from the shadowed street, assisting a third. Safely out of the factory, Samíah and Gideon had met their dawn appointment.

ACID WATER HAD LONG AGO BEGUN TO ERODE AND dissolve the limestone. The roof and jagged walls of the subterranean passage steadily closed in upon the travelers. When they had reached the first tier, at a place not very far from the secret door to the fireworks factory, Gideon and Habib paused to allow the others time to catch up.

Samíah came first, her breath labored and heavy, as she strained to see in the shadows. Above, the new day's sun was brightly shining; here, though, few streaks of light seeped through the cracks and fissures. Save for the occasional ray slanting down from some unseen crevice, the tunnels remained as bleak and dark as they had been at midnight.

Behind Samíah, the genie was stumbling. He held one hand against the wall for support while cradling Lucifer tightly with the other. He cursed brusquely below his breath, appalled at the indignity of it all—not to mention the discomfort. The chill and drafts made him shiver, the foully reeking stink of open cesspools accosted his supernatural sensibilities. And the minor but constant aches and pains that came from walking in a half-squat position tormented his unhoned muscles. It was quite undignified, he decided, and how he ever became involved in this whole sordid affair was rapidly becoming a mystery to him. Nevertheless, here he was. Entangled—for the first and final time!—in the uneventful affairs of lowly mortals, with little or nothing he could do about it. After all, a bargain was still a bargain. Fortunately, though, there was no way other members of the Guild might come to learn about it. Still, in his mind's eye he could picture them if they did find out. They would never let him live this down. Never. Not through all eternity, by Allah! He would be the butt of endless jokes from one side of the universe to the other.

"So what do you think?" Gideon was saying as the small party gathered together.

Habib wet his lips as he glanced down at the first fork and downward curve of the tunnel. "It's been many, many years since I sloshed a slop mop in the sewers," he confided, gently stroking the stubble below his lip. He placed his hands on his hips. This journey seemed so preposterous to him; Gideon and Samíah had babbled incoherently beneath the arch at the Street of the Harlots, urging him away and into the manhole before he had time to ask a single question. With the injured Flacco quickly taken to safety in the Gypsy *ofisa*, Gideon had forced him to hold off his unanswered questions, claiming that time was so short and vital there wasn't time. Now, he found himself back in a place he'd all but forgotten.

"Do you still remember the way, Habib?" Gideon's voice was anxious, reverberating slightly.

The dustman scratched his head. "This sounds crazy to me. Are you *sure* we'll find something down there?"

"No question of it, my friend. The attack against Marrakesh will come tonight. That's why they've taken Rosa. We have to find them—now. Put an end to the messiah once and for all."

"Please, Papa," implored Samíah. "Do as Gideon asks. There's no time to lose."

The dustman shuddered at the memory of these shafts. Yes, there were ways to reach the inner sanctums below: dangerous tunnels. More than once some unwary sewer worker had become lost, wandering until he starved and died among the labyrinthine mazes. Many false tunnels had been built by the early sultans to confuse and trick an enemy trying to find them.

Slowly, Habib studied the tunnel before him. He might be able to take them safely through. But what if he took a single misstep? What then? They would all be doomed.

"All right, I'll try."

Gideon heaved a thankful sigh. "We'll need to mark our passage so Wanko will be able to follow us. Anyone have a piece of chalk?"

Habib shook his head, so did Samíah. Her eyes were fixed on the genie. He certainly *was* a peculiar fellow. He didn't look like anyone from the village, and she had absolutely no idea where her father knew him from. What with his gleaming turban, white robes, and hairless skin that was slightly green even in the dim light he seemed a character indeed. And why was he now looking back at her in that funny sort of way, as though she were not a stranger to him at all. As they stood facing each other she had the feeling he could read her very thoughts, look into and through every fiber of her being. His expression may have been impassive, but somehow she had the feeling he was inwardly smiling at her, as if two long-lost acquaintances had been brought together at last. Her father's friend didn't exactly frighten her—but his stare did make her uneasy.

"Chalk?" said Habib, breaking the moment of silence. The dustman looked sharply at the genie. "You can help us find some, can't you?" His manner was cryptic.

With a frown, the genie made a gesture with his fingers. According to the rules, he'd already done his part by granting Habib one wish. Still, if there was any hope of quickly getting out of this damnable city and back to sleep in the bottle, he would have to bend the rules a bit. Magically, although no one saw it, a piece of clean white chalk appeared in his hand.

"Here," he said, handing it to Gideon. "Just so happens that I always carry some with me, er, for emergencies."

Gideon took the chalk gratefully and made his first marking—a large X in a circle—in an obvious spot on the wall, followed by a small arrow.

"Lead on, Habib. As fast as you can. I'll leave the next marker before we reach another level."

A loud clang echoed from the shadows. Gideon spun, drew his knife expecting to find an Assassin ready to spring. "Who goes?" he demanded, stepping in front of the others and wielding the blade menacingly.

"Only me, Gideon—don't worry." The voice seemed distant and shaky. The secret agent narrowed his eyes to get a glimpse of the emerging figure. But if it wasn't an Assassin, then who? Surely not Wanko—the king would by now be only beginning to muster his forces. The rag man? No, he would be leading the Karshi for the coming assault. Then who?

To his astonishment it was a soldier's glittering epaulets he noted first.

Captain Enos stepped out into the open and sheepishly looked at the knot of people.

"You!" gasped Samíah. "How did you get here?"

"I—I followed you. When the fireworks began, I was on patrol, as you instructed, Gideon, but then I noticed him." His gaze drifted to the dustman. "I saw him crouching beneath the arch with the other fellow and became suspicious. Knowing the dustman to be Samíah's father I realized something was afoot. So I hid on the other side of the Street of Harlots and waited. Then, when you came," he was speaking and looking to Gideon again, "I knew something had gone wrong. When I heard Rosa's name I couldn't control myself—"

"So you followed us down here?" It was less a question than a statement.

Captain Enos nodded. "I had to, Gideon. Forgive me for disobeying, but I couldn't live with myself any longer, not while Rosa is still in their hands." He sheathed the sword which had fallen and caused the commotion.

Gideon sighed. What was he to do now with the lovestruck soldier? By all rights, the captain should never have risked coming down here like this. But, he couldn't blame the hapless captain for his worry and distress. Surely if Samíah had been whisked away, Gideon would have felt the same.

"I suppose there's no point in telling you to get back above ground?"

The bold soldier shook his head. "I heard you say that Rosa is still down there somewhere. If you intend going after her, then I'm coming too. Besides," and here he smiled wanly, "you'll probably have need of an extra sword."

Gideon grinned. A good man lik Captain Enos would indeed be useful where they were going. "Don't just stand there gawking. If you want to follow, then come on. Allah knows we've wasted far too much time already."

Habib took the lead and, single file, they began the descent.

A STREAM OF BEFOULED WATER LAPPED GENTLY against the stone embankments. The walkway beside it was becoming increasingly narrow but remained wide enough to walk on. Vitrified clay pipes poured their fluids into the conduit from beneath the surface and caused minor ripples in the steady flow. At random intervals along the wall were unlighted torches set in place for the sewer workers. As the dim brightness of the shafts turned to velvet black with the deeper descent, Habib took a torch in hand and waited while Gideon struck Flacco's flint and lit it. Smokey orange flame burst into life. Samíah cringed at the sight of a furry rat darting from the sudden light.

Stoically, the dustman continued on, his companions single file on his heels. Here the ceiling was a cracked and rotting dome scarred with layers, each telling of a time rock had come crashing down. The last fall had been quite recently, Habib could tell from the tiny flakes of mica which continued to float in a light drizzle.

"Most of these tunnels regularly collapse," the dustman noted gloomily.

At length the conduit flowed into a great gaping hole through which there were no walkways. The catch basin ahead rested like a dark lake amid its cavern, still and silent. For an instant it appeared they had reached a dead end. Captain Enos shuddered involuntarily and was about to protest their being led on a fool's errand when Habib twisted himself knowingly along the edge of the walkway and held his torch high. As if out of nowhere an entrance appeared. Aged frames of rotting wood carved squarely into rock granted access into yet another grotesque tunnel, this one blacker still. The dustman poked the flame inside the opening. A sickly pungent smell came to his nostrils, and he peered down the set of winding stone steps. "This way," he mumbled, moving inside first and testing the sturdiness of the first step. Then boldly, without waiting for the others he began the descent.

Gideon, holding Samíah's hand, was right behind. The genie looked to the soldier; Enos indicated he should go next. With a grunt and a hidden moan he followed the girl.

"There are handholds along the wall," Habib pointed out. "Walk slowly and carefully." As if to give testimony to his warning, a shard of rock was dislodged from a step, and the dustman nearly toppled.

"How much longer?" Gideon wanted to know after they had descended for a long time.

"Not too much more. In fact, I think I can see the landing

now." He thrust forward his torch and bared his lips in what was going to be a smile. The sight of what he saw turned it instead into a grimace. Along the cracked floor a pack of rodents hunched around the maggot- and worm-infested corpse of what once had been a man. Only now it wasn't a man at all, merely bones and thin layers of meat around the crown of the skull and arms. The rest had long since been picked clean.

At sight of the strangers and the torch, the rodents dashed away in different directions. Samíah wretched at the ghastly corpse, burying her head against Gideon's chest whild Habib and Captain Enos came for a closer inspection. Eyeless sockets stared harrowingly up at the visitors.

Habib felt his stomach turn. He knelt. "Probably a sewer worker. Look at the way his leg is bent. My guess is that he lost his work gang. He must have followed the stairway in his panic, hoping to find some way out. Maybe he fell, broke his leg and was unable to move. Who can say? One thing is certain, though: he spent his last days right here, fighting off the rats, starving. But in the end," and here he sighed, "they over-whelmed him."

Captain Enos looked away in revulsion, wondering if he, too, might soon become a feast for rodents.

"I warned you the sewers weren't a very pretty place," said Habib. "Do you still want to go on?"

"We have no choice," said Gideon.

The dustman straightened his shoulders and nodded. Then he walked around the body and continued on.

For some time the tunnel remained on a straight, unbending course. Suddenly, though, it started to turn, then turn again. Soon there stood before them a whole complex of new tunnels, one leading to the left, another to the right; two more spiraling downward, two along the other side seemingly providing an upward channel back toward the surface. Habib wasn't fooled by any of them.

"All are false routes but one," he told his companions as they gathered around him. He winked at Gideon. "If you had to guess, which one would you choose?"

Putting his hands on his hips and searching the maze slowly,

Gideon used a combination of logic, deduction, and intuition. He immediately discounted the entrances leading upward. "Those must be counterfeit," he announced. "We're looking for a way farther down, not up."

The dustman chuckled. "And if it had been you constructing such an elaborate hoax, wouldn't you want your enemies to deduce precisely the same thing?" He smiled with a gleam in his eye. "Ah my young friend, you haven't done your homework well enough. You surmised exactly what the sultans of old would have hoped. Look here," he marched quickly toward the seemingly false entrances. "First they go up. His torch poked inside. Silky spider webs gleamed in the light. "Then they turn and go down. Straight down."

"Amazing," mumbled Captain Enos.

"All right," said Gideon. "I'm convinced. But which of the two leading up do we take?"

Habib looked from one to the other of his companions. Sighing, he said, "I don't know."

The dustman shrugged. "I told you; it's been years since I was last in the sewers. And this chamber I've never seen at all."

"Then how do you know the tunnel leading up is the right one?"

"From what the gang bosses taught us long ago, as a precaution should anyone ever become lost."

Samíah groaned. "So what do we do now?"

Gideon looked at her expressionlessly before turning back to Habib. "I suppose we'll have to make a choice."

"It's a fifty-fifty proposition," reminded the dustman. "One will be right, the other wrong."

"Do we take a vote or what?" the soldier wanted to know.

"Flip a coin," offered Samíah. "Unless," and here she looked quizzically to her father's green-fleshed friend, "someone else has a better idea."

The genie studied the entrances with a jaundiced eye. "The one on the right," he mumbled as Lucifer hissed.

Gideon nodded and started to move. "Hold on," complained Captain Enos. "How do we know he's correct? Why, he's not even from the city. He's an, er," he sought for the proper word, "an *outsider*. Why should we listen to him?"

Habib huffed and swelled his chest. "If my friend says go to the right, then that's the way we go." He said it with an air of finality. And, nudging Samíah, he moved off.

It was a steep climb, long and hazardous. Habib counted off his upward steps, and with time began to despair. The tunnel twisted, with so many new turnoffs and sudden side entrances that already it appeared impossible to retrace their steps. So far—and the number of carefully counted steps neared the one-thousand mark—there appeared no sign of the hoped for descent. What if the genie *were* wrong? Each new fork made it increasingly apparent how confusing the journey had become.

Unexpectedly, while mulling these somber, unshared thoughts, Habib reached a landing. Terrible down drafts of wind shot from the fissures, scattering the torch flame and nearly extinguishing it. Sheltering the licking fire with a cupped hand he peered about. The weak flame glinted off mica and reflected in the rock walls. Pale light pushed back the absolute black that surrounded them. With an unsure step, the dustman pressed forward. They had come to the top of the shaft with nowhere to go—nowhere save a wide, gaping hole that spanned the narrow floor before him; an almost circular shaft, stepless, that led straight down. Habib knelt beside the edge. Rusted sets of handholds glimmered dully when he poked the torch inside. A bottomless hole.

Gideon came to his side. The whistle of the draft was so loud that Habib had to raise his voice to be heard. "This is it," he called, his hair blowing wildly. "We'll have to lower ourselves down."

"Down there?" said Samíah, aghast.

"We need some rope," said Gideon, as he noted the shaft's jagged outcroppings.

"And where are we supposed to find cord for a descent like that?" said the soldier. All faces turned blank and expressionless. Where indeed?

Habib narrowed his gaze as he regarded the genie.

With a long sigh the green-skinned stranger reached deep

inside the folds of his white robes. To everyone but the dust-man's amazement he tugged out a circular long shank of hemp. "I, er, always have some of this handy," he tried to explain as he handed it to the dustman. "I keep it, er . . ."

Samíah shot him a curious stare. "I know, I know, you keep it for emergencies."

Without losing time Gideon proceeded to wrap one end of the taut line securely around his waist. He didn't know where the dustman's friend had found the rope, and right now he didn't much care. When the cable was secure he tossed the line over to Captain Enos. "Can you support my weight until I reach a landing?"

The soldier seemed hesitant. "How—How do you know the line's long enough?" he stammered. "That hole seems mighty deep."

"He's right," said Samíah weakly. Her eyes were filled with dread and a plea for Gideon to reconsider such a hasty action.

Standing with folded arms, his stubby hand stroking Lucifer behind the strange cat's ears, the genie said simply, "The line is long enough for the drop."

"How can you be so sure?" Captain Enos rejoined.

Dryly, the genie looked at the soldier. "The line is long enough," he repeated; inwardly appalled at having his word questioned.

"We'll find out one way or the other soon enough," said Gideon. He rested himself at the edge of the hole and let his feet dangle over the side. The dustman knelt beside him. The torch would provide small light for at least part of the way down. After that, Gideon would have to feel his way alone.

"Once I've touched the bottom I'll yank twice," he told Habib. "That will be the signal to haul the rope up. Loop it around yourself and let Captain Enos lower you. Then repeat the procedure for Samíah and the others. Last man to drop will have to loop the rope around a handhold and hope it's strong enough to support him. Understand?"

Both the soldier and the dustman sourly nodded.

Samíah saw Gideon smile briefly at her; then he drew a deep breath and slipped over the side. Captain Enos and the genie held the hemp slackly. Gideon lowered himself to the first handhold and tested it. It was strong, he realized thankfully. So far, so good.

His feet searched for the next hold. The rope became taut as he maneuvered himself slowly toward it. When he tilted his head, the flickering brightness above the opening threw a shadowed image of Samíah as she strained to see over the side, mutely following his careful progress.

Deeper and deeper he descended, growing more assured. Soon the outlined circumference above was little more than a distant circle. His hands began to blister as they closed tightly around the metallic holds. The heavy rasping of his belabored breath became his only companion as he continued the precipitous drop. He pivoted to avoid a dangerous outcropping, made a jacknife squeeze between it and another slightly below. For an instant he dangled in mid-air, then the heel of his boot sought purchase and found it as it nudged another hold. Gideon paused to catch his breath.

Progress was slow but steady. His vision had all but become accustomed to the lightlessness of his surroundings when, hardly aware of it, his feet scraped along the landing.

Grimly he touched the bottom. It didn't take more than a quick, inspection before he found what he was looking for. Deep within the shadows there was a crawl space like a huge mole hole. He dropped to his knees and burrowed his head and shoulders inside. An entire new tunnel greeted him on the other side. Wide and tubular on a descent gently angled, he could see glimmers of light in the distance. He stood back up with an expression of satisfaction. The final leg of the journey was before him; there was no doubt in his mind that the distant lights were the lights of the ancient inner sanctum—the fortress of the messiah.

Gideon whispered a quick prayer and with a single motion unlooped the hemp from his waist and yanked it twice in the prescribed signal. The line was hauled up. Patiently Gideon waited for the others to reach him.

PEEKING FROM THE SCREENED DOOR ACROSS THE narrow chamber Rosa could see the first double line of cowled fanatics as they hurried across the courtyard below in sinister procession. Torch flames danced in their hands, beating back the darkness and revealing the vast area between the massive structures which loomed incredibly high on either side of the courtyard. Rosa, for the first time, became aware of the enormousness of this underground fortress. Almost as huge as the grand palace of Marrakesh itself, it was like a city in miniature, with high steeples and towers with lookout posts, and severe portcullises of iron now raised but ready to drop shut on a moment's notice to cut off any breach of an advancing enemy. Complete with moat—a circular deep river of sewer water that surrounded the fortress—this haven of the messiah seemed inpenetrable indeed.

It was an eerie, surrealistic sight to the Gypsy girl. From her window in the tower room she had seen the underworld panorama of the cavern, and now from the screened door she was looking inside, down at the central courtyard where the army of her captors were busily on the move.

A chill draft nudged her matted hair; she brushed it impatiently away from her eyes as she scanned the scene below apprehensively. The movements of the armed hosts of the messiah could only mean one thing: that the attack upon the city above was about to commence in full force. Spurred by Blinco

Rascola's treachery, the army of the messiah was on the march toward the tunnels, ready to swarm like insects over the un-suspecting city, ready to overwhelm opposition and take the palace itself as a declaration of their power.

Rosa bit her lip in anger and frustration. It all seemed so futile. She, Gideon, and Wanko, and the others had come so close to smashing the threat once and for all, and now because of Blinco Rascola they were doomed. A few precious hours more might have made all the difference, caught the fanatics unaware, and allowed the counterattack to halt the assault be-fore it began. But it was too late. She shuddered and tried not to cry. The forces of evil had outwitted the forces of good. The Black Empire was about to win.

Sickly horrified by what she was witnessing, Rosa turned from the sight and disconsolately heaved a bitter sigh. She knew the hopelessness of the situation, and it broke her heart to realize that she would never see any of those she loved again. Not Wanko or the queen, not Samíah or Gideon, not even her bold and brave lover, Captain Enos.

Why they were keeping her alive now she didn't know. Whisked from her prison in the fireworks factory, she had half expected to be killed right then and there. Then, after her arduous journey kicking and screaming as they dragged her down to the inner sanctum, they had promptly imprisoned her in this foul place. Surely even death was preferable to this, to the torture of being able to watch while the world collapsed around her. Or perhaps it was for this very reason they had left her unmolested: so that she could indeed witness the fall of everything she loved. If this had been the messiah's intent, then it had worked all too well. Rosa was all but broken. Had she a knife or a razor or a sliver of glass at hand, she knew she would have willingly taken her own life.

A key fitted into the lock; the screened door opened behind her slowly. She didn't turn as a figure emerged from the hallway and stood malevolently eyeing her beneath the frame.

"So you are the Gypsy woman," came the gravelly voice, a voice that sent waves of ice shooting through her.

Slowly, she looked around. The cowled figure stood in

shadows, arms folded, his face hidden within the depths of his hood. Only his eyes were apparent to her: cold and merciless, flickering with evil.

She threw back her head and faced him evenly, unwilling to let this latest tormentor know how frightened she really was. "I am the Gypsy," she acknowledged with all the pride and defiance she could muster. "I am Rosa, daughter of Wanko the king."

"Ah, yes, Rosa, daughter of the king. You are named well for one so lovely and young."

She backed off a pace with her heart thrumming. "Touch me and I'll gouge out your eyes!" she flared.

His jawline tightened. He let his gaze linger over her young and vibrant body, frowning at the sight of the bruises that marred her perfection. Her captors had been clumsy to flaw her like this. Heavy-handed, uncouth oafs. He had warned them to be careful, not to blemish her in any way. Still, they had disobeyed: handled her roughly when she kicked and screamed and fought them. It was an affront to his sensibilities. His gods would not be pleased having an imperfect woman brought to them on the altar, a gift of a woman whose flesh had been damaged, even if only slightly. The oafs would have to be punished for their infraction. Yet, despite the flaws, she was still a prize to him above all others but one—the woman Samíah. And upon the sacred altar she would, as planned, be handed to the Gods of Night as his first sacrifice, her heart plucked from her chest still beating, her blood drained and sipped by his high priests, her body offered in purity to the stone statues of the deities whose appetites were insatiable, constantly demanding new life's blood.

The clatter of footsteps marching over the marble became louder. By the hundreds now they were crossing the courtyard and under the portcullis. The sound of it was more than pleasing; the thought of vengeance stirred him to the verge of ecstasy the way no woman's flesh ever could. Soon the victory would be complete: the fabled city of Marrakesh humbled before his might, the clown of a sultan and all those who blindly followed him prime blood for further noble sacrifice. How splendid it would be! Empire after empire would grovel at his feet. Soon he would have it all. A new world order would prevail, spanning continents and oceans. It was now so close, within his grasp, that he could almost touch it. His will would reign supreme!

"Can you hear them marching, dear Rosa?" he asked, chortling, looking straight through her and not seeing her at all. "Does my army entrance you as they march to eternal reward?"

At first she thought him to be speaking metaphorically. Then suddenly the weight of his words hit her. *My army...My army*... She became cold, colder than ever before.

"It's you," she whispered. "You are... the messiah...."

He repeated the words slowly, answering now not to her but to the other whispered voices that were always with him, always there to instruct him. "Yes, Rosa. I am he. The one who is come, come back from the dead to lead. See, my Rosa, see how they do my bidding." He lifted his arm and pointed toward the window. "They gather at my bidding, Rosa, drugged and at one with the gods who speak to me. To the tunnels they go, Rosa, to the light of day and the birth of the New Dawn. Yes—but first shall come the Black Night. The darkest night that ever the surface world has seen. Bow, Rosa! Cringe before the all-seeing Eye of Darkness."

She stood shivering, afraid now not merely for her life but for her eternal soul.

"They didn't listen to me the last time, Rosa," he went on, babbling almost incoherently. "The fools! They fought my will, turned against the all-seeing Darkness, forced me to flee and hide below the streets. But I was not defeated, not even then. It was a sign, dear Rosa, don't you see? I was being put to the test, the ultimate test of my gods. They had deemed me worthy but untried, but now they know the truth even as I know it. This time the peoples of the world shall heed my call, shall bow unto me and the new order that is to come! And a wonderful world it will be, Rosa. And you"—his eyes flamed with burning insanity—"shall be twice blessed. Yes, from afar you shall witness my coming, among the gods who take you to their bosoms and cradle you as one of their own. Your death shall be glorious, Rosa! Upon the sacred altar of afterlife!"

He began to laugh, gesturing at the window, then lifting his arms above his head and balling his hands into fists, "See, Rosa; see what my madness has brought to the world. An army like never before! See, Rosa, then come with me to the altar. The flames of eternity await."

Against her will she peered from the window. The messiah had not lied. Grim high priests even now invoked the incantation while what seemed to be hundreds—no, thousands!—of demented fanatics stood humbled and bowed. She put her hand to her mouth and gasped at the sight. For surely the madman before her had been right. This was an unstoppable army, determined to right the wrongs imposed by the forces of light and bring about the New Dawn of Darkness.

GIDEON RESUMED HIS CAUTIOUS PACE UNTIL, WITH a few quick strides, he reached the portal entrance. Crouching, he sucked in air to fill his lungs and, with his eyes stinging from the sudden unexpected flood of artificial light, gazed from the portal to the looming cavernous walls. The fortress rose high: massive towers of cold gray stone above the crenellated fortifications, grim steeples and watchtowers aglow with eerie torchlight. It was a mind-boggling sight, this armed castle, and only now did the secret agent truly begin to comprehend the magnificence of the feat of the ancient sultans.

Twin towers, turrets of streaked black stone, jutted along either side of the portcullis beyond the deep waters of the moat. From his clandestine nook he could make out the shadowy forms of hooded fanatics as they spilled over the bridge in small numbers. A feeling of panic nearly overwhelmed Gideon as he realized what was happening. He had come too late— too late to halt the assault. The messiah's forces were on the march.

With Habib and the genie at her back, Samíah knelt next to Gideon and stared through the portal in abject wonder. Her thoughts were numbed both by the chill of the subterranean world and by the appearance of the devilish castle.

"Blessed sultan!" wheezed Captain Enos. "What are we to do now?"

Regaining a measure of composure, Samíah became aware of dim and distant voices, singing like a choir. Her eyes darted anxiously from the portal toward a dark stairwell twisting up to the castle proper. At regular intervals along the upward flight catwalks jutted outward from the walls until they finally disappeared somewhere within the fortifications. With a finger to her lips she stopped Gideon from speaking and cautioned her companions to listen. The resonant murmurings echoed hollowly, the unclear phrases of the song making her shudder.

"The priests," mouthed Habib in barely a whisper. "The priests must be invoking the blessings from their gods."

Gideon nodded knowingly. It was a ceremony, he was sure. A grim liturgy to signal the coming battle. In his imagination he could picture it; dozens of unholy monks gathered at their altar, giving sacrifice to the evil harbingers of the new world order. And Gideon knew he was powerless to stop it.

Samíah focused her attention upon the bridge where more and more fanatics were assembling. It would not take the Assassin army very long to work their way to the surface, she realized, and then to unleash their destruction in a tempest. It would be terrible.

"Time," growled the secret agent. "We need time."

"Aye," agreed Habib. "But how do we buy it?"

They all knew that both Wanko and the rag man would by now have gathered their forces for the counterattack, but it would still take a while before they could follow Gideon's scrawled markings and lead a vanguard through the sewers.

Not fifty meters in front of the secret agent, unobscured by any visible impediment, stood the castle's portcullis, the goal of the night's venture. But how were they to reach it? How to gain access to the bridge when numberless fanatics were fully armed and prepared to stop them?

"The ceremony," said the genie.

Samíah turned to the white-robed, peculiar stranger. "What did you say?"

"The rites, girl! Stop the rites. The Assassins cannot march to battle before the invocations are complete."

"He's right!" rasped Gideon, snapping his fingers. "That's it." An icy chill ran up Habib's spine as he continued. "If we can reach the sacred altar, stop the completion of the sacrifice . . ."

Captain Enos picked up the thought. "They'll have to hold off the assault and turn their attention to us. Brilliant, Gideon! With luck we can stall them for hours—more than enough time for a counterattack." Then suddenly his cheer turned definitely sour. The implications of the ruse sank home. "That means we," and he glanced around at the pitiful band facing him, "will have to fight this whole army by ourselves."

"First, though, they'll have to catch us," answered the genie with a strange twinkle in his eye. Lucifer hissed in his arms.

"I never dreamed of winding up a martyr," said Habib gloomily. He looked at his daughter. If he was to die for the cause of freedom, then so be it. He was old, his life behind him anyway. But it broke his heart to think that his beloved child would also have to pay the ultimate price.

"None of us want to be martyrs," Gideon replied with a sigh. "But we have to hold the fanatics off for as long as we can."

Captain Enos stiffened his shoulders and his resolve, thinking not of personal safety but of his home, his land, and loved ones, and of Rosa who perhaps was beyond saving now but who still cried out to him in his troubled mind. Dourly, he looked at the portal and the gathering, then back to the stairwell. Those catwalks would be heavily guarded, he knew. Even trying to reach the altar was perilous in itself. "We'll have to tread carefully, friends. We don't want any alarm bells signaling our approach."

With a cold smile Gideon said, "On the contrary. Our best hope is to be as loud and obvious as possible—a big enough diversion to stop these proceedings in their tracks." He searched the faces of his companions, gratified to find no objections. Then with a flurry of activity they drew their weapons. The soldier drew his sword from its scabbard and clutched the hilt with both hands. The dustman took the small knife from his sleeve. Samíah had the dagger retrieved from the fireworks factory, while Gideon grasped his own glinting blade.

"Ready?" he asked, moving from the portal and toward the spiral stairwell, blinking as he gazed along the small upward tunnel to the first level and the cross passage.

One by one they all nodded, dry mouthed and serious. The secret agent set his lips in a tight line. "Then let's go."

He took the first step and began to bound up them two and three at a time. The others raced right on his heels. Up to the first tier they hurried, brightness from the ensconced torches growing correspondingly closer. The flat level was wide and ventilated. Gideon ran across it, oblivious of the fact that they were approaching the viaduct that led straight to the highest tower. The chanting voices were still muffled but growing steadily louder. Through random portals in the wall they could peer down at the ever-enlarging gathering of the fanatics below. Soon they would be above the moat.

It was when the next set of steps was reached and the second tier hazy with dancing torchlight before them that a brace of loud bells began to jangle.

"We've tripped a wire!" shouted Gideon. "Keep moving!"

Metal was grating loudly behind them. Samíah glanced back over her shoulder. From the high ceiling a lumbering steel cross-barred portcullis started to descend and cut off the avenue

behind. Ahead, a second steel gate started to fall. Without time
to breathe, Gideon yanked Samíah forcefully and lowering his
head and shoulders, pulled them both safely through. Captain
Enos, followed closey by Habib, hurtled forward and made it
through. The genie, huffing and puffing, sprang forward in a
low crouch, plopping on his belly as the rapidly falling gate
neared the stone floor. Steel prongs *thunked* into place, the
gate shut tight and immovable.

The genie rose slowly to his feet, and spun at the clink of
boots. A startled Assassin, eyes aflame with fervor and the
effects of drugs sprinted with dagger in hand toward him. From
the other side came several more shaven-headed fanatics.
Tongueless—as were all guardians of the inner sanctum—they
lurched to stop the advance of the trespassers. Gideon dodged
a wild thrust and punched his blade through the rough fabric
of the robe. The guardian faltered, then moaned. Captain Enos
made short shrift of his companion, heaving his sword above
his head like a battle axe and cleaving his skull. Membrane
oozed as the Assassin slumped.

As the third fanatic rushed for the genie, the white-robed
creature of the bottle poked an index finger into the air and
blinked. It was like the wind of a hurricane that hit the advancing guardian. He was knocked back powerfully, the blade
flying from his hand, and sent dumbly careening backward
where he catapulted into the grim bars of the portcullis.

From the corner of her eye Samíah had seen—or thought
she'd seen, what her father's curious friend had done. "How—
how did you manage that?" she asked.

The genie smiled wanly in response; there was little time
for explanations. More bells rang, and from the recesses of the
ceiling came the screaming of sirens. Along the catwalks and
side passages behind and beyond more gates began to descend
while others began to rise.

Gideon scrambled forward into the wide corridor ahead. A
tangle of granite ramps, blocks, and ungraceful columns spanned
the dizzying route. Habib turned at the drone of a whizzing
knife. The blade smacked against the column to his right and
clattered across the floor. A glassy-eyed guardian, whose sleeves

bore the sacred markings of his order, surged blindly, then leaped for the dustman like an ape swinging through the jungle trees. Habib pivoted, sidestepped the flying figure. He lifted one foot high and tripped the assailant mid-flight. The fanatic tumbled head over heels and yowled and his head crashed into a block of granite bulging from the wall.

The chanting was continuing ever louder, Gideon noticed as he paced quickly between the rows of pillars and strange statues. He saw a mystifying glow of brightness ahead, a pyramid doorway of solid iron covered with a mosaic of fiery crimson stones embedded in the surface. He surged toward it, instinctively sure it would prove to be the entrance to the ceremony chamber.

From the ramps and side portals came a stream of fanatics, daggers in their hands. Captain Enos quickly dispatched the Assassin on his heels with a furious elbow to the attacker's jaw, and spun around in a single motion ready to greet the onslaught and give Gideon time to reach the doorway.

Bounding down the ramp they came, knives agleam, desperation written into their faces. The bold soldier met the first surge with an overhand smash of his sword that crushed the cowled head. With each successive blow came the crunch of bone, the wailing of tongueless screams. Bodies choked the narrow gaps between the columns. Slashing and hacking insanely, Captain Enos routed the advance, turned the surviving attackers scurrying backward. Partly in confusion and partly in the need to defend the bejeweled doorway, the new line of racing fanatics circumvented the sword-heaving soldier and strove for the door. Habib blocked one with a flashing knife; a spurt of blood stained his shirt, and he looked on while the enemy crumpled at his feet. The genie dropped to his knees and lifted his left hand. Two fingers, like horns, poked into the air. Three fanatics suddenly stumbled, and those behind them tumbled across a floor that had turned as slick as ice.

"The door, man, the door!" called out the genie to Gideon.

Fending off yet another grisly foe, the secret agent banged his way between two tackling Assassins and reached the pyramid. A bolt of blue steel held firmly as he tried to slip it aside.

It wouldn't give. With every ounce of strength he could muster he yanked at it again and again—but the bolt held fast. "I can't open it!" he shouted back above the growing din. "It won't give!"

The entire floor of the corridor had become too slippery to walk on. With a measure of satisfaction the genie watched the sight of fanatics come stumbling off the ramps only to slip and slide like novice ice skaters upon a winter pond. A knot of guardians was crawling on their knees, falling flat on their faces. One used a pillar for support and made it to his feet. Stepping away, though, his arms windmilled for balance, his feet sought purchase. He skidded on his backside and tumbled over a group of belly-crawling guardians. The genie chuckled and scratched Lucifer behind the ears.

With the fanatics held temporarily at bay Captain Enos and Habib reached Gideon's side. Together with Samíah they were all tugging and pulling furiously at the bolt. The genie sauntered over slowly, his green features oddly colored by the bath of glowing red light. "That won't work," he announced, his eyes examining both the bolt and pyramid-shaped door.

"It has to work!" cried Samíah in frustration. Fanatics were beginning to swarm the ramps now, sliding down to the level of the corridor. Many had come from the courtyards at the calling of the warning sirens and, slippery floor or not, sooner or later they would reach the door.

"We need a ring," said the genie after his observations were complete.

"A ring? What are you talking about, man?" rasped Habib.

The genie rubbed at his chin, scanned the bevy of slain bodies between the pillars. His gaze focused on one particular bony hand extending from a sleeve. Losing no time he placed Lucifer on the floor.

Lucifer scurried toward the pillars, nudged his face into the slain fanatic's hand, and bit down hard. A moment later he was back, ringed finger clamped between his jaws.

"There's a good fellow," beamed the genie. He took the bloodied finger and pulled off the ring, holding it high for all to see "Aha!" he exclaimed. "I was right. Excuse me." He elbowed his way to the door, extended the rough surface of the ring and aligned its clustered design of strange triangles and cubes carefully into a matching indentation above the latch. A tense instant passed with nothing happening, but when the door started to hum everyone drew back. "It wouldn't open without the proper code," the genie explained to his astounded companions. Then to Gideon, "Go on, try the bolt now."

In no mood to demand explanations, Gideon did as told. To his surprise the bolt slid quite easily this time. The genie placed a hand against the largest of the embedded gemstones and impatiently waited. Humming with the pressure, the door of iron slowly began to ascend. Samiah stood amazed.

"Quick," called the genie, mopping his brow. "Get through— we don't know how long it will remain open."

No sooner had they cleared the entrance and entered a narrow vestibule than the pyramid groaningly started to come down. The last thing Samíah saw as she glanced behind was the frantic scrambling of sliding mutes trying to gain access. The door touched bottom with a thud, locking the guardians out.

"Here," called Gideon, rushing to the far side of the antechamber where a second pyramid entrance stood—this one unlocked. Again the genie used his palm to apply pressure. When the iron screen lifted it did so silently, and moments later they all found themselves looking down from a theater gallery into the most sacred ground of the subterranean world: the chamber of the altar of sacrifice.

A DIM, DIFFUSED LIGHT SPILLED ACROSS THE CHILLY oval chamber; butter-yellow flames danced from the braziers, casting surrealistic shadows over the raised marble altar and the hideous granite statue that hovered demonically over it. A gargoyle, wingless and clawed, whose flaming ruby eyes seemed omnipresent and alive. A deity of unfathomable cruelty, insatiable in its desire for human sacrifice. Lifelike it rested on its haunches, peering downward in grim satisfaction.

Around the base of the altar dozens of bareheaded priests gathered in a semicircle. Glazed eyes unblinking, they chanted the invocations, paying homage to the awful creature looming above them. Breathlessly, Samíah watched, uncertain whether or not the grim priests were aware their liturgy was observed. The proceedings were frightening enough, but it was when she saw the altar itself that she truly gasped in horror. There were four raised slabs of marble before the base of the terrible statue— and upon each lay the near naked form of a victim prepared for sacrifice. One was a woman.

"Rosa!" she cried, trying to lurch forward. But Gideon's strong hands held her back. "Wait—not yet."

Clad in a flowing velvet robe which extended from neck to foot, came yet another figure, small and wispy. At his approach to the altar steps, the voices of the priests lifted in unison. He wore the sacred cowl and markings of high priest, but it was the shudder in Samíah's breast that made her realize who he was: the messiah.

He climbed the platform of marble, lifting his gaze directly to the bestial face of the gargoyle while the other priests shivered from it. Then reaching deep within the folds of his sleeve, he withdrew a knife—but a knife like Samíah had never seen before. A long, thick surgical tool, razor sharp, whose edges glinted in the dimness. He flicked the blade upward, into the face of the gargoyle, and, it seemed that the demon, bathed in soft ethereal haze created by the rows of tallow candles, suddenly stirred to life, its shapless body beginning to sway, ruby eyes flickering excitedly, chiseled head nodding in well-pleased acceptance of the offerings. Samíah recoiled in horror.

Methodically, the assembled priests one by one reached into the animal skin placed on the floor of the platform and drew small empty drinking cups. The largest vessel remaining was a bowl, carved from stuff the hue of starlight and encrusted with black, gleaming pearls. This artifact the messiah himself took and carefully, respectfully, placed at the foot of the statue.

The chanting became more fervent now, the knot of priests rocking back and forth on their heels, faces alight with expectation. The messiah lifted his arms in a florish; his robe swayed as he turned. "The time is come!" he shouted. The singing ceased abruptly. A wicked smile parted the lips of the messiah. Slowly, the blade flashing in his hand, he indicated for his acolytes to prepare the first victim. The high priests came to the platform and approached the first slab. The semiconscious victim squirmed, tried to scream. But the gag in his mouth nearly choked him and, with the veins bulging from his neck, his hands pinioned and tied, his sweaty body spread-eagled across the stone, he watched with heart-thrumming terror as the acolytes began to rub an oily substance over his body.

The messiah stood over him and smiled dementedly. "Be not afraid, Blinko Rascola," he muttered, the surgical instrument twisting in his hand as he held it over the brazier's spiraling flames. Tonight you shall dwell at one with the gods of the dark."

The bound gypsy strained like a hound on a leash. His eyes

were wide and pitiful, his fingers bending like lobster claws, scratching futilely over the marble surface of the slab. Blinco Rascola struggled as hard as he was able, kicking out as much as his bindings would allow.

"Remove the cloth from his mouth," commanded the messiah, "so that our gods may hear him when he comes."

Blinco Rascola's face already had taken on the pallor of a corpse. He stared at his master with mottled and degenerate features, the effects of the numbing drug taking hold. "I . . . I have served you well, master," he croaked.

The messiah nodded as he lifted the white-hot instrument from the flames. "You *have* served our cause well, Gypsy."

"Then why? Why?" He was trembling all over, a miserable, wretched, soul. "Free me, master, free me to serve you again. I can be useful still . . . you'll see."

A cruel, curt smile broke on the messiah's lips. "Why do you fight me so, Gypsy?" He mouthed the words mockingly. "Cannot you see that you are blessed, blessed as no other of your kind has ever been before? Eternal and everlasting glory awaits you, Blinco Rascola. This is not death but the beginnings of glorious afterlife."

Whimpering, spittle forming at his lips and mucus running from his nose, the traitor sobbed and begged.

"Have you no shame, man?" cried the messiah. "Face your destiny with pride!"

"But my reward, master. You promised me my reward!"

The highest priest of all the Assassins looked down at the crumbled, broken figure with contempt. "Reward, Gypsy? For your failure to deliver the woman into my hands? Yes! *This* shall be your reward!" He lifted the surgical knife and held it expertly above the Gypsy's bare, heaving chest. "In the name of the New Order I send you to hell!"

"Noooooooo!" shrieked the traitor, his scream so ear-piercing that it sent shockwaves across the unholy chamber. With a steady hand the blade came down. Blood spurted as the knife cut through flesh, first severing the artery in Blinco Rascola's throat, then slicing downward in a single fluid motion to where it parted the chest cavity. Vocal chords severed, the gypsy still tried to scream, a soundless yowl of pain and fear. Tearing open the arch of the aorta so a river of blood pulsed, the messiah's sure hands plucked the beating heart from its home and lifted it high above his head for all to see. The gathering of priests stood in excitment, holding out their cups and jockeying for position to gain the trickle of scarlet drops. With the organ still pumping, the messiah gingerly placed it in the bowl at the statue's base: the first offering. And in the grimness of the oval, misted chamber the gargoyle seemed to roar with pleasure. Blinco Rascola's lifeless body twitched in spasms for a long time.

Samíah buried her face in her hands and tried not to vomit. Gideon turned from the sickening sight in revulsion. No man deserved such an abysmal death, he knew, not even the traitor.

The messiah's robe and hands were splattered and stained. He dipped his fingertips into a waiting bowl and cleaned the blood from the cooled instrument. After this was done he lowered the knife back into the brazier's flames to purify it for the next offering. The acolytes grinned like idiots in anticipation of the coming joyous procedure.

Rosa, her eyes dimmed and her head foggy from the drug, turned away from the corpse of Blinco Rascola with fear and disgust. Which of the victims would be next, she wondered? She, or one of the other two poor souls spread-eagled on the slabs?

"Sweet, sweet child," mumbled the messiah when the burning knife was ready. "Be not afraid. Immortality awaits you."

Black hair spilled in waves across her face as she shook her head vehemently. Above the slab the ruby eyes of the monster gargoyle seemed to be staring straight down at her. She wriggled her wrists and arched her back; the leather cords tightened. With her feet and ankles secured by double-knotted coils of hemp she could barely move her toes, much less kick out in freedom. The messiah once more held up the gleaming surgical knife. Rosa twisted wildly, eyes frenzied with terror at what was about to be done. The acolytes silently surrounded her and began their ritual of the oils. All the while she could see the messiah grinning down at her with a special twinkle in his eyes.

"Sweet, sweet Gypsy girl," he rasped, "I promise you, dear child, that the gift of your own heart will be far more pleasing to the lords of the darkness." When the acolytes had finished and her supple skin was smeared totally with the thick, foul-smelling mixture, the messiah brought forth a strange talisman and placed it gently between her heaving breasts. His glare lingered momentarily on her rounded nipples while he made a gesture over it.

"In the world beyond this realm, sweet child, in the universe of eternal darkness, you shall stride even more nobly than when you walked among mere mortals. Yes, sweet thing, there shall be no pain, no cause for alarm."

The gags were removed and she gasped to fill her lungs with the incense-laden air.

"Come, my Rosa." He drew his face closer to hers. "Kiss me, sweet child. Taste upon my lips the nectar of divine afterlife among the gods." Her lips trembled feebly as his wide mouth drew near hers. The smell of him nauseated her, the touch of his hand as he cupped her breasts and fondled her. Again she squirmed, wanting to scream. He forced her mouth open and darted his thick tongue inside it. Rosa clamped her jaws shut.

With an animal yowl the messiah flung himself away, blood curdling from the corner of his mouth. He reeled with the sting, the pain of what she had spitefully done, then returned with a sadistic smile, no longer benign.

"You should not have done that, Rosa," he said, spitting the words, wiping his mouth with a bloodstained hand. He reached out and allowed his fingers to massage the vibrant texture of her young flesh, the round, full curves of her womanly form. She was a masterpiece, but now one who had shamed him before his gods—and for that she would pay dearly.

Rosa agonized beneath his touch, her eyes slitted and dimmer than before. He pressed his palm over her with renewed urgency, each touch a purposeful violation. Through the fog of her delirium she could still hear him ranting, but somehow it no longer mattered. Perhaps she was lucky; for her the ordeal would soon be over. No one would hurt her anymore. More than anything she felt sorry for the other victims, the poor souls still bound, gagged, and waiting their turns.

"Your death will be slow and painful, Rosa. You will beg me to kiss you before you die." His teeth, perfect and white, shone when he laughed. The surgical knife danced in his eager hand.

"You can do with me what you like," she hissed. "But nothing's gonna make me kiss you, see? You're doomed— you and your whole filthy army!"

His chuckle was malevolent. "It is too late for that, sweet child. Far too late. The ceremony is all but complete, my army of the night already on the move." He clenched his fist. "Soon all will be mine? A pity you could not have shared the glory with me."

Defiantly she looked straight at him, lifting her head and glaring, "*Up yours*, messiah!"

"Blasphemer!" The knife lifted high, ready to plunge.

"Rosa!" came the cry from behind. The messiah turned in amazement.

Tearing through the pyramid door came the bold captain of the sultan's guards. Sword lifted high above his head, the frenzied soldier bounded into the haze-filled chamber, kicking over braziers and rows of tallow candles, surging for the platform and the bedeviled altar. Right behind raced Gideon, Habib only a half pace on his heels.

"They have violated our holy ceremony! Stop them!" The messiah stood bellowing at the top of his lungs. The high priests snapped out of their stupors, discarded their bloody cups of sacrifice, and rallied. Poisoned daggers whipped from their belts.

Out of his mind with worry and love for the captured Gypsy girl, Captain Enos daringly charged into their midst. His swinging blade slashed off the head of a priest before his dagger could thrust; the severed head caromed one way, the torso another. The soldier banged his way onward, wreaking havoc in the line of defending priests. Gongs and alarm bells rang madly everywhere.

Several acolytes dropped back in confusion. The floor before the altar became a crazed swirl of movement. The first of the drugged priests atop the platform bounded down with his poisoned dagger clutched in his raised hand. Before he could plunge it into the captain's back, Gideon rammed the heel of his hand hard against the base of his nose. Cartilage cracked; the blow dropped the acolyte like a bird arrowed on its perch. Gideon caught him before he swooned to the ground, pivoted him around, shoved him forcefully into a rushing group of fevered priests leaping from the near side of the marble altar. The glaze-eyed priests fell back. Then, stumbling back up, they sought to cut off the intruders before they could gain the steps to the statue.

Scrambling for cover, Habib caught the swinging arm of one, rammed his knife point-blank. He lashed out again in a swift horizontal arc, felt but did not see the cutting edge bite into soft flesh. With the priest's moan, he ducked a sailing dagger and toppled a flaming brazier. White-hot coals danced across the floor; priests began to howl as the coals singed their bare feet and set the hems of their robes afire.

The mute guardians, having successfully slid their way to the first pyramid door and unlocked it, were now regrouping and rushing helter-skelter through the antechamber. With a flourish of his hands the genie turned that floor to ice as well, then pulled Samíah away from the second door and used the stolen ring to lock it. Guardians banged and pounded on the iron, blocked from gaining entry.

The melee continued amid the clatter of crossed knives and screaming priests. With the coals lighting small fires all about, the haze and smoke grew thicker. Gideon heard someone scream and fall; he glanced to his right and saw Habib stomp the writhing figure who had nearly blind-sided the secret agent.

"Thanks, dustman."

"Forget it. It was no favor. Unless we can hold that door shut, they'll be swarming us in a minute."

He was right, Gideon saw. True, the guardians were temporarily locked outside the evil chamber, but at the same time he and his friends were locked in. Trapped.

Captain Enos struggled his way to the marble altar. Beneath

the frightening gaze of the lifelike gargoyle, he dispatched two more acolytes and hurried to the slabs. One chop of his weapon snapped the bonds holding Rosa's feet; a second and third freed her hands. While Gideon and Habib protected his flanks, he lifted the barely conscious girl, cradling her in his arms. "Rosa, Rosa," he cried, forgetting the tumult around him. "Speak to me, Rosa. Speak to me!"

The Gypsy princess hung limply with her arms at her sides. At the call of her name, her eyelids parted and she peered up into his anguished face. Her eyes saw him dimly, but a spark of recognition was there. She awoke as if from a trance. "Enos! Is . . . is it . . . really . . . you?"

The bold commander hugged her with tears streaming down his face.

Gideon thrust and parried with a priest at the steps. As Habib blocked more attempts, Samíah and the genie made it safely up to the altar. Another acolyte lurched from the side. Samíah cried out in warning; the genie spun around, Lucifer leaping from his arms. The cat clawed like a mountain lion at the acolyte's face. The dagger dropped from his grasp, and he wailed like a banshee in torment. Blood poured between his fingers as he covered his mangled features.

Gideon kicked high at his assailant, and caught him in the groin. The priest let out a weak croak, and in that instant the secret agent's blade slashed his throat from ear to ear. The priest was instantly dead. The sound of loud and wicked laughter assaulted Gideon before he could wipe the blade. Turning, he saw the hooded figure brazenly standing at the base of the statue, the bowl containing Blinco Rascola's heart clutched to his bosom.

Time stopped as the secret agent stared at his hated adversary. Within the cowl the messiah's eyes smoldered with crimson fires, identical to the flaming rubies of the fiendish god.

"Say your prayers, messiah!" growled Gideon amid the swirl of the mist. Suddenly the entire chamber gave the appearance of being lost within the deepest reaches of a hellish void.

"You have come too late, master spy!" hissed the messiah. In his hand he lifted Blinco Rascola's beating heart, fed by the surging powers of the stirring gargoyle. "My army is un-leashed—and Marrakesh shall pay the price!" He howled with laughter like the madman he was, his visage so frightening that Gideon blanched.

"I am invincible!" rattled on the messiah. Robe aswirl, he backpedaled onto the base of the statue, standing beneath the glare of the lifelike eyes. "See for yourself!"

A band of exploding color nearly blinded the secret agent. It lasted only an instant, and when it was gone Gideon blinked to clear his vision. The entire section of marble wall directly behind the statue had vanished, and he found himself looking as through a great window upon the panorama of underworld beyond the oval chamber. Nestled beneath the black-streaked turrets of the castle towers, he could see the antlike movements of the messiah's marching army crossing the bridge and moat, on the move toward the tunnels. They had not turned at the warning of the bells and sirens, had not been deterred even by the intrusion on the sacred ceremony.

The highest priest of the Assassins roared with mirth as his enemies stood mute and gaping. Samíah gasped at the realization of what see was seeing. They had failed to halt the assault, and now the futility of their bold strike hit home mercilessly, draining her of any remaining courage.

"Did you believe that I could so easily be defeated?" the messiah demanded. "That twenty years of careful planning could be overturned by a single rash action? No, my army is blinded to you. Each and every soldier has drunk from the potion and marches with one purpose alone: to destroy your city!"

Gideon wanted to lunge, to plunge his blade straight through the maniac's black heart. But it was as if he were caught in the grip of unseen hands; he wanted to attack but could only stand powerless, looking fixedly down upon a force of drugged fanatics who lived for this night and this night alone.

The messiah's voice raved with contempt. Aglow with the life-force of his god's pervasive presence, his twisted mouth perverted into a sneer, he gazed intently upon the woman with a cruel gleam in his eyes. "And for you, Samíah," he intoned, "there shall be a special place in the world yet to come. I have vowed it a thousand times and been thwarted nearly as many. But this time my wish has been answered. This time it is you who have come to me. And this time there can be no escape."

Mesmerized, Samiah watched as his hand drew the surgical knife from within the folds of his sleeve and, with Blinco Rascola's heart cradled in the other, lifted the instrument high as if to strike the girl.

"Pray for the resurrection," cried the messiah.

Habib snapped from the stupor that held them all transfixed. He threw himself between the girl and the thrusting madman, his weight deflecting the downward thrust, sending the messiah toppling backward. The cowl flew off the messiah's head. Habib made to charge for him, but at sight of the depraved, drugged face he stopped, stared unbelieving into the warped and distorted features somehow so familiar.

Through the hatred of his blazing eyes the messiah met the stare with a cruel, sadistic smile.

"You!" Habib blurted, frozen, reeling with uncertainty. "You are . . . the messiah?" An awful, glacial frost penetrated deep into the dustman's soul, turning him almost to stone. The man he knew but now hardly recognized threw back his head and laughed with bitter malice, the joke of it somehow all the more pleasing during this moment of impending glory.

"Yes, Habib. Do not doubt your senses. It is I, Kubla, the messiah, one and the same."

Dazed, shaken with incomprehension, Habib tried to grasp the truth of what his eyes were seeing. The dreaded leader of the Assassins was a man he had called a friend and confidant, the man he had trusted with his life in times of need and pain. Kubla, the dentist, who had been more than a neighbor, who had been part of the fabric of the Old Quarter.

Like a wheeling scavenger the physician's laughter floated; Kubla flung his cape aside and glared at the hapless dustman. "Now do you believe?" he chortled, forcing Habib to look directly at him. The disguise had been more than fruitful, Kubla knew, serving his cause well enough so that by daylight he could walk freely through the city, openly and defiantly passing under the very noses of the sultan's soldiers. But by night he would return, crawl back into the sewers to his underworld haven, resume his true identity under the watchful eyes of his evil gods. For a generation he had beguiled and deceived them all, the fools who sought to catch him. Plotting and scheming, defying them to find him, while his fanatic followers instilled the city with fear and dread. Now, though, there was no longer need of disguise. It no longer mattered that he had at last been exposed. Now the time of glory had finally arrived, the sacred hour of revenge that would sweep him to heretofore undreamed-of triumphs.

Within that hellish chamber the gargoyle god seemed to share the messiah's demented laughter. Habib felt his mind slipping from him, madness tempting him away from the world of reality. Before him he could see the feared tray of surgical tools that the Syrian had used with such precision, remember the almost sadistic grin when the knives were wielded and fresh blood spurted. Unable to stand it any longer, the dustman raised his fists and roared in shrieking madness. Bathed in the crimson shadows of the statue, he lurched unprotected, surging for the taunting figure.

"Papa, no!" cried Samíah.

The lash of the surgical blade tore through the cloth of the dustman's shirt, ruptured the artery in his bicep. Habib staggered. Crazed, the messiah flicked his arm and charged for Samíah. Gideon blocked his path, and the two of them grappled for only a moment. The messiah broke free and, frothing at the mouth, flung Blinco Rascola's heart into the secret agent's face. Then he pivoted and jumped back onto the statue's broad base.

Gideon dispatched the houndish acolyte yapping at his heels and bounded for the frenzied messiah. It was then that he heard the blare of trumpets.

Kubla climbed monkeylike into the folded arms of the gargoyle and stared through the translucent wall. Way, way below, along the spit of land jutting from the moat, a horde of new figures had emerged from the nearest of the tunnels.

Samíah gaped with widened eyes. These were not Assassins,

she saw, but a new army, an army of ragtag whopping Gypsies and Karshis streaming through underground shafts to confront the marching fanatics. "Wanko and the rag man!" she gasped. "They've reached the castle!"

A phalanx of Assassins roared forward to meet the assault. The clash of battle sounded like sweet music to her ears. Along the gutted paths leading to the keep, the sides joined battle, Gypsies in loose formation interlocking with the front lines of Assassin forces. Though many of the Gypsies fell, the bulk of the attackers successfully edged the fanatics backward to the river surrounding the castle. A wing of fearsome scarlet-clad Karshi scissored down from the main body and sought to outflank the front ranks of charging fanatics. Their spears flew, and a mass of Assassins crumpled like wheat in a hailstorm. The fanatic flanks disintegrated beneath the awesome weight of the fire. As they staggered and dropped like flies, a second wing of devout Karshi, shouting war cries and wielding scimitars, crushed the column and turned to meet the next advance.

The bridge from the castle swarmed with hundreds of glaze-eyed fanatics thundering from the inner keep. Contact was quickly made, and Samíah cried out in anguish when it became apparent that the overwhelming enemy numbers would cut down the brave fighters.

The filthy waters of the moat were already clogged with bloodied corpses. Pinioned on the left and right, the Karshi forces vainly sought to hold their ground. Slowly they were forced to yield from the bridge. Though three fanatics fell for every one of their own, the Karshi position seemed hopeless. With the din of war shrieking all around, a knot of bow-carrying Gypsies formed a double line and took up strong positions along the path. Their ranks swelled quickly, and moments later a torrent of arrows came singing down into the main force of rushing Assassins. Defilers wheeled and yowled, shafts piercing their bodies, sending them spinning this way and that.

Still the fanatics came on. The planks of the bridge became an insane swirl of knives, swords, and spears countered by Gypsy arrows. A thin line of Assassin troops drew up close to the shore; as they did a fresh shower of shafts, well directed by one of Wanko's lieutenants, hailed through their midst. Five and six at a time, the fanatics fell to their knees as arrow after arrow pounded their already pincushioned flesh.

The momentum started by the Karshi vanguard finally soured. More forces of Assassins hurried blindly from the keep, and with them a strong counterattack quickly developed and over-whelmed the few survivors holding the bridge. Converging from three sides, the Assassins gained the upper hand swiftly, regained the bridge in short order, and positioned themselves for an all-out thrust against the Gypsy bands along the shoreline. Vigorously the men under Wanko's steady command continued to repulse them; but without reinforcements the battle would surely be lost.

Captain Enos, Rosa huddled beside him, flexed his jaw and watched in anguish. Then suddenly his eyes began to brighten. For, from the closely guarded tunnels directly behind the jutting towers of the castle, a new and most welcome element entered the fray. It was the sultan's guards, banners aflutter, his own proud regiment leading the forefront.

Another Assassin phalanx formed, turned on the land to face the newest threat. Shouts of glee rose from the Gypsy and Karshi ranks. And with it, renewed courage. A furious hand-to-hand combat erupted on all sides, only now it was the fa-natics who were being steadily pressed back.

Captain Enos beamed at the sight of his regiment, led by his own top sergeants and lieutenants, breaking free of the pulsing mobs and tearing onto the bridge. The Assassins fell back, stumbling over the limp bodies of friend and foe. So swift was the retreat, that within the space of a few halting breaths the vanguard of the sultan's soldiers had not only gained the bridge but secured it.

Wanko lifted his knife arm and rallied his men to follow. Tens of dozens of stout Gypsies charged fearlessly from the shore and dived into the remaining knots of surrounded fanatics. A brief but deadly fight ensued, and when it was done the victorious Gyspies broke through cleanly and swelled the ranks of the remaining Karshis. The taste of victory in their mouths, they thundered forward, straight for the castle's gate.

Thick rows of kneeling crossbow archers fired in rapid succession both from the open gate and from high above along the walls and tower turrets. The sultan's guards paid a deadly toll, fully one quarter of their number falling by the wayside long before the entrance to the unholy castle had been gained. Undeterred, though, they hurried ahead, shields held high brightly reflecting the torchlight.

A force of Night Masters, the most terrible of the messiah's troops, hurled themselves from the approach into an all-but-suicidal attack. Heedless of their lives, the zombielike stalkers of the night threw themselves among the advancing squadrons of tight-lipped Marrakesh soldiers. Bloody violence reigned; mortally wounded, one soldier shrieked as first his face and then his body was hacked. A second soldier caught a blade that stuck through one side of his head and protruded out the other. Dead on his feet, he continued to cling to the savage Assassin, slowing him enough so that they both careened amid the next arrow barrage.

From his lofty position, the messiah looked on with horror at the sight of his carefully nurtured army being ravaged. He bolted down from the arms of the statue and sought to run clear of the platform. Gideon's coarse voice stopped him short, sent him wheeling around to face the hated adversary.

"Not this time, messiah!" The secret agent crouched and lifted his blade to eye level. One on one he faced his enemy, an encounter he had prayed for since he could remember. "There's nothing that can save your doomed soul now. Look about you, messiah. You've finally lost—and this time there won't be any escape."

With the mists still whorled at his feet, the madman glanced around at his once-opulent altar chamber. Everywhere were littered the mangled corpses of acolytes and guardians; tiny fires burst ignominiously in pale yellow brightness from the overturned braziers. The bloodied floors and marble slabs gave grim testimony to the terrible struggle that was all but ended, and he saw in Gideon's eyes the glint of victory.

"I am not vanquished yet, master spy!" Kubla spat the words defiantly. He twirled his surgical knife anew, poking and jabbing it through the air to keep his foe off balance. Then he uttered a venomous cry and thrust the instrument with all his crazed strength. Samíah was yelling at Gideon, but the secret agent seemed deaf to her warning. He threw himself sideways, and the razor-sharp weapon sliced a clean slash across his shoulder. A dark stain rapidly developed. Gideon grunted and lurched ahead, but his legs gave out from under him and he staggered. The messiah's eyes were gleaming with depraved fires. He pulled yet another surgical tool from the folds of his sleeve and made to hurl it.

Outside, the wail of trumpet blasts shattered the air; it took but a cursory glance through the broken wall to realize that the sultan's soldiers, had breached the sniper line at the gate and were now thrusting in loose formations into the courtyards, across the inner keep, and up to the crenellated walls. A few Assassins struck up a battle cry to meet the onslaught, their voices only to be smothered by the rising roar of opposing combatants. Up and down the castle, in and out of the courtyards, on the bridge and land and even amid the reeking waters of the moat, the battle raged, the din of close combat punctuated by the shrieks of the dying.

The messiah winced at the sight; his arm fell, and he began to flee.

"Don't let him escape!" yelled Gideon.

Beringed hand outstretched, the messiah pressed the indentations in a hidden recess of the gargoyle's belly. A small trapdoor opened, and he crawled through it with the speed of a lizard. Weaponless, Habib crouched and followed after. Inside the gut of the statue he managed to stand and peer into the darkness. There was a narrow set of steps ahead; he couldn't see the messiah climbing them, but he could hear the frantic clatter of footsteps. Sightlessly, the dustman gave chase. The messiah spun, kicked savagely. Habib caught the blow in the chest and, momentarily stunned, fell sideways against the inner wall. It took only a second to regain his senses.

A pinprick of light grew larger. There was a portal at the top of the steps, and through it he saw the messiah squirm like a snake. Huffing, Habib reached it as well. He compacted his broad frame and barely managed to squeeze through. The shouts and cries of battle greeted him. He was on a gallery now, he realized, outside of the dreaded altar chamber, directly above the courtyards. Before him loomed the massive stones of the tallest tower, behind him only the statue's secret portal. Of the messiah there was no sign. Cursing, his wound beginning to throb, he rushed toward the tower. The rail-less gallery was like a narrow bridge suspended in midair. One bad step either way, and he would tumble fifty meters below. Fighting vertigo, he kept his gaze steady and straight ahead.

The lash of a whip bit into his wrist. The messiah appeared from the unseen entrance to the tower and stung him again. Fire spread up his forearm, the whip-coil's lash stunning him with searing pain.

The messiah was laughing at him, taunting him, daring him to come. Habib sheltered his face and strove forward. Once more the whip cracked; the pain nearly sent Habib staggering; his feet sought purchase and found it—only inches away from the edge of the walk. The messiah stood waiting for him, coiling the whip, this time ready to lash the dustman over the side. One cautious step at a time, Habib pressed on. And there, high above the fray, with the shouts and cries and clash of weapons all around, they confronted each other, two solitary figures far above the mayhem.

"I'm going to kill you, messiah," the dustman hissed.

Kubla grinned at him like a vulture circling his prey. "You, Habib? You, when the whole sultan's army has failed for years?" Streaking arrows of flame darted above their heads and cast the underworld panorama in a strange parody of daylight. By the score, Assassins were falling from the walls, splashing into the already corpse-dammed waters of the moat.

"You are finished, messiah. The army you trained and nurtured has been decimated." For an unmeasurable time nothing else was spoken, no further attempt was made by Habib to close the gap separating them. All the while the messiah stood with his back to the tower wall, his hand clutching at the whip. The terror of brutal war around them continued unabated, and with each mournful cry another nail had been driven into the coffin of the messiah's dream of conquest.

"Look about you, Kubla," the dustman said, breaking the silence with a mirthless smile of satisfaction. In truth he hadn't been so certain of the defeat of the messiah's black army, not with his own allies paying so dearly for every inch of ground achieved. But now, standing above the battle, he could see that the tide had irrevocably turned. While the remaining vestiges of Assassin power stood isolated in their pockets of resistance, fighting to the death in a mindless cause, bit by bit the castle was being secured by the combined Gypsy and Karshi forces.

Kubla's anxiety seemed to increase. By the light of the torches and flaming arrows he saw that what the dustman had said was true. His forces were crushed, his sanctuary overrun, his dreams and plans shattered like a pane of glass.

"Come, messiah," dared Habib, beckoning to the twitching figure. "It's only you and me now. No one can save you. Not your army, not your gods. Kill me, messiah—before I kill you."

With a scream of rage, the robed scourge of Marrakesh cracked his whip. Though the vicious stroke tore through flesh, Habib's calloused hand caught the whip-coil on the downstroke and clutched it fiercely, his ferocious pull yanking Kubla toward him like a hound on a leash. The cut burned like white fire. Habib grappled with the weaseling figure along the center of the precarious span. A smash from his bloodied fist sent Kubla reeling back. The whip dropped, and Habib scooped it up triumphantly. All the dustman's pain and rage broke to the surface: the wanton death and destruction wreaked upon his peaceful city ringing in his ears, the murders, the kidnappings, the threats to Samíah.

He saw Kubla, the fearful messiah now groveling like a rabid dog, on his knees and whimpering, shielding himself from the lash of the whip, trying to scamper back toward the tower like a gutter rat finally cornered. He would shred Kubla's flesh layer by layer, inflict upon him the torment that others had suffered for so long. Their ghosts cried out for revenge to Habib, and he would wreak it.

"Papa, don't!"

The shrill cry of his daughter's voice snapped the burning insanity from his mind. He turned to find Samíah distraught, stepping from the portal and onto the bridge.

"Go away, child!" he barked. His face was twisted now, as twisted and demented as the man's he was going to kill.

"Please, Papa! Don't do that! Take him alive. Don't turn yourself into the animal he is!" Tears were streaming down her cheeks. "Please, Papa, *please*!"

Habib fought against her pleadings, unable to control his surging lust to flay the cringing figure to death. "Leave me, daughter! Begone!"

"I can't leave you, Papa! I love you!"

Habib stared at the girl, his mouth quivering. Suddenly, all the rage was gone, vanished, melted away like the first snowflake of winter. Samíah threw herself into his arms, and Habib dropped the whip at his feet.

Opposite them, Kubla lifted himself shakily. The keep was blazing with small fires everywhere, his once-invincible army lay scattered in pools of blood for as far as he could see. "Kill me then, dustman!" he shrieked. "Go on, finish it!"

Habib met the madman's wild gaze and shook his head. "No, Kubla," he whispered. "I'll not add another death to so many."

The messiah grinned in fury. "I knew you were a coward, Habib! You were always a coward!" Then, with his laughter raging, he stretched out his arms and held them high, stepping to the edge of the precarious walk. "Let Marrakesh be my epitaph!" he screamed.

Habib bolted to grab him. Kubla forcefully threw himself over before the dustman could even get close. In horror the father and daughter watched him sail down to the courtyard below, where his body splattered among the corpses of his followers.

Badly shaken, Habib let Samíah lead him back down into the altar chamber. When they arrived, they found Gideon back on his feet, directing orders to the squad of the sultan's soldiers who had finally broken through the last resistance. At the sight of the girl, Gideon stopped what he was doing. Samíah came slowly forward, and when they kissed it was as though all time stood still.

Captain Enos cleared his throat. "Er, isn't it time we set free the other captives?" he said sheepishly.

Gideon hit himself lightly in the forehead. "By Allah, I nearly forgot!" With Samíah beside him, he hurried to the two remaining figures gagged and spread-eagled on the marble slabs. With a quick stroke he unbound their ropes and set them free. "Up you go," he said, lending each a hand. Samíah stared long and hard at the first captive, a chill returning. The man, humbled and tearful, she recognized as the very same she had seen abducted from the marketplace so long before. The palace noble.

Weakly, the fellow fell to his knees before Gideon. "My lord," he rasped, kissing the ring on Gideon's right hand, "I never dreamed I'd live to see you again."

The secret agent helped him up, led him slowly to the arriving troops. "Nor I you, minister. Thank heaven we arrived in the nick of time."

The kidnapped noble sniffed and hung his head. "Thank you, my lord, thank you. You do your father great honor."

Perplexed, Samíah stared at the pitiful scene. Why did the man call Gideon, 'My lord'? she wondered. And what did he mean about doing honor to his father?

The squad of soldiers fanned out and secured the grim chamber. Their commander came and greeted Gideon, looked with worry to his wound. "My lord, you've been hurt!"

"It's nothing, commander. See to the others first."

"But my lord!"

Samíah shook her head in bewilderment. Nudging Captain Enos by the elbow, she said, "Why are they all bowing to Gideon like that? Calling him 'lord,' protecting him with a bodyguard as though he were the most important man in the world?"

The soldier looked at her with a curious expression. "Why? Don't you know?"

She shook her head.

At that Captain Enos's face broke into a broad grin. "You mean you really don't know? *Really?* He never told you?"

Samíah didn't exactly know why, but suddenly she was beginning to feel rather stupid.

Captain Enos scratched his head in wonder. "Well," he said, drawing a breath, "I guess there's no point in keeping it from you any longer. My Lord Gideon is the younger son of our beloved sultan."

THERE IS NO PARTY ANYWHERE LIKE A GYPSY party, and no Gypsy party was ever like this one. "Everybody is welcome tonight!" the king had proclaimed—and from everywhere they came. The peaceful meadow beyond the city walls shook with the throngs attending. There were Berber tribesmen from the Atlas Mountains mingling with the folk of the desert, city folk from the Old Quarter as well as the New, high-ranking officials side by side with the platoons of street-sweepers and dustmen, weary pilgrims and travelers from all corners, invited distinguished guests from the palace and dignitaries and ambassadors from other cities and other lands. Actors, poets reciting verse, fire-eaters, magicians, snake charmers, wandering balladeers, and wandering holy men in search of Mecca. Shepherds, goatherds, orchard tenders. Butchers, bakers, and candlestick makers. There were those who came to eat and those to came to stuff themselves.

Those who came to drink and those who came to get drunk. Those who came to partake in the merriment, along with boorish fellows who attended soley to boast about their own small part in Marrakesh's victory. Rascals and liars and politicans (which to many were all the same category, anyway), jokesters and clowns, entertainers of every size, color, and description. Fishermen and fisherwives, sailors, children galore chasing and being chased in turn by dogs and chickens and goats and geese and, well, just about every farm and domestic animal in the Gypsy camp. Physicians, faith-healers, the charitable and uncharitable, dowagers, landlords, tax collectors, bill collectors, the well-heeled and the ill-mannered. Scholars who ceaselessly debated life and afterlife, mullahs, rabbis, Christian theologians, and a special place of the fanatical Karshi. The bold and the timid, the high and the mighty along with their endless entourages of flunkies and hangers-on. Yes, and even a genie was on hand—although few realized it. It was a marvelous medley of humanity drawn together with amazing goodwill and good feeling. A celebration not so much of victory as of life itself.

Succulent meat hissed and dripped on spits over the scores of camp fires. There was fruit from the orchards; fresh fish from the sea; fresher bread, hot and buttery, provided by a dozen of the city's most renowned bakers, spice- and garlic-peppered to Queen Yana's own secret recipe. And there was wine. Barrels of it provided by the king. Yes, and even some 'Gypsy poison' as well, although most would forever deny partaking of it. Strange, though, how it so quickly disappeared.

Now, Samíah was there also, of course, dressed in the finest Gypsy boots, skirt, and ruffled blouse the queen could provide. Happily she ate and drank and laughed and carried on and had as good a time as she'd ever remembered.

Gypsy violins hummed and guitars strummed. Crowds gathered and watched with joy as Rosa danced, the Gypsy princess twirling, clapping her hands while the drums beat and the tambourines clattered. Beside her, a host of Gypsy children gyrated in imitation of the stunning girl. With hands on hips, King Wanko joined her in a Spanish-Gypsy fandango, and many a widow's eye widened and brow rose in speculation as he charmed his way to their hearts.

Speaking of widows, the widow Anna was there also, invited by Habib and hanging onto his arm every moment, proud of her hero and his own special role in saving Marrakesh—and even prouder when she heard the envious whispers of those many who wished they could have been in her place.

As for good, brave Captain Enos, he found himself besieged by fellow officers who made him tell over and over again how he broke up the unhallowed sacrifice and saved the life of his darling, while almost singlehandedly routing the devilish priests and guardians. Enos was so preoccupied that for most of the party he hardly had a chance to dance with Rosa. But when his commanding officer spoke of the promotion to come, he leaped to his feet and joined the Gypsy princess in her dance, whisking the poor girl off her feet and spinning round and round. His future father-in-law, King Wanko, looked askance at the jovial soldier, wondering if the *gadjo* would ever make a good Gypsy son. Still, Wanko had to admire his courage, and with a contented sigh figured that Rosa could have done worse. Captain Enos might never make a good horse thief, but having such a respected and admired son-in-law was certainly going to add to Gypsy prestige. Wanko only hoped the good soldier had enough money put away for a fitting dowry. After all, a princess was worth the highest price.

In the wee hours before dawn, the party finally began to wind down. Snoring Gypsies and guests rested leisurely around the ebbing fires, bellies filled, thirsts quenched, tomorrow's hangovers and headaches yet to begin. Guitars softly strummed, a few lilting voices now singing tender and beautiful ballads. Many of the guests had gone home, and for some it was to be good-bye forever.

Habib finally managed to tear away from the widow Anna; he roused himself and ambled over to his friend. The genie was sitting alone, resting near the flames of the dying bonfire, busily mumbling to Lucifer who purred in his lap.

"Ah, Habib," said the genie, looking up at the bulky figure, "I was hoping you'd stop by before I left."

The dustman's brain was cloudy from the wine; he scratched his head and gazed at his companion. "Are you leaving?" he asked.

"A bargain is a bargain, Habib. It will soon be time to return to the bottle. After all, I still have my nap to finish, remember? Do me a favor, there's a good fellow. Carry the bottle somewhere far away, toss it beneath a heap of your rubbish in the dump when you go back to work. Lucifer will take care of the rest." The cat hissed and nodded.

Habib didn't know what to say. The events of these past weeks had been so dramatic, had made such a permanent impact on his life, that it seemed the genie and he had been together for years. In a peculiar sort of way they had become, well, almost like brothers, as if the green-tinted visitor were indeed his long-lost relative from the village come to stay with him. It was with shock and sorrow that he'd been snapped back to reality. His friend was leaving.

"Must you go?" he asked.

The genie nodded. "My work is done, Habib. There's no longer any reason to stay."

The dustman grabbed at straws. "Now listen, my friend, our bargain was to find my daughter a husband. As of yet there hasn't been any wedding I know of, so as far as I'm concerned, your work here isn't done. Not by a long shot!"

The genie smiled his impish smile, teeth flashing. "I will miss you, too, Habib. But"—and here he sighed—"I suppose I should clarify your daughter's status before I go."

"Hrumph!"

With a flourish of his hand, the genie pointed to the swaying trees along the edge of the camp. Two figures sat together, quietly speaking beneath the moon and flickering stars. It was a private conversation, one which neither he nor anyone else had the right to listen to. One last time he would bend the rules, allow the dustman to overhear what was being said. Besides, he was a little bit curious himself. He put a finger to his lips. "Shhh, Habib. Listen carefully."

Cross-legged, her back against the bark of a juniper tree,

306

Samíah lowered her eyes from Gideon's gaze. "Forgive me, my lord, for speaking to you with such familiarity."

"Calling me Gideon will do very nicely, thank you. Too few people do it, and to tell you the truth I hate to be referred to by my title."

Samíah smiled, a tiny sparkle of firelight reflecting in her eyes. "You *are* lucky, Gideon. And I do envy you. And, er, should we not meet again after tonight I want to say that I'll never forget the experiences were shared. They will live with me forever."

"Mine also, Samíah. But what's all this talk of never seeing each other?"

"How can it be otherwise my lo—Gideon? You have your duties and obligations and I have mine. You'll go back to the palace . . ."

"And you?"

"To my work, I suppose." She groaned, adding, "Do you have any idea how far behind I am? Why, there are three dresses that should have been completed long ago, and six more that I haven't even had time to buy cloth or patterns for!"

"The life of a dress maker is a difficult one," he said solemnly.

You bet it is! Likely as not I'll lose my clients for being so tardy."

"No, you won't. I'll give you an official letter, signed under my own seal, saying that you were preoccupied with special assignments for the palace." He gazed up at the waning moon and scratched his chin. "Not only that, but I think I'll speak with my mother about having some gowns made for the next royal affair."

Her eyes grew wide. "You would really do that for me, Gideon?"

"It's the least I can do. Anyway, it'll ease your work load and, er, free up some of your time for us." He chuckled. "That should solve the problem. In fact, I think I'll even find a place for you within the palace grounds so you can work there full-time."

At first she burst with happiness at the idea. She, Samíah,

daughter of the dustman Habib, to be bestowed with such honor! It was unthinkable! Suddenly, though, she frowned.

"What's the matter?"

"Thank you for your gracious offer, Gideon, but I'm afraid I'll have to turn it down. No, no, it's impossible. I can't accept."

"Why on earth not?"

She bit her lip in consternation. "It's not that I wouldn't enjoy it, but what about Papa? He's getting on in years, Gideon. Soon he'll be retiring with a pension. Someone will have to be here, take care of him, look after the household."

The secret agent, youngest son of the sultan, glanced back toward the party. "Seems to me that your widow neighbor can handle that job well enough," he observed. "And I'm sure Anna shall be delighted to become the dustman's wife."

"Papa married?" She was incredulous. "He wouldn't want that! Never! I'm sure he—"

"And I'm sure this Anna has it all planned out to the letter," he rejoined, cutting her off. "If there's one thing I've learned, it's that a woman won't be put off by anything—once she sets her mind to it."

Samíah stared at him; he was speaking about Anna, of course, but somewhere behind his words was a statement about her.

"What about you, Gideon? What are you going to do now that this sordid affair is finished? Will you go back to the job? Become a spy on some other case?"

Gideon leaned back and kneaded the muscles in his injured arm. "I think I'm getting too old for this line of work. It's time I changed careers and found something more mundane to do. I'll keep myself busy, though." He laughed. "Of that you can be sure. I don't very much like the idea of spending my days in idleness. Guess I'm too much like you."

Now it was Samíah's turn to grin.

"First things first, though," he went on. "I'll have to settle down with a proper home and place to live. Maybe by the sea. I love the sea, you know, Yes, a nice house, not too opulent, but tasteful enough to spend my years. Which reminds me, I'll need someone to decorate it. You know what I mean—pick out curtains and carpets and furniture and the like. To be honest, I know absolutely nothing about such matters." Samíah giggled and he grinned. "Then," he continued with a sigh, "I'm going to need someone to look after it. A maid, I suppose. Someone to scrub the floors, wash the laundry, cook my meals, make the bed, provide conversation when I'm lonely, and nag me when I need to be nagged."

"Sounds like you don't need a maid but a wife."

"A wife?" He looked at her with curiosity. "Hmmmm. A wife, eh? I've never considered one. But maybe you're right. Perchance do you know where I might find one?" He leaned forward.

Samíah shrugged and shook her head. "I can ask around if you want."

"Yes, please do that. I would be most grateful. Most . . . Say, er, you wouldn't want the job by any chance, would you? I know I'm hard to live with, but it could be worse. I don't get drunk or spend my money frivolously or beat up children."

"Me?" she gasped in shock. "How could I? Oh Gideon, I'm afraid I wouldn't be very good at it. Not after so long." She shook her head again. "Too much has passed in my life. I think it's better for me to stay alone."

"Do you mean that?"

"Yes."

A lump rose in his throat and his heart sank like a pebble in a pond. "Am I supposed to believe you?" he asked.

Tears fell helplessly from her eyes. "No. No, you're not! And if you dare even glance the wrong way at another woman—!"

They flew into each other's arms and kissed. Slowly the image of the lovers faded in Habib's eyes, their words no longer heard. Habib wiped away a tear of his own and looked back at his friend. You did keep your promise," he said.

The genie nodded, thankful it had all worked out so well, exactly as planned. But then he had no reason to believe it wouldn't. The stars never lied.

"Will . . . will my daughter be happy?" the dustman wanted to know.

The genie mused at the question. "Well, Habib, knowing Samíah's temper and willfulness—"

"You mean they'll fight like cats and dogs?"

"They are both stubborn, you know. Demanding, assured, self-confident." He could see Habib's face go pale as he spoke. "But on the other hand, they love each other very much—and when it comes right down to it, love is enough. Wouldn't you say?"

"And grandchildren for me?"

"A whole brood of them, Habib. Satisfied now?"

"One last question. I don't think my old heart can take any more of what we've been through. Tell me, genie, will there be other adventures? New dangers and perils they'll have to face? If I know Gideon and my daughter as well, in a month they'll both be searching for some new wrong to be righted."

With a condescending smile at the ways of mortals, as well as a touch of genuine surprise at how prophetic this dustman actually was, the genie only replied, "That, my good friend Habib, is another tale to tell."

About the Author

Graham Diamond has been writing tales of adventure for as long as he can remember. Today there are well over one million copies in print of his many books, which include THE THIEF OF KALIMAR, CAPTAIN SINBAD, and MARRAKESH. At the age of 37, he is the most prominent American author writing stories in the Arabian Nights tradition, and he plans to write many, many more.